ZANE PRESS

T0130861

FLESH *to* *Flesh*

AN *Erotic* ANTHOLOGY

Z ANE PRESENTS

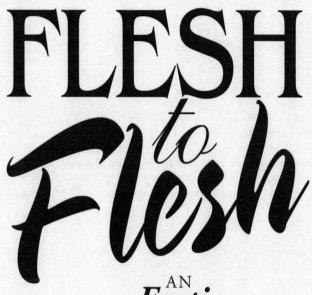

FLESH to Flesh

AN *Erotic* ANTHOLOGY

EDITED BY
LEE HAYES

SBI

STREBOR BOOKS

NEW YORK LONDON TORONTO SYDNEY

Strebor Books
P.O. Box 6505
Largo, MD 20792
http://www.streborbooks.com

© 2008 Edited by Lee Hayes

ISBN-13 978-1-59309-164-4
ISBN-10   1-59309-164-8
LCCN 2007943467

First Strebor Books trade paperback edition May 2008

Cover design: www.mariondesigns.com
Cover photo: Nathan "SEVEN" Scott

10 9 8 7 6 5 4 3 2 1

Manufactured in the United States of America

For information regarding special discounts for bulk purchases, please contact Simon & Schuster Special Sales at 1-800-456-6798 or business@simonandschuster.com

COPYRIGHT NOTICES

THIS BOOK IS DEDICATED TO
all the people who aren't afraid to add some spice to their lives.
This book is meant to delight, entice and entertain.

The stories in this anthology are diverse, clever and ultra-sexy.
It was important to me to include stories from a variety of
authors, both novice and seasoned, so that *Flesh to Flesh*
can fulfill your sexual fantasies.

Special Note: These stories are works of fiction.
The characters within these stories cannot contract a sexually
transmitted disease because these people are not real—you are!
If you engage in sexual activity, always use a condom!
Always!

TABLE OF CONTENTS

I Can't Tell You What He Looked Like

MAURICE MURRELL

(cover model for *Flesh to Flesh*)

He came to me in a dream, chocolate light-skinned
Green, brown-eyed, his body thick and thin
His behind was flat and bubbly, his hair was shaved and long,
  his legs stopped but never with an end
I can't tell you what he looked like, but I can describe him
  perfectly
He was my man, the man of my dreams; he was a reflection of me

I can't tell you the color of his eyes, all I can tell you is they
  burned my soul
I can't tell you if his touch was rough or smooth, but it turned all
  the necessary areas hot and cold.
I can't tell you the thickness of his lips, just that his kiss filled
  with passion
And, I can't tell you what his hair was like, all I know was he was
  my bald Samson

I can't tell you if he was tall or short, only that he could look me
  in the eye
I can't tell you if he was thick or thin, but laying on me was
  subliminally sublime

I can't tell you if his skin tone, reflected the night or the day
All I know is, it was the perfect shade to my own tone, every time
  we would play

I can't tell you if his teeth were crooked or even if they were
  straight
All I can tell you is his smile was the first thing I saw when I fell
  asleep, or the first thing when I would awake.

I can't tell you if his style of clothes was expensive or even cheap
Because all I wanted to do was take those clothes off and lay
  them next to the fireplace in a heap.

I can't tell you if his smell was either pungent, masculine or
  feminine sweet
All I know is it was intoxicating, one whiff and I was forever
  knocked off my feet.

I can't tell you if he liked to go out all the time or liked to stay
  at home
All I know was whatever we did was fun; with him I was never
  alone.

I can't tell you what he looked like, but I can describe him
  perfectly
He was the man of my dreams, you couldn't label him
  aesthetically
I can't tell you all those things that most people first list
But on my man, and my only man, my dream, my virgin,
  my first kiss

He was my everything; I was his—that was never misunderstood
I can't tell you what he looked like. I wouldn't even try if I could.

He never had a label, he was here for my soul and I
He couldn't tell you either what I looked like, but for me
  he would die

I was his everything, he was mine, we were him, he was I
And we don't even know what each other even looks like, 'cause
  love has us blind.
Blind to the superficialness, blind to the shallowness of it all
See 'cause when I close my eyes I see him, in his reflection I
  can recall
See I can't tell you what he looked like, but I can tell you this
He was mine, he was mine; never ever a love like this

I can't tell you what he looks like, neither can he describe me
But we will be written in history as blind lovers forever to be...

"Dream with no limit; they're yours to make any way you want."

৪০েি

With a bachelors in marketing, never did Maurice Murrell think he would be a model (Clik Magazine, JMT, Time, etc), actor (Finding Me, Ski-Trip series, B-Boy Blues), or dancer (hip-hop, street jazz), and now never did he think he would be a published writer. While being a guest writer for magazines and winning poetry nights, this will be Maurice's first work ever published in an anthology. "Writing has always helped me express the way I feel about love, life, and perseverance. It's a way for people to connect with you; they can't judge you with their eyes, but with their thoughts, hearts, and souls." Visit www.mauricemurrell.com for more information on Maurice.

Making Heat, Jazz and Love
LM ROSS

There was a cool blue hue to the room, as the assembled jazz crowd sipped their martinis and smoked their cigarettes. I was slowly imbibing my Courvoisier and slyly checking out the place. This was my scene, my haunt, my NYC jazz dream, and the elements felt just right. I perused the locals and the few heads who boldly nodded in my direction. But this was a typically straight crowd. I made sure I did nothing, said nothing that would arouse unwanted suspicion. I had many friends in the city, but a scant few really dug jazz with the same fervor as me, so it had become my style to usually roll on the solo tip. This night was no different. So, there I sat, sipping and waiting for the show to begin as a feeling of anticipation rose in the air. I could almost taste it, feel it buzzing on my skin.

I needed this escape. I'd been dealing with some deeply emotional stuff that comes with residual heartbreak. Steven, my lover of almost seven years, had fallen for the charms and assumedly the younger dick of a co-worker. I'd suspected something developing between them, but Steven chalked it up to my "crazy insecurity." Well, a few weeks later, I arrived early from a business trip, and my crazy insecure ass caught them, going at it, in the bed Steven and I purchased and shared. They jumped up, naked and ashamed, with apologies and explanations tripping from their lips. I'd never once cheated on Steven, and there he was, in our bed, fucking some acrobatic bitch on the slide. That betrayal ended it for us. I mean, what good was a relationship if the motherfucka lacked trust?

I had, for all intents and purposes, given up on men. I denied all temptations from that point onward, and trust, there were more than a few! I needed to work on me. I needed to love me again. I needed to spoil me, and accept all my good, bad and bullshit parts. I had been doing just that…for months. My only reprieve was a little entertainment, by way of jazz.

Showtime: The piano player appeared in a shaft of golden light. Brotha with dreads, attired in a natty-blue suit, his long nimble fingers caressed the keys slowly as if he had at his disposal, eighty-eight different lovers. He played and the crowd swayed to the strains of his smooth bossa nova. Gradually the light increased, and in the corner was a stout cat, on bass. He began to thump in slow and sultry jazzy tones, and soon he and the pianist were grooving in song. I dug the vibe they manifested. I nodded my head to their potent fusion. Soon, the drummer appeared, beating those snares in a nasty counterpoint that made something inside us jump as everyone tapped their feet. The sound the three of them manifested was sweet, tangy and saucy to the point of sounding sexual. And then, in a brazenly blue neon glare, the man on the sax appeared.

The bleat of his horn transformed the room. I detected the sighs and swoons. I heard a woman release an orgasmic cry of: "Damn, that brotha be fine!"

I must admit that the sista didn't lie. Brotha was fine, in a winter-white turtleneck sweater and matching trousers. Tall, bald, madly broad-shouldered, he had a presence and a gravity that could not be denied. He played like quiet fire. He played sooooo slowly and soulfully that he conjured up visions of hot Nawlins nights, the cry of alley cats, the bite of bourbon on the tongue, and the sweet caress of an amorous lover. He played as if he'd crawled between my thighs and discovered the clue to my carnal paradise. I felt both shook and hooked on this sound he made. And still he played, as the jazz-heads nodded and ladies swooned. But some part of my senses made me think, he was blowing for me, just me...and that blue-bruised hurt lodged deep within me.

I flashed back to all of those hot and sensuous times Steven and I shared when our bodies would grind in perfect sync, and it seemed we'd shared one mind. Damn! That brotha on the horn, killing me jazzily with his song! And the more he played, the more of a towering black Adonis he became.

Sometimes inside of his performance, I swear he'd made serious eye contact with me. Not the people at the first few tables, not those women he'd given a case of the screaming thigh sweats... but to me!

The whole set felt like I was sitting in a den of audible sex. It made me moist. It made my dick harder than the Empire State.

After the performance, the band was signing their latest CD for all who purchased it. After the mood I'd just experienced, there was no way in hell I could resist copping it. In fact, I asked for three: one for my stereo, one for my car, and one for my portable CD. The brotha who blew smiled as I approached the table where he and his band mates were seated. I glanced causally over my left shoulder to see if that luminous smile was for someone else. But no, it was a smile directed at me. As I drew closer, I felt something strange and warm, and familiar, too. I didn't know him, but it was as if we both knew each other's core secret. Odd, sometimes, how you just simply know. This brotha was family. And what a big bald and finely talented addition he made to the brood!

"Tight set. I was really digging the vibe, yo." These were my first words to him.

"Thanks, mon. Guess ya be a fan. Three CDs?" he asked with a smile brighter than a noonday Jamaican sun that made him even more intriguing.

"Ummm...yeah...when I dig something, I mean reeeeeeeally dig it, I don't wanna be caught someplace without it."

Damn! That sounded like I was trying to come onto the cat! I wasn't; at least not consciously. But then he set his slow sable-eyed glow-in-the-dark ray on me.

Oh shit! It was a look I knew by heart. It was that "yes-I-like-men-and-if-given-the-chance-I'd-love-to-fuck-the-shit-outta-you" look!

"I'm Colin," he said, still flashing that mega-watt smile. "Colin Elliot," he added, and my dick jumped inside my suit pants as he said it.

"I'm Lance," I uttered.

He extended his large, dark jazz-talented hand. I took it, and in that moment, I almost heard music. The wail of a faraway trumpet, the beat of torrid congas, and the sounds of jungle music played in my chest.

I watched that hand as he signed my CDs. And despite the surroundings, I could not seem to take my eyes off him. Just as he was signing the third one, someone tapped his shoulder, whispered in his ear, and his eyes widened. "Ya kiddin'! Duh mon is 'ere?" Colin asked excitedly. And his excitement made me strangely jealous that some person had suddenly broken our spell.

"Hell! I betta jwaun talk to him, mon!" he said. "Been nice… re-e-e-e-eal nice meetin' ya, Lance." He quickly shook my hand again. And though disappointed, I was pleased that at least he'd remembered my name.

When Colin stood, he was a tall drink of water: six feet five inches, buffed, and tantalizingly chocolate. He had wide sweeping shoulders, a proud jutting chest. His perfect posture and smooth shaved head gave his whole presence the look of a long, tall dick.

I shrugged off the spell, and made my way outside the club. I took the subway back home, musing on the night's events. I reached inside my coat pocket to read the CD, to stare at his picture and daydream. And there, on the last copy, that jazz-hot player had scribbled his phone number!

Sly fox! I wanted to call him. I was tempted. But damn it! The last thing I needed was a jazz cat constantly on the road, doing what musicians do: fuck small tribes of groupies. So, I passed on calling this intriguing new man. Besides, in my ongoing campaign of treating myself to the pleasures of life, I'd booked a vacation in Jamaica.

It was a pleasant eighty-five degrees when I arrived on the island. A balmy breeze greeted my skin, as I detected the scent of citrus fruit in the air. The palm trees stood tall and phallic, their full ripe coconuts hung like large brown balls, surrounding me in shade and sultry possibilities. My hotel was nestled just off Long Bay in Negril. Everything within eyesight was white, blue or green. Steven and I had planned to sizzle together in that paradise, to see Jamaica as a twosome. We'd had daydreams of gazing longingly at the sunset, walking barefoot in the sand, and making sweet passionate love under one of the island's waterfalls. But that fantasy ended when the bastard cheated on me!

So, for my first night alone in Jamaica, I thought of Steven, and ruthlessly masturbated as the cool balmy breeze blew in, caressing every pore of my nakedness.

The next day, I awakened to the light of a blazing saffron sun. Gazing over the terrace and along the beach, the island men were godlike—tall, gorgeous black sculptures with neatly braided dreads and blinding smiles. Everyone smiled. It appeared to be contagious. I quickly showered and went downstairs to have breakfast among the living. On the way, I saw a poster of the jazz band which would be playing in the showroom. And there, right in the middle, stood a tall, bald, elegant-looking Colin! I couldn't believe it! Was fate placing us both in Jamaica, at the very same time? Well, that was definitely one performance I planned to catch!

After breakfast I changed into my trunks and hit the beach. As luck or fate would have it, I saw a man who looked just like Colin, talking to some people as they strolled along the sand. The closer I came, my heat began to quicken. It was him! Yes. It was Colin, in a white shirt and matching shorts, his lovely complexion accented sharply against the blue and white of the beach. I wanted him to remember me. I didn't think he would. But as I approached the small group, Colin's eyes darted toward me. I knew from the gaze that he did, in fact, remember.

"Ey you! What ya doin' in my neck of dee woods?" His Jamaican accent seemed even thicker than I'd recalled, or perhaps it was an effect, or an osmosis thing.

"Just enjoying the scenery, man. How are you, Colin?"

"I be good...beautiful, mon. Just 'ere tuh play a few gigs, ya know," he said, totally ignoring the people he was conversing with earlier. "I hope ya plan to see dee show. I'll even play sum'm special just for ya." He winked.

Amidst all that lush and beautiful scenery of the beach, I sat obsessing on Colin, his music, his friendliness, his hotness, his white shorts, housing this mysteriously meaty iguana. That night, I twisted out three nut-busting loads, haunted by buck-naked fantasies of Colin. Hell, I needed the distraction—even more since Steven was gone.

The next day, I happened upon a vision stretched out like some chocolate colossus against a snow-white blanket on the beach. It was a long, dark, stunning picture of rugged masculinity. That vision turned out to be Colin! The warm Jamaican sun shone down on the peaks of his russet nipples. Like magnets, my eyes were drawn to his chest, and the rest of him.

I nodded as I passed, and he smiled the brightest white smile in that land of smiles. I thought to myself, please…just let me chill and lounge beside you!

And, as if he'd heard my private thoughts, with the sweep of a long strong arm, he graciously invited me to sit and hang out with him. In a flash, I accepted and plopped down beside his utter cocoa-butter godliness. My hungry eyes perused him as he lay gazing at the beach. The water was limpid and exquisite with its varying shades of greens and resplendent blues. But my view of nature was obscured by the vision of Colin in his leopard bikini. The more I looked, the hotter I became. Was it the sun, a trick of light stretching out the spots of his bikini? Whatever it was certainly cast a mighty shadow.

"So, 'ave ya been? 'Aving a good time, mon? Ya been to any fun places yet?" he asked.

I was far too busy covertly gazing at his shrouded manhood. For a moment, I thought his voice had come from it. "Fun places"? Hell, I couldn't think of a more "fun place" to be, than taking a long hot joyride down his...

"Well, it's lovely, great. But where can a gay man get laid in this place?" I asked. I hoped I hadn't shocked him. But, fuck! I was just horny enough to let him know.

Colin remained eerily quiet. Had I turned him off by being so candid? I checked his face. His eyes were closed. Had he fallen asleep? Maybe he hadn't heard me. But then, my wandering gaze peered down at his member, and shit! Right before my eyes, I witnessed an amazingly powerful swelling in that nylon bikini. That fucking leopard print was beginning to move, shift and, shit! I expected it to ROAR! The hot, primal pulse of his man-sex beat there, pounding like some urgent drum. I wanted to grab it, unleash that giant into the cool air to breathe free, unencumbered.

But it was broad daylight, and hundreds of people surrounded us. Still, it was getting awfully hot on that beach.

"So...Ya like what ya seein', mon?" he asked, in a low and lazy, yet deeply sexy, voice.

I gulped as the bulge just kept growing, enlarging—beginning to shoot sideways and then across his large brown thigh! Did I "like" what I was "seein'"? Somewhere between my labored breaths, I might've managed a "yesssss!"

"We've got Hedonism II, if ya like it straight and crowded. But ya no group playa...bet ya like it 'ot an private...," he discerned. "Well, doncha?" he asked. I nodded yes. "Well, I gwan to give ya special pass to my show, mon. Afterward, we can talk, an 'ang out, privately. Would ja like dat?"

Of course, I'd like it. That would be lovely. But, his invitation left me feeling conflicted. Whatever he had in mind, I was very sure sex would eventually be a part of it. I hadn't been sexual since my last fit of angry sex with Steven—which was almost six months ago. I liked this Colin cat. I felt I could really vibe with him. What if we got together, and fucked, with no emotion—just fucked because the island, and the sand, and the hue of moon and the mood of the place cast some sensually sinful spell on us? I didn't want this to be some crazy freaky episode of: what happens in Jamaica, stays in Jamaica!

"Ya know, dat night in duh jazz club, I wanted tuh get to know ya better, mon. But circumstances got in duh way."

That statement alone was like steel drum music to my ears. So, he didn't extend the invite for some quick and meaningless fuck. Cool. Very cool.

"Well, your playing really captured my imagination. Man. It's so sensual...and knowing...and dangerous, too. What do you think of when you play, man?"

"Angels...sometimes. And sometimes I imagine a lover from dee past... But that night...when I saw you, I closed my eyes an thought of you...only Lance."

Stop it! This mofo was trying to charm the towel off my naked ass! It was sweet, though.

"I want ya..."—he paused seductively—"...at dee show tonight. And evvvvvvvvery night we play, mon. Promise me, yah come, my Lancelot!"

"I promise, Colin."

No one, not a soul, could have stopped me.

I attended both performances, and quickly noticed how his band abandoned jazz and catered to the crowd with a set of mostly reggae music, and other island-inspired sounds. I rocked, like the others rocked, lively to their beat. They also flipped the script on their choice of attire, choosing outfits that reflected an island flava: long, flowing printed shirts and pastel-colored trousers. But for the final limbo number, Colin dressed the most provocatively of all. He wore a boldly blue-and-white-printed sarong. Oh, my God! The legs, the arms, the chest, the body on him! Shirtless, shoeless, every lean black muscle gleaming under the lights, he was practically asking to be sexually assaulted, right there, on that stage!

Finally, once the show came to a close at midnight, I, with my backstage pass, strolled, as I was told to, beyond the dressing room into that narrow hallway. There stood Colin, still wearing that damn sarong! He looked like a tall, dark king from another time, a King direct from the Isle of Lust. Shirtless was his best look, and the caps of his wide shoulders were dusted with sweat. He saw me, and grinned the most mischievous of all the grins in his arsenal. He motioned me to the back door. He had things to take care of with the band, but agreed to meet me there. I waited outside, as the warm air filled me with longing and that strange trace of heady excitement. Then, Colin appeared. Still clad in that sarong, his pumped biceps and hairless well-defined chest caught a trace of moonlight as he approached me. His nipples resembled jujubes.

"Ready for a lil' island dee-light, mon?"

I nodded an enthusiastic *yes!*

The air was thick with the dick of promise. The ocean breeze eased the humidity, yet didn't do a damn thing for the heat I was feeling.

We boarded a bamboo raft and Colin stood, rowing us to parts unknown. He knew the island like the back of his strong hand, rowing us to the darkest end of the beach, cognizant it would be completely uninhabited.

"Must be verrrrry careful on my island; ya know, batty-boys are much despised here," he said with a whisper.

"Yes. I'm aware. There's much homophobia in this place."

But did Colin consider himself a "batty-boy"? Did he embrace his gayness, or was he in deep denial?

"Ah…the main reason I left. In New York, I am free, to be all of me…no hiding, no secrecy."

I nodded in agreement as he continued rowing, to where, I'd no idea.

Finally, we'd reached the spot. Of all the places in paradise, this by far was the most heavenly—a small lagoon, where the moon lit against a lush waterfall. I could hear the gurgling waters; smell every scent the island offered: the allspice, the sugar cane, the mangos and the coconuts.

Once onshore, he suggested we go swimming.

"But I've no trunks, man," I protested.

"Aye! On dis private tour, no trunks allowed, mon. Now, ya strip!"

Shrugging, I kicked off my sandals and very quickly removed my tank.

"Ooh, you're a beauty, mon. Lean, an not a ounce of fat on ya." He reached out one large hand and playfully pinched my nipple. "An these were made for suckin'."

There was a tower in my Bermuda shorts before they fell. Colin's fingers played along the fine hairs descending my belly. "Lemme git a look at dat ass," he demanded, gripping my trembling globes. "Ah! It's a round, tenduh an it be taut too, just the way I like," he appraised.

As I was about to remove my briefs, Colin briskly shoved them to my feet. My dick was a piece of shameless granite. Colin grinned, then fell to his knees. All at once, his tongue teased my burning head. I shivered to the warm wet friction. He gobbled me whole. The cool breeze, his warm tongue caused a rush of tingling sensations. He licked me slow and methodically. I palmed his shaved spinning skull. He took me to the back of his moist throat. My knees buckled. I fell, and we positioned ourselves into a heated 69. Yes! He was my food; my rich ripe banana, throbbing on my tongue. He ate my lust, whole. Those lips plunged down my shaft, as Colin commenced to suck and savor. Oh! He blew me as lewdly as he blew his saxophone. All a brotha could do was sigh, and twitch and moan. Touching him, sucking him, feeling him shiver, I know I was coating pleasure all through his being. I began to thrust my hips as his hungry throat caught my dick, pitch for eager pitch. "Gooood deek, mon… Good deek," he sighed, between breaths, between sucks, between slobber. The weight of his full Jamaican boner surged down my throat. I groped the slopes of his thighs. Oh! Colin seemed to suck me more wildly when I gripped the slabs of his ebony ass. Moments passed.

Colin's sucking ceased. All at once, he grabbed my bobbing hard-on, pulled me by the hub of it, then ran, with me in hand, leading me in a dash to the bay. We jumped in and began our buck-naked midnight swim. Ooh! The tepid water felt so brisk to my dick. The rushing currents calmed my throbbing meat and soon everything grew more serene.

Colin shot me a mischievous leer, and dove beneath me. Quickly he playfully wrestled my buoyant dick inside his lips. "Oh! Yes!" I treaded, shivering as he sucked me warm and wet. Water boiled up around me. His tongue and throat rattled against me. It was bliss! A few luscious moments of this, and in a huge splash he came up for air. Shit! He looked so hot— drenching wet and bathed by moonlight. Then, grabbing my shoulder, he led me down.

His thick floating dick awaited my air-sucking lips. Bloated and full, it entered and quickly jammed my mouth. Oh! I gobbled, gurgled, and nearly drowned trying to contain it, as he laughed uproariously above me. Suddenly, he pulled me to the surface, and we swam back to shore. As we emerged, shivering and drenched, Colin shouted, "To the waterfalls!" He ran ahead of me, naked and dripping, his ripped ass flexing, his long broad dick slapping thigh to thigh.

Colin made it there first, and as I joined him, he slowly pushed me to my knees. "Lick it. Lick dee rim!" He sighed.

I licked, I sloshed, I feasted, and a man could get drunk on it! Peeling back the long russet skin made him shimmy in my hand. My palm was full of wild pulsations. The long cola-colored dick flexed and stretched like elastic in my grip. As he fed me his bloated manhood, his natural musk mixed with my slobber, its taste only hardened me more. I licked and lacquered him in smooth slick circles. Shit, he was big! I drew back a wild gag. I traveled down its grossly thick ridge, lapping seven, then eight velvet inches. I jacked the lower half with both hands as my mouth assaulted the top.

Surrounded by the crash of water, I gazed upward and saw Colin's pleasured face. Beyond the big wet blur of his uncon-querable meat, he was smiling down at me. My tongue slithered back and forth across the massive head, like a slurping carnivore gone hog-wild for his meaty feast! By the sounds I made, Colin could surely tell, I was ravenous!

Making a treat of him, my lips fell to his low loose-hanging balls which hung like ebony ornaments between his thighs. I made an effort to suction them both into my jaw. It was useless. Still I licked, lapping his bulging sac. But soon he groaned, lifted my chin, and brought my lips back to his wet and waiting boner.

"Ya like it? Oh yeah! Eat that cock, mon. Yes! Whatta mouth! Mmmm. Eat me, mon!" he cried, his eyes rolling in his head. He was warm and tangy and growing hotter. "OOOOH! That feels, fuck, fuck, f-f-fucking FANTASTIC, mon!" he purred.

We made it to the sand and tumbled down, contorting in a luscious 69. His massive prick pressed at my lips, as mine did to his. He then braided his long tongue around my throbbing cock, and the moment he slithered down, it sent a wildfire through my scrotum. I was treated to Colin's warm wet throat as I pistoned through his full, slick lips. He licked me up and down, saturating my shaft with cool, wet swirls. I thrust, and his soft generous lips cushioned my slide. A sigh, a touch of his teeth made my cock drum some near orgasmic beat. He mouth-fucked me with a long throbbing cock so thick, so hard it felt like a slab of lead, pumping on my tongue.

I grabbed his dusky globes, kneaded them, and his thrusts increased. His flopping nuts slapped rhythmically beneath my chin. I licked them as his cock rode across my face. The pulsation in his balls extended up his shaft. I wanted his every stupefying inch pumping up my ass. I stopped. His suction ceased. Colin could see my lust to be fucked coupled with the fear of a dick the size of his, splitting my asshole in two.

"Think ya can handle it, mon?' he asked, shaking his long spit-soaked prick at me.

"It's a fuckin' monster! I don't know, but I'm willing to try..."

He pulled me in close. He licked two long fingers and jammed them up my hot asshole. As he parted my nervous cheeks, his lips floated up, and he kissed me with a yearning as strong and urgent as my own. Oh! My skin, cock, every part of me caught fire and light when Colin kissed me.

He spread me out on a blanket, and ran a slow tongue across my toes, calves, thighs and balls! Oh! Yes! I turned, and Colin's long tongue swiped the building sweat beading at my burning crevice. He darted inside, fluttered, and I ground my cock into the blanket, thrashing and swirling my pleasured butt! Two fingers, then three was enough for him to determine I was deep enough. But knowing the length, width, breadth of his own cock, he smeared globs of lube inside my puckered anus. Then he coated his long thick threatening member, as I stretched spread-eagle on the blanket.

I was dizzy with heat as I pulled my cheeks open in a horny invitation for him. Colin sighed, held his long, condomed piece in both hands and mounted me. I felt the poke as he guided forth, his thick crest brushing at my breech. Oh! He moved in so fucking slowly, I ached for him. But then, his fierce knobby crown probed and pricked and it broke soundly into my flesh. "YEOW! SHIT!" It was instant anguish!

He kneaded my blistering cheeks around a long staff of shaft meat, which was only halfway inside, and still lengthening. Oh! I felt the slow and steady sting, and grunted as it went deeper. "AWW! Shit!" My straining anus flexed to enclose his malicious measure. My whole body sizzled with rough heat-filled painful pleasure. He wiggled there. I felt it all as the sweet pain of it made me jabber.

"Oh, Colin! You, you gotta monsta! Easy! Please!" I growled.

He dismounted me, and I wondered why.

He gestured to the falls. We waded through the churning

waters and over to a group of rocks. Colin steadily beat his rigid measure, as he positioned me against a wall. "Bend over, mon." I did, gripping the stones facing me for extra leverage. Holding my globes, he led his big invasive pole in a slow pulsating probe up my ass. "Aww! Oh! Ah! Yes! Yes!" Still lodged inside me, Colin walked us closer to the rocks. "Bring ya one leg up, an put ya foot on top, mon." He sighed.

I placed one foot on a jagged stone. This position spread me wider for him. He pushed. I felt a boiling heat push past my coil, as it snaked past my prostate, then deeper still. My moan withered into his sigh. A violent groan rose between us. He commenced to slide, to move, to thrust and throw me a mean almost tribal fuck. It was hard, rhythmic and he bucked with emotion as he pushed past places no other man had ever been. I sighed, I grimaced, and I took it. The water from the falls tumbled down, washing down over us. He molded his torso to my wet back, and bucked with a violent thunder. "Oh! Aww! Yes!" I bellowed. He found a new rhythm and set a feverish pace, his thick legs crashing—his thickness banging me sore. Sore, yes, but utterly satisfied. "Oh yes!" I chimed. Colin was born to pound a man's ass, to fuck it with heat and sweat, wind and sexual lightning.

"Mmm! Yes! Ya got some good stuff, babeeee!" He sighed, before his motion began to slow.

The rhythm he'd set only made me hot, so hot, I wanted, needed, desperately to DO HIM!

"You wanna give me a go at that sweet ass of yours, man?" I asked, not knowing what he'd say, but hoping he'd say, YES!

He pulled out of me, slowly, and whispered, "Ya think ya can handle it, mon?"

Before I knew it, I was sliding a rubber down the length of my dick, and slowly aiming it to his sweet puckered starfish. Moist, pliable, warm, giving, it was like entering a dark unknown cove, where a tight cave of skin awaited to bring me pleasure. I gave it to him soft and slow, at first. Oh, I felt his insides squeezing me, teasing me, letting me in deeper, gradually. He rolled his hips in that sultry Jamaican wine, and I just went all wild inside it. It was like my passion unzipped its careful coat of behavior. My dick sliced inside him, hard and quick, catching his slickest rhythm. The sounds of our sighs collided. My sultry effort brought forced choppy breaths from him. With an occasional smack to his cheeks, I loved when he jumped and shivered, and said, "Fuck me, mon!"

The falls trickled down and around us. Drenched with sweat, water and lust, we moved, engulfed and lunged and enveloped, as each jolt I made inside him sent his manhood swinging. I sent hot, tender kisses slowly along his neck. Colin shivered with a vibration centered deep in his gut. We locked into an exacting rhythm, rolling our hips in lusty unison. I swooned. Colin groaned, and I went in so deep, both our bodies stiffened.

I felt him shudder and I shuddered with him. I pulled my piece slowly from his deepest recesses. Ripping off the condom in a flash, without even tugging, I erupted. And just then, Colin turned to face me. With his manhood long and rigid, let loose a Jamaican holler, and the great slab just sputtered! As hard as the falls surrounding us, our cream shot in warm and milky torrents, pelting each other's skin in a deluge.

Under the rushing waterfalls, we stood gazing and breathless and kissing, kissing like we meant it. I watched his huffing moon-lit silhouette. A feeling of utter consummation welled up in me so strong. Oh! In that instant, I erupted, again, not knowing I would. But a thick soul-cleansing load charged to his wet, heaving torso.

"Oh, shit, yes! Yes!" I puffed, my lust, at long last quenched.

"Mighty 'ot one, mon." Colin sighed, as he re-tied his sarong and carefully tucked that beauteous Jamaican jumbo away.

For the rest of my stay, there was jazz, and vibe, and neon and Colin.

That last night, we made love on the white sands of another beach, off a secluded section of Jumbee Bay. I thought of plantains, ripe mangos, and the rich fortifying milk of coconuts. After he climaxed, Colin lay on his side, and I pondered what would become of us. Was he ready to be more than a secret he wore inside his pants? Was he man enough to own who and what he was?

"Lance. I don't want it to end, mon. I been feelin' ya. Feelin' ya deep...and not jess ya deek, but ya heart."

Those words were sweeter than all the cane in Jamaica. Colin let it be known that he was ready to step out, and more importantly, to step out of his private closet. It was easier in the States, and he was already a New Yorker, like me.

Three months later, this beautiful musician cat moved in with me. And now we make heat and jazz and love, almost nightly. Maybe Stella went to Jamaica and got her groove back. But me? I found Colin, and got the whole damn musical suite!

ଞଙ୍ଗ

L.M. Ross is a New York writer and a jazz poet of immense musicality. His work, which has appeared in over 270 magazines, journals and anthologies, echoes the best of lyric writers, and yet contains brutal slashes of honesty. His haunting novel Manhood...The Longest Moan *is a story of youthful ambition, maturing success and heartbreaking disappointment. It is a deep, wistful, brave and sexy story. It's follow-up,* The Moanin' After, *is a look at life in the big city, after the party, after losing friends, and after the onset of AIDS. Ross, as a writer, possesses the innate quality of making his characters* breathe.

The Snake Handler
ARMAND

The first day I stepped onto the zoo grounds as an employee was like walking on a cloud. As a zoology major at the local university, my lifelong dream was to work with animals—saving rhinos on the Serengeti Plains, capturing and releasing problem bears, running a sanctuary for endangered cats, rehabilitating injured horses, tagging wild eagles. I wanted more than anything to work with animals and people who love animals. Having grown up on a farm in rural Illinois, I was accustomed to being around both livestock and wildlife, and the zoo was a perfect place to combine my love for animals and my training in zoology.

Because demand was high, it was tough to get a job at the zoo, but I finally scored an interview and was offered a position as an assistant handler. Though I preferred to work with mammals—primates, marsupials, ungulates, ursine, lupine—I was assigned to the Herpetarium, the Snake House. Very few people requested jobs with bugs and reptiles, so they were usually the last positions to fill, but I had agreed to take any opening in order to get my foot in the door. I was even willing to tend to serpents, if it got me the job. After all, back home I had removed many troublesome cottonmouths, rat snakes and racers that had the misfortune of coming in contact with scared humans. I knew I could handle the Snake House until something better came along.

On my first day, after a brief orientation by an administrator, I was escorted by a lackey, some non-communicative sixteen-year-old girl with freckles and braces, to the Herpetarium, where I was deposited in a feeding and handling room behind the scenes. While I waited for someone to come and tell me what to do, I furtively looked around.

By snaking (no pun intended) through the walkways, handlers could get to the backs of each cage to feed and care for their ophidian charges. At the north end of the building, out of view of the visitors, was the handling room where I had been unceremoniously abandoned. In this room, food was stored and prepared and snakes could be weighed and examined. A large dry erase board listed the feeding schedule of each animal. I could see from the board that a rhinoceros viper was on loan to another zoo, that the Burmese python was gravid, and that the green mamba wasn't eating and needed close observation.

"So you're the new guy," a deep voice called from behind me.

When I turned, I could not have been more surprised. Before me, wearing the ubiquitous zoo uniform of khaki shorts, a button-down shirt and work boots, was the most beautiful Italian man I had ever seen.

"Uh, yeah."

I was reduced to caveman speak.

The hunky man began to walk toward me and I felt my knees quiver beneath me. He extended his hand as he said, "Tony."

I read his nametag—which actually said "Antonio"—took his hand in mine, shook forcefully and responded, "Samson."

"Well, Samson, let me show you around." He smiled wide,

showing the most perfect teeth behind full lips. When he turned to give me the tour, I finally took a breath, and I wondered if he had read the desire on my face. "Here are the live rodents," Tony said as he pointed. "A couple of our snakes won't eat euthanized prey, so we have no choice but to feed them live. Keeps us from having to force-feed them."

The snake handler could have been reading the Dead Sea Scrolls to me—in Aramaic—and I would have been rapt with attention. He had a deep voice with a slight rasp and a hint of an Italian accent. It was so fucking sexy that I felt my cock twitch just hearing him speak.

As he led me through the corridors, I stayed close behind and never took my eyes off of him. While I had the medium build of a soccer player, green eyes and auburn hair, Tony had the stocky build of a rugby player, brown eyes and black hair. The khaki fabric stretching over his muscular frame highlighted his manly physique. As he walked ahead of me, I admired his thick calves and round ass. When he turned to make sure I was listening, I snapped stiff as a board, afraid that I'd been caught gazing at him with lust in my eyes.

As time went on and Tony trained me in the art of snake handling, I had the opportunity to learn a great deal about the reptiles from Tony, and I was amazed by his knowledge about and comfort with his charges. He loved the snakes and handled them (only as much as was needed) with deft precision and an almost spiritual intuition. Through his gorgeous, soft brown eyes, I learned to appreciate the serpents in a new way. From the massive reticulated python to the stocky puff adder, from the highly toxic Egyptian cobra to the non-virulent kingsnake, from the green Emerald Tree boa to the yellow eyelash viper, he loved his snakes.

For more than one reason, it was exciting to watch Tony work.

On occasion, another keeper would joke about the way Tony "handled his snake," and the puerile, obvious double entendre always made me smile. At night, I dreamed about how Tony might indeed "handle his snake."

After a month at my job, I had learned how to feed most of the animals and to clean their cages, but I was still not allowed to go near the highly toxic snakes, like the fer-de-lance and the tiger snake, unless Tony was there to supervise. While trying to learn to handle snakes, I made some mistakes. Once, while trying to put the female rock python away, I looked away briefly, and she swung back and bit into my arm. Because of my shock, I really didn't feel much pain, but Tony had to pry her jaws apart to release my bruised arm. Thankfully, she was a juvenile and had only grown to about eight feet, instead of her potential twenty feet. I knew she had no intention of trying to kill me, but she was preparing to shed and wasn't her normal placid self. I should have known better.

My pride was hurt more than my arm, but I was able to keep my composure, and Tony commended me on not losing my cool. He merely put the rock python in her cage, got out the first aid kit and calmly washed the small puncture marks on my arm with antiseptic. He made no disparaging remarks while he cleaned my wound; he merely pointed out that bites happened to all snake handlers. While he held my arm it began to tremble, not because of the snake bite but because of the touch of the snake handler. Our faces were only inches apart, and I felt a slight swoon. Tony bandaged my wound, patted me on the back and then told me to finish my daily tasks. So I got right back in the proverbial saddle, and handled the next serpent, a much more cooperative common boa. Tony rewarded me with an approving smile and said, "You'll make a great snake handler. You've got what it takes."

Damn, I could eat him up.

After about three months at the zoo, I was invited to hear a lecture in the series being hosted by the zoo. The speaker was a naturalist who was touring the country with his animal photos from around the globe. The zoo remained open late and staff was able to attend the lecture for free. Tony and I sat together and afterward we went to the Snake House. He said that he wanted to check on the newest addition, a Gaboon viper from Africa, and I merely wanted to follow Tony.

After checking the animals, Tony turned quickly and ran into me. I stumbled backward against the stainless steel counter. He apologized and I froze in place. The sheer contact of his body made me raw and exposed, and my cock began to grow.

Tony looked up and down my body. I remained still, leaning against the cold counter with mice scampering in bins behind me.

He licked his lips.

I took a deep breath.

Then he lunged at me and began to devour my mouth with his. Our tongues explored as our pelvises ground together. Next, I did what I had imagined doing since the first time I laid eyes on him: I slid my hands over his round ass.

Tony ripped my shirt open and began to lick my nipples. He was like a hungry animal about to tear me apart. I tugged at his shirt and was able to untuck it from his pants. Then I pulled it over his head and caught sight of his naked torso, which was exquisite. A cleaved chest with a sparse dusting of black hair, dark nipples and a glorious trail around his navel made me salivate with desire.

"Damn, you're hot," I uttered.

"I was hoping you were gay," he said, "because I've been dying to do this to you since the first day I walked in and you were standing here."

He ran his hands over the blond hair on my chest. My nipples were standing at full attention and felt like they might explode. He kissed me hard and caused the stainless steel counter to creak under the pressure of our bodies pushing against it. In the distance I heard the sibilant rattle of a snake's tail. I reached for his belt, adroitly unfastening it, and yanked his fly open.

There straining against black cotton briefs was his fat cock. Without delay, I reached inside his underwear and wrapped my hands around it.

"Fuck yeah," Tony moaned.

His cock was the thickest one I'd ever seen. It was hard and arched up against his body. The description "beer can" came to mind. On the end of his dick I could feel pre-cum, and I wanted a taste, but before I could Tony tore at my shorts until he had me standing there buck naked in front of him.

Not to be outdone, I dropped to my knees and yanked down his khaki shorts. For a moment, I stared at the bulge in his briefs and time began to run in slow motion. I reached for his underwear, folded them down and watched his hard cock come into view. It was fucking glorious. I grabbed the elastic band and pulled his underwear all the way down to his ankles.

Once the shock wore off and I realized that I was actually going to have sex with Tony, I went into action, taking his cock in my hand and squeezing the pre-cum out of the tip. Then I leaned over and licked his cock from base to tip and sucked on the end of it, tasting the pre-cum. He moaned as I slid my lips over the crown of his thick dick.

His member was definitely thicker than any I had ever sucked before, and at first I found it difficult to work the entire cock into my mouth. While I stretched my mouth over his organ, Tony reached down and rubbed his hands through my blond locks, and before long I was taking his dick deep into my mouth.

"Fuck yeah, buddy. Suck my cock. That's so hot."

I looked up at him as I sucked. His eyes were drifting up in his head as if he were lost in a drug haze, but it was just intense orgiastic pleasure overtaking him.

"Yeah, that's it," he moaned. "Fuck, that feels good."

I couldn't quite get my lips all the way to the end of the base of his cock because it was just so damn thick. So I wrapped my thumb and index finger tightly around the base and squeezed while I vigorously licked the sensitive spot on the underside of his dick, and Tony went fucking nuts. He gasped and his legs buckled.

"Oh my God. Shit. Ohhhh. That's it."

I let go of his cock and stroked it in the tight grip of my fist. As I stroked it, I slapped the head of it against my cheek.

"I love your dick," I said. "I love your body."

"Yeah. You're fucking hot, buddy. I hope you got some time to do this right."

My response was a wide grin and a nod.

"Let me get my boots off." So I let go of his tumescent penis, and he madly tore at the laces of his work boots. Once he had them off, he kicked his pants and underwear aside and then lifted me up. We began to kiss like we were insatiable for more. His lips were so heavenly.

Tony suddenly dropped to his knees and took my own stiff cock in his mouth. Within minutes he was devouring my entire cock, and it was wet and warm, and I was lost in ecstasy. With my left hand, I reached down and brushed the stubble on his cheek, and it was surprisingly erotic and made me shudder with pleasure. With my right hand, I played with one of my erect nipples.

I was moaning loudly. The cold steel against my ass could not distract me from what he was doing to my cock.

"I want to lick your ass," I heard myself say.

Tony stopped sucking. "Yeah?"

"Is that okay? You have the best ass."

Tony turned around and bent over showing me his glorious, rock-hard ass. It was the most perfect butt I'd ever laid eyes on, and I wanted to dive in, so I reached out and rubbed his massive globes.

"You like my ass?" he asked.

"God yes."

"I fucking love having my ass eaten. You going to fuck me too?"

Could I have heard right? Was I hallucinating? Was this fucking Italian stallion going to actually let me poke my dick inside his tight pucker? Now I knew I must be dreaming.

Well, if he was going to let me fuck him, I knew that I'd better get started loosening him up with a good rim job.

Tony bent over the island in the center of the room and I knelt behind him. His cheeks were covered with sparse black hair. I licked each cheek in turn and then pulled them apart. Eureka! There was the pink rose surrounded by small curly black hairs. I tickled my tongue lightly against the tight muscle and heard Tony moan. He pressed his ass back toward me, and I dove in with gusto.

Nothing could have stopped me from licking avidly at the snake handler's pink pucker. My tongue toyed with it playfully, poked at it aggressively and lapped the surrounding skin.

"Oh fuck, Samson, you're gonna make me cum just licking my hole," Tony called out.

"Hold on. Don't cum yet. I got more for you."

With that, I wet my middle finger and slid it into him slowly and felt his hole grip tightly.

"Yeah. That's it. Damn, your finger feels good."

Fuck, he was tight. I reached between his massive thighs and grabbed his cock. It was still arched, rock hard, up against his belly. Once again I felt pre-cum, so I used it to lubricate my hand and I began to stroke his dick while I fingered his ass.

Suddenly, Tony looked back at me and said, "Let's six-nine." I slid my finger out of his ass, and he jumped atop the island and lay on his back. I crawled atop him in "69" position and immediately felt his lips around my cock.

While he sucked my dick, I lifted his legs and continued to finger his ass like I was a child with a new toy. Eventually, I worked two fingers inside of him. I had never been so turned on.

"I'm going to cum," I said.

"No," he insisted. "I want you to fuck me."

"Okay." If I must, I must.

I jumped from the table and Tony followed suit. Before bending over in front of me, he gave me another long, deep kiss.

"You got a condom?" I asked.

"In my bag," he said as he pointed. Rather than get it for me, Tony just bent all the way over the island, his torso at a forty-five-degree angle, his ass pressed back out, and waited.

I all but ran to his bag and flipped open the flap. Inside I found a strip of condoms. I tore one free, ripped at the wrapper and then slid the lubricated condom onto my tumescent dick.

"You ready?" I asked.

"Fuck yeah. I'm usually more of a top, but I've been wanting your dick in my ass for a long time now. Give it to me."

What could I do but oblige?

I approached him and marveled at his glorious ass. I rubbed the head of my dick up and down his crack and then teased his hole by poking at it lightly.

"Here it goes," I warned.

Then I stepped forward and felt my cock pressing hard against his tight hole. Tony shifted his ass and bent his back slightly. I knew my cock was in the proper place, so I pushed harder and then felt the tightness enveloping my dick. No way would I rush this, so I eased up the pressure and watched as my cock slowly buried itself farther into his ass. Before long, my prick was completely out of sight.

"Damn, your ass is tight," I marveled.

"I don't get fucked often."

"Are you okay?"

"Start slow."

Just as he commanded, I began to ease my cock out of his ass and then slowly worked it back inside. After about ten slow strokes, I stopped and reached down again for his cock.

Damn! He was still hard as a bat!

"Oh yeah," he groaned. "That feels good. That's it. Fuck me, Samson."

"Yeah, buddy. Take my cock."

"Give it to me, buddy."

"Tell me what you like?"

"I like your big cock in my ass. Come on. Give it to me."

Tony looked back and I could see the ecstasy in his eyes. His mouth moved as if he was kissing the air, so I leaned over and pressed my dick fully into him and began to kiss him passionately. While I chewed on his lips, I stroked his hard cock furiously. Then I began to fuck him in earnest.

The Italian god began to moan like I had never heard before. Could he really be enjoying this as much as me? I watched his head bob with each thrust and his eyes rolled up. He began to chew on the knuckle of his thumb.

I looked down and saw my cock sliding in and out of his ass. For a moment, I had an out-of-body experience. Was that really my cock sliding into that perfect muscled ass? I came to my senses and realized it was.

As if driven by an invisible force, I began to buck my hips hard against his ass and watch the globes dance with each thrust. I was pounding him like I had a grudge and his moans encouraged me until I was beyond control.

"Fuck yeah," he cried. "Keep it up, buddy. Pound my ass."

"Oh yeah. Take it for me, Tony."

"Oh, Samson, it feels so good. Come on. Fuck me. Give it to me. Fuck me. Fuck me."

His ass was taking all I had. The fucking was so forceful that I could hear the slap of my body against his cheeks, and the thwap excited me even more.

Without thought, I reached for his right knee and lifted his leg. Tony followed my lead and put his leg up on the table. Now I had easier access to his tight hole, so I continued to work his ass over good as I watched my dick invading him deeply.

His cock was tensing and I knew that he was going to shoot soon, and so was I. I pulled my dick all the way out and plunged it back in once, and then twice, and then a third time. Neither one of us could last much longer, so I just began to piston my cock inside of him with all my might.

"Oh fuck," he yelled. "Oh fuck yeah. Fuck me, buddy. Fuck me good. Give it to me. Give it to me. You're going to make me cum. I'm going to cum. Keep pounding me. Keep fucking me. Oh yeah. Fuuuuuuck yeah."

And then I felt his cock convulsing in my hand and his body jerked in ecstatic spasms. Somehow I lasted all the way through his ejaculation before I let go of his cock, pulled my dick out of his ass, yanked off the condom and shot all over his beefy ass.

For a moment, the only sound was our heavy panting. Then Tony turned around and kissed me tenderly.

"That was amazing, Samson," he said.

"The best sex I've ever had," I responded.

I lifted my hand and saw some of his cum on my fingers, so I licked it off instinctively, tasting his man juice. Then he rubbed his hand over his ass, wiping up some of my cum, and then licked it off of his fingers.

"So you liked it?" I asked.

"Oh yeah. Did you?"

"Oh yeah."

"It was fucking hot."

"You took it like a champ."

"It takes a special guy for me to bottom, but when it's right, it drives me fucking crazy and I cum like I've never cum before. I cum buckets, as you can tell. Usually I top. I'd love to top you sometime."

"Yeah," I said with a smile. "I'd like that."

"So you want to get out of here and go back to my place?" Tony asked.

"Sure."

As we dressed, Tony asked me about my future at the zoo. "I hear a job's opening up in the Cat House. Do you think you'll request to transfer there?"

"Nah," I responded coyly. "I think I've come to like the snakes." I reached up and pinched his nipples, looked him in the eyes and added, "And the snake handler."

Then we kissed again.

෪෬

Armand works full time and spends much of his free time writing short stories, essays, poetry and novels. He's had nearly a dozen stories—ranging from sports erotica to superhero stories—published in a variety of anthologies. Writing sexy adult stories comes easily to him, because he has so many fantasies to put down on paper. He is working hard to publish his first novel and lives by himself in Ohio.

Stress Relief

DAYNE AVERY

"Why can't the mirror be kind tonight?" he wondered. Any other night he could endure the vicious taunting from the man in the mirror, but not tonight. Tonight all he wanted was to crawl up in bed with a big slice of red velvet cake, a glass of milk and make all the stresses of today fade away.

"Cake…hmmmmm, yeah right. Dream on, chunky trunks, you know you can't have cake—try some water and a salad!" the mirror teased.

In front of him stood the reflection of someone new he'd reluctantly accepted as the aging version of his former self. At twenty-eight, Jair Mitchel was far from his father's wrinkles and gray hair, but his appearance had undergone a metamorphosis, changing from the sexy twenty-one-year-old physique he used to know.

"Can't I trade my metabolism for one that isn't broken? My metabolism is just as shot to hell as my love life," he said out loud.

"Maybe if you'd hit the gym once in a while that would solve both problems," the mirror insulted again.

Jair, hopeless romantic and workaholic, was finally facing his fears. Nights like this he wished he could be straight. So many of the straight couples he saw had men with less than stellar physiques. In those same heterosexual pairings, it seemed the women loved having a man with a few extra pounds of meat to hold on to; however, in the image-obsessed city of Atlanta, a gay man who was overweight was better off single. Jair was not straight, and he wasn't in a dating pool of women who liked "healthy" men. He was as gay as the day is long and his dating realm could be more vicious than swimming in a tank full of hungry sharks. He knew he would be devoured, chewed up and spit out if he went searching for love. So, he stayed home and sulked.

About the only thing he liked about his weight was the big ole booty it helped create. Having a big ass was definitely a hot commodity for the boys. Unfortunately, that valuable asset also came with signs of a double chin, man boobs, and a potbelly that he couldn't wait to rid if only he'd kept his promise to get back in the gym.

As Jair rubbed the place his six-pack used to be, he thought back to the years everything was on point, before the recent breakup with his ex-boyfriend Tim, and before his busy schedule consumed him, which left no time for the gym.

"Another New Year's resolution undone." The mirror was relentless in its teasing. Jair had been swearing to himself to get back in shape, but there were two things standing in his way: a busy schedule and a healthy appetite.

"Thank God for a cute face," he exclaimed, still studying his reflection. Jair knew that in the shark-infested waters of gay Atlanta, at times it seemed to be all about a cute face, big dick and hot body. Now, he was left with two out of three—good odds in gambling, but horrible in trying to find love.

After Tim, Jair threw himself into his job, swearing off men completely. On the plus side, he was now one of Atlanta's best entertainment lawyers, but the drawback was a social life that was null and void. Not only was he faced with the lack of a life, but on nights like this, he actually missed Tim. Those big gentle arms wrapped around him used to ease away his stress and make him feel like a supermodel. Now, the yearning made his body scream out silently for someone to come and love the pain away— or at least sex him good enough to make him forget about it.

After being with Tim for three years, the comfort of the relationship manifested with a pound here and a pound there. Before he knew it, Jair had put on fifteen pounds and completely gave up the struggle of trying to maintain a gym body when he had a man who loved every pound. Besides, it was so much easier to just keep the weight. Now, he was single and though he looked full, his life was empty.

Luckily, the extra pounds he carried weren't enough to show through his clothing. When fully dressed, the spare tire and slightly saggy pecks didn't show and he held it together nicely. But, when the clothes came off, so did that façade and the confidence layers of clothing helped create. He wasn't at the point where he'd be let into the fat boys club, but he was far from the thin and hot clique he used to know. As Jair continued to view his birthday suit in the mirror, it took everything inside of him not to get toasty off a few glasses of Grey Goose, get drunk, pick up the phone and dial Tim, hoping for a hot round of pity sex.

Lucidly, Jair came to his senses and decided to forgo the mercy fuck, even though he had had one of those days, which left him longing for just a taste of relief. Even if he couldn't savor the sweet taste, just a sip or even a sniff of the aroma it could bring would have been enough. He wanted someone to make him feel special, make him feel wanted—to make him feel. Passing the bar, and being one of the best lawyers in the city, didn't mean a thing if he had no one who could share his success. He stood still, naked with just his insecurity as a shield, and longed for a change.

He looked on the table near the mirror and saw the small golden certificate with his name in gold ink and the words *LES ESTIQUE* in large, bold script across the top.

Les Estique was Atlanta's best-kept secret. Owned and operated by black men, fully staffed with black men and catering to a clientele of mostly black men—it was definitely a candy shop: Hershey's Kisses, Almond Joys, M&M's, Mr. Goodbars and many other samples of delectable chocolates filled the place. Les Estique was the place to pamper yourself, network, sightsee, and most importantly, relax. Though it was not a gay spa, it was a known fact that most of the men frequenting the establishment played for the home team and the atmosphere was definitely gay friendly.

He wanted so badly to use that certificate. Hell, it was free and he needed a massage more than anyone. Jair had knots on his body in places he never thought they could be; however, just thinking about the gorgeous men at Les Estique made him feel super self-conscious.

Tonight had been weeks in the making. With his busy schedule, Jair had to plan this outing weeks in advance. Missing this opportunity would mean probably missing out forever. The spa pass was a birthday gift from his best friend Seth and with November 14th creeping dangerously the certificate would expire. It was now or never.

As he exchanged glances of his taunting reflection and the unused spa pass for the thirtieth time, Jair battled himself for courage. Could he let a couple of unwanted pounds keep him from enjoying an all-expenses-paid visit to one of the hottest places in town? Would he waste his best friend's money because of an unused gym membership and fleeting self-esteem?

"Surely not!" he exclaimed after finally convincing himself to get dressed and go.

After all, Seth was far from Mr. Universe. Kindly described, Seth was more than just a little overweight and had already been to Les Estique three times. Not only did he go, but he had raved about it ever since. If Seth could be secure in all three hundred pounds of his glory, surely so could Jair at a modest 195.

❉❉❉

He arrived to heaven on earth. The decor was an amalgamation of modern elements that converged into a picture-perfect spa that could have been the centerfold of a magazine. Earth tones, sparkling whites, polished silvers, and frosted glass were the color palatte. The waiting room looked like the lobby of a four-star hotel and smelled of lavender and jasmine. Jair felt like royalty as soon as he stepped inside.

A tall honey-colored statue of a man with short auburn locs swayed back and forth singing to a Maxwell song playing softly through the speakers from behind the desk in the lobby. Ironically, the host bore a strong resemblance to Maxwell. He had the hair, the complexion and even a similar vibe—he just couldn't sing.

As Jair surveyed the landscape, it became increasingly difficult to make eye contact with the Maxwell look-alike after seeing some of the patrons. Good God, the men! Short, tall, buff, slim, all shades of brown, model types, and even those sexy rough-around-the-edges types that Jair liked best. For a short while,

Jair lost focus of reality and purpose. But, the chocolate around him was bittersweet. Yes, it was beautiful. From white chocolate to mocha latte, right down to darkest of the dark. The spa was a melting pot of beautiful shades of brown. All that fineness had Jair suddenly wanting to ditch his appointment and run to the nearest gym. He suddenly felt a sense of urgency to do 1,858,045 sit ups, 548,124 pushups, run eighty miles and then come back in a few months when he didn't look so different than the other gorgeous men surrounding him. He knew that running wasn't his thing; his missed sessions on the treadmill were exactly why he had put on the extra pounds in the first place. Instead of making a mad dash for the exit sign to his left, he sucked in his baby gut, forced his shoulders back, chin up, chest out and tried to create a makeshift physique.

"Jair Mitchel, here for my six-thirty appointment," he said, trying to keep his stomach tight in between words. The host smiled while noticing a familiar gaze of enchantment deep in Jair's eyes.

"Have a seat and your masseur will be right up."

As he waited in the lobby, Jair tried to ignore his feelings of inadequacy, but that did not stop his eyes from dancing around the lobby, taking note of every man in the room. He was caught up in his lust until he heard someone calling his name.

"Junior Mitchel?" Jair looked up to see the most intriguing set of cat eyes. They belonged to a man who looked too gorgeous to be breathing. For a split second, as they shook hands and introduced themselves, Jair's heart stopped beating. Never had he shared time and space with someone so attractive.

"Junior, my name is Terrance and I will be taking care of you tonight. Have you ever been here before?" Terrance asked in a smooth baritone growl. Jair continued to glass into Terrance's eyes, oblivious to the question that had been posed to him.

"Junior, are you alright? Junior!"

"Huh?" Jair questioned, entranced by Terrance's grayish-blue eyes and sexy timbre. Everything about Terrance was just so damn sexy. And his eyes were real, none of that artificial beauty from a box going on. He was the real deal. Dressed in all white with the smile of an angel and body of a god, this man was the finest thing in the building. His physical beauty was astounding, so much so that Jair couldn't hear the words coming from Terrance's full pink lips. He could only trace the movement with his eyes, further blinded by a set of sparkling white teeth. If a heart could melt, in that moment Jair's heart dissolved.

"Is this your first time?" Terrance asked again.

"Yes."

"Oh, so you're a virgin?" Terrance spoke with seduction, sex appeal, and a dangerously high level of confidence. The way he stood so secure in his skin, smiling with the assurance that he was the sexiest thing in the room, was enough to make Jair almost wet his pants. The mere thought that this god-in-flesh form could be flirting sent chills racing and blood flowing from Jair's brain. Every function stopped, sending all thoughts, movements, feelings, and comprehension to a spot growing beneath the zipper of his jeans. *If only fate could be so kind*, Jair thought. However, reality whispered in his subconscious that Terrance was just trying to break the ice. Maybe he was trying to get a big tip, but it was still nice to dream.

"My name is Jair, like air with a 'J.' You were close but it's not Junior—it's Jair."

"Oh, I'm sorry. They had you down as Junior."

"It's cool. I'm used to people messing up my name."

"Well, I'll make sure I get it right. This way—Jair."

Terrance led the way and Jair followed. It was difficult for Jair to walk with the sudden growth in his jeans. His eyes zeroed in on Terrance's unbelievable ass. The view didn't make the situation any better. Just like every other part of Terrance, his ass was a thing of true beauty. Its motion was enough to cause a stroke. It looked like two perfect orbs suspended in air like planets moving on their own axis, defying gravity.

"Right in here, Jair. There's a changing room off to your left. You will need to take everything off and get comfortable. Fresh towels are to your left and there is a bathroom on your right. I'll be back in just a sec." Terrance pointed to a room with almond-colored walls, fresh linens, a massage table, candles and three aloe plants.

Damn, damn, damn! Jair thought. The moment Terrance had turned around to show him into the room, he couldn't look away fast enough. He was caught with his eyes on the cookie jar. It was blatantly obvious that he was staring. Jair felt his cheeks getting redder by the second. By the way Terrance smiled and winked slyly in response, Jair knew that he was accustomed to the attention.

Make yourself comfortable indeed, Jair thought as he stripped, threw on a towel, then hopped on the table face down, covering only the areas he was most self-conscious of. Everything else was exposed to the cool air in the room. *Two can play this game*, Jair thought as he pulled his towel down a little lower showing just enough to find out if Terrance was serious or not. He still wasn't sure if Terrance had been flirting but the sly comments and winking left Jair feeling a sudden burst of confidence. As he stretched out on the table, he heard a knock on the door.

"Ready?"

"Ready!"

Within a minute's time, Terrance was using his gifted hands to smooth away every problem Jair could ever imagine. His hands felt soft like a woman's but there was no doubt that Terrance was all man. His touch was better than a mother's hug, better than a lover's kiss, and even better than the moment during sex when the sting of penetration finally subsides and you're left with bliss. His touch rubbed away the hurt and gently kneaded the insecurities until they faded. Jair felt beautiful and whole while Terrance took complete control. Jair's eyes closed as he felt the cares of the world dissipate. It had been months since he felt the touch of a man, but a lifetime since it had felt so good. The forbidden high he felt as he breathed in Terrance's cologne and masculinity caused tiny drops of wetness to ooze from the tip of his penis and the massage had just begun.

Ordinarily, Jair would have tried to hide his erection, but in Terrance's care he felt comfortable, beautiful and complete. In that moment, nothing mattered.

His eyes opened as hands moved underneath his towel, shaking his spell. The small drips underneath his towel grew as his body began to quiver.

"Are you okay?" Terrance asked.

"I think so."

"Just relax… Free yourself, this is a massage. It's supposed to be enjoyable."

Jair was already having the time of his life but, at Terrance's command, he lost himself inside daydreams of those large biceps wrapped around him without the white uniform. In a close-eyed, sensual world of endless possibilities, Jair no longer fought the jerking of his body. Reality dissolved once again leaving Jair inside the only place he wanted to be—submission. It felt so surreal, so right, so necessary. He swore he could feel the soft caress of Terrance's lips on the back of his neck—the same spot that always made him lose control. The chill delivered by a single kiss gave Jair the courage to do the unthinkable.

He threw the towel to the ground and grabbed the hands of his masseuse, pulling them into him harder, and lower to touch all the spots the material once shielded.

Now naked, touches turned to French kisses on his thighs, leaving them wet with moisture. The kisses worked their way upward. Pulses of white light bathed in ecstasy tickled the spot where the wet spot and the tip of his dick silently met to talk about how good it felt.

Right cheek parted.

Left parted.

His ass was now open and being massaged for the first time. Tim never touched him there. Jair felt the gentle pressure of a tongue exploring his insides as his own pressure continued to build. With Terrance's tongue inside him, Jair wondered what flavor he was. His complexion was a butter pecan, but did he taste as good? Apparently, he was better. He moved his hips like he was riding Terrance's tongue, and as Jair's ass met Terrance's full pink lips it felt like they were telling him the secret to ecstasy.

Terrance savored it giving it a soft peck with his lips.

Then, a single kiss turned to French kissing deep inside his ass.

He liked it.

He devoured it.

And from the reaction, he loved it.

Jair may have looked like butter pecan but from the noises

Terrance made as he tongue-fucked him over and over again, it had him feeling like Campbell's soup—mmmm-mmmm good! The feeling of Terrance's five-o'-clock shadow and hard tongue was like twenty-four-karat gold against his skin. Terrance continued to taste the sweet, saltiness of Jair and seemed like he couldn't let go.

Twenty-eight years and his body had never been explored like this. He'd never let anyone eat him out but couldn't resist someone as fine as Terrance. Jair rolled over onto his back and his eyes met a spot they'd never known in the back of his head. Suddenly, he could feel his precum being washed away by the warm comfort of Terrance's saliva. The heat of his mouth introduced itself to Jair's dick and as the two met for the first time, Jair had to let out a shout.

"Oh shit!"

Jair couldn't help but squirm. He tried to brace himself as he felt the back of Terrance's throat. It felt so good that all his movements had him scared he would soon fall from the table. Terrance was working it. Not only was he a skilled artist of massage but his tongue should be in the *Guinness World Records*. With his tongue, Terrance made figure-eights around the head of Jair's dick and used both hands to massage the rest slowly. Every now and then he would delicately trace the outlines of the veins with his fingertips, causing more clear liquid to ooze.

Terrance took turns focusing the attention from head, to shaft, then balls, playing hide-and-seek with his mouth. He made sure each area of his client was fully serviced. The feeling of his dick as it repeatedly touched the back of Terrance's throat had him ready to explode. Now, every inch of him was being consumed and he was using his hands to tickle Jair's extremely sensitive sac.

Dick and throat fit like lock and key and would soon unlock his orgasm if the pleasure continued. Jair's hands caressed Terrance's head and gently pushed him lower on the pulsing, fully engorged eight-and-a-half-inch, veiny, butter pecan delight.

"Take it."

"Word?"

"Yeah, I saw you staring earlier. If you want some, get some," Terrance demanded.

Suddenly, that heavenly frame was bent over the massage table and Jair wasted no time in studying the curves. Every inch, every line was flawless. From his neck down to his sculpted back to the arch his body made where the top of his ass and back blended. He was perfection. Two irresistible dimples lay in the nook of the small of his back. Jair kissed them, slowly taking his time on each before attacking what he longed for. His ass not only looked perfect; it felt twice as good. It was just the right combination of firm and soft like his favorite pillow. Jair couldn't help but bury his face in it.

Terrance handed Jair a gold condom that looked like a coin. He removed the foil and quickly rolled it on while using his other hand to get Terrance open. He wet Terrance's ass once more with his mouth before sliding in, nice and easy. Slowly easing his way inside, a smile broke out across his face. Terrance welcomed him in with a soft moan that made Jair's dick sit up like concrete inside him. The two felt like they were made for each other. Jair went deeper, then deeper still until his dick was all the way inside and his thighs met the back of Terrance's ass. His insides felt as if he'd been waiting for this night all his life. It was just right.

"Take it," Terrance commanded again.

"You sure you want it like that?"

"Hell yeah!"

Jair had been prepared to take it slow and gentle with Terrance. Ass wasn't something you could just go ramming any kind of way. But, from the demands, he could tell that gentle wasn't Terrance's style. He wanted it hard, unforgiving, and he wanted it all. Terrance grabbed the back of Jair's thighs and then pulled him into him deeper and harder.

All requests were honored as Jair began to pound away at the flesh around him and anything standing in between. The inside of Terrance's ass was like a vacuum pulling him in deeper with each forceful thrust.

Over and over.

Deeper and deeper.

Each thrust felt better.

The harder he went the more Terrance seemed to love it. Jair discovered that Terrance was a moaner. The sounds made him go faster, which turned them both on even more. Soft moans grew louder as Terrance's grip grew tighter. He loved to hear a man let him know he liked his sex. It let him know he was putting in work. Jair couldn't stand quiet sex, but he didn't have to worry about that tonight. Terrance was yelling from his guts, not giving a fuck if anyone could hear. The moment seemed to last forever and yet that wasn't long enough. Both men wanted to continue, but feared that they couldn't take much more.

Pressure was building inside Jair and he could feel the skin around his nuts growing tighter with each thrust. As he slapped his ass, leaving pink marks on Terrance's beautiful tan skin, the moaning grew louder and Jair's dick grew harder still.

The sound of his thighs smacking against Terrance's ass created the sound of a standing ovation. He knew it was about time for him to cum. He could feel the grip around his dick starting to loosen and he knew Terrance was close to climax, too.

"Where you want me to cum?" Jair asked between heavy breaths.

"You decide."

Jair thought for a moment about all the places he could bust and wondered just how many of those places Terrance would actually let him. How much of a freak was he?

On his face?

On his chest?

On his back?

On his thighs?

So many places, but so little time to decide.

Just then he pulled out from the vacuum-like seal they had made. He used his hands to take off the condom and finish releasing what had been building inside ever since he first looked into those pretty eyes. In less than a moment, Terrance was wearing hot passion all over his back and ass as they both smiled as Terrance was climaxing, too. They let out deep breaths of satisfaction before Jair collapsed on Terrance's back. It felt so good lying there in the pretty mess they made.

"Jair. Jair. Jair, wake up!"

Jair's eyes stung as they met the bright, overhead fluorescent lights that illuminated the room. As Jair's eyes adjusted, he looked around to see Terrance looking as sexy as ever, but still wearing his uniform. How did he get it on so fast?

The fantasy ended simultaneously with his first massage. As his pupils finished adjusting to the light of reality, so did Jair. Reality was back to rear its ugly face. Sadly, there were no more orgasms or ecstasy. He was still on the massage table with the towel barely covering him. He could feel the familiar wetness of excitement soaking into the white terrycloth material on him. Those same pretty white teeth and bluish-gray eyes greeted him. Terrance smiled as if he held a secret between his lips. But that secret was far from what Jair hoped it was.

Jair's smile shrank to half its size as he realized what he'd had was his first wet dream since junior high. The encounter the two men shared only existed in Jair's daydream. He should have known it was too good to be true. This wasn't the type of establishment that looked like its clients would get happy endings. But, the way Terrance smiled, Jair had to wonder if he could tell the many thoughts which still swarmed about in his head.

"How was your first massage?"

"Great!"

"So this won't be the last, now will it?"

"No, I will definitely be back."

"Cool, be sure you come see me again."

Terrance spoke in his usual confident voice, making Jair wonder if this conversation was just another attempt at a larger tip or a genuine interest. Either way Jair soaked up the attention like the towel absorbed the remains of his fantasies. This was the most attention he'd had in a long time. Even if the good time came by way of a gift certificate, he hadn't felt this good in what felt like years. He wasn't ready for it to end.

Before excusing himself so that Jair could get dressed, Terrance smiled again and slipped him a business card. On the back of the card, he wrote his cell phone number, then slipped out of the room. Jair felt tingles under his towel as he watched Terrance walk away. He placed the card close to him and imagined the first time he would call the number on the back. Jair knew that somewhere in the very near future his busy schedule was going to have to make some time for Terrance. After all, what was life without a little daydreaming every now and then?

෩ൠ

Dayne Avery is a Delaware native and the author of novels I Wrote This Song *and* Details. *His works are steadily receiving attention. They have been featured in magazines, numerous websites, and* I Wrote This Song *won the award for 2005's National Best Fiction by a SGL Author. While following the path of literary trail-blazers like James Baldwin, Essex Hemphill, and Langston Hughes—Avery aspires to create art in written form.*

A Daydream at the Beach
LANDON DIXON

Brandon dove for the spike, and missed it.

"Sorry, Cole," he said, looking up at me and spitting sand out of his mouth.

That was it. We were officially eliminated from the two-on-two beach volleyball competition. "No problem, dude," I said. "There's always next weekend." I helped him to his feet, and helped him brush some of the sand off his round, firm buttocks and his sweat-soaked back.

Brandon and I had been V ball partners ever since we'd hooked up at an impromptu competition a couple of months earlier. That was the first time I'd ever met him. We hadn't won a tournament yet, but each week we got just a little bit closer as we got to know each other better. We'd made it all the way to the semi-finals this time around.

He was a tall guy, about six-six, with a lean, powerful, dark black body. His muscles glistened under the hot sun on the hot sand. His ass was big and bold and powerful, and his cock was rigidly outlined against the thin material of his red Speedo. I kept my appreciation for his body in my mind, and away from my hands, for the time being, at least. Until I could feel him out a bit better, so to speak.

"Why don't we go for a swim to cool off?" he suggested, once we had downed a couple of consolatory cold ones in the crowded beer tent.

"Sounds like an idea," I said. I ran my hand through my long, blond hair that was bleached almost white from all of the hours I'd spent in the sun chasing balls around. My smooth, hairless skin was tanned a deep, golden brown for the same reason. Even with all the exercise, however, I was no muscleman like Brandon; in fact, a lot of people said that I still looked like a boy, despite my twenty-two years. Part of it, of course, was due to my innocent-appearing, baby-blue eyes.

Brandon and I walked out of the stifling shade of the tent and back under the blazing sun. It must have been a hundred degrees, with only a hint of a wind to push the super-heated air around. I was headed for the packed beach beyond the volleyball courts when Brandon suddenly grabbed my arm.

"Not here. I know a better place," he said, smiling, his strong teeth flashing a brilliant white, his brown eyes twinkling.

"Okay," I replied. I was game for anything with this guy.

We hot-footed it through the parking lot and climbed into his sun-baked jeep. He pulled out of the lot and pointed the vehicle south and drove for about a half hour, the traffic getting lighter and lighter, the cottages farther and farther apart. Finally, he turned off the highway onto a grassy road that led into the bush. Five minutes later, the road abruptly ended and we sat on the cusp of a small, secluded beach. The beach was maybe twenty feet by one hundred feet, and hemmed in by birch and poplar trees which came right down to the water's edge on either side.

"No crowd here," I commented, as we piled out of the jeep.

He nodded, pointed at the lake. "There's a sand bar a ways out. Before that, the water's pretty deep—but nice and cool."

Sounded good to me. I bolted away and bounded into the water, with Brandon in hot pursuit. We were soon up to our necks in the cool, clear water. It felt great.

After splashing around for a while, Brandon swam farther out into the lake. I dove underneath the tranquil surface of the water, and when I came back up I saw that Brandon was standing on top of the water fifty feet away from me. "Hey, I didn't know you could walk on water!" I shouted at him.

"Come and try it yourself!" he yelled back.

I started to swim out to him, and then found myself crawling and then walking on sand. The water was only up to my ankles on the highest point of the sandbar. "Hey, this is cool!" I said.

"No doubt. I'm gonna lie down and catch some rays."

"I'm with you!"

He grinned. "Sure you don't need some more lotion? You white boys get burnt awful easy."

"I'll survive. I'm almost as dark as you."

He laughed and said, "You wish," and then lay down on his stomach on the sand.

I stared longingly at his plump, athletic ass, and at his broad, muscular shoulders, then sprawled down next to him. The shallow water acted like a cushion and the feeling was sensational—totally relaxing. As the hot sun beat down on me from a cloudless sky, and the water rippled gently against my body, pushed along by a soft breeze that blew in off the lake, I found myself getting drowsier and drowsier, until…

I felt Brandon's hand on my back. It felt good there—warm and strong and reassuring. Then it drifted lower down my back, lower and lower, caressing me as it traveled down my goose-bumped flesh, until it reached my lower back. And my heartfelt prayers were answered when his roving hand didn't stop there.

His big mitt slid underneath the elastic band of my swim trunks and came to rest on my taut, tingling ass cheeks. He began squeezing and fondling my ass as my mind screamed, *yes*! And my cock jumped six inches in length and buried itself in the sand.

I turned my head and gazed dreamily into Brandon's liquid brown eyes. "I've wanted to ever since I met you, man," he said, smiling gently. "How 'bout you?"

I answered his ridiculous question by scrambling to my knees, rolling him over on his back, and diving on top of him.

"Easy, tiger," he said, laughing.

I covered his mouth with mine and kissed him long and hard. His thick, sensuous lips were soft and receptive, then open; and I crowded my tongue inside of his mouth. I ground my heated body against his, our hardened cocks pressing together, and an electric shock shot through me and made me gasp into his mouth. He grabbed my head, forced it back an inch or so, and then painted my lips with his impossibly pink tongue.

"Yeah," I murmured, rhythmically pumping my rock-hard cock against his, as he attacked my mouth.

"Stick out your tongue," he said. I did. He caught it with his strong, white teeth, then replaced teeth with lips and began sucking on my slimy tongue like it was an engorged cock.

I moaned and stuck my tongue out as far as it would go, reveling in the dizzying feel of his lips and his cock and his body, and the sun and the water. Our total exposure on the water-swept sandbar only heightened the excitement.

He released my tongue from his loving mouth and said, "You wanna sixty-nine, baby?"

I looked down at him and kissed him on the lips. "You have to ask?"

We stood up on shaky legs and hastily stripped off our swim suits. His cock sprang out into the gentle summer breeze and my heart almost stopped. It was blue-black and big—like a thick, thick stick of eight-inch-long licorice. And it was still growing. He stared at my own arrow-straight dick and whistled; I go about seven super-sensitive inches myself.

"Heads or tails?" he asked, grinning.

"Heads," I called quickly. I'd need all the leverage I could get to swallow his massive organ, if swallowing it was at all possible.

He lay back down on the sand and I climbed over top of him. I positioned my twitching erection just above his face, and he firmly gripped my ass cheeks and pulled me down into his mouth without hesitation. "Yeah," I mumbled, the sensation of his warm, wet mouth engulfing my swollen cock virtually unbearable. He sucked and sucked on my mushroomed cockhead, then took more of my dick into his mouth, vacuum-sealing my cock in his heated maw, sucking long and hard, over and over, up and down. He obviously knew his way around a man's cock.

And so did I. I held his massive rod by the base, then flicked my tongue across his gigantic hood. He groaned, and the sound coursed through my mouth-wrapped cock and through my body, setting me ablaze. I cupped his big, black balls, played with them, and then lowered my head farther down on his pole, letting his cock sink into my mouth. I bobbed my head up and down on his dick, sucking his raging member, licking it, biting it.

"God, that feels great," he moaned, momentarily pulling my dripping cock out of his velvet mouth.

"You ain't felt nothing yet, brother," I told him. I sucked his cock deep into my mouth and my head went down like the setting sun.

"Sweet Jesus!" he cried.

Inch by massive, rock-hard inch I slid that giant cock into my mouth. He cried out again when I'd buried half of it and his bloated cockhead slammed against the back of my throat; cried out yet again when I determinedly lowered my head even farther and gulped his cock down to the gag point and beyond. I jammed it into my throat.

His body tensed, quivered, and he frantically sucked me off in an effort to divert his lust-addled mind from the towering sexual pressure on his cock, as I crammed more and more of him into my greedy mouth. His body jerked when my nose plowed into his balls and my tongue snaked out to explore the pube-covered skin at the base of his mighty dick. I had deep-throated his entire cock.

He abandoned my cock, all senses lost. His head lolled about in the sand and the water, and his body flashed repeatedly with the erotic shocks of heavy-duty cock-swallowing. His breathing was hard and erratic. His cock was buried deep within my throat, to the hilt, and breath whistled out of my flared nostrils as I desperately tried to hold onto the perfect moment for as long as I possibly could.

"Jesus Christ, I'm gonna cum!" he yelled, his fingers digging into my butt, clawing for a grip on reality.

I didn't want him to cum just yet—I had something else in mind—but it's tough making your feelings known when you've got a man's monster cock plugged to the balls inside your mouth and throat. So I grasped his muscled thighs and pushed back, and he and I watched feverishly as his slimy, glistening cock slid out of my mouth. Inch by sopping wet inch I disgorged his humongous erection, until, finally, his cock popped out and I gasped for air; my mouth stretched but triumphant.

"I want to fuck you," I croaked, grabbing his slick dick in my hand and pulling on it.

"Anything you want, baby," he answered hoarsely. "After that performance, anything you want."

I smiled. "I want you to stroke your big, black cock while I fuck you," I said, filling in the details of my fantasy. "I want you to stroke your dick while I fuck you in the ass—until we cum together."

"Let's get it on," he responded.

I swung around until my cock was on top of his. The contrast between the white and dark meat was stunning, exhilarating. He grabbed hold of his huge cock and began stroking it with practiced ease, polishing the engorged head with a flick of his powerful wrist. I cupped water onto my own cock until it was good and wet, then spread his legs farther apart and pressed a finger against his asshole.

"Don't be shy," he said, grinning up at me as he tugged on his cock.

I slid my finger into his ass. He groaned, closed his eyes. I shoved a second finger inside his butt—in search of the first. Then I began to gently finger-fuck him.

"Fuck my ass!" he urged, stroking the length of his incredible cock, faster and faster.

I pulled my fingers out of his ass, twisted my knees around in the wet sand until they were partially buried, and then lifted his long legs in my arms and placed his slim ankles on top of my shoulders. When I felt that we were all set for entry, I gripped my straining cock with my right hand and steered it up against his pucker. I swallowed hard when cock-flesh met ass-flesh, and then shoved my dick against him as he lifted his hips. My cock-head broke the plane of his asshole and I was inside.

"Fuck me hard, baby!" he coaxed, his voice drifting across the placid lake, carried along by the light wind into the far-off bushes. "Fuck me hard!" He raised his ass farther out of the water and the sand and shoved against me. My cock slid halfway inside of his tight butt.

"Oh, yeah," I said, closing my eyes—the incredible sensation of heat and tightness from sticking my swollen cock into this man's beautiful ass beating against my brain.

I thrust forward recklessly, and the rest of my seven inches slid inside of him and I was buried to the balls. He groaned, and his hand became a blur on his rigid shaft. My hips took up a rhythm as ancient as the Grecian Olympics, and I began pounding his ass—shoving my cock in and out of his glory hole, slowly at first, then faster and faster and faster. My balls spanked his butt shamelessly as I buried and re-buried my cock inside of his ass. His eyes were closed and his mouth was open, as he clung to and stroked his cock for dear life as I rode his rump harder and harder.

My head started to spin and I gripped his fleshy thighs against my gleaming chest in a desperate bid to cling to reality. My world collapsed down upon me, until it encompassed only his ass and my cock, my cock in his ass. I banged him like a drum, over and over and over again, the only sounds the splash-smack of my balls against his butt, and his low animal moaning as he flailed his cock to orgasm.

"I'm gonna cum, baby!" he screamed, gritting his teeth, his face contorted in sheer sexual agony as he pounded his cock with his hand, while I pounded his ass with my cock.

"I'm cumming, too!" I screamed back.

His eyes shot open, and they were misted with uncontrollable lust. "Pull it out and cum all over me!" he pleaded, and then moaned in mind-blowing ecstasy as his huge, ebony rod began shooting ropes and ropes of sizzling semen.

I watched in awe as he jacked jets of white-hot cum out of his straining cock, raining jism down onto his body, all over his body—some of the thick, milky jizz even splashing down onto his ecstatic face. His mouth gaped open in a silent scream and he took it all in.

It was too much for me. I plundered his ass with some more frenzied thrusting, and then, with cum boiling to the blasting point at the bottom of my balls, I ripped my raging cock out of his vise-like ass and frantically stroked myself to apocalyptic orgasm. "Fuck almighty!" I shouted out to heaven and earth, as cum rocketed out of the flaming tip of my cock and smacked down on top of Brandon's rippling body. He was getting it from both ends now—cum spraying out of both of our cocks and coating his night-shaded stomach and chest and face.

"Yeah!" he cried, tugging a last torrent of super-heated sperm from his massive cock, and then watching, wide-eyed, as I painted his undulating body with my own jism.

My body jerked each time a thick jet of scorching cum burst out of my pumping cock, and that was many, many times. I threw back my head and grunted in time to the devastating blasts of pure, unadulterated sexual satisfaction. I came like I never came before, shooting goo like there was a goo shortage that I just had to fill, until, finally, my cock stopped spewing its sticky goodness, my body convulsed one final time with the after-effects of ecstasy, and I leaned hard against Brandon's sweat-drenched legs, teetering on the brink of unconsciousness.

After a blissful eternity, I pried open my weary eyes and gazed down at my cum-soaked lover. He was rubbing the simmering semen all over his body, smearing his muscles with it, a satiated smile on his saucy lips. "Kiss me," he whispered.

I fell on top of him and mashed my lips against his, tasting the cum that he had yet to swallow—mine and his both. I licked cum off his face, shared it with him, our wasted bodies glued together, the warm waves of the lake gently lapping at our dazzling nakedness.

I felt his hand on my back, and...

He was shaking me.

My eyes popped open. "Huh, what?" I mumbled, dazed.

"You were sleeping," he said, grinning. "Have a good dream?"

"Huh?" I couldn't believe that it had all been a dream. It had seemed so real. I squinted at him, felt my hard cock pushing into the hot, wet sand. "Yeah, it was—"

I cut off the chatter when I felt his hand drifting lower and lower down my back.

ಏಞಿ

Landon Dixon's writing credits include Options, Beau, In Touch/Indulge, Men, Freshmen, [2], Mandate, Torso, Honcho, *and stories in the anthologies* Straight? Volume 2, Friction 7, Working Stiff, Sex by the Book, *and* Ultimate Gay Erotica 2005 *and* 2007.

Last Call

DEMOND MAURICE

Normally, I'd never run to catch the train, but on this Friday evening after the work week from hell, I decided to get my Carl Lewis on as I headed over to D.C.'s Union Station. I needed to get as far away from my office as fast as I could. Most people couldn't wait for the New Year to begin, but I wasn't one of them. My job's work load was always hectic at year's end and just as bad at the beginning. Today, I was determined to leave at five p.m. like most normal people. Somewhere in the city at some bar, there was a stool anticipating the warmth of my tired, overworked ass. And, I knew just the place. I could almost taste the smooth lubrication of a Grey Goose martini coating the back of my throat and if I hurried, I could take full advantage of the Happy Hour Special—all you can drink for $25 until eight o'clock.

Nine drinks were the most I'd had during one sitting, and I was pretty much comatose for the remainder of the evening. I remember waking up in my apartment with my pants and boxer briefs down around my ankles. Since I lived alone and didn't feel as though I had been violated, the only explanation was that I had to go to the bathroom and afterward couldn't bend down to pull them back up.

❀❀❀

There was a train on the platform as I made my way down the escalator, brushing past those who didn't understand the rule of the D.C. Metro system which required people to stand to the right and let folks walk down the left. *Damn it!* I thought just as the doors to the train closed. I was about to stick my new Ferragamo shoe in the door and I quickly came to my senses. Three minutes for the next train was better than losing my shoe or my foot.

There was a craving in the depths of my soul and I didn't know if it was the drink I had on my mind or the fact that I hadn't had sex since the new year began and the first month was about to be over. I usually bring in the New Year with a bang—literally—as a promise to a year filled with lots and lots of hot sweaty sex. I hoped tonight I could satisfy both cravings. There were always a few good-looking men in the crowd on Friday nights at the T-Spot, but everyone usually stayed close to the crew they came with, only allowing their eyes to venture to different areas of the bar. However, after a few drinks, I usually made my way around the space to see the familiar faces, but mainly to get a closer look at the new ones. It was not uncommon for me to become quite friendly after a few drinks and kiss a few unsuspecting men throughout the course of the evening. It wasn't a particular goal of mine; it just always seemed to happen.

As I sat on the train, I tried to collect my thoughts and my mood shifted from work to play. The day was over and my night was about to begin. I let my head rest against the window as the symphony of sounds began to entertain me; the steel-on-steel sounds from the train against the track; the chimes of the opening and closing doors; the pre-recorded monotone voice announcing the station stops from the overhead speakers. Ordinarily it would be annoying, but today I was so numb that it put me in a zombie-like trance instead. As the train moved down the track, my eyes became heavy and I had to fight to keep them open. My head bobbled loosely back and forth with the rhythm of the train. As I caught myself for what seemed like the fifth time, I noticed I had an audience of one staring at me as if he had placed a silent bet that I would be out in a matter of seconds. When he noticed that I had caught him, he quickly looked away with a boyish shyness and pretended to be interested in the newspaper in his hand. The deep dimple in his caramel cheek let me know that he was humored by it all. The color of his skin reminded me of the Sugar Daddy candy we used to get from the corner store when I was a child. It was basically a wad of hard caramel on a stick. We used to suck and lick on this candy for hours—most times in vain. I can never recall actually finishing one of them.

My voyeur's smile was contagious and I smiled as he turned back, blithely unaware I was still focusing on him. I felt that familiar tingling in my loins and began to mentally assess his attributes. By the way he wore his suit, I could tell that his body was taut and hard—just the way I liked. He had the kind of body that I imagined would look good in almost anything—or nothing— but, his gray, pin-striped Armani suit was tailored to a perfect fit for his massive body. His flat front dress pants didn't leave much to the mind's eye and I could clearly see he was a *tool man*. In order to be a tool man, not only did the dick have to be at least ten inches, but it had to have the girth of a good cucumber as well; the kind of dick that required skill versus talent; the kind of dick that required a plan of attack instead of just jumping on it any kind of way. A tool man's dick was that dick you could still feel the next day. Like I say, "If I can't still feel it the next day, he ain't do shit."

❊❊❊

My eyes lingered a little longer than I thought due to the smirk he had on his face when our eyes locked on each other. He had this look on his face as if he knew what was running through my head. Regardless, my eyes continued with the assessment as I caught the bling from his ring and I jumped to the conclusion that he was married, but I realized the ring was on the right hand, not the left.

Just as I tried to end my thoughts, he bent down, picked up his briefcase and headed in my direction. *Oh shit!* I thought to myself. *What if he is coming over here?* Before I could finish my thought he was standing right in front of me.

"Excuse me, is this the Red Line?"

The sound of his voice sent chills throughout my eager body; it was a masculine voice with just enough confidence. I took a quick second to compose myself. I'm quite sure that he knew what train he was on because he was already on the train before me. But if this was his pickup line, then I'd play along.

"Yes, this is the Red Line."

"How many more stops to Metro Center?" Normally, I would have pointed to the almost life-size map on the train wall behind him, but I was intrigued by his game.

"Two stops—Judiciary Square, then Gallery Place." He hovered above me and I got a whiff of his scent—he was wearing my favorite, Le Male by Jean Paul Gaultier. I tried to keep my cool even as the smell of my favorite cologne filled my nostrils. I was hoping that I was only imagining that my eyes were rolling back into my head, revealing the whites of my eyes, as I quietly inhaled and exhaled. This was some real Savannah, from *Waiting to Exhale* type of shit.

"Are you okay?" he asked with some concern.

Blinking repeatedly, I pretended I was trying to bring my eyes to a clear focus. "Yeah, I am just a little tired. That's all," I said, almost embarrassed.

"I know how you feel, man. I have never been so happy to see Friday. *The man* got his money out of me this week for sure."

With each syllable he spoke, his masculinity became more evident, as did his scent.

"By the way, I'm Preecher," he said as he extended his hand.

"Preecher?" I asked in a curious tone. "That's an unusual name."

"For the record, I am not a preacher; it's P-r-e-e-c-h-e-r, although I have been known to get an amen or two on occasion," he said with a devious grin.

I was thinking more like "Hallelujah."

"I am a Southern man," he continued. "My grandmother had high hopes for me. You know that whole lawyer, doctor, preacher or teacher thang." Even though he was engaging me in conversation I was trying not to miss my stop so that I could transfer trains. I could choose between him and a martini, but since he wasn't naked, the martini was in a strong first place for the evening.

"Well, it doesn't look like you destroyed her high hopes too badly—Armani, Cole Haan, Tumi. I would think she would be satisfied. Now all you have to do is get married and she will say that her work is done." Damn, I had just given myself away to the fact that I had run him through my mental scanner and by the look on his face he knew it, too.

"So do you have my credit score, too?"

"If we were going one more stop, I'd be able to process and deliver that for you," I said with a laugh as the train reached Metro Center.

"Let's just say that I didn't miss the mark by that much," he said with confidence.

I stood up as the train stopped, forgetting about that extra jolt that almost always happens when the train comes to a full stop. Stumbling a few feet forward, I landed right under his nose, instinctively bracing myself with my hand on his chest. We were so close that I could feel his breath on my bottom lip. Call me delusional, but I swear I felt the warmth of his breath creep down my V-neck cashmere sweater and glide across my overly sensitive nipples. He had the perfect set of pink-grapefruit lips. I felt like pulling something straight out of a fairytale like kissing him and running off the train, but I remembered he was getting off at Metro Center, too. For that half of a second, we stood on the edge of each other's personal space in a moment on pause; the train was on pause; our words were on pause and so was my breathing. The fluttering of the butterflies in my stomach made me lightheaded and I needed some air quickly. The moment was awkward, full of unspoken words and potential.

The expression on his face changed to a very serious and focused look as if he were doing research on a term paper and I was the subject. His eyes told a story of a passionate, patient, yet persistent man. For a half of a second, I felt like the leading lady in one of those Harlequin romance novels in the arms of her secret lover who had come to her with an ultimatum—leave him or lose me.

The opening of the doors brought us out of our moment. I proceeded to exit the train. From a few steps behind me he called out, "Do I get a name?"

I turned back looking slightly over my shoulder and said, "It's Randal."

Why was I was running from him? Why was he standing there with this defeated look on his face like a puppy that wasn't selected at the pound? I wanted to turn around, but my feet were steadily going forward and something within me told me to keep moving. I looked back and saw him going in the opposite direction and within seconds, my feet had led me down the escalator and out of his sight. *Fuck!* I can be such a bitch sometimes. This fine-ass man was clearly trying to pick me up and I ran away like damn Cinder-fucking-rella, knowing damn well that I did not leave one of my Ferragamos behind for him to romantically find me later like in the story.

"Preecher," I said to myself. The name sounded good rolling off my tongue. I could easily hear myself echoing that name in between moans as he was in between me. "Preecher… Preeeeeecher!" I wondered if it would be a sin if I pretended that he really was a preacher and I was the one who brought him to his knees, sacrificing his collar to satisfy my lust. I slid my hand in my pocket to hide my protruding erection. My thoughts had seriously heated up my commute.

I boarded the next train while focusing on the escalator hoping Preecher would come running down after me, but the doors closed and the train began to move forward. The smell of his cologne lingered in my nasal cavity which made me scan the train just to make sure he hadn't boarded.

As the train arrived at Eastern Market, I still had Preecher on my mind. I tried to rewrite the event of a moment's past. I pictured myself sitting down to dinner getting to know more about Preecher and discussing politics over a glass of Chardonnay, but

I quickly erased that. I then pictured myself pressed up against the wall in the foyer of his house with my pants around my ankles and my shirt above my head. I had the feeling we wouldn't have made it much farther into the house. My fantasy provided a much better ending to this story than the one etched in reality.

As I exited the train station, I braced myself for the January chill that was in the wind. The bar was about five blocks from the station and I wanted to make sure I didn't freeze before I got there. Winter is my least favorite season. If it wasn't for my obsession with coats and sweaters, I would move west.

The T-Spot was relatively new to D.C.'s Capitol Hill area, but quickly attracted a regular crowd for Friday's Happy Hour. It wasn't officially a gay bar, but all it takes is for two or three of us to go on a regular and then to start spreading the word. Before you know it, it's a regular watering hole for the rest of the gay community. I am not sure what initially attracted us to the T-Spot—maybe it was time for something new; maybe it was the art deco interior with various colored lighting that gave it an upscale feeling unlike most of the other gay bars in the city. You knew you were somewhere different. You knew you were not in an old warehouse or a pimped-out row house which was typical of the black gay bars in D.C. With a few booth seats and a couple table tops occupying the space to the right and left, there was only a narrow aisle for pageantry, but I made great use of the space.

When I entered, I was surprised to see the size of the crowd for it to only be around six o'clock. Usually, the crowd filtered in later, but I presumed everyone was feeling the week's work load and had the same urgency as me. Hugs, greetings, kisses, smiles and waves were the norm for my entrance. I always felt like a local celebrity. Once I found my friends in our usual area, I disrobed from my winter garments, and got the attention of the waitress with a nod and a smile which implied, *I'll have what I always have, a Lime Coconut Martini.*

For the next hour and a half, I let every stress and worry fade into the evening. The laughter drowned out any thoughts of work or work-related issues. My friends and I carried out our usual routine of being the center of attention and drawing the attention of most people within an ear's distance. We made new friends every week—mostly straight women who couldn't resist the fun we seemed to be having.

As the evening began to mellow down, thoughts of Preecher began to fill my mind. I couldn't shake thoughts of him out of my head. I wondered what he was doing at this very moment. Was he thinking about me as I was thinking about him? Thinking about him had my mind in a state of mild delusion. I began to smell him in the air as if he had walked past me unnoticed. What were the chances of that happening? As the last call was made from the bar for the last round of drinks for the Happy Hour special, I decided I would make my way to the restroom. I'd try to empty some of the alcohol out of my system so that I could make it through the rest of the evening. As I steadied myself for the narrow walk through the crowd, another whiff of Preecher's scent spun me around causing me to crane my neck over the crowd, but to my dismay I didn't see him.

With carefully planned steps to hide my toxic state, I made it safely to the restroom. Looking in the mirror, my eyes reflected that I was past being buzzed and edging closer to being just plain ole drunk. I decided to splash some water on my face to help get myself together for the walk back to my friends. The cold water sent me into a mini shock causing me to take a deep gasp for air, but it did the trick. As I lifted my head and looked into the mirror, I saw that I wasn't the only one looking back at me. I quickly jerked my head around to make sure that my mind and the mirror weren't in cahoots with a cruel joke. Next week, I'd have to limit my drinks to three instead of five. He handed me a paper towel to wipe my face and I could see through the water in my eyes that he was just as real as he was when I had seen him a couple hours ago on the train. In fact this time he was even more real because he had come out of his Armani suit and was wearing a baby-blue, form-fitting sweater with some low-rise jeans that put everything on display. I didn't know what to say or do because his smile had me frozen. I think he was saying something to me, but I couldn't hear him. His pink lips were moving and his deep dimples were showing. Whatever he was saying must have been quite humorous because he appeared to be laughing a little. He reached out and touched my face and I melted. His words were no longer on mute.

"You still had a few drops of water left on your forehead; I didn't want it to run into your eyes."

"Is this really happening? I have been thinking about you since I ran away from you at the train station," I said just above a whisper. Preecher moved in closer to me and gently kissed my lips.

"Did that feel real?"

It felt so real that I felt my body began to tremble. I felt my hands and my fingers tingle a bit in anticipation of what was going to happen next. All I knew was that I was not going to let him slip away from me twice in one day. This was not going to be another Cinderella moment. With one hand, I pulled him closer to me and with the other I locked the door. Our tongues tangled together from the deep passionate kiss we shared. Preecher wrapped both his arms around my waist. The feeling of his flexed biceps weakened my spine causing my body to become limp in ecstasy. Feeling that I had succumbed to the strength of his grasp, he lifted me off my feet with my legs wrapped around his waist and carried me over to the sink. Lust and alcohol are a dangerous combination because the fact that I was about to do the unthinkable in a public restroom didn't faze me at all. Without taking a moment to untie our tongues, we began to undress each other. I lifted his sweater over his head and let it hit the floor. His pecs stood up through his wifebeater like the peaks of Mount Rushmore. I wanted to keep this image in front of me, but I also wanted to feel his flesh against my flesh so I lifted his shirt over his head, allowing it to rest on the back of his neck. He did the same with both my sweater and shirt. Preecher took to my nipples like a starving breast-feeding infant. Chills ran up and down my body as he licked and sucked the most erotically sensitive area on my body. My mouth was open, but air was the only thing coming out of it as he held my nipple between his teeth. I wanted to scream, but the feeling of his tongue took me to a place beyond a scream. Our bodies were so close that all of the space that once existed between us was no more. The beating of our hearts united with a powerful pace as the moisture on our chests caused us to stick to each other. I reached for the buckle of his pants and as my hands brushed across his abs, I read his six-pack abs with my hands, as if reading a message in Braille. Preecher pulled back and began to watch me as I released his manhood from his fitted briefs. He looked down as if he were waiting just as I was to see the unleashing of the captive one.

My assessment from earlier was so on point. Preecher was no doubt a tool man. His slightly curved caramel, thick dick just hung there. For all I know, it could have been dipped in gold. I hopped down from the sink onto my knees to idolize the prize that was before me. As I looked up at him, he ran his dick across my lips glossing them with his precum. Without hesitation I took him deep into my mouth and felt a slight trembling in his legs. My combination of deep throat sucking and licking caused spasms throughout his body as he held himself up by holding onto the walls. Feeling that this would be my only moment to prove my skills before he had his way, I showed no mercy while cupping his balls and slipping my thumb into his ass. He was going to remember this as the best head he had ever received. I could hear him breathing as if he were practicing with a Lamaze coach. I knew that if I was going to feel this gorgeous dick inside of me that I needed to get off my knees really soon.

Preecher was thinking the same as he bent down to help raise me from the floor. With an aggressive force, he turned me around pressing my face against the mirror and entered me slowly, inch by inch, until I could feel his soft pubic hairs on my ass. We stood there for a moment while allowing my body to adjust and conform to its guest. I gave a slight push back to signal that I was ready for take off and Preecher took me for a ride that I would never have imagined in my wildest dreams. His rhythm; his passion, his thrust was executed with such style and precision that I forgot that I was pressed against a mirror in a public rest-room. His working-man hands were suctioned against my ass as he pleasured me. The changing of his rhythm from slow, variable strokes to quick repetitious thrusts, let me know that he was about to relieve the pressure holding in his scrotum. Glancing in the mirror between moans I could see his contorted face as he worked toward his finale. I began to jack my dick with intensity to make sure we both enjoyed the experience to the fullest.

Preecher began to pound my ass like a madman, causing our sounds to become more audible than we had been all night. Before the other could scream with passion, we quickly covered each other's mouths. Preecher pulled out turning me to face him and we covered each other's chest with the warm contents that had worked up in our bodies. Exhausted and in a state of ecstasy, we began to laugh with what little breath we had left.

❂❂❂

As the sunlight crept through the blinds, Preecher reached over and pulled me into his arms. We were still naked and drained from the episode at the bar last night and the episodes that followed once we got home.

"It's good to be home," he proclaimed.

"If I had known the welcome home was going to be like that, I would have cut that trip back a couple days and gotten here sooner."

"I cannot believe that I let you talk me into that, but trust me, I have no regrets."

"I love you."

"I love you more."

"I can't wait until the next last call."

☒☒☒

Demond Maurice is proud to make his writing debut in Flesh to Flesh. *Sparking a popular interest in his writing through his blogs, Demond Maurice has retained the following of a faithful few. In the near future, Demond Maurice plans to complete and publish his highly anticipated first novel,* 90 Degrees in the Shade. *Demond Maurice currently resides in Prince Georges County, Maryland.*

Don't Touch
JAMIE FREEMAN

I thought for a moment it was him, ducking out of the men's room on the main concourse, about twenty paces ahead of me. Even after a decade, I see him sometimes: in New York coming out of a restaurant that serves only rice pudding; in that London bookshop across from the National Gallery; in that Budapest McDonald's in line and, now, in snowy Salzburg, ducking out of a men's room after midnight. Those same dark features; the same short muscular build.

I imagine I can see the thin nose, the small perfect hands. But now I am surely succumbing to the lure of memory. I imagine him turning to take another look at me, then, seeing who I am, drop his bag and coat on the platform and fly into my arms. We will hug like Ilsa and Rick would have in that Paris train station, if the world had been a simpler place. But Ilsa will always leave Rick standing alone on the platform.

The man coming out of the men's room does look at me, his enticing eyes capturing mine for a moment too long. Then he hurries down the corridor in the direction of the trains. And it is not who I thought it was after all.

I stop off at the men's room for a piss, the sad sound echoing through the empty tiled room, then make my way to my train. It is nearly one a.m. by the time the train starts rolling north toward Berlin, and I am ensconced in an empty compartment, long coat tucked around my shoulders, legs propped on the seat opposite me, thinking of him. I lay aside my copy of Isherwood's *Goodbye to Berlin*, flip out the overhead light and stare into the cold night.

❋❋❋

Grove was perfect. And I'm not just saying this because he was my best friend and my first love. He was one of those people whom everyone loved, whom everybody wanted to be with and, for a time, he was mine. He made me feel special, winking at me when people said stupid things, touching my shoulder when we stood together listening to a new song on the radio, rubbing his leg absently against mine in our favorite booth at the deli near our apartment. He was so alive, so physically entrancing. No wonder people love him, I used to think; no wonder, when he moves like that, body sinewy and graceful as a dancer, small and solid with muscle.

He would sometimes stand next to me on the Metro, when the train was crowded or when he was too keyed up from the movie we'd seen to sit, and his arm would be wrapped around the pole, small hands grasping the smooth metal like a lover. I would watch his arm muscles flex with the slowing of the train as we approached each station, the ropey vein sliding along the pale inside of his forearm. I would pray that we would somehow never reach our destination, that we could somehow ride on in this hot compartment forever, my throat dry and full of my desire for him. But our stop would come and he would look up and smile at me. I would be pulled along in his wake, out the doors, through the turnstiles and up the towering escalator into the night.

The first time I saw Grove naked, we had been out dancing at one of the clubs in Southeast D.C.. We were at Tracks, probably, and the men had circled him like jackals while I watched him dance alone on the dance floor alone or close to me, while I brushed my hands seductively against his sweaty mesh shirt and listened to him sing along to the music. Our bodies meshed together that night like they never had before, and I felt certain that it would be the night he would pull me into his bed and begin things with a kiss.

But when we staggered back into our apartment, we were only roommates again. He was back to talking about Lucy, his girl-friend, whom I reluctantly loved and who was in Boston visiting her parents for the weekend.

"God, Chris, I love her so much," he said, pulling his shirt over his head, muscles aligned in an inverted triangle that pointed to the thicket of pubic hair that peeked out the top of his loose jeans.

I pulled off my own shirt and watched him kick off his shoes, feet pale and perfect against the dark carpet; toes digging into the shag as he stretched long and wide. I couldn't bear it any longer when he reached for the zipper of his jeans, and I staggered drunkenly into the bathroom. The shower was biting cold and it sobered me somewhat, flushing the alcohol and the cocaine and the desire I had burning within me for Grove down the drain in swirling circles. And I stood there for a long time under the icy rush.

"*Fahrkarte, bitte.*" A voice startles me and light suddenly floods the compartment.

The man is tall and plain, cheeks a little too full, stomach a little too heavy, but he has the Austrian precision of dress, and he is smiling as he holds out a gloved hand.

I hand him my ticket, which he punches and hands back to me. "*Gute Nacht,*" and I am again in darkness.

"*Bitte, ist hier frei?*" another voice says even before my eyes have fully adjusted to the darkness. The silhouette stands tall in the doorway, a large duffel bag on his shoulder.

"*Genau,*" I say, pointing to the empty seats across from me. The stranger comes into the compartment, stowing his duffel bag on the overhead shelf and pulling a paperback out of his coat pocket. He drops down on the seat opposite me, propping his feet up and leaning his head back against the headrest. His eyes close as his head touches the cushion, and I think again of Grove and that night after the club.

❈❈❈

I was in the shower for what seemed like a long time when I heard him open the door. "You're gonna waste all the hot water," he said, padding across the room and flinging open the shower stall door. "You," he says grabbing my arm, "out." He pulls me out onto the bathmat and steps past me into the shower, our bodies colliding for an instant, the hair of my chest brushing against his shoulders, the tip of my cock sliding lightly along the top of his buttocks. "Jesus, Christopher, it's fuckin' freezing," he groans. Then he flips the hot water on in a swift sure motion and pulls the door shut behind him.

I've thought about that moment a lot over the years, as though it was a moment of great importance, a moment of potentiality, when it was simply a moment of drunkenness and misplaced desire. I had stood there for a full five minutes, cold water dripping off of me onto the fuzzy bathroom rug and the old orange bathmat as I considered just opening the door and stepping back into the shower with him. I watched him soap himself, hands running along the muscled planes of his legs, reaching up between them to the dark triangle that was obscured by the steam and the textured glass of the shower door. But I couldn't get past Lucy and all their history and finally, defeated, I left the bathroom, soaking wet and climbed into bed, burrowing under my comforter and wishing myself into oblivion.

When I woke the next morning, Grove, in a pair of my boxers, was sleeping next to me in the bed. He was lying on his stomach, snoring slightly into the pillow. I reached out and grabbed his shoulder, shaking him awake. "What are you doing here?"

❊❊❊

"*Bitte?*" The response is from the man opposite me in the train car. I realize I have spoken out loud.

"I'm sorry," I say in English. "I was dreaming."

"No problem," he says, smiling and shifting slightly in his seat, his crossed legs resting next to mine.

"You're American?" I ask.

"*Genau,*" he says, laughing.

We talk for a while, laughing and recounting travel stories in the dim confines of this train compartment, hurtling north through the snowy night. There is a sliver of moon and, when the train reaches higher ground, it occasionally makes its presence known, light sliding across the man's lap, his arm, the stubble on his chin. He is animated, with hands that tell more of his story than his rumbling voice cares to, but he wears a gold band on his left hand, barring my way to more intimate discourse.

We lapse into silence after a while and I watch him shift in his seat, searching for a comfortable position to sleep in. His long legs stretch next to me, rolling against me as the train turns, then rolling away from me as the train shifts direction.

❖❖❖

I was the best man at Grove's wedding. He and Lucy were married on a cruise ship somewhere off the Pacific coast of Mexico. Lucy and I planned the wedding on the living room floor of the apartment I shared with her fiancé, watching *Mad About You* and leafing through glossy magazines. To our twenty-year-old sensibilities, it seemed the most romantic thing in the world to be married in a simple shipboard ceremony. We pictured the three of us standing with the captain in his dress whites at the railing overlooking the sunrise and the Mexican Riviera. But by the time Lucy's mother had wrestled control from us, it became a lavishly produced affair involving over three hundred seasick guests crowded into the Acapulco Ballroom.

The first thing Lucy's mother did was to find out the name of the travel agent and demand that the couple-to-be be split up. So, for the three nights prior to the wedding, Lucy roomed with Genie, her maid of honor, and Grove bunked with me on the far side of the ship.

We spent the first two nights of the cruise drinking and dancing.

Genie and I ended up passing out together in the oversized bed in her room while Grove and Lucy slept in mine. But the night before the wedding was different for some reason. The traditional last dance at the disco was an old Sinatra version of Almost Like Being In Love. Genie and I had just stepped out onto the floor, her skirt flaring up as I swung her out to the end of my arm. She laughed and twirled back to me, but then Grove was there, tapping her on the shoulder and bowing formally, asking to cut in. I stepped back and held out Genie's hand to him, but he took my hand instead. Meanwhile, Lucy bowed to Genie and the two of them danced around in lazy circles. Grove and I danced close, his chest pressed against mine, as he laughed and breathed alcohol onto my neck.

"You're the best friend I've ever had," he said. "I hope you know that, hope you know I'd do anything for you." And my stomach fell through nine decks to plunge into the ocean.

We did a couple of Jäger shots with the bartender after the girls went back to their room, then did a couple of lines of coke before we stumbled back to our cabin.

"I can't sleep with her tonight, Chris," he slurred as we staggered down the corridor, "It's my last night being single, you know? And I just can't do…"

He lurched as the ship slid to one side beneath us, caught himself on my shoulder, then righted himself and pushed open the door to our cabin.

"Coffee," he whispered, so I called room service and, within minutes, we were sipping hot creamy coffee together on the tiny sofa. Grove drank a cup and a half of coffee, then staggered into the bathroom. He was gone a long time.

"You okay?" I asked, knocking gently on the door.

There was a long silence, then he opened the door and looked out at me. He had washed his face and straightened his clothing.

"You look better," I said.

"I feel better. I'm sorry—Christ—you shouldn't have to baby-sit me." He pushed the bathroom door open a bit wider and walked out, remarkably steady. He turned back around and looked at me with eyes so full of emotion that I wanted to run away. "I love you, man. I could not do this without you standing beside me every step of the way. I'm terrified. I mean, my God, I'm getting married tomorrow, I mean today, man. I...I don't know what I would do...you mean so much to me. You're my best friend in the world."

He was standing there with this indescribably mournful look in his brimming eyes and all I wanted in that moment was to hold him so close to me that he would feel safe and loved and a little less terrified. So I reached out a hand across the distance to touch his chest and he stepped back—quickly, deliberately.

He must have seen the shock on my face because he said, "No—you don't understand. It's not what you think."

And I stood there and looked at him, still and silent.

He watched me with those green eyes of his and I felt dizzy, a moment of déjà vu that hit me with such force, I stepped back and sat on the foot of the bed. And he took a step back from me and landed on the sofa.

We sat there facing each other for a long moment.

"It's not what you think," he said again.

"What exactly, am I thinking?" I asked angrily, cheeks flushing red.

He stared at me for a moment then I felt his eyes slide through me into the far distance. "I think," he said from behind those dreamy, unfocused eyes, "I think sometimes I want one thing and then sometimes I want something else." His eyes snapped back to me, fast, startling me. "I'm not afraid of you."

"I know that," I said, slightly disoriented.

"There are lines, Christopher. Lines between things, between this and that…." His voice trailed off and he ran his fingers through his hair. "Lines that divide what we do and who we are from what we don't do and who we're not."

"Grove, I wasn't trying to—"

"Oh, I know," he said, waving his hand dismissively. "I know you weren't doing anything. It's just that there's a line. Here. Tonight."

I watched him in silence, feeling the distance opening between us like a sudden chasm.

"And I've already made my decision about who I am and what I'll do. I mean, I'm getting married tomorrow…"

"Look, Grove, I'm not trying to do anything here—"

"I know, I know," he said again, his voice quavering for a moment. He captivated me with eyes that bore into me. "This is about me. I'm the one standing on the edge."

I locked eyes with him for a long time, waiting for this moment to pass. But it did not. We sat, staring at each other across two feet of beige carpet, across the greatest divide that can ever separate two people. I loved him. And I was completely immobile, knowing that if I moved a millimeter, I would leap across the chasm into his arms and this moment would end with one of us walking out the door forever.

But then he startled me, reaching down and pulling off first one shoe, then the other.

"No words," he said, flashing me his nervous smile.

He kicked his shoes toward me, then reached up to unbutton his shirt, tan fingers, moving slowly from top to bottom against the white cotton, unhooking each button, then moving on to the next, pulling the tails of his shirt out of his pants, then taking the shirt off and tossing it over the back of the chair next to him. He peeled his tight T-shirt up across his belly, his abs, his hairy chest. He pulled it over his head, then threw it to the side.

I could feel the pressure of my erection breaking through the alcohol-induced moment, rubbing against the inside of my boxers.

He looked at me for a long moment, and I didn't dare breathe until he leaned forward and reached down to peel his right sock slowly from his foot. He let his fingers trail along the naked arch, flexing his toes, grinning up quickly at me, then peeling his left sock off as well. When the socks were off, he stood up and began to unbuckle his belt.

I stood up and reached out to help him, but he caught my hands in his. He pushed them back toward me and said two words: "Don't touch."

And suddenly I understood.

❍❍❍

On the train I feel the incremental slowing of the braking systems that signal the approach to a station. Along this part of the route, the stations are little more than a platform and a ticket booth, standing in the middle of a cluster of ten or fifteen buildings. So, less than five minutes after the train coasts to a stop, we are underway again.

I look across at my companion, who appears to be asleep, and I see the impressively long thin outline of an erection against the denim of his jeans. The jeans are tight enough, and his ardor bold enough, to see the contours of the head outlined like an invitation beneath the worn denim. I shift uncomfortably in my seat, pulling my coat over my own lap and my own rearing erection. I am not wearing underwear and the friction feels like the tickle of flames along my shaft.

❍❍❍

And there Grove stood, less than two feet from me, unbuckling his belt and watching me with those eyes. He tugged on the belt, pulling it away from him, the leather holding on to each belt loop for an instant until he finally ripped it free in one broad movement, brandishing it in the air like a whip, then flicking it across the room.

He pulled his pants down to his ankles and stepped out of them in a swift motion, then stood back up, leaving a mere sheath of white cotton and about two feet of empty space between my raging erection and his.

He stood for a moment, then grinned foolishly and crossed his arms, tapping his foot in mock exasperation until I began to pull off my clothes in a flurry. When I was down to my underwear, I took one look at him and pulled them down to my ankles, kicking them away from us and standing completely naked in front of him, my erection bobbing and bouncing between us.

He looked up and down my body for a long time, his eyes beginning at my feet and traveling up my muscular legs, across the planes of my thick toned thighs and into the dark tangle of hair that clustered around my balls. He looked carefully at my cock and for a moment, I could feel the shadow of his regard across the length of my shaft. I shivered involuntarily, drawing his focus up to my face.

He wore a look that I had never seen before; an expression of desire and humor plus a tinge of something else, something like resignation.

He grinned again and dropped his underwear, kicking it to the side.

I drew in a quick breath and concentrated on not touching his cock as it bobbed in front of him. I had seen it before, but not quite like this. It was short, but thick, with a pale shaft that extended to a particularly thick purplish head. The head was straining like a creature trying to escape the tiny cluster of pubic hair. His balls were large and heavy, hanging low in their shaved pouch.

Grove reached down and gave himself a couple of strokes, a left-handed grip that was loose and exact at the same time, a practiced move that made my cock jump in response. He grinned at that and began to rub his abdomen with his right hand, pumping with one hand and, with the other, rubbing circles along his belly, then his chest, circling his tiny dark nipples for a moment, then sliding back along his treasure trail for a two-fisted massage of his cock.

I watched him rub himself and reached down with my right hand, pulling lightly on my balls, sliding my fingernail down the length of my cock, enjoying both the sight of him touching himself and the feel of my own gentle solo prelude.

He started stroking himself more rhythmically, eyes roaming across my body as if he was storing every contour, every muscle for later recall. He reached up absently and spit into his hand, sliding the spit along the hot length of his cock, rolling the saliva across the head with the palm of his hand as though he were chalking a pool cue. I smiled at this, spit in my own hand and mirrored his movements.

We stood there stroking ourselves and watching each other, our movements synching as the heat began to build in my stomach. Suddenly, in an instant, his eyes snapped shut and he shuddered, then came in a torrent, globs of searing hot cum hitting my stomach, my legs, my toes, and the carpet between us.

He looked supremely embarrassed and uncomfortable as if he did not expect this to happen, or was chagrined by the speed with which it did.

I let my hand slack off, but when he saw my erection bobbing there, he said, "But you didn't come."

I shrugged. For a moment, he looked as though he would drop to his knees and take my cock into his mouth. This thought sent a pulse through my cock and, seeing my continuing excitement, Grove stood up, turned around, put his feet together and bent himself at the waist, palms stretched out against the floor in front of him. "Don't touch," he reminded me as I moved behind him.

I dropped to my knees behind him, my face hovering less than a foot from the spectacular sight he had just thrust at me. His limber body doubled over on itself, thrusting his ass cheeks up and apart and there, buried in a damp wisp of hair, his rosebud sphincter stared out at me. It pulsed slowly in an odd, sentient pattern and the hair around it trembled slightly under my breath. He shifted a fraction closer and it was all I could do not to plunge my tongue into him. But I kept just enough distance between us to keep us from touching and I grabbed my rearing cock with renewed vigor.

The musky odor of him was both sweet and rank, drifting across the slight divide and invading my senses as I pumped myself faster and faster. I breathed deeply, licked my hand and stroked myself. I groaned in spite of myself, breaking the silence awkwardly, like a tourist in a foreign library. And I endeavored, in spite of my growing excitement to memorize the line of fur that ran along the very innermost crevice of him, the tantalizing scent of him, the tiny purple sphincter that winked its carnal code at me.

And I stroked myself, my breathing becoming ragged, catching in my throat. Heat rose off my cheeks in waves, and I felt the first explosion of ether behind my eyes that presaged my orgasm. Then it was on me, like a wave, creeping up the startled hairs on my arms and legs, and smashing its way out of me. I started to cum in spurts that crossed the distance between us, splattering the back of Grove's thighs, calves and heels. I let out a long sighing groan and the ether behind my eyes engulfed me for an instant sending everything else into a flash of blackness.

And then it was over and, somehow, Grove was up and laughing and toweling himself off. And I smeared his cum across my chest and stomach, and let it dry there as we stood naked on the balcony, staring at the sky and finishing off the lukewarm coffee. I watched Grove's animated smile as he talked about the stars and the dark outline of the Mexican shoreline in the near distance. And I new that somehow, despite his clear design, despite his careful construction of the demarcations, we had somehow stepped across the line.

And so he was married to Lucy and I toasted the happy couple at their reception and I slept alone the next night, curled around a pillow stuffed with feathers and memories. And the next night I slept with a performer from one of the lounge acts, missing breakfast and lunch and, finally, that evening in Mazatlan, missing the boat altogether.

✪✪✪

And now, a decade later, I still feel the sting of loss and the menace of boundaries and the sadness of empty train platforms, holding me rigidly to my seat, despite the fact that the man with whom I share this lonely compartment is toying playfully with his long thin cock, eyeing me speculatively and licking his lips. I watch this moment unfold before me in the flickering cinematic images that play in the blank spaces behind my eyes. I am a camera, I think, as I begin to record the moment, not on the permanent stock where Grove resides, but on a tape whose quality is marginal, whose images dance with the static of disconnection and shimmer slightly, making it difficult to see the lines that divide individuals. Is that mine? Is that his? Is that me? Is that him? Do I care?

I unbutton my jeans, unzip my zipper and pull my hard cock out of my jeans. I watch the smile spread across his thin lips. "*Nicht berühren,*" I whisper, don't touch. I glance at my reflection in the window, then look back at this stranger as he kneels on the floor in front of me.

ཀ ཀ

Jamie Freeman lives in North Florida. He divides his time between his day job and the solitary joys of reading, running and writing. Although this is his first published short story, he has previously published a children's book and has a completed novel manuscript waiting patiently on the edge of his desk. He can be reached by email at JamieFreeman2@gmail.com.

Thickness
NATHAN JAMES

Have you ever discovered something about yourself that excites and astonishes you at the same time? I'm talking about a moment when every neat, preconceived notion you've held in your life gets turned on its ear? Let me see if I can put it all together for you. My name is Brian Watkins, and the last couple of days of my life have defied all the nice little conventions I'd become so comfortable with. Okay, I admit it, I'm still kind of young—only twenty-two—and I haven't begun to discover all of life's wonders yet. Well, let me dive right in.

Two days ago, I was at my friend Manny's gym. Manny and I had been friends all our lives. His dad had passed away a year ago, and now Manny owns the gym. It was late, and Manny was tired, so he tossed me the keys and told me to lock up when I was done.

I was pleased to have some quiet workout time, and I was waiting on the last few patrons to leave so I could do my reps in peace. I came out of the locker room and there, on the treadmill, was a man of about six-two. I'd never seen him in the gym before. He was bald-headed, with a neatly trimmed goatee, full lips, a wide, flat nose, deep-set brown eyes, and he was solid, thick, but not fat. He looked like he was in his early thirties. His caramel-hued skin shone in the bright, white overhead lights as he ran, glistening with sweat. I watched his long powerful legs working as he jogged.

I was transfixed by his beauty, watching his graceful stride, even as I wondered about my strange attraction to this man. In contrast to him, I stood five-eight, with a close fade, thin mustache, medium lips, and a square chin. My dark-brown skin showcased my sculpted body, which I was inordinately proud of. I was solid muscle from neck to feet, and I made the gym my second home to keep it that way. Biceps, pecs, delts, quads, glutes, lats, all were honed to the best of my ability.

Naw, I couldn't possibly want this guy, could I? Yes, he was handsome, but I'd always thought big, thick, non-muscular men would turn me off. Too many muscle guys in muscle mags reinforced that notion in my head. I was becoming conditioned to only appreciate physical "perfection." Besides, he looked to be about ten years older than me, and I wasn't into older men…was I?

I watched as he got off the treadmill and stretched out. Seeing him extend his limbs so effortlessly, did something to me. I felt that familiar stirring in my groin and hoped no one saw that embarrassing bulge in my shorts. The man started toward the locker room and smiled as he passed me. Suddenly, I became weak in the knees. Almost involuntarily, I followed behind him. I pretended to look through my locker as I watched him undress out of the corner of my eye.

"Hey, man, could you pass me that towel?" His voice was rich, deep, and captivating.

"Sure," I said, passing him the towel from the bench. "By the way, my name is Brian. I'm in charge of the gym. I thought I knew everybody, but I've never seen you before."

"I'm Rudy. Rudy Nesbitt," he replied. "I just came in to check the place out. Somebody recommended it to me."

Rudy peeled off his T-shirt, revealing his big, beautiful body. Wide, strong shoulders; massive, round pecs, with the most exquisite gold nip rings. Rudy was thick, with a gentle roundness to his belly that hinted of softness without being flabby. He had a deep navel that my tongue desperately wanted to probe. I watched him, trying not to let my jaw drop as he toweled the sweat off him.

"How—how do you like this place? Do we have a satisfied customer?"

"Yeah, you do." Rudy smiled, lighting up the room. "I think I'll join."

Oh, would you? What was going on with me? I'd never been this awestruck by a guy, especially someone like Rudy, who I thought wasn't "my type." I'd always shied away from the thick "daddies," preferring the muscle men I usually hooked up with instead. But listening to Rudy's deep voice, watching him move with quiet confidence, feeling the power of him just wash over me, well, this was different.

Rudy pulled his shorts off, and I thought I might faint. He had a big, round, perfect bubble ass. I was so hard by this time—and trying my best to hide it—that I imagined my dick might just burst through my shorts. Rudy stood there naked in front of me, and I'm sure my eyes were as big as dinner plates. I tried not to gawk, but...

"Hey man, are you all right?"

"Umm, yeah, I kinda got distracted for a minute... I'm okay."

"Oh." Rudy chuckled softly. "Did I distract you?" He winked at me playfully, then walked off to the showers, leaving me speechless standing by my locker.

My mind was screaming at me to strip and follow him into the shower, but there were a few other people still on the gym floor. Being caught in the shower, ogling Rudy with a huge erection, might be bad for me and the gym. So, with almost superhuman strength, I went back out to the desk, willing my dick down so I could work.

Within ten minutes, the other three patrons had finished their workouts, showered, dressed, and left. Rudy, however, was still in the locker room. I decided to check on him. I found him still in that hot, steamy shower, luxuriating as cascades of water rushed over him. Beads of water clung to his every curve, making me hungry for his sweet thickness. Almost on impulse, I ran out of the locker room, grabbed the gym keys off the front desk, and locked the front doors. I hurried back to the locker room, practically tearing my shorts and wifebeater off as I went, and strode into the shower. Rudy turned and smiled at me. Without a word, he stepped toward me, dripping wet, bare skin shimmering.

"Rudy, I...," I began.

"Shhh. Don't say a word," Rudy whispered.

Rudy wrapped his big arms around me, and I could feel his long hardness against my six-pack. I pressed my own rock-solid dick against his thigh, and began to caress his shoulders. Rudy's torso slid wetly against me as I let my hands explore his curves, and feel his softness. I couldn't stop myself. I kissed Rudy's neck, letting my tongue lap the beads of water from his skin. Rudy hugged me tightly, and his mammoth pecs felt so amazing against my smaller body.

I writhed against him as he squeezed my ass, holding me in his meaty palms. I was getting weaker and weaker as Rudy drew me deeper into him. I began kissing his pecs, licking those sweet nips, flicking my tongue around those nip rings of his! I couldn't contain myself any longer.

"Rudy, oh, yes, man. You're so awesome!"

"Go ahead, man." Oh, that deep, sexy voice! "Kiss me, man. Lick my body like I know you want to."

"Oh, yesss, please, yesss, I must…" My words failed me as I kissed Rudy's pecs, and felt my knees giving way as I worked down his body, licking the roundness of his belly, probing that delectably deep navel, tickling Rudy's bushy black pubes.

On my knees now, with Rudy stroking my head gently, sensually, I licked Rudy's generous nine-inch shaft, which was, like the rest of Rudy, thick and meaty. Water dripped onto the tip of my tongue from the head of Rudy's dick, and that was it for me.

Pursing my lips, I took him inside me, delicately at first, then engulfing him, feeling the fullness of him inside my mouth. I rolled my eyes upward as I serviced him, to gaze at his massive body towering over me. I flung one arm around Rudy's left thigh, and it was like holding onto a tree trunk. I held Rudy's dick in my other hand as I sucked him furiously, my head bobbing.

I felt the clouds of steam around me as I went on and on, thirstily drinking his pre-cum as Rudy threw his head back, his hips gently thrusting as I worked his shaft. Just when I thought I was going to swallow pints of sweet Rudy juice, Rudy gently guided my head away from him with those big hands of his. Pulling me back to my feet, we kissed fiercely, our tongues intertwining, hands ravishing each other.

Suddenly, Rudy broke away, with a look resembling terror on his face, and stepped back to the shower, rinsed himself off, and wordlessly, scurried off to the locker room. I sank to my knees again, wet, naked, weak, overwhelmed by the experience. I could hear Rudy dressing frantically, but I was too drained to pick myself off the wet tile floor and chase after him. Besides, the front door was locked. He'd need me to let him out.

I sat on my bare bottom in the steamy shower, trying to compose myself. I was giddy, aroused, amazed and…scared. Rudy was so big, so comforting. Like the daddy-type he was, I felt secure in his arms. But what had I done to make him break away and dash off like a jack rabbit?

I heard Rudy coming back toward the locker room. His footsteps were fast paced, angry. Well, I had locked him in. Just as I was about to summon the strength to pull myself to my feet, Rudy came into the shower, his face showing annoyance. Damn, he was an imposing sight! Tall, stern, with a black Sean John jacket, white dress shirt, deep blue Rocawear jeans, black boots, and Nautica Navigator watch, Rudy was a sight to behold. I sat there, still wet, small, naked and weak, hoping he wasn't too pissed off with me.

"You know the door's locked, right, man?" Rudy growled.

Uh-oh. "Uh yeah, Rudy. I'm sorry. Let me get dressed, and I'll let you out."

"Why did you lock me in?"

"I didn't want anyone…to, you know, see us," I managed. "I just wanted you so bad."

Rudy's expression softened a little. "I guess that makes sense. Sorry I snapped at you. Let me help you up." Rudy took my hand and effortlessly brought me to my feet. I felt so vulnerable standing there, bare and helpless, before this massively attractive hunk of a man.

"Rudy," I asked, "what happened? Did I do something wrong?"

"No, you didn't. Not at all. I think I did, though."

"You did? How?"

Instead of replying, Rudy walked out of the shower and sat on a bench in the locker room. I followed him, and leaned against the wall. In spite of myself, I had no desire to cover up. I liked being naked in front of him.

"Can I ask you something, Brian?"

"Of course."

"Are you a top or a bottom?"

"Well, I prefer being a top…"

"I'm a bottom. Always have been. But usually, everybody expects me to be a top. I thought you would, too, so I tried to leave before I… embarrassed myself."

Instantly my heart went out to Rudy. I understood exactly what he was getting at. Being big and thick, guys had automatically pegged him as a "top." Rudy felt ashamed for being a "bottom," which, in his mind, guys associated with smaller, weaker men. I was guilty of making assumptions, too. Rudy was not, as I mentioned before, "my usual type." I'd read all the "no fats, no fems" lines on the hook-up sites I visited and had bought into the negative stereotypes about "thick" men for quite a while. I was still surprised at the intensity of my attraction to Rudy, and I felt a little ashamed at how long I'd held on to my preconceptions.

"Rudy, man, you have nothing to be upset about. You were incredible in the shower! I can't begin to thank you enough!"

"Thank me?"

"Yes! You set me free of my close-minded ideas…about big guys like you."

"Oh, I did, huh?" Rudy allowed himself a little chuckle. It was good to see him smile again.

"If you're a bottom, Rudy," I leaned in close and whispered in his ear, "I can think of a few things I'd like to do with you."

"Really?" Rudy eyed my rising erection.

"More than you can imagine, man…really."

Rudy stood up and embraced me, and I could feel all his tension melt away. I held him for divinely long moments, savoring the feel of his leather coat against my bare skin. I breathed in his scent deeply, which was musky, yet sweet, and pressed my bare body tightly against him. We kissed passionately, this time with a tenderness I didn't fully expect.

Rudy reached down and cupped my ass in his hands. He squeezed me, and as I gasped with pleasure, he gripped my thighs and picked me up off the floor. I wrapped my legs around his waist, and pressed my hardness against the contrasting softness of his abdomen. Rudy held me with ease, caressing my back and shoulders as I squeezed my legs around him.

I began humping Rudy's belly as he held me. Wildly, I kissed Rudy's neck again, sucking deeply this time.

"Oooh, yeah," Rudy moaned. "That feels so, so good."

"Rudy," I panted, "let me lick those gorgeous nips again, please."

"Go for it, man."

I pulled my arms in toward me and unbuttoned Rudy's shirt. Exposing Rudy's chest, I went right to work on his right nip, feeling the roundness of it, and his massive pec on the tip of my tongue. I pulled at the ring on Rudy's left nip with my right hand, making him shudder with delight. I let my tongue dance on his nip, feeling Rudy's big body undulate in waves of pleasure. Finally, he let me down, and as I stood there, hot with anticipation, he threw his coat off and started to undress.

I couldn't wait that long. I stepped to him and unbuttoned the rest of his shirt. Just before I could undo his belt, Rudy bent over (oh, that ass!) and withdrew condoms and a smack packet of lube from his coat. I like a prepared man.

Handing them to me, I got myself together while Rudy took

off his tight jeans and let his boxer briefs fall to the floor. I pulled the rubber on in breathless anticipation. I took pride in being so well endowed that I could see the lot number on a condom when I put one on. Rudy embraced me again, and I felt his heavy breathing on my shoulder.

Gently, I placed my hands on his hips, and guided him to the space between the bench and the lockers. I stood up on the bench while Rudy spread-eagled himself, facing the lockers. I looked down at his beautiful, full butt, and marveled. I want this…oh yes, I really want this!

Have you ever been abreast of the moment, when all your ideas and thoughts about the way things are avail you nothing? Have you ever felt a sense of wonder at the newness of an experience that took your power of speech away? Can you fathom the cascade of ecstasy that accompanied that first, tenuous entry into a new sexual dimension? I was rushing headlong to that wonderful place as I knelt on the towel-covered bench, and spread Rudy's cheeks apart.

I let my tongue do the talking as I explored that soft man-hole, feeling its juicy wetness as I probed Rudy. He jiggled with delight as I rolled my tongue against his walls, and I reached around his waist and stroked his diamond-hard erection. Rudy was panting hard as I snaked my tongue deeper inside him, and I felt my whole body tingle as he moaned and writhed under my ministrations. Finally, I let my tongue find its way out of his hot, wet ass, slowly, teasingly, while Rudy gasped.

"Ohhh, ohhh, damn, man, please, please. I want you inside me, please!"

"Rudy, your wish," I giggled, "is my command."

I stood up on the bench, got us both ready, and slowly, sweetly, advanced myself into Rudy's willing, quivering man-hole. I could feel him contracting himself as I plunged deeper and deeper inside him. He tightened his walls around me, and it felt so good!

I began to work Rudy's ass, reveling in the feel of those huge cheeks slapping up against me, as I pumped furiously, and Rudy moaned, a single long utterance of total ecstasy that came from deep within him. I had this big, strong, masculine hunk under my complete control as I rolled my hips in a grinding motion, making my dick hit Rudy's every pleasure spot.

I bent forward, and hugged him around his thick, soft waist. Pressing my chest against his massive back, I moved him around with my hips, letting my dick do this fantastically sensual slow roll inside his juicy ass.

"Oh, Brian, don't stop. You're so good. Don't stop!"

Rudy thrashed his head around wildly, as I kept at it, drilling him with an intensity I didn't know I could muster. All those "muscle gods" I thought were the height of sexual desirability just faded away. Rudy was such a generous, enthusiastic lover!

I pulled down on Rudy's nip rings as I felt my climax coming, and I felt Rudy bucking and contracting. I came in a blasting release of rivers of cum, filling Rudy up with my sweet white juice, even as Rudy shot his load onto the lockers in front of him. I held on to Rudy for dear life as the power of my orgasm threatened to sweep us both away…

Finally, spent, drenched in sweat, Rudy hung limply in my arms. I guided him down to the bench, and straddled his waist to sit in his lap. We held each other, too overwhelmed to utter a sound. I looked into Rudy's eyes, and found there a profound relief, a gratitude that needed no words. He was, in fact, a kind, giving lover, something most of my muscled lovers lacked. They, unlike Rudy, were too impressed with themselves.

I was glad that Rudy had found in me, a partner who wanted him without judgment. I could see he'd been searching for one for quite a long time. I was happy we'd found each other, and amazed at how, in such a short period of time, Rudy could lead me on such a journey of self-discovery.

"I guess we need to go back to the showers." I giggled.

"Yeah, we do," Rudy replied, affectionately kissing me on the forehead.

We showered together, lathering each other up, and admiring each other's bodies. We lingered under the warm water, in a wet, slippery embrace, then finally, dried each other off and got dressed. We exchanged phone numbers and e-mail addresses, and made a dinner date for the next night. I let Rudy out, locked the gym up, and started for home.

I closed my eyes as I lay on my bed. I thought about Rudy, and the ways we so arbitrarily put people into neat little "boxes" in our minds. As the breeze floated in through my window and caressed my naked body, I reflected on all the things Rudy had taught me that day.

I'd learned not to assume things about people based on their appearance. I'd discovered that bigness does not a top guy make. I'd been pleasantly surprised by the way I found big, thick Rudy to be so electrifyingly hot.

To think I'd let my head be filled up with all that "perfect body" garbage! There was softness, together with a strength and sweetness that defined Rudy, and made me want to rest my head for hours on his massive chest, and just listen to his deep, sexy voice forever. I imagined lying in Rudy's protective arms, feeling him against me, wrapping my legs around his massive thighs and holding on to him, holding on, holding on, holding on…

The alarm hammered my ears, and I bolted up in my bed.

Damn. Morning already! But it wasn't such a bad thing. I'd awakened to a new day, my mind open to all its immense possibilities, unchained. Rudy had, with a "thickness," set me free. I couldn't wait to see what else he had to teach me...

ഋഝ

Author and activist Nathan James, called the "philosopher-prince of erotica" by reviewers, began his bibliography with the novel The Devil's Details *(S-Ink, 2005), the short stories "Enchanted Morning"* (Muscle Worshipers, *STARbooks Press 2006), and "Ten Days"* (Love In A Lock Up, *STARbooks Press, 2007). His e-books,* In His Court *(Forbidden Publications, 2006) and* Check Ride *(Forbidden Publications, 2007) have enjoyed bestseller status. Nathan was nominated by fellow authors in 2007 for the Clik Magazine Awards. He is a passionate activist, speaking at antiwar protests and gay-rights rallies across the country. Nathan is a regular contributor to local papers and www.kuttinedgeonline.com, where he writes articles of interest to the LGBT community of color. Nathan is a lifelong resident of New York City, and he will be traveling widely in 2008 as a director of the Black Pride Experience Project. Nathan enjoys hearing from readers, and can be reached at nathan@nathanjamesonline.com and he encourages people to visit his website at www.nathanjamesonline.com*

That's Not What This Is About

M.K. LEIGH

He brushed against me so casually I wasn't sure it meant anything. The hardware store aisle was narrow, cluttered with electrical wires and plumbing elbows in overflowing bins; a touch could have meant nothing at all. Why would it? At the time, I was a young schoolteacher in a mid-sized town, with students with names like Timmy and Wendy, who had dogs called Lassie and Scoot, whose mothers packed them peanut butter and jam sandwiches in painted tin lunch boxes, and waited for them after school on the porch with a tray of cookies and milk, a snack before their daddies came home for dinner from selling insurance or appliances. A brush-past simply didn't mean then what it does now. But when he passed me on his way out of the store and squeezed my groin, the meaning was clear. I paid for a light switch I didn't need and slid into the passenger side of his Ford Fairlane wagon.

We drove in silence to a deserted baseball field at the edge of town. He stopped at the far end of the gravel parking lot, by the outfield fence, where he unzipped his pants, leaving them buttoned and buckled. The engine idled loudly, shaking the car, but he left it running anyway. I lowered my head to his lap, while he watched nervously for interruptions. I was confined by the steering wheel, and I could only get to him through the opening in his pants. But once I caught his scent I forgot about everything else. I coaxed his cock hard with my tongue and was able to get three fingers into his pants to massage his balls. He gasped and urged me along with his hands. I slid my lips over the head and down the shaft. I sucked his cock, increasing the tempo as I felt his body tensing, until he raised my head by the chin and I got a close-up of his violent orgasm.

I was short of breath and trying desperately to undo my belt, but to my surprise he shifted out of park and we rolled past the bleachers toward the exit. Steering with one hand, he tucked himself back into his pants with the other, ignoring my protests. Frustrated, I distracted myself by rapidly flicking my newly purchased light switch on and off, much to his annoyance I hoped. I glanced at him only long enough to notice a tattoo on his left forearm, obscured by the rolled-up sleeve of his work shirt. I debated starting a conversation but before I could overcome my irritation with him, we were back on the main street, where he let me out without saying a word.

That evening, I ate dinner out of a can, while leaning against the counter in my kitchenette. I decided, on reflection, that while the afternoon hadn't been fulfilling, it had been thrilling. I enjoyed uncomplicated encounters with unceremonious conclusions much more than sentimental love-making with cautious but tender good-byes. When I finished eating, I settled myself into a corner of the couch and fantasized about him—in a motel room, unbridled by the worry of detection, free to focus his sexual energy on me. Had we, I would have treated it as one continuous date so it wouldn't have violated my once-or-twice-only policy, my rule for avoiding the complications of emotional bonds. Life was difficult enough for a gay schoolteacher then; I didn't need the problems that came with a relationship. Sex was what I was looking for and I found enough of it to keep me happy.

And sometimes sex found me.

I was window shopping, not far from Jessop's Hardware, where weeks earlier I had been groped, when my tattooed stranger pulled up to the sidewalk and threw open the passenger side door. I hesitated, only long enough to be certain I wasn't being watched, then got in. "Where do you live?" he asked with an accent, possibly Italian. I told him my address and we drove the short distance to my apartment.

Leading him to my bedroom, I stripped while I walked, leaving behind a trail of clothes, then sat back on the bed propped up on my elbows. He stood in the doorway filling it with his shoulders. He wasn't tall but he was broad, with muscular arms and big hands with thick fingers. He unbuttoned his shirt and kicked off his shoes, before undoing his pants and letting them drop to the floor. His stomach was hard and flat, his legs powerful. On his barrel chest was a small patch of thick hair, dense like the black curls on his head. Tattoos spread across his body: a crudely drawn mermaid swam up his right arm, over his shoulder and across his chest just below his collarbone; on his forearm was an ornate dagger, the tattoo partially covered by his shirt at the ballpark. I was trying to make out the others when he hooked his thumbs into his briefs and tugged them off. He knelt over me, thrusting his groin in my face, rushing again. I played with his cock slowly, trying to relax him, letting my tongue flick gently along skin that was oddly translucent for a dark man. I searched his face for emotion but it was stern, his eyes closed tightly. I licked his balls, then went down on his cock. He wavered and then opened his eyes, the glassiness giving way to intensity. When I thought I had calmed him, I lay back and brought up my knees, but he entered me roughly. I wrapped my legs around his back, grabbing a handful of his chest hair and giving it a twist when he thrust too hard. He smirked and slowed to a smooth rhythm. I realized as he fucked me that he was a brutish dangerous stranger, who could harm my much smaller boyish body and there would be nothing I could do to defend myself. The thought got me off moments before he shuddered and fell on top of me.

We lay on the bed not talking. He stared at the ceiling while I examined his skin. "Tell me about your tattoos," I said finally.

He turned toward me. "I will tell you next time."

There won't be a next time, I thought; this was date number two.

"My name is Viktor," he said. "You?"

I considered not telling him, but did anyway.

"Randy, I must go. I am in town for afternoon only and must make sales calls. Maybe again I see you," he said with an accent I now thought was Russian.

"Maybe," I said. I watched him dress, thinking it would be a shame not to see him again. A third time would be such a small exception to the rule.

Viktor came by regularly after that, about every month or so. I wasn't interested in a relationship, but, I told myself, I had to be careful because of my job. My once-or-twice-only policy increased the risk of picking up an undercover cop or someone who would out me to the school board. Besides, what we had wasn't a relationship. I knew he was Russian and a salesman from another town but I didn't know which, and he knew my name and address but that was all. I regarded it strictly as a convenient arrangement for sex, though, as his visits became more frequent,

I began to wonder if he saw it the same way. Then, about a year after we first met, as he mopped his forehead with my sheets, while I tidied the room from his much appreciated wild tear, he asked: "Do you go with other men?"

I laughed and continued clearing up.

"Do not laugh at me," he said.

"Of course," I said and righted a toppled chair.

"While we are together?"

I folded his pants and dropped them on the chair. "You need to get this straight: we aren't 'together.' That's not what this is about."

When he leapt off the bed I cowered, sure he was going to strike me. Instead he grabbed his clothes and dressed, slamming out of the apartment shouting a tirade of profanity, some of it incomprehensible, all of it mean-spirited.

❖❖❖

I did my best to forget Viktor and reinstated my once-or-twice-only policy, his rage confirming that anything more leads to complications. I became more discreet and stopped taking dates back to my apartment. Still, the joy I felt with other men reminded me that what I had with Viktor was about sex, so, while it was regrettable he didn't see it the same way, I moved on.

My life was back to normal when almost a year later I bumped into Viktor in the doorway of a diner not far from my apartment. I edged past, pretending I hadn't noticed him, and sat on a stool at the lunch counter. I ordered a coffee and when he sat next to me I acted as if running into him was nothing out of the ordinary. I casually motioned for the waitress to make it two coffees. He glared at me while I sat awkwardly silent, thinking about what I should say. I was grateful when she placed cups in front of us. "How have you been, Viktor?" I asked and sipped my coffee, focusing my attention on the waitress lining up fresh pies in a glass display case before heading back into the kitchen.

When she was gone, Viktor grabbed my collar, forcing me to face him. My cup rattled, spilling coffee onto the counter. "I wait in car," he said and marched out the door. Only an elderly couple had noticed his outburst. I smiled at them and they turned away whispering. I tried to mop up the coffee with a handful of napkins but only managed to make a greater mess. Defeated, I fumbled through my wallet and placed a ten-dollar bill under a ketchup bottle and rushed out to the street. My intention was to go to get away from Victor, but, after a moment of indecision, I got into his car.

At my apartment, Viktor threw me down on the bed, turning me over so I was facing away from him. I buried my head in a pillow, screaming into it as he fucked me. When my knees became raw from rubbing against the linen, I turned over onto my back. There was fury in his eyes and he grunted so loudly I was worried the neighbors would hear. I grabbed him by the back of the neck and pushed my tongue into his mouth to quiet him. He mashed my lips with a kiss before breaking away, gasping for air. He held me down to the bed with a hand that spanned my entire chest. The tension in my stomach was building, when I noticed it. I shouted for him to stop, then planted a foot into the middle of his chest and shoved him off me.

He stumbled from the bed.

I pointed to his chest. "What the hell is that?"

He looked down at the name "Maria" freshly tattooed above his heart. "Maria? She is my mother's name."

"Liar," I shouted.

He hesitated, then said, "She is my wife."

I crawled to the edge of the bed, bringing us face to face. "You're angry because I fuck other men when you have a wife?" Viktor looked confused, unable to make the connection. "Look," I said, stepping off the bed, "I really don't care if you're married or even if you have kids…" He looked away. "Figures. I don't care. But let's get this straight: don't you dare get mad at me for having my own life when you go back to your little hick town and your little happy family when you're done with me. Do you understand?" He conceded but he was jittery. "You want to fuck when you pull into town, that's fine, but you stay out of my business."

"I live across town," he said, then named the immigrant district. "I work in factory there."

I threw up my hands. "I don't care. You have your life; I have mine."

He nodded but said, "My name is not Viktor." Then he told me his real name, his accent changing. "I am not from Russia. I am from Malta."

Italian, Russian, Maltese, it didn't matter to me. "You should go now," I said, handing him his pants.

He let them fall to the floor and extended a trembling hand toward me. I shook my head and mouthed, *No.* He looked helpless. Then his erection, lost in the argument, came twitching back. I was inclined, again, to tell him to go, but his sad look and his hard-on conspired against me. I sat on the bed with my feet on the edge of the mattress. "Okay, one last time," I said, "but you'd better make it worth my while."

He did.

❋❋❋

I continued to call him Viktor and didn't care that he wasn't Russian or a salesman or any of the rest of it. I didn't ask him about his wife and he didn't ask me about my sex partners, though there were fewer of them as the years passed. In middle age, I was becoming more preoccupied with my health and finances; I certainly wasn't entertaining fewer lovers because I was becoming sentimental about Victor. Even after a couple of decades, I never expected to grow old with him, I never asked him to leave his wife, and I never asked for anything beyond what we had for the span of his brief visits. It was about the sex and, if he wasn't around, I went out and found someone else to be with.

Then one night I was in the bathroom of a noisy bar, with a pretty young man on his knees before me, bringing me to orgasm. I caught a glimpse of a small tattoo on his wrist, when it occurred to me that I had never wondered whether Viktor had other male lovers. I had always assumed that I was his only one, though I had no reason to—after all, he was the one who had brazenly approached me in the hardware store so many years before.

I lifted the new wave head off me, careful to avoid messing the sculpted hair.

"What's the matter?" he asked.

"I have to go," I said, zipping up my pants. I pushed past him and made my way out of the bar, walking quickly down the street toward home, confused and angry at myself for being so ridiculous. Why did I care? I knew he had a wife and that didn't bother me. But this was somehow different. I was a block from the bar when I came to my senses and decided I wasn't going to confront Viktor about his other partners. By the time I was curled up on my bed, I had convinced myself it was hypocritical to expect to be his only gay lover when I had others. Then, I convinced myself that if there were others, I would have sensed it. My intuition, admittedly, comforted me more than my sense of fairness.

I didn't tell him that he was now my only lover. I didn't want to revisit the issue because I didn't want him to think we were "together." But by then, things had already begun to change between us, yet so gradually I hadn't noticed them as they happened. Viktor had became more conscientious, letting me know when he'd be by and calling if he couldn't make it; and I would prepare dinner for us and he would stay later to watch television before going home. And more changes were to come. When, early on, he told me how proud he was of his son and daughter starring in their grade-school plays it irked me, but when he showed me pictures of Robert's graduation from law school and Sonia's wedding I felt an irrational sense of pride. And when Maria died of an aneurysm, I was grief stricken, and distraught I couldn't be there to comfort him.

❀❀❀

A different Victor came back to me after his wife's death. He had lost some of his aggression over the years but now he was an old man. He ached after sex and sometimes during he had to rest to catch his breath. But the sex was good, until the time came he couldn't keep his erection, and that was okay since he still pleased me. I was even accepting when he lost interest in sex altogether. He would lie on the couch roaring with laughter at *The Simpsons*, despite my having to explain the irreverent parts to him. Yet, I remained unsentimental, reminding myself that, despite the absence of his wife for almost a decade, all we had together were his visits—we never ate at restaurants together, we never went on vacation together, and we never did the things that straight or even gay lovers did in public together. It didn't matter to me. I had decided long before that I wouldn't become a dependent queen with pathetic dreams of eternal love and happiness in the arms of my man. That's not what this was about.

Then one afternoon he arrived at my apartment with a silly grin on his face. He opened his shirt to reveal a tattoo of my name in blue script on his chest, close to the fading tattoo of "Maria." I threw a pillow at him, catching him off-guard. He repeated, "But you don't like?" over and over, trying to make sense of my tantrum, just as he had tried on the day he stabbed me in the heart with his wife's name, as if with his tattooed dagger. I pushed him down on the couch, and though I was smaller than him, I held him down, tears dripping off my face onto the fresh ink, hitting him weakly, angry with him for cutting the last string binding together the illusion of my emotional detachment.

ജന

M.K. Leigh mostly writes short fiction. Other projects he is working on include a crime novel and an experimental collaborative murder mystery. When he isn't contemplating philosophical or community issues, he is either wandering around exploring the city or hanging out in the Village, where he lives in Toronto.

Class Reunion

RODNEY LOFTON

I couldn't believe that twenty years had passed before this moment arrived. I had avoided the incremental five-, ten- and fifteen-year reunions just for this one. Hell, it had taken that long to overcome the ridicule and rejection. As I stood in line waiting to take my turn at the meet-and-greet table, every cliché popped in my head, ranging from the Biblical "Revenge is mine, said the Lord," to the all-time classic, "Don't fuck with me, fellas," spit out by Faye Dunaway in *Mommie Dearest*. In my mind, I had played this scenario over and over. I would take center stage like Celie in *The Color Purple*, and with rage and condemnation, state for the record, "Ya'll made my life here a living hell." The line continued to move, as my eyes shifted. For effect, I would pound on the podium, when they all kissed my ass to bestow upon me the achievement award. Yes, this would be my defining moment.

I had received the invitation just a few short weeks prior to this night. As I read the request for my attendance, the thoughts of high school brought back so many bad memories. It was as if I was back in time and hearing the word "fag" greet me each time I entered with Ms. Taylor's geometry class, or the intimidating looks in Mr. Freeman's gym class. Back then, I was a frail child, weighing no more than a buck twenty soaking wet and wearing boots. I dared not dart my eyes while in the showers at the guys I would go home and beat off to. If fantasy had served me well, the steam in those showers would hide the caressing tight little bodies of young men, walking toward me to borrow the liquid soap I chose over the more traditional bar. I would squeeze a little into their hands as they reminded me my arms were too short to reach my back. They would offer their assistance, by applying some to my already smooth skin, watching the suds slide suggestively to the crack of my ass.

Wait a minute, I digress. Those were just dreams, but the harsh reality was the hurt I felt when I arrived home, thankful that I had made it there with no signs of a bloody lip or a punch-sore body. Yes, I had survived. I survived the words, the looks and the whispers. Now it was my time to inflict a little pain.

It was my turn to receive my name tag. Before I could announce myself, I heard her voice. "Oh my God, Chris, it is so good to see you!" It was Alicia Raymond. I remembered how that voice served as salve from others. Her face was a little rounder and hips a little wider, but she still looked the same. Before I could acknowledge her, her arms were around my neck, embracing me. I felt smothered but warmed by her genuine sincerity. She jokingly whispered in my ear, "Don't show your ass tonight," and we both laughed. Over the last few years she had attempted to get me to come to the reunion, but I wasn't ready. Now I was. It was our little secret of my revenge plans. Before I could apply the nametag to my lapel, she had grabbed me and whisked me into the ballroom.

As I entered the banquet hall, the years I had spent in therapy to overcome the hatred from these fuckers had vanished. If anything, pity had replaced it. Here I was doing my thing and doing it well. I looked around and the once jovial faces now had been replaced with scowls. With therapy, came the endless hours in the gym to tone and define what was there. I didn't care about being buffed, just enough cardio to hit me in all the right places. I no longer walked with my head hanging. I glided, eye-balling every muthafucka who called me a punk. I could still see some lingering effects in their eyes, but I didn't care. I was the shit.

As Alicia took me from table to table to remind me of everyone in attendance, I heard over the blaring of the eighties music, the questions in everyone's mind: "Are you married?" "Where have you been? "Do you have kids?" It was as if my responses were pre-recorded and played in loop for them: *No, I'm not married. I've been around. And no kids, as far as I know of.* My hardened heart softened a bit, as I wondered how our lives in this room had taken different paths. I reminisced with old friends from the drama department, was saddened to hear that favorite teachers had passed, and celebrated baby pictures shown in abundance. I was beginning to feel what high school could have been like, until I saw him.

If one person could monopolize your thoughts, serving as both tormentor and dream, it was Terrell Johnson. Time had definitely been kind to him. His high-riding cross-country shorts had now been replaced by dress slacks that highlighted that perfect ass. His shirt pressed against the developed pecs I so desperately wanted to rest my head on in high school. And as I continued to admire his perfect frame, I was reminded why I avoided these reunions.

Terrell was the ringleader of the gang of assholes in high school whose mission was to let everyone know I was gay. From the name calling, to the drawing of dicks in my English class chair, I was the brunt of his jokes. I remember sitting in class and having him ask me what it felt like to get fucked. Embarrassment always led me in the opposite direction when he made his way toward me. And now he was doing it again.

He danced through the crowd making his way toward the table where I sat with Alicia and her husband. As I had done in the past, I found a reason to escape from what I assumed to be another round of his fag-bashing statements. Before I could run away as I did in the past, his hand grabbed my shoulder.

"Hey, Chris, how the hell are you?" he asked as if we were old friends. I couldn't believe the balls he had. How could he think I would give him an answer that suited him? As I turned to face him to tell him the rehearsed speech, he smiled. I melted like a little bitch. His smooth, cute face in high school was now replaced with a rugged handsomeness. He sported a perfect mustache and goatee, which showcased and highlighted those pearly whites. I had longed to taste his full lips in high school and now they were teasing me once again.

I managed to reply a standard "hello" with a bit of coldness. He sensed my reluctance in greeting him but continued to smile. *Don't do this to me*, I thought to myself. I wanted to hate him, but I couldn't. Without an invitation, he pulled out the chair next to me and sat down.

As the words freely left his mouth, I couldn't believe he didn't remember the hell he put me through. I wanted to be angry, but he had an air about him that melted the icy façade I wanted to display. I held on to his every word as he shared with the table the events of his life over the last twenty years. Time had been good to him and it clearly showed.

Throughout the night, glasses clinked and drinks were spilled as everybody made their way to the dance floor. Some huddled in corners catching up and it became clear that old rivalries became newfound friendships. I realized that it was getting late and the drinks I had enjoyed were now taking their toll on me. I made promises to keep in contact with old friends and new acquaintances. I hugged Alicia and thanked her for encouraging me to come. As I made my way out of the ballroom, I was happy that I had attended the reunion. I had finally buried the past and the anger with it.

"Where ya going, Chris? We're just getting started," a voice called out as I felt fingers tap me on the shoulder. It was Terrell. I informed him that it was getting late and I'd had way too much to drink. He asked where I was staying while I was in town and I shared with him the hotel in which the reunion was being held. I said good night and told him it was good seeing him.

As I made my way to the elevator, he continued to follow me. "You got a minute?" he asked. I was puzzled, searching for an answer on his face. I said, "sure" and invited him back to my room. My feet were hurting from dancing and I just wanted to chill for a bit. We rode the elevator in silence. I couldn't imagine what he wanted to talk about, but I humored him.

We made our way to my room and I immediately kicked off my shoes. Terrell took the one seat located near the picturesque window. In my travels, I always made sure to take a bottle of something with me, because of the high-ass prices in the mini fridge. On this trip I decided on tequila, figuring it would help give me the courage to face the former foes of my graduating class. He reached for the bottle. "Do you mind?" I shook my head no and he poured two shots of the Cuervo. He raised a toast to the graduating class of 1986 and we both laughed, swallowing the burning liquid. He chased the toast with another as he offered me one more. We sat there in silence, until his lips parted to say what I had hoped for in high school.

"Man, I am sorry for fucking with you so much back in the day." His eyes pleaded for my forgiveness. "I know it must have been hell for you, but we were kids." This time, I had to take another swig before I could respond.

"Terrell, it was fucked up, it really was. Do you know what it felt like to have everybody call me names?" I felt myself back in the halls leaving gym class. My eyes started to glisten as he walked over to me. He stood above me.

"I know and I am sorry." He reached for my hand. I stood up and braced myself from falling. Before I stumbled, he caught me in his arms and held me. "I know."

What the fuck was happening? As I felt myself attempt to squirm out of his grasp, his body that I dreamed of felt so good pressed against mine. The more I tried to get away, the tighter he held me. I felt his hands begin to caress the small of my back. I pleaded with God: *please do not let my dick get hard*. I could only imagine that this was the next step in his cruel games to embarrass me. Outside in the halls of the hotel room would be his boys to laugh at me once again. I pushed him away.

His hand grabbed me as I made my way to the door to show him out. He swung me around once again to hold me. He smelled of the tequila and light perspiration from the summer heat. Damn, I wanted this man. Everyone knew that I was gay. There was no hiding it—not because I was flashy. It was something that I was open about and Terrell knew it. "Don't do this, Terrell," I pleaded. "Don't." He rubbed his goatee against my face.

"Not all of us are as open as you are," he whispered, placing his tongue gently beneath my ear.

With that, he ran his tongue across my lips. I closed my eyes to drink in the remnants of the lingering alcohol on his breath. I closed my eyes as his tongue searched to find a way into my closed mouth. It was the sweetest kiss I had longed for.

Our mouths danced in synch with each other, as his strong hands had found their way to the cup of my ass. He gently squeezed my cheeks, as he made a circular motion, taking in the hours I had spent in spinning class. My hands traveled the length of his torso to the opening of his shirt. I unbuttoned the remaining buttons revealing the neatly trimmed chest hair. I lowered my mouth from his, exploring his neck, to the manly protruding Adam's apple. I licked and sucked the firmness, giving him a sample of what I would do later. I continued to open his shirt, exposing the nipple I eventually took into my mouth. I gently bit it, as he removed his shirt allowing me full access to the massive chest I would savor. With his chest completely exposed, he grabbed my chin to bring me back to his lips. We kissed once again, while his body leaned toward me forcing me onto the bed.

By this time, he had removed my shirt, exposing the jewelry-adorned nipple to my left. He was fascinated by the silver hoop that he found his lips massaging gently. I never really got the full pleasure of having the ring played with, but the fantasy of this man took me to new heights. The nights I had lain in bed waiting for this, dreaming of this, sent me. As I arched my back in delight, he stopped. Damn, it was a dream, so I thought.

He stood up to remove the rest of his clothing. He stood before me in his form-fitting black boxers, with a hard-on I could imagine would hurt me. It was better than I had ever dreamed. I removed the remainder of my clothes and waited for his return.

His hard body pressed me into the mattress, kissing me passionately. Although I was not as strong as Terrell, I had skills. I was able to reverse the positions of our bodies, with me now on top of him.

I picked up where my exploration left off. I drizzled his body with the saliva of my tongue, searching spots I had hoped would turn him out. I followed the chest hair to his belly button, taking a whiff of his crotch as I lowered myself.

I didn't want to appear eager, so I ran my tongue against the cotton boxers, tracing the outline of his dick. I could feel his excitement, as the pulsating heartbeat bounced eagerly against my chin and the few droplets of oozing pre-cum. I lowered the band of the boxers, exposing the fully engorged head. I was glad that I had waited for this moment, for the teenage dick had been replaced by that of a man.

I ran my tongue across the head, feeling it jump toward my lips. I did this a couple of times, noticing the act generated more juice to taste. Like the tequila, I swallowed. I opened my mouth to take Terrell in. I felt the head of his dick expand more as I continued to lower the boxers and take more of him into my mouth.

With slow precision, I licked this delicacy. I savored the taste of his sweat, avoiding a mishap of grinding my teeth into his meat. My hands ran across his chest, as I searched the jewels of his nuts. I took one in at a time, and eventually expanded my throat to accompany both. The smooth pubic hair tickled my nose, as I inhaled his scent. Damn!

I removed his nuts from my mouth, tracing the vein of his dick with my tongue to taste the accumulated nut dripping. After this, I made my way back to his mouth, to share with him his taste. He grabbed the back of my head, forcing his tongue deep in my mouth. Before I knew it, he had flipped me over and reciprocated the act.

Although it was a valiant effort, I could tell that giving head was not his forte. I would hope if the situation should ever arise again, that he would allow me to teach him how and where to place his mouth. But, it wasn't all bad.

After he returned the favor, he made his way back to me. We shared more kisses and caresses. His hands made my body quiver and long for his touch.

What skills he lacked in giving head, he definitely made up in other areas. In the area of getting fucked, I gave as good as I got in return. But this night, I wanted to act out the high school fantasies I had jacked off to many a night.

I excused myself to the bathroom to retrieve the bottle of lube and condoms I traveled with. In the past, the lube only got a workout with me taking matters in hand, but not tonight. As Terrell lay there in all of his beautiful black glory, I poured more than enough to lubricate not only him, but me as well.

I expertly warmed my hands before I placed them around his huge dick. I moved my hands slowly, making sure not to miss an inch of this dream. He moaned, "Damn, that feels good," as I massaged him. When he was ripe and ready for the taking, I grabbed the condom. I had hoped that it would fit. He was bigger than I remembered and fatter than I was used to.

Although it was a snug fit, the latex encased this glorious piece of flesh. Terrell allowed the time and effort to lower myself on him. It had been a while since anyone had hit this, so I was careful to take my time to enjoy the moment. I felt the head beg for entrance, as I braced myself and guided him in. I kept it there for a moment to get situated. I raised my head, pleading with my own self to be able to do this. I took a deep breath, holding it in, as I slowly and painfully expanded to accommodate him. I felt my hole tighten around his dick. I purposely did this to get back at him for those years of torment. He grunted with this sensation and I smiled a sinister grin with this control I had.

When I felt he was completely inside, I eased myself up and down his shaft. I felt Terrell's hips wriggle beneath me, finding places that had not been discovered before. At times, I had to remind him of my control, by squeezing tightly to signal him to slow down. Each time I lowered myself, he met me by raising his hips to meet me. His hands were firmly placed around my ass, as he grabbed me to open me more. With time, came comfort.

He raised himself up and held me as he placed me on my back. He slid me to the edge of the bed, where he had proper footing to brace himself. He arranged my limber legs around his broad shoulders, as I caught a glimpse of the cross-country thighs he possessed. As he stood there, I felt his lips brush against my hairy legs. He removed several inches of himself, with enough still intact for me to enjoy. He slowly filled me once again, pushing me way beyond my limits. He continued this intrusion, with perfect timing. Every now and then, I felt his head brush against my prostate, sending tingles up my spine. He removed himself slowly, as not to hurt me. He motioned for me to turn over, as he entered once again, hitting it from the back. I bounced back, his hands tightening around my waist. Damn, he felt good.

We continued this for a moment. My body ached but I didn't care. He leaned forward with his thrust to kiss the back of my neck. With him still inside, he meticulously flipped me on my back again, and this time wrapped my legs around his waist.

He placed one hand behind my back, the other on my neck as he held me close. I bit down on his ear so not to scream. When my moans grew louder, he silenced me with his mouth. With one last thrust, I felt him lunge deep inside. If the condom had not been in place, I would have drowned from the nut of love he released deep inside.

His sweat-drenched body fell upon mine, spent and depleted. But this was not over. I needed to show this brotha I was no bottom bitch. His limp dick slid out and rested between my pained hole. I shifted from beneath him as he crawled onto the bed. His perfect specimen was sprawled, with his left leg slightly higher than the other. While he attempted to recuperate from his trek, I made my way to his ass.

I tasted the sweat of his muscular dimpled ass. I was strong enough to seize this opportunity, but spreading his cheeks and thrusting my tongue deep. He was startled at my boldness, but he allowed me the savory taste. Baby, it was the best salad I have ever eaten.

He looked at me from the side as I placed the condom on my own hard dick. I released the lube in the crack of his ass, as I sought my revenge. When I pushed at the opening, he reared back. "Damn, yo, be gentle."

I smiled. "This is for the hell you put me through in high school." I placed my arms on his shoulders and mimicked the rhythmic motions he had just enjoyed in my hole. When I felt he had been punished enough, based on his writhing beneath me, I took pity and started to really enjoy what the reunion had done for me.

We lay there as we saw the sun rise over the city skyline. We chatted more about where our lives had taken us and apologized to each other one last time. I knew time was coming to an end for the two of us, but glad things had worked out the way they did. We eventually showered and enjoyed some coffee from room service. As we parted ways with a gentle kiss, we vowed to keep in touch.

As he headed out the door, he turned to me. "Chris, man, if I knew then, what I know now…damn, can you imagine?"

I nodded. "It's not too late for you, my friend."

That was five years ago. We laughed about it, as we headed to our twenty-fifth class reunion, and *our* five-year anniversary.

ဆာ

Rodney Lofton has been a voice and face for those living with HIV for the past ten years. He has served as a keynote speaker and requested facilitator by the New Jersey World AIDS Day Celebration, the U.S. Conference on AIDS, and many others. He is a former freelance writer and public relations professional. The author is currently a columnist for the online GBMNews (www.gbmnews.com) which focuses on issues related to the African-American gay community including health and entertainment. His debut offering, The Day I Stopped Being Pretty: A Memoir *(Strebor Books), was nominated for a 2008 Lambda Literary Award. His second outing,* No More Tomorrows: Two Lives, Two Stories, One Love *(Strebor Books), is scheduled for release September 2008. Visit the author at www.rodneylofton.com or www.myspace.com/rodlofton*

The Summer of the Hippie
NEIL PLAKCY

"There's a hippie moved in next door," Brian McNulty's father said one evening in early June, one of the few days that summer his father hadn't been in Harrisburg on important state business. His father was a lawyer and a state senator, and it was his parents' fervent wish that Brian would follow in his footsteps—complete his senior year at Phillips Exeter, the prep school his father had attended, then follow his dad to the University of Pennsylvania, and then Columbia for law school.

He'd work for a few years for a big-name firm in Manhattan, then return to their small town in rural Bucks County to take over his father's small-town practice and his senate seat when he was ready to retire.

"A hippie?" Brian's mother had asked. "You mean like on one of those communes?" She looked frightened, as if they'd have to start locking their doors and inventorying the sheep and chickens.

At sixteen, Brian was a year younger than his sister Amy and her diametrical opposite. She was the wild child, but he was the good boy, president of his junior class at Deerfield, a letterman in three sports—football, baseball and lacrosse. He'd never caused his parents a moment's worry. His wheat-blond hair was a shade lighter than his sister's and only an inch shorter. He had blue eyes and blond lashes the girls swooned for, and his slim body was already beginning to develop wiry muscles in his legs, arms and chest.

"He's moved in with Eleanor O'Donnell for the summer," Brian's father said. Their next-door-neighbor taught English at the regional high school and had a reputation for bringing home stray kids. "He's half-Mexican, the son of her best friend, and the parents don't know what to do with him."

"Maybe Eleanor can straighten him out," his mother said.

His father snorted. "Cut his hair for one thing. She's already gotten him a job at the Tasti-Freeze."

"Is he cute?" Amy asked.

Senator McNulty shook his finger at his daughter. "I ever catch you going out with a long-haired hippie like that, I'll shave his head myself."

The next night Brian was in the living room watching TV when Amy returned from a date. "Eddie and I stopped by the Tasti-Freeze and the hippie Daddy was talking about was at the window," she said. "His hair's all pinned up in a net, but you know, Eddie said he's a homo."

"Really?" Brian looked up. "Eddie has experience with homos?"

Amy pouted. "You're disgusting." She stalked away.

Brian looked at the clock. It was nine-thirty, and he knew the Tasti-Freeze stayed open until ten. If he hopped on his bike, he could be in what passed for the center of Lumberville in ten minutes.

He wondered why his heart was beating so fast when he pulled up at the drive-up ice cream stand with a giant plastic soft-serve cone perched on the pointed roof just the way the cross sat atop St. Mark's Episcopal Church. It hadn't been that tough a ride, certainly nothing like he could do at school. Maybe it was the warm night air.

There were no cars in the parking lot, and inside the small lit building he saw a slim young man cleaning up and getting ready to close for the night. He parked his bicycle and walked up to the window. "Is it too late to get a cone?"

The boy came to the window. He had smooth caramel skin, and spoke with a slight Spanish accent. "Not for you, *guapo*," he said. "That means handsome, you know. Let me guess, vanilla and chocolate swirled together?"

Brian nodded. "Somehow I knew you liked it both ways," the boy said, and picked up a pointed cone and a square-bottomed one. "Regular or sugared?"

"I'd like some sugar," Brian said.

Oh, my God, Brian thought, as the boy picked up the sugar cone and turned to the machine. *He's flirting with me, and I'm flirting back. What the hell is going on?*

The guy brought the cone to Brian and handed it to him. "So what do a couple of guys do for fun out here in the boondocks?" he said.

Brian pulled a crumpled dollar bill from his pocket but the boy waved it away. "On the house," he said. "If you're gonna hang around here, I might just join you."

"Sure," Brian said. He stood at the window while the boy pulled his own cone, then swiped a rag over the counter, turned off the machines, and flipped off the lights. He walked over to the picnic bench at the back of the parking lot.

There was no traffic on the local road in front of the Tasti-Freeze, and under a stand of pine, he was sheltered by shadows even if someone did drive by. He was sitting there licking his cone when the boy came out the back door, carrying his half-eaten chocolate cone. He'd taken off the hair net, and Brian saw the straight brown hair, which reached down to the boy's shoulders, then curved just a little.

He wore a T-shirt with a picture of Chicago's Sears Tower, a pair of cut-off jean shorts, and sneakers without socks. There was a fluidity about the way he moved, like he was a guy who danced well. Brian was wearing perfectly pressed chino shorts, deck shoes, and a Brooks Brothers polo shirt with the hanging sheep crest. The only thing they seemed to have in common was that he, too, wore no socks.

"I'm Franco," the boy said, sitting down across from Brian, who introduced himself. "You live in this boondock town?"

"All my life."

"You have my deepest sympathy."

"You're from Chicago?" Brian asked, motioning at the T-shirt.

"The Windy City. See this building on my shirt? It's the largest erection in the Midwest."

Brian giggled. He'd never heard anyone use the word "erection" outside of health class. In the locker rooms at Deerfield they used words like "stiffy" and "woodie."

Though Brian had grown up in Lumberville, his family had moved out to the big house just before he left for Deerfield at the start of seventh grade. He'd lost touch with all his hometown friends as they went on to junior high and then high school, and his prep school friends were spread across the globe. Aside from the occasional phone call, he was on his own, with only his sister for company. And while she liked boys a lot, she preferred those who weren't related to her.

"I heard you're my next-door neighbor," Brian said. "Is Miss O'Donnell your aunt or something?"

"My mom's best friend," Franco said. "My parents got divorced last year and my mom needs some time on her own to chill out. All my mom's family is back in Mexico and she says I'm too much to handle on her own."

Brian nodded.

"That's what they say," Franco said, licking his tongue along the side of the chocolate cone. "But it's really because I'm a homo."

Brian caught some ice cream going down the wrong way and started to cough. Franco didn't seem to notice. "Yup. I started letting Father Paderewski jerk me off after Mass when I was thirteen. Last summer I spent most of my time hanging around Navy Pier, giving blowjobs to horny sailors. My mom liked the extra money I was bringing in but eventually the Catholic guilt got to her."

Brian was holding his ice cream cone so hard that the shell cracked. Franco laughed and said, "Come on, I'm just joking."

Brian's shoulders relaxed and he laughed thinly. "Not about the homo part, though," Franco said. "My mom thought maybe getting out of the city would cure me." He tossed the remainder of his cone into an open trash can next to the table. Then he looked directly into Brian's eyes. "You think it will?"

And Brian McNulty, the good boy, who'd never done a thing he couldn't tell his parents, looked back at Franco and said, "Doubt it."

Kissing Franco, Brian realized what it was all the other guys had been saying about kissing—how it gave you a stiffy, made you feel like you were king of the world, wiped away your inhibitions faster than booze did.

Brian had kissed a few girls, most at school dances, and he'd always been able to stop whenever he wanted—happy, almost, to get it over with. But now, he mashed his lips against Franco's and felt intoxicated, more than he'd ever felt with a shot of Johnnie Walker stolen from his dad's liquor cabinet or a couple of beers smuggled into the dorm.

Of their own accord, his arms found their way around Franco's back, and they held each other close. Then Franco's hands were pulling at the hem of Brian's shirt, working their way up his chest to massage his stomach, his pecs, his nipples. "Man, you are one sexy fucker," Franco said, and the dirty talk excited Brian even more.

"You, too," he said. Franco's hand found its way to Brian's chino-covered crotch and began rubbing. Brian had jerked himself off before, many times, but it had never felt so good as when someone else's hand was doing the work. He gingerly put his hand down onto Franco's dick, which was pressing against the denim, and started rubbing. Too, too quickly, Brian felt himself losing control, spurting cream into his briefs, and he could tell from the way Franco whimpered and then stiffened that he'd done the same.

"Oh, man, my mom is gonna freak," Brian said, pulling back. "My shorts must be full of jism."

"I do the wash at Eleanor's," Franco said. "Give 'em to me."

"But my mom will notice a pair short in the wash."

Franco laughed. "Man, you are one straight arrow. Take a clean pair from your drawer when you get home. Sleep in 'em overnight, then put 'em in the wash. She'll never know the difference. She doesn't keep an inventory, does she?"

Brian shook his head. "Only for the wash. My sister throws her clothes under her bed so my mom's always checking up on us."

Franco laughed. "I'll bet you wear pajamas, don't you?"

"What's wrong with pajamas?"

"With Superman on them?"

"They're striped. From Brooks Brothers. What my dad wears."

"Whatever," Franco said. "So? What are you waiting for? Give me your shorts."

"You gonna look away?" Brian said, standing up.

"Hell, no," Franco said. "This is what I get in exchange for washing your shorts. Course, probably won't be much of a show. You probably still have a little boy *pinga*." He smirked. "That means dick in Spanish."

"Do not," Brian said. He stood up and dropped his chino shorts. There was a big wet spot on his white Jockey briefs. "Yuck," he said, pulling them down, careful not to smear the jism down his leg. He stood there facing Franco, who was watching with that same smirk on his face. Brian took the wadded-up shorts and used them to wipe the cum away from his dick, stroking it as he did to make it harder. He had to show Franco he had a man's dick, not a little boy's.

Franco's smirk turned into a smile. He slid across the picnic bench and took Brian's warm, stiff dick in his hand. Neither said anything. Then Franco bobbed down and took Brian's dick in his mouth, licking and sucking it clean.

He backed off when he finished, leaving Brian standing there with his stiff dick out in the light night breeze, his shorts on the picnic bench. "Anything to do around here during the day?" Franco asked.

"There's a pond at the back of our property," Brian said. "Sometimes I go back there and skinny-dip. It's real private. My sister's leaving tomorrow for six weeks in France, and after my mom drops her at the airport in Philly, she's going to the art museum all day. My dad's up in Harrisburg. So nobody will bother us."

"Sounds like a plan, *mi amigo*," Franco said, standing up. Brian realized he had exposed himself but hadn't seen the other boy, and snatched up his shorts. "See you tomorrow," Franco said. "I'll ring your bell."

He jumped into an old VW Beetle parked at the back of the lot and drove off. Brian sat on the bench for a while in his chino shorts, savoring the feeling of the rough fabric against his skin, his dick tender, and then he rode his bicycle back to the house, whistling off key the whole way.

The next morning Brian helped load his sister's luggage into his mom's station wagon, and stood at the end of the driveway waving good-bye. Only a few minutes later, Franco was at the door, and Brian had the feeling the other boy had been waiting somewhere in the line of trees by the street.

"Hey," Brian said, opening the door. "It's kind of early for swimming."

In response, Franco stepped inside, closed the door behind him, and enveloped Brian in a passionate kiss. Franco's lips were chapped, but his skin was smooth and almost soft. With Brian's deep summer tan, they were almost the same color, though once their clothes were off Brian's tan line was visible, the white skin against the brown. Franco's body was the same color, golden in the light, all over.

They stripped down right there in his mother's perfect living room, and enjoyed each other's bodies every way they could think of—there, in the kitchen, on the stairs to the second floor, in Brian's bedroom and in his bathroom, in the tub, Brian on the bottom in the hot water, Franco bobbing up and down on Brian's dick, the way greased with lots of his sister's lemon-scented soap.

Franco sometimes whispered Spanish words into Brian's ear, things Brian had never studied in school, but which excited him.

In the spring there had been a Puerto Rican gardener at Deerfield, and once Brian had lurked in the woods watching the man, shirtless as he cut the grass.

They ate lunch in the kitchen, naked except for towels around their waists, which dropped when it was time for dessert. Finally they collapsed on the sofa in the den, watching old movies on TV, both of them sated for the moment, yet relishing the nearness of each other's half-naked bodies.

Two days later, Brian announced that he'd taken a job at the Tasti-Freeze, to make extra pocket money for his senior year at Deerfield. His father thought the job was beneath him, but grudgingly applauded his son's industry. Little did he know that Franco was the reason Brian wanted to be at the Tasti-Freeze. It wasn't like he was saving up to buy a corsage for a special girl to wear to the fall formal.

Brian and Franco talked all the time. They met up each morning, either at Miss McDonnell's house if she was out, or at the McNultys, or sometimes at the swimming pond in the back. Brian was amazed that they had so much to say to each other. He learned that Franco's real name was Frank Scalitti, but he'd changed it the year before to sound more exotic. His father was Italian and his mother Mexican, and he had a grandmother in Guadalupe Hidalgo. That Franco was smart but a bad student, because he skipped class a lot to avoid teasing. That he was the only child of a nurse who worked extra shifts to pay the bills now that Frank's father had flown the coop.

Brian told Franco things he'd never told anyone else, about feeling so lonely at Deerfield, different from his classmates and teammates in a way he couldn't identify until he met Franco. About all the plans his parents had for him—college and law school and taking over his father's seat. "You want to do all that?" Franco asked.

Brian shrugged. "My parents know what's right for me."

"They do? They know about us?"

Brian's eyes opened wide. "No."

"So I'm just your summer fling, before you go back to Deerstalker and get on with your real life?"

"Deerfield. And this is my real life, here."

"Uh-huh."

The old VW belonged to Miss O'Donnell, and she usually used it during the day, so if the boys wanted to go anywhere they rode their bicycles. Once a week or so they made the long trip down into New Hope, the one place in Bucks County where Franco's long hair didn't stand out. Sixties retreads and artsy types congregated there, in the little wood-framed town along the Delaware. Head shops crowded against ice cream parlors, antique stores and Italian restaurants, and they found one dim place called La Roma, lit only by candles in Chianti bottles, owned by an old gay couple. They could sit in the back and hold hands and even daringly lean across the table to kiss when no one was looking.

They had sex every chance they could, and yet just spending time together was almost as important. Brian felt he'd found the one person who could see deep into his soul. The one thing he refused to see, however, was the date, looming ahead, when his parents expected him to return to Deerfield for his senior year.

"I'm going to tell my parents I don't want to go back," he said to Franco one night at La Roma. Two months had spun by and it was early August. He was set to return to Massachusetts at the end of the month, heading up a week before the start of school for football practice.

"And do what?" Franco asked.

"Transfer to public school," he said. "We'll be together."

"Eleanor says maybe she can home-school me. I'll just get my GED."

"Then she can teach both of us," Brian said.

"Get real. Your parents are never going to let you get out of going back to Deerstalker."

"Deerfield. And they can't make me do anything I don't want."

"Course they can. You think they're going to let you throw away everything they have planned for you—college and law school and all?"

"I don't care. I want to be with you."

"You gotta live in the real world, Brian. This has been fun but it's not going to last."

"You just have to have faith," Brian said. "Even if we go to different high schools for senior year, you can still apply to Penn. We can be roommates."

"You gotta be smart to get into a school like that. They take one look at my grades, they'll laugh themselves silly."

"My father's a state senator. He can pull some strings."

"I don't want to talk anymore," Franco said. "Kiss me, you jerk."

Riding their bicycles back up to Lumberville that night, Franco was like a wild man, darting in front of oncoming cars and laughing. Every time he turned into the road Brian's heart nearly stopped beating, but they finally made it back without incident. "What was up with you tonight?" Brian asked, when they pulled into Eleanor O'Donnell's driveway. "You were acting crazy." He pushed lightly against Franco's shoulder.

"Don't push me," Franco said. He pushed back against Brian. Before they both knew what was happening, they were flailing against each other, until finally Brian, who was bigger and stronger, overcame Franco and locked his arms around the other boy's back, pulling him into a bear hug and kissing his cheek, which he discovered was wet with tears.

They kissed passionately, and then Franco pulled away. "I gotta get to sleep," he said. "I'm going to Philly tomorrow with Eleanor."

"So I'll see you in the afternoon?" Brian asked.

"I'll call you." He kissed Brian one more time and then hurried up the driveway.

He never did call. That night, getting ready for work at the Tasti-Freeze, Brian finally called Miss O'Donnell's house. "I'm sorry, Brian, he went back to Chicago today," she said. "Didn't he tell you?"

"Um, yeah, I guess I got the dates confused." Brian hung up the phone and rushed up to his room, where he buried his head in his pillow and sobbed until his stomach ached.

❁❁❁

Gradually the memory of Franco hurt less and less, and as he'd always done, Brian threw himself into his schoolwork, into athletics and activities. Though he'd never have admitted it out loud, he went through life like a horse with blinders on, focusing only on the straight and narrow path ahead of him. Three years after his law school graduation, while he was working at a top law firm in Manhattan, Brian got an emergency call from his mother. The senator had suffered a fatal heart attack, she said, and she needed Brian at home right away.

His mother met him at the Trenton train station, and kissed his cheek. "Your sister is on her way in from California," Mary Ann McNulty said. She looked like she was on her way to an elegant cocktail party—simple black dress, black pumps, her graying hair piled up on her head. "I'm meeting her at the airport tonight. I need you to go to Harrisburg for me."

"Harrisburg? Why? Can't the funeral home bring Dad's body home?"

"I want you to bring his things home," she said. "I don't want to have anything to do with that—that woman."

"What woman?"

"Here's the address," his mother said. "There's an Avis counter on the upper level."

And then she turned and walked away.

Ever the good boy, Brian watched her go without an argument. It was nearly six p.m. by the time he pulled up at the address his mother had given him, a Colonial-era stone farmhouse just outside the Harrisburg city limits. He rang the bell, and was greeted by an elegant, dark-haired woman with an Eastern European accent. "You must be Brian," she said. "You look just like your father."

Like Alice falling into the rabbit hole, Brian fell into his father's alternative life. Mina Gerulaitis was originally from Latvia, she said. She and Brian's father had been together for nearly twenty years, though as a Catholic, Frederick McNulty would never divorce his wife. The house was filled with photos of Fred and Mina smiling, laughing, attending government functions, even on vacation in what looked like the California or Arizona desert.

Mina had already packed his father's clothes—three suitcases full. "If you think it's appropriate, please tell your mother that he always loved her," she said.

Numbly, he put the suitcases in the car and headed back toward

Lumberville. All the way there, he reflected on his father's hypocrisy—expecting a standard of behavior from his wife and children, a standard he flouted himself. And as he drove, he found himself thinking of Franco Scalitti, and wondering how different his life would have been if he'd been able to flout his father's conventions and reach for the love that mattered to him.

By the time Brian found himself on the station platform at Trenton, waiting for the train back to the city, he'd made up his mind. His mother wanted to sell the house and move to a retirement community in Florida where she could start over again, and he agreed to buy the house from her and take over his father's legal practice.

Eleanor O'Donnell had died two years earlier, and a young family had moved into her house. Every time Brian drove past her house, he wondered what had happened to Franco Scalitti.

Then one day he had to hire a private detective to help with a client's case. On an impulse, he asked if she could find missing persons.

"I can try," she said. "Sometimes people don't want to be found, you know."

"I know." He told her what he knew about Franco Scalitti. "He may be going by Frank again," he said. "Or he may be dead."

With Franco's passion for sex, he might have contracted the AIDS virus early. The thought wrenched his heart with a pain he hadn't felt since the day he'd discovered Franco had left. What if he'd wasted all this time and Franco was dead? What if he'd moved on with his life, found a man who wasn't afraid to love him?

He gave the detective a check for a retainer and then closed the office and went for a walk along the Delaware's banks. It was a gray, windy day, and the rough, turbulent water reflected his mood. Franco was his unfinished business. For years, he'd been Brian's dirty little secret, as Mina Gerulaitis had been his father's. If Franco was dead, or if he'd moved on in life, Brian knew he would have to let him go. But if he was still out there, Brian wanted to know. He had to try, even if he didn't like what he found.

The next day, the detective called. It had been a pretty simple search, she said. A man named Frank Scalitti, who had the right birth date and background, was the chef at a Mexican restaurant called La Hacienda, in Buffalo Grove, a Chicago suburb. As soon as the call was finished, Brian booked a flight to Chicago for Saturday morning. He arrived at O'Hare in mid-afternoon, rented a car, and drove to Buffalo Grove, a busy suburb of strip malls, office buildings and townhouse complexes.

He drove around for a while, half hoping to spot Franco standing along the side of the road, waiting for him, though he knew that was a foolish hope. What would he look like? Would he remember Brian at all?

The restaurant opened for dinner at six-thirty, and Brian was the first customer seated. It was warm and dark inside, tables lit by the glow of candles stuck into old tequila bottles. Brian was stabbed by a memory of La Roma in New Hope, that Italian restaurant where he and Franco had held hands in the dark so long before.

He ordered a Tecate, an appetizer of shredded pork taquitos, and chiles rellenos with shrimp. His stomach was in knots, but even so, he recognized the food was delicious. Then, his hands held under the table to disguise their shaking, he asked the waitress if the chef that night was Franco Scalitti.

"You mean Frank?" she said. "Yeah, he's back there. You want to talk to him?"

The man in the white chef's jacket who came out of the kitchen was nearly bald, and no longer had the slim physique of a six-teen-year-old. Yet even without the long, flowing brown hair, and in the flickering candlelight, Brian recognized the boy he'd loved, the man he realized he still loved more than anyone.

He stood up and held out his hand. Then he saw recognition flare in Frank's eyes. "Brian?" he asked.

"Franco," he said. "My father died, and I had to come see you."

Even as he said it, he realized it didn't make sense, but some-how Frank understood him completely. "I hoped you'd come," Frank said, and he enveloped Brian in one of those big bear hugs, both of them insulated by more flesh and muscle than they'd had at sixteen. But all that mattered was the touch, feeling Frank's arms around him once again.

Frank took Brian's face in his hands and kissed him, deeply, a kiss Brian returned fervently. "The first man I ever loved," Frank announced to the restaurant, his arm around Brian's shoulder. "And he's come back to me!"

The customers applauded. "Kiss him again, then get back in the kitchen," a man called. "I'm hungry."

"You don't know what hunger is," Frank announced, and kissed Brian again, then dragged him back into the kitchen with him.

"I have a restaurant full of people to cook for," Frank said, "but I don't want to let you out of my sight."

"I'll sit over there in the corner," Brian said. "I'm not going to let you get away from me again."

Frank had fallen in love with an older man, who'd convinced him to go to cooking school, and who'd seen him established at La Hacienda before succumbing to the virus. Frank had felt guilty for his negative status, unable to commit to loving anyone else who might die, until Brian showed up in the dining room and he felt the ice around his heart start to melt.

They shared their dreams for the future. "I just want to be with you," Brian said. "I'll take the bar in Illinois. I'll sell the house in Lumberville and close my practice."

"Hold on, cowboy. You own that big house now?"

Brian nodded.

"And all those acres?"

"My dad had an agreement with a farmer but that guy sold out two years ago. No one's farmed it since."

"I've been wanting to grow my own food for a while," Frank said. "I think there's a real market for organic produce. From Lumberville I could sell to restaurants in New Hope and Phila-delphia."

"Mister," Brian said, squeezing Frank's hand, "I see the begin-ning of a beautiful friendship."

"Friendship is good," Frank said. "But two men don't live together on friendship alone."

Brian leaned across and kissed him. His heart swelled and his dick rose. "You and me, baby," he said. "We can have it all."

And the seeds they'd planted during that summer fling so long ago finally took root, and grew and blossomed.

§©Q

Neil Plakcy is the author of Mahu, Mahu Surfer *and* Mahu Fire *(April 2008), mystery novels which take place in Hawaii. With Sharon Sakson, he is co-editor of* Paws & Reflect: Exploring the Bond Between Men and Their Dogs. *A jour-nalist, book reviewer and college professor, he is also a frequent contributor to gay anthologies, and editor of the forthcoming gay construction worker erotica anthology,* Hard Hats.

Social Studies
DONALD PEEBLES

Rashawn Thomas ran all the way to the first-floor lobby of Urban University in Harlem, New York. His heart beating rapidly, he clutched his chest while taking a deep breath. He took his student ID out of his backpack before the black and Latino security guards had a chance to justify their jobs by exerting their authority over him. He didn't have time for that bullshit. He had enough on his mind, wondering if he was going to flunk out of his class, due to his chronic lateness. He wasn't in the mood for some ignorant-ass security guard getting up in his face.

He flashed his student ID when he noticed a brand-new security peace officer at the booth. Expecting shade from the guard, he kept his student ID out until it was made clear to the security guard that he was a graduate student. During their exchange, Rashawn noticed the security guard's dark brown eyes staring at him curiously. He was used to some of the other security guards giving him mad attitude with their disapproving gazes, pitiful stares, and gas faces. He couldn't believe how the new guard stared dead at him.

"Wassup, brotha? How you doing tonight?" the security guard asked, breaking apart Rashawn's paranoia.

Rashawn couldn't believe that the security guard actually spoke to him. "Fine," he replied, putting his student ID away into his backpack. Although he tried acting all coy, he found himself gazing at the security guard. He couldn't help but notice his bright skin, bald head, dark brown eyes, and full pink lips. Rashawn had always considered himself a gym rat with his well-developed body, but the security guard had him beat. The security guard's massive chest and arms couldn't hide under his dark blue shirt. Rashawn's eyes rested on the bulge in the guard's tight pants. Realizing that he was caught looking at the bulge, he quickly averted his eyes to something else.

Damn, I want him, he thought to himself.

"Is everything okay, brotha?" the security guard asked.

Snapping out of his euphoria, Rashawn looked at his watch and noticed the time. "Oh shit! I gotta go to class or my professor will fail my ass," he whined.

"Have a blessed night."

"You too, brotha!" the security guard said as Rashawn ran up the escalator to the second floor.

❈❈❈

Rashawn had dinner with Daniel Adrienne, his best friend and classmate, in the cafeteria while going over their first term-paper assignments. Finishing his pink lemonade, Rashawn spotted the security guard of his dreams, walking into the cafeteria with Forrester, the other security guard.

"Look, Daniel," Rashawn whispered, tapping his best friend and classmate on his left arm. "Look!"

"Who do you want me to look at now, Rashawn?"

"That's my baby daddy over there. You see the muscular light-skinned security guard?"

Daniel scanned the cafeteria until his eyes focused onto the two brothas.

Rashawn pointed him out. Clearly uninterested, he faced Rashawn with a pitiful look.

"What is it? You don't think he's phyne like I told you?"

"I hate to be the bearer of bad news, Rashawn, but there's something that I must tell you."

"What, Daniel?"

"He's not your type."

Rashawn couldn't believe what he heard. "My type? What exactly is my type?"

"Well, his name is Sinbad and he isn't gay. According to a girl I work with, he goes out with women—only women. I'm sorry, but it looks like he's off-limits to men," Daniel said nonchalantly, biting into his tuna fish sandwich.

You're such a miserable bastard, Daniel, Rashawn thought to himself as he chewed into his Philly cheesesteak. He couldn't believe Daniel had the nerve to cockblock him from getting with Sinbad. From that point on, he promised himself that he wouldn't confide to Daniel about his crush on Sinbad or any other brotha ever again. Not wanting to tell Daniel off about himself, he continued staring dead at Sinbad and Forrester as his erection decreased as the possibility of getting fucked by Sinbad faded slowly out of his mind.

❊❊❊

Back at the library, Rashawn pulled his student ID out of his backpack to show the security guard on duty at the booth. He didn't want any problems with him or her. He just wanted to be on his way to study for his African-American LGBT History final exam. He was relieved to see Forrester sitting at the library booth, checking student IDs.

"What's up, Rashawn?" Forrester asked, giving him a pound.

"I'm fine, Forrester," Rashawn replied, putting his student ID into his backpack. He was glad to see him, always feeling that Forrester was one of the coolest security guards on campus. They spoke to each other whenever they had the chance.

"That's good." Forrester smiled, always giving Rashawn a comforting feeling. He wasn't all hard-looking, defeated, nor bitter like how some of the security guards were. He was a thirty-seven-year-old brotha who always wore his dark blue cap, sported clear glasses which circled around his dark brown eyes, stared with his pointy nose, and smiled with his semi-thick purple-pink lips. He wasn't as muscular, buff, or built like some of the other security guards, but he still held his own whenever he needed to. "Where are you on your way to?"

"I'm on my way to study for my history exam. I'll probably find a nice quiet spot in the basement and chill there for two hours or so." As he stood talking to Forrester, he couldn't help thinking about Sinbad. He craved the touch, smell, and taste of it. He couldn't easily erase the thought of Sinbad banging the shit out of him as his hands held onto his muscular ass to allow him to fuck him deeper and deeper. His face produced a smile and his body vibrated a little at the thought.

"Rashawn, are you all right?" Forrester inquired.

"Yeah, I'm good." Rashawn grinned, snapping out of his daydream. He decided that he wasn't going to allow Daniel to cockblock him from getting Sinbad's dick. *It's now or never*, he thought to himself, staring at Forrester. "I have to ask you a question."

"What is it?"

"Who is that light-skinned security guard you walk with in the cafeteria sometimes?"

"Which one?"

"He's really tall, bald, and built. I think his name is Sinbad."

"You're talking about Brooks. Sinbad is his first name."

"Yes, that's him!" Rashawn yelled with enthusiasm, unable to hide his crush on Brooks.

Forrester walked away from the booth over to Rashawn. His mouth covered Rashawn's right ear. "Why do you want to know about Brooks for? You want him to fuck the hell out of you, don't you?" he whispered.

Rashawn couldn't believe Forrester went there. It was like he knew what was on his mind; however, he still wasn't sure about Brooks' sexual orientation, thinking about what Daniel told him the previous mouth. "Is he only into girls?"

Forrester crossed his arms across his chest. "Who the fuck told you that?"

"Umm...Umm...my friend Daniel."

"Never mind about that. Anyway, I'll tell you from my own mouth. Read my motherfuckin' lips: Brooks goes both ways."

"Stop! You're lying, Forrester! Get the fuck outta here!" Rashawn gagged, covering his mouth.

Forrester inched back to Rashawn's right ear. "I wouldn't lie about Brooks going both ways. I should know because he sucks my dick every chance he gets in the security locker room. He also jerks me off as well."

Rashawn found himself taken aback by Forrester's confirmation of Brooks swinging both ways. Yet, it piqued his curiosity.

"Earth to Rashawn! Earth to Rashawn!!" Forrester called out, snapping his fingers.

"Oh shit. I just got lost for a minute." Rashawn apologized, wiping his sweaty head with the back of his right hand. He felt his body vibrating with that hot flash feeling again. He looked at his watch, realizing how fast the time went by. "Oh shit, Forrester! Look at the time! I gotta study before class starts. I'll talk to you another time." Rashawn walked quickly to the staircase leading to the basement and disappeared.

After the exam ended, Rashawn walked down the escalator from the second floor after finishing his final exam. Glad that the spring semester was over, he took a deep breath and exhaled. He planned on celebrating by going out to a few clubs and cruising the thug brothas at Chi-Chi's, having dinner at the Pink Tea Cup, and shaking his ass at Escuelita with Daniel and their other friends.

As soon as his feet landed onto the first floor, he searched through his backpack to make sure he didn't leave anything back on the sixth floor. He stopped in his tracks when he realized what he was looking for wasn't in his backpack.

"Where the fuck is my journal?" he yelled, noticing that some professors and students were alarmed by his sudden outburst. He flipped his backpack upside down as all of his pens, books, peppermint balls, business cards, and papers landed onto the floor. He scavenged through his belongings, but to no avail, whatever he searched for was nowhere in sight. "Where's my journal?"

Putting his belongings into his backpack, he headed to the first-floor lobby booth, where Forrester sat.

"Are you okay, Rashawn? You don't look so great."

"I lost my journal. I thought I had it when I took my final exam tonight."

"What did it look like?"

"It was a light-blue book with a picture on it."

"Are you sure you lost it in this building?"

"I had it when I ran in here tonight."

"The only suggestion that I could advise you on is to file a lost item claim."

"How do I do that?"

"You must file it in the security office on the fourth floor. What I can do for you is to let the security guard on duty know that you are on your way to file a lost item claim."

"Cool. What's the room number?"

"Room 420."

"Thanks, Forrester. You are a lifesaver," Rashawn said, quickly walking to the escalator.

Rashawn reached Room 420, the security office and hoped to retrieve his journal and celebrate the rest of the night away. He couldn't believe it when his eyes met those of Sinbad Brooks, who just happened to have been the only security guard on duty in the office. Brooks smiled and stared intently at him.

"How can I help you, brotha?" Brooks asked, crossing his strong hands.

"I am here to file a lost item claim," Rashawn replied, looking in his eyes.

"What did you lose?"

"I lost my journal. It was a light-blue book with a picture on it."

Brooks suddenly got up from his seat behind the desk, and walked to a huge white box with the sign "LOST AND FOUND" pasted onto it. He pulled a light-blue book out of the box. He took a close look at the picture of porn stars Bobby Blake and Flex Deon Blake in their naked black male glory and smiled. "It looks like your journal isn't lost after all."

Rashawn took a deep breath and exhaled when Brooks produced the journal. "Get the fuck outta here. That's it! Thank you! Where was it found?"

"A student found it on the second floor and returned it to this office."

"I wish I could thank whoever turned this in," Rashawn said, relieved that his journal, which consisted of entries about his ten years of gay sexual encounters, wasn't revealed to the entire Urban University faculty, staff, and student body. "Can I have my journal?"

Instead of handling the journal back to Rashawn, Brooks nodded his head and opened the journal to take a look at some entries. Turning the pages, his face became intrigued by what he read.

"Please give it back to me now," Rashawn pleaded, trying to snatch his journal away from Brooks. Irritated and fed-up, he attempted to leap over the desk to retrieve his journal. Somehow, he lost his balance and came close to falling, but Brooks quickly caught Rashawn helping him regain his balance. "Can you please give me my journal back? I'm asking nicely."

"I'm sorry, but I can't do that, brotha."

"Oh, fuck this! If you're not going to give me my journal, then I'll call your supervisor. You have a fuckin' good night, Sinbad Brooks," Rashawn threatened as he moved toward the door to leave.

"Oh no the fuck you're not," Brooks said, hurriedly jumping up from his seat to shut the door, blocking Rashawn from leaving.

Although he felt completely turned off by Brooks at that moment, his dick began getting hard in his jeans. He couldn't bring himself to admit that he'd been waiting for that moment for three months. He dropped his guard when Brooks suddenly forced his tongue into his unsuspecting mouth. His hardness intensified when Brooks grabbed his bulge. He found himself turned on more when Brooks nibbled on his left ear for several minutes.

Brooks turned away from Rashawn before locking the door. Making sure it was locked securely, Brooks' tongue moved from Rashawn's left ear to his mouth. After kissing him for several minutes, Brooks stopped in order to open up the journal.

"I really want my journal now. I'm not fuckin' playing anymore," Rashawn protested, feeling like kicking him in his nuts, grabbing his journal, and running out.

"I bet you Francisco never did this," Brooks cooed, his mouth caressing Rashawn's neck. His touch gave his body a pleasurable jolt. He unbuttoned Rashawn's yellow-and-black plaid shirt as his fingers squeezed and pinched his dark nipples. He nibbled his tongue on his ears from front to back. Feeling Rashawn's nipples get hard, he glided his right hand down his stomach until he reached his pubic area. His hand played with Rashawn's bulge in his jeans, slowly massaging his thighs. He smiled as Rashawn let out a moan. "I know Anthony-Basil never got this close," he whispered into his right ear before biting into his neck.

Brooks bent down to untie Rashawn's black sneakers. He took them off and placed them at the bottom of the desk. He unrolled Rashawn's socks off his feet and threw them next to the sneakers. His hands glided up Rashawn's legs until they stopped at his bulge. Looking up at him, he slowly unbuttoned his jeans and allowed them to fall down to his ankles. Rashawn lifted his feet to make it easier for Brooks to remove his jeans off his toned legs. Brooks threw them across the office. He stroked Rashawn's seven-inch dick through his boxer briefs. He smiled when Rashawn let out another moan. He pulled the boxer briefs down Rashawn's leg as the dick slammed against his right thigh. He threw the boxer briefs over to the sneakers and socks. His right hand rolled down Rashawn's dick as a little pre-cum dripped onto his fingers.

Having managed to take Rashawn's clothes off, Brooks got up to move the journal off the desk and onto his chair. He took Rashawn's hands into his and walked him over to the suede couch. Positioning him on the couch, Brooks turned him around in order to take a bird's-eye view of his bubble butt. He knelt his knees on the carpet as his hands spread Rashawn's ass cheeks and his tongue licked around his tight hole. Rashawn let out another moan when Brooks' tongue dug into the small black hole, pulling onto the soft brown flesh. Brooks pulled Rashawn's ass cheeks wider apart, slobbing his mouth all over. He enjoyed feasting on Rashawn's chewy caramel so much, he spat saliva around the hole. His moustache smudged up the mixture of his saliva and Rashawn's juices as it dripped onto his lips.

After feasting on Rashawn's bubble butt for several minutes, Brooks inserted one finger into Rashawn's asshole to see if it opened up for his eleven-inch dick. He took it out and placed it in his mouth, licking the juices off his finger. Rashawn turned his body around to see Brooks take off his black shoes, blue socks, snuggly tight pants, shirt, and white wife beater. Not only was Rashawn impressed with Brooks' massive body, but he was also enamored of his white jockstrap which held back his throbbing dick. Unable to contain himself, Rashawn reached down and freed Brooks' massive member from its bonds. Holding it whole in his right hand, he inspected it for several seconds. The beautiful dick's veiny texture was a wondrous sight and Rashawn had to taste it. His tongue rolled from the pink tip all the way down to the pubic area. He wet it up entirely with his saliva. He didn't want to stop squeezing his tongue around the tip as his teeth held on tight. He enjoyed taking the entire length as it touched his throat. He pulled it out of his mouth as he jerked it a little. His mouth grabbed onto his huge hanging nuts, licking and sucking on them. He grinned up at Brooks, who grunted out several pleadings.

"Suck that dick!" Brooks commanded. He knew that Brooks liked his dick-sucking skills. After a few minutes, he placed the dick back into his mouth as he rolled it clockwise along his gums. He bobbed his head up and down on it, dripping saliva from the corners of his mouth. He was far from exhausted when he pulled the dick out of his mouth, dipped one of his fingers into his watery mouth, and played with Brooks' tight asshole. He slowly plunged it into the soft pink flesh, wiggled it around a little, and pulled out when Brooks tightened his ass muscles around his finger.

They moved to the carpet where they continued their own game of lost and found. Rashawn laid himself down flat on his back while Brooks lowered his muscular ass over his face. Rashawn spread apart Brooks' cheeks as his nose dove far up the tight black hole. His tongue lapped all around it, gnawing onto the small pink flesh. He loved how Brooks' manhole smelledand tasted while Brooks sucked Rashawn's seven-inch dick. He bobbed up and down, making deep crevices on the sides of his jaws. He took a slight detour to grab, lick, and suck Rashawn's nuts, wetting them up with his saliva. They got a chance to taste each other's fruits for nearly a half-hour.

Convinced that Rashawn was finally ready to take his elevenincher, Brooks jerked Rashawn's throbbing dick as his cue to get up. Rashawn squeezed and smacked his ass. Brooks spread Rashawn's thighs wide apart as he inched up onto him. He slowly got his dick into him through the front, holding Rashawn's legs over his shoulders.

"I knew you wanted this dick from the first time you saw me," Brooks said as he slammed his dick against Rashawn's walls. "I saw you checking out my dick when I was at the desk. "

"I don't know what you're talking about, Brooks," Rashawn replied coyly.

"I know that you're talking shit right now, but I'll let it pass. You were able to play that little boy shit with those tired-ass bustas you used to fuck with, but guess the fuck what? I'm about to lay it down on you," Brooks said.

"Oh yeah?"

"Hell yeah," Brooks boasted, quickly jamming his dick back into Rashawn's juicy asshole. "I bet you all those tired-ass bustas never got you open like this. Well, I'm going to put it down on you, brotha."

Brooks pulled out after banging the fuck out of Rashawn. Getting up from the carpet, he knocked everything off the desk with his hands. He placed his body flat onto the desk as Rashawn hovered his ass over his dick. Gently easing Brooks' dick into his moist hole, Rashawn jumped up and down on it like he was on a carousel ride at Coney Island. He held his dick as Brooks thrusted at a rapid speed repeatedly. He felt his asshole expanding with the dick's frenzy. Looking down, the sight of Brooks' muscular thighs popping and slamming against his boy pussy got him hotter. He didn't want him to stop filling him up, enjoying the *plop-plop-plop* sound. As soon as Brooks felt his entire body shake and quiver, he gently lifted Rashawn off his dick. Rashawn watched as extra large mounds of cum erupted out of Brooks' dick. Brooks grunted like a lion when Rashawn's mouth covered the tip of his dick, scooping his cum all the way down his throat and licking the sides of his mouth.

Used to being treated like the mistress by men throughout his ten years of gay sex, Rashawn got up to gather his black leather sneakers, boxer briefs, yellow-and-black plaid shirt, jeans, socks, backpack, and journal. As soon as he approached his belongings, Brooks pulled him by his waist back over to the desk. Brooks laid him flat down as two of his fingers dipped into Rashawn's ass. Feeling Brooks' fingers explore and finally hit his prostate, Rashawn shook uncontrollably until a year's worth of sexually frustrated cum flew onto his stomach, dick, and pubic area. His eyes popped inside of his head when Brooks licked and swallowed all of his cum down his throat. They took a breather on the desk, where Brooks held Rashawn in his massive arms.

After Brooks straightened the security office back to normal and sprayed all over with a potpourri scent to rid the aroma of sweaty gay sex, he and Rashawn put back on their clothes.

"I believe this is yours, brotha." Brooks smiled, giving Rashawn his journal back.

"Thank you, Brooks!" Rashawn replied. He gagged when Brooks tongued him down for a minute. Looking back to make sure they didn't leave incriminating evidence of their sex session, they took their belongings, turned the lights off, and locked the office for the night.

"Don't tell anyone about this, brotha," Brooks begged, looking into Rashawn's eyes.

"Our secret is safe with me." Rashawn smiled, clutching his hands onto his journal.

Although they left Room 420 together, they went their separate ways. Rashawn exited the building from the third floor as he went on his way to his apartment to get a good night's sleep. Having celebrated the semester's end with Brooks, he went to bed a very happy camper.

❂❂❂

Forrester sat at the first-floor lobby booth, flirting with a young Asian woman. As soon as Rashawn approached him, the Asian woman quickly left the building and Forrester acted as if nothing happened.

"Did you ever find your journal, Rashawn?" Forrester asked, filling out his timesheet.

"Yes, someone found the journal and returned it to the security office," Rashawn replied.

"I'm glad that you got your journal back, especially since the spring semester is over. Well, it looks like Brooks is coming now to relieve me from my post. Rashawn, I'll walk you outside."

Rashawn walked over to Brooks, who proceeded to take his place in the booth. "Thank you for everything regarding my journal, Brooks. I wish more men could be just like you." He smiled.

"It's been my pleasure, brotha," Brooks responded, slipping him a small white piece of paper into his hands.

Rashawn and Forrester walked outside of Urban University into the warm weather. "Forrester, it's been a long semester. I'm going to let you go now. I'll see you in the fall."

"You take care of yourself, Rashawn."

"You too, Forrester!" Rashawn said as he walked away. He turned right back around and walked over to Forrester. "By the way, thank you for arranging my lost and found session with Brooks."

Forrester nodded his head in silence as Rashawn walked away. Sifting his right hand into his chest pocket, he pulled out the small white piece of paper Brooks slipped into his hands. His mouth produced a wide smile when he noticed that not only did Brooks jot his phone number but also wrote down Rashawn's final grade for his African-American LGBT history class: A+.

THE END

৪৩০৪

Donald Peebles is a proud African-American Same-Gender-Loving brotha who lives in Jamaica, New York. He holds a masters degree in history from City College in New York. He is currently employed as a vendor services eepresentative at Ogilvy & Mather. His interests include reading, writing, film, music, television, soap operas, Black History, working out, spirituality, and spending time with family and friends. He has been published in Urban Dialogue, ShoutOut!, SBC, and Writes of Passage USA. He is working on two novels, Hooker Heritage *and* Bastards and Bitches. *He can be reached at donald.peebles@yahoo.com and www.myspace.com/donaldpeebles*

Pendulum Swing

TIM'M T. WEST

Nights like this are grounded in the perfection that stars fall into. Soft and welcoming, the ground teases some unnamed constellation until one of its leading lights dashes its way to visibility—wanting to be seen beyond clear night twinkling, distinguished as alive within the mass of depth and uncertainty. Sometimes stars are lucky enough to fall alongside an Other—both taking the simultaneous leap into whatever lies beyond their heroism. When a falling star is lucky enough to find such a complement, magic happens in the world, if only for that night. And sometimes there are people whose rhythms are guided in parallel fashion—uncertain as what brought them out of their darkness and into night or, for what, but certain that it was meant for them to search, wander, fall into someone else falling.

❂❂❂

Malik Dixon was driven to the Bay Area some five years earlier as a hip-hop journalist to explore this place where both racial and sexual politricks collide. He appreciated, as much as anything, how the moderate climate in the Bay complemented his fashion sense. An ex-dreadlocked exemplar of the aesthetic some have called bourgie boho, intricate layers of clothing were a necessity that was perfect on warm days that chilled instantly with the coming of moonlight.

The exterior layers of clothing somehow reflected the various shades of Malik's personality. It was the accessorizing of Macy's or Banana Republic with rare thrift store finds, so as to appease both those who wouldn't be caught dead in a vintage store as well as those who required thrift rags as a political marker of whatever was left of center. His dress was as deliberately complicated as his politics. But this night would not be about style or politics. Tonight was about hunger. And the rare calling to feel another's flesh against his was a hunger that was as perfectly predictable as full moons. On nights like this, he was neither an intellectual nor an activist; just an animal longing for the unfamiliar pleasure of the perfect stranger.

A muscular six feet two inches and 240 pounds, his presence alone made him a conversation piece in most social settings. Still, in his mind, going to the gym was purely cathartic, though he welcomed the results and understood the attention it drew. He was not a Southerner but could be mistaken for someone rooted in Texarkana or Macon because of his mannish soul-swagger. He always walked with the humility of one of those archetypal Negroes who worked hard in the fields for very little, and who returned to their families proud of their honest living.

He was Jack Daniels, dark and strong—so much that a dose of him was intoxicating. Mandingo was in his bloodline, as well as the polish and charisma of our most beloved intellectuals; traceable back to Du Bois or Douglass. Beyond his physicality, Malik's charisma was so powerful that the people he caught staring seldom stopped thereafter. It was the self-entrapment of those spellbound by a confidence he seemed so oblivious to.

"Sexy" was the name given to him by those who didn't—and wouldn't—know his name. He had no idea what people found sexy about him, but had come to learn over the years that to not use it to his advantage was to waste a gift from God. Malik had landed the position of editor-in-chief of *The Realness*, an award-winning hip-hop quarterly lauded for its focus on cutting-edge editorials about fashion and politics. This position called for regular "code switching," so as not to disarm the rappers he interviewed or the label executives fighting to position their artists as hip-hop's "next shit." He was not a pretty boy, gym rat, or thug, yet his charm was bound up in his ability to blend yet stand out in any of these settings.

His sex appeal was significant, given that he was one pair of glasses and two gadgets away from being a stone-cold nerd. No one would know this from looking at him; though he carried an awareness of it in clumsy gestures that still ironically added to his sex appeal. Still, in spite of the burden that came with being effortlessly sexy, he could not retract the inevitability of stubborn genetics.

His walk was among the gifts he inherited. The product of a long line of bowlegged, well-fed men who cheated because it was shamefully expected, Malik did not easily identify with such promiscuity or the womanizing made ritual by older brothers and uncles. At the edge of the twenty-first century, he had different options; and he was decisively and unapologetically homosexual—often and regularly "outing" himself as a way of shocking and awing even the least suspecting.

People most desired this strange Mandingo of a man because he was such an open book, yet people still struggled to figure out what made him tick. There were, however, occasions when he was just a Dixon, both horny and needing affirmation that he still had that touch. Nights like these tap into the carnal, unconscious parts of men whose sexual thirst gets quenched as surely as the sun will arrive with dawn.

Tonight, Malik would give in to the hunger of loins and longings; would prey on bended knees, if necessary. Still, his desire for romance and companionship would color even his rare slips into one-night stands. Those who arrived in his space to "trick," never forgot that they were made love to, even when names got disremembered as inelegantly as how the men met. Malik was a precise and skillful lover who took great pride and excitement in how he made others feel.

"You got eyes that love to catch people watching," a voice as deep as his own reverberated, cutting through the maze, smoke, and mirrors of San Francisco's Pendulum. In Frisco, this was the only spot for colored boys seeking pleasure beyond what their hands, boyfriends, or wives could provide. While it wasn't D.C. or Atlanta, Malik would surely find somebody handsome enough there. The Bay wasn't known for grand numbers of black gay men, but it had its share of good-looking brothas—though most traveled across the bridge from Oakland to color the Castro on Saturday nights.

"So, you just gonna ignore me, huh?" the voice said with a force a tad stronger than the initial comment.

"What was that?" Malik replied, pretending not to be able to hear above whatever Top 40 hip-hop hit of the moment was being played…again.

"I guess you caught me looking. That's why you came over here, right?" The voice, like butter on oven-baked bread, made a part of him melt, though he chose to pretend that it didn't. Still, its reverb alone teased Malik's hunger.

There are times when a voice is so seductive that you pray it is attached to a body that is as attractive. This was one of those moments. The guy's "game" was a tad above average but there was something honest in it, so Malik indulged. "Naw, man, I just came to the first available space in this auction block of a bar. Do the drunk old white men always have to grab at brothas?" Fully giving in to the curiosity of the silhouette he had only caught out of the corner of his eye, Malik turned toward the voice to be assured that his prayer had been answered. Fully facing this handsome brotha, he became more hardened than the voice had already started to make him.

"Todd's the name, yo. And yours?"

Todd stood about five feet eleven and 215 pounds of thickali-ciousness. Packed so tightly in the space, Malik became quickly embarrassed by the throbbing in his pants on his new friend's midsection.

"So, I take that as a good sign," Todd whispered looking down at Malik's crotch, which seemed to graze his modest love handles. "I don't get out but a few times a year, but when I do it's always my hope that some handsome brotha will be hard pressed to talk to me."

Malik blushed, taken by how quickly Todd's lines had gone from nervous cliché to the most playful innuendos. But Malik quickly pulled his face together. Blushing wasn't very manly; for an anxious top that was most often attracted to other tops, every gesture counted for or against satisfying the night's hunger.

There was a necessary silence. Each man held onto the other, heavy breaths accelerating. It started with the eyes—each recognizing in the other a mirror unlike anything experienced before. A smile or two was returned between the two as confirmation that permission would be given for almost anything. They had a chemistry that was a formula of gods, so touches and glances were a perfectly choreographed dance as passionate and carefree as if no one else were looking. This night that called them both from the shadows of solitude had already offered its share of pleasure in this looking game that minutes after their introduction still entranced them.

"Can you stay here for a bit?" Todd whispered in Malik's ear, his hand gently caressing the small of Malik's back. "You ain't gotta answer…," he continued, gently though firmly pulling Malik's body into him. "Just stay here pressed close. Feels like home."

Malik could feel a train of butterflies shuffling up his back and down to his stomach, where they would rest. This was where Todd's hand belonged. It was home. Could this hunger be about something more than flesh, this body next to him more than the usual suspect? "Do you say that to everybody?" Malik sharply asked, feeling deep down that he might be experiencing yet another moment that was too good to be true.

"I plan to say it every time I'm as close to you as I am now," Todd returned.

Malik's cool began to unravel as the soft force of Todd's breath further warmed his soul. His charm was so magnetic that Malik would have married the guy on the spot if Todd had popped the question. Feeling too open and vulnerable, Malik used his quick wit to break the prowess of Todd's seduction. "Well, if I feel like home, wait 'til I get you into my house."

The humor of the moment lightened what had quickly become too perfectly intense to be just a hunt. *This one could get it*, Malik thought, grinning as Todd responded with a beautifully full smile. It cut through all the machismo, revealing both men as enchanted, as if each other's first crush. It was a man's smile—a smile man enough to recognize a man strong enough to smile; to be man enough to appreciate and mirror that vulnerability.

Together, standing there, they were an Urban Outfitters billboard for Bay Area homie-sexuals. Malik was so beautifully black that it was never used against him in games of the dozens. His mask was chiseled by the gods, with sharp features that further heightened his masculinity. "That black-ass negro is phyne," women would often say, as if a dark-complexioned person had to be exceptionally good looking to warrant attention, underscoring the color-struck mentality that still weaves its way through color lines in colored sections.

Malik wasn't thought to be handsome in the standard ways—he was beautiful because no one could ever approximate his imprint: deep cut eyes that suggested Africa or the Caribbean, with a sharp jaw line and a chiseled nose that men wanted to brush during kissing games. The shine off his bald head was an additional marker of strength and often intimidation.

Todd, on the other hand, was what some would call a typical Berkeley, Cali poster child—often drawing questions like "what are you mixed with?" Like many Bay Area natives who are the offspring of Black Power and Hippie Free Love, he was one of those brothas whose gigantic, uneven afro actually worked for him.

"You black?" Malik asked.

"Of course," Todd replied, seeming slightly irritated by the question. "Why'd you ask that?"

"With such full features, I thought you might have been Polynesian or something," Malik replied, creating conversation where silence had become uncomfortable.

"I get that a lot. But I'm just black, plain black with a plain black mama from East Texas and a black daddy from Baton Rouge. I'm sure there's something mixed in back there, but I ain't grow up around much extended family, so who knows."

"You out?" It was a question that was crucial for Malik to ask. He expected the answer to be "no." And that's how he'd know the men he'd met would be no more than flings. He had expectations of a grand commitment ceremony, adoption, and shared family holidays. So with this question of being "out" or not, he had slipped out of his carnal mode to consider how his politics might align with this guy who he seemed to be falling in love with tonight. Could Todd be a prospect for boyfriend or husband, or would the memory of him be the only trace left after this perfect night?

"Naw," Todd replied. "I ain't got no issues with liking guys, but given what I do, I can't really be out."

"And what do you do in 2003 that prevents you from being out?" Malik asked.

"I rap," Todd declared. "I figured when you came in that you might recognize me from some of the industry parties."

"Oh really?" Malik pondered, lamenting for a moment, his friend's answer. But disappointment would quickly become a challenge. The right man would come "out" for him, he'd always thought. "Hmm. I used to rap, but now I just interview rappers. Don't worry, I respect discretion, so you ain't gotta worry about seeing yourself on the cover of *The Guardian* with a rainbow-colored microphone in your mouth. I've already covered the Deep Dick crew."

"You funny, you know?" Todd said, laughing. "But I like it. I like you. Sometimes I think about coming out, but I ain't met nobody yet worth doing that for."

"And I'm supposed to fall for that?" Malik asked.

"Not exactly," said Todd. "You're supposed to fall for me. I'm worth it."

"So spit something. You can do it over this Neptunes beat. I wanna hear you flow."

"But I can't stand this damn song," Todd complained.

"A good emcee can rap over anything/Can parlay about bling or simple things/Cream and ghetto dreams/My flow hunts sucka-emcees like Jeff Dahmer/So quit stalling/Save the drama for the baby mama."

"Oh! It's like that then, huh?" Todd said, laughing, seeming only slightly impressed.

"Yeah…it's like that," Malik said, glad that he didn't fuck up the freestyle and aware that if he had continued, he would have tripped up and said something even more corny.

The energy of the place seemed to pick up as the track bounced beneath the feet of these men whose only dancing happened between their eyes.

"How bout me and you take this cipher to your house/Since you opened your mouth/Presented that route and option/Got a brotha stalking/Pressed against your thigh/Throbbing like my man ready to break out my fly/I never imagined bustin rhymes in gay clubs/Not with banjee boys or homothugs given some love/This brotha stay straight blunted but right now you my drug/So where's this house you been talking bout, let's un-plug/You nervous?/ I'm DL trying to lock lips with a journalist/Write a pretty mess on this treasure chest, I've earned this/Gimme something to think about when I lay to rest/My lyrics put your game to the test/this flo's blessed/And we ain't gotta tell a soul/but this night knows/I'll cum for you baby boy any way the wind blows…."

The idea of finding a suitable place in which to indulge this attraction was scrapped. The two had become a spectacle of sorts, pleasing white and colored men alike who were watching their bodies unfold between breath and beats. After a few drinks from one of the stronger and generous bartenders, Malik found courage to gently grab the back of Todd's neck, giving him a full, wet tongue kiss that would have been considered sloppy if it weren't for the passion and force behind it, lasting a good minute or two before pulling away with more tender peck-kisses on the periphery of Todd's full lips.

"Don't stop there," Todd said. "I want you."

At that moment, the pendulum had swung. It was time to go home. And Todd understood that "home" was wherever Malik was taking him…

❖❖❖

Malik was one of a rare few brothas who preferred to live in Frisco's Castro, not because it was gay, but because of its beautiful scenery and convenience to work on the MUNI train. Once outside, Malik took Todd's hand, daring him to resist. If he manned up, he wouldn't really give a fuck. Todd's boys, if really straight, wouldn't be caught dead in the Castro anyhow. And being an indie rapper, few people at the gay joint would have ever been exposed to his work. Only serious underground heads would have recognized Todd.

"I'm up the hill," Malik tugged. After a few hand-held stops and taking a pause at the corner of Nineteenth and Collingwood, Todd picked the larger Malik clean off his feet. "Damn. So you gonna really act gay and try to sweep a brotha off his feet, huh?"

After some feigned protest, Todd put Malik back on his feet, kissing him in the center of the crosswalk. "Tonight, I just don't give a fuck, you know. Sometimes I get tired of givin' a fuck."

There was something very powerful and emotional in the statement, but Malik knew better than to probe. Crossing the street, they locked eyes again.

"I ain't scared to hold your hand," Todd continued. "Some of my best friends are gay," he belted, sharing knee-slapping laughter with Malik, who threw caution to the wind, let go of his demands that the men he date be "out," and let himself fall alongside Todd. Besides, Todd was not yet even a date, just a moment of perfection in a life filled with more drama and pain than peace of mind.

The short three-block walk up the Hill was tiring, not so much because the men were winded, but anxious to wrestle and rest with each other. Not soon after Malik opened the door, did Todd push Malik to the sofa and drop to his knees. In the same moment he reached for Malik's zipper, not even taking a moment to inspect the place, since he had learned on the walk that Malik lived alone.

"Easy now," Malik said. "Let's take our time with this. Besides, I don't really even know if we're compatible."

"We are," Todd replied, taking Malik's fullness into his warm mouth for a tease before saying, "You're a man. I'm a man. You diggin' me, right? We're compatible."

"But I'm a …"

"You're man enough to let me make love to you tonight. So shut up with all that categorizing! This ain't Paris' ball."

Todd forcefully interrupted Malik's laughter, who was surprised that Todd would even know anything about gay ball culture. He kissed Malik passionately before there could be any protest of his hand gripping Malik's ass. And while Malik had not been one to give up control in such situations, this was a different test of his manhood. He knew that he'd reach new plateaus if he could only be man enough to be vulnerable with this man. As gay and out as he'd been, he still had his hang-ups and masculinity issues but, somehow, Todd disarmed them all.

Bending over to break Todd's focus on his nine with a kiss not unlike the one in the club, Malik let go of top/bottom preoccupations that even he believed to be silly. He'd always believed that the right guy could get inside of him, but was unwilling to let just anyone. And since this night had been so perfect and a conversation even with this brotha beyond tonight was not promised, he trusted Todd with his body.

Malik never cared much for being sucked, but did like the look of it: submission, full lips, dick worship. It was one of the more narcissistic things about his sex because it became a moment where he'd watch himself play porn daddy to some wanting mouth. But Todd was different. He wanted to please; wanted to give into impulses he'd only considered when self-pleasuring. He wanted to make love and be made love to.

He led Malik to the kitchen and set him down on the kitchen counter, and in an instant flexed both of Malik's legs back toward his shoulders, his back on the countertop grounding the gravity of his massive body. It was uncomfortably wonderful for Malik; letting go of inhibitions. Todd was man enough to elicit a relaxation he'd never known. And pleasures too.

❂❂❂

"Right there, right under my nut sac," Malik instructed.

"I know what I'm doing. Just relax," Todd replied as the warm wetness of his fibrillating tongue made its way past Malik's nut sac and lingered on his perineum. Malik's body jolted with resistance for a quick moment before giving into a pleasure that, in all his years of selfish "toptitude," he'd never experienced.

Todd was a tad smaller, but just as strong, doing with Malik what he wanted, with little resistance. From the glide of a finger to even deeper probing, Malik's back and legs gripped Todd's back, his left arm grounding their thumping, his right arm pulling Todd's head down for intermittent passion kisses.

"Damn, boy...you feel good," Malik said.

Todd could not reply, so focused in his pleasuring that he gave himself fully over to the task or making it a night both he and Malik would remember...

❈❈❈

Todd woke in sweat and sheets that carried Malik's scent, some mix of amber and frankincense from the Ashby Flea Market. There were two opened Trojan wrappers as evidence, perhaps, that they two had played safe, even under the influence of intoxicating romance and alcohol. Todd was hedonistic enough to want the best of both worlds that night and dressed quietly while taking reflective moments to adore Malik's slumber. Often he'd stand above Malik, for minutes at a time, watching the rise and fall of his chest with each exhale.

❈❈❈

Malik would wake a few hours later, terrified that he'd lost track of the only man, besides his father, that he'd been vulnerable with. Would such a perfect moment be reduced to sweat-tainted sheets cooling with morning, the bite of alcohol resting on the roof of his mouth, flesh tenderized with the bump and grind of mansex, or the echo of Neptunes' beats that rang in both his memory and eardrum? Malik hopped up with urgency, hoping to find some trace that Todd was not just one of the few names he'd remember after a night feeding his seasonal hunger. Scanning the entire place to notice that he hadn't been robbed of anything beyond his sexual stubbornness, he arrived in the bathroom to see a note on the mirror:

Gone to get changed. Call if you want to do brunch.

Was gonna cook, but your mothafucking fridge is empty, pa.

Thanks for the perfect night. (510) Hella Me.

Laughing at Todd's obsessive iteration of his independence, Malik smiled. *So very Beyonce for a rapper; so Destiny's Child,* he thought, a widening grin spreading as he rushed to his cell phone. Anxiously dialing the number, he awaited Todd's answer, unsure of exactly what he'd say.

"I'm hella me, and who the hell are you? Holla," Todd answered.

"It's Malik."

"Yeah, I know. You buy some groceries yet? I ain't coming back home until you do."

"And I guess I gotta clean up a bit to make room for a studio too, huh?"

"I ain't say all that. Just get some food. I hope you're free today. Was thinking maybe we could cook dinner or something, watch a DVD. Just chill."

"Sure," Malik responded, his smile noticeable across the miles that separated the blacker part of the Bay from its more popular complement. "Whatever you want to do."

❋❋❋

And they did whatever they wanted to do, throwing caution and fear to the wind, building on the courage provided by someone else struggling with how black men can love one another in a culture so fearful of it. They would continue to fall, night after night, until others, moved by their example, would too fall.

Months later, on a warm blanketed evening in Golden Gate Park after a Spearhead concert with The Coup, Malik and Todd would watch the night sky. At a most peaceful moment they would sight a falling star, and another, falling just moments after.

"Yeah, superstar, you the slow-ass one. If it wasn't for my DL ass, we wouldn't even be here now, Mister Activist."

"Don't get too proud, baby boy. You still got a ways to go."

Both men found meaning in the courage to fall—to shed assumptions and notions that had robbed them of the perfect night and perfect complement. Looking into each other's eyes with a most passionate resolve, they both knew that no challenge would be audacious enough to break their bond. They would also know, without the words to speak its full understanding—their backs against ground and heads to the blackening sky, each with a hand clenching his most beloved—nights like this are grounded in the perfection that stars fall into.

ℰℭ

Tim'm T. West is an author/publisher, poet, emcee, scholar, educator and activist who in 1999 co-founded Deep Dickollective and established himself as one of the more dynamic and influential Renaissance artists coming into the 21st century. In 2003 he released a critically acclaimed poetic memoir Red Dirt Revival; *in 2005 a chapbook* BARE, *before "Flirting" (June 2007). Musically, he released his solo debut,* Songs from Red Dirt, *on Cellular Records. Alongside "Flirting," Tim'm released* Blakkboy Blue(s) (Family Ties), *the highly anticipated followup to his debut, as well as* On Some Other, *DDC's third full-studio album project. A cultural critic, he is widely published in academic and literary anthologies, journals, and other publications, including but not limited to: Freedom in This Village, Self Organizing Men, Voices Rising, Total Chaos, and If We Have To Take Tomorrow. Tim'm is also featured in two critically acclaimed hip-hop documentaries: Alex Hinton's* Pick Up the Mic *(LOGO) and Byron Hurt's* Beyond Beats and Rhymes *(PBS). While he tours nationally and internationally, since its origins in D.C. in December 2004, Tim'm has been the founder and host of "The Front Porch" open mic/feature series in D.C., Atlanta, Brooklyn, Chicago, and Oakland. He resides in Atlanta, GA. More of Tim'm's work can be found at www.reddirt.biz*

The One
JAYDEN BLAKE

The moment I opened the front door and saw Andy standing there, I knew something serious was brewing. These days my best friend never dropped by without calling first, not since that time he'd walked in and caught me underneath that Latino bartender. He looked sober and I surmised that, whatever he'd come to discuss, he felt it was too intense for the phone.

I scrutinized his expression, so at odds with his usual sunny visage, and my brain immediately conjured up visions of catastrophe. Was Andy sick? AIDS? Tumor? Some type of cancer. Hadn't a cousin of his died of Hodgkin's Disease? Maybe it was Parkinson's. Either way, wasn't it something genetic?

"Noah," Andy said, derailing my train of thought, "can I come in, or are you going to make me stand on the porch all day while you try and figure out why I'm here?"

"Oh. Of course." I stepped back, holding the door wide. Andy preceded me through the kitchen, pausing when he reached the living room. I'd been in the process of folding laundry and the couch was covered with tidy, color-coordinated piles. Andy looked at the neat stacks, then looked at me.

"I was just doing the laundry," I explained. "Here, let me make some room...."

"That's okay," he said. "I'll do it." With that, he picked up several piles and flung them into the air. Then he sat down in the empty spot, grinning up at me as a colorful mélange of shirts and pillowcases fluttered down around him.

"Dick," I said, but couldn't suppress a chuckle. Andy has always taken exception to my penchant for orderliness. He thinks I'm uptight and obsessive. I think *he's* scattered and undisciplined, and have told him so on a number of occasions. He never even balances his checkbook. "Doesn't it bother you not to know how much money you have?" I asked him.

"Doesn't it bother *you* that it takes you an hour and a half to iron a shirt?" he responded.

Andy loves to twist my tail about it and he was enjoying himself thoroughly just then, looking up from amidst the melee of clothing with a grin the size of Texas. A flush of pleasure bloomed in my chest, which is the effect Andy's smile always has on me. It's like a shot of liquid sunshine.

I sat down in the armchair across from him, grinning and beaming like a fool. From this vantage point I had a marvelous view of him. I loved looking at Andy, the way his shaggy blond hair hung into his deep blue eyes, the lean lines of his long, hard body, and he was giving me a similar scrutiny. I was in my usual early morning attire—running shorts—and his gaze lingered on the dark mat of hair on my bare chest. He's a sucker for hairy men, Andy is, and the spark in his eyes was enough to make the glow in my chest move to a lower part of my anatomy.

At moments like this, I have to wonder why we split up. I've had more intense relationships and longer ones, during the half-dozen or so years that have passed since Andy and I were a couple, but I've never been able to replicate the sheer joy of the six months we spent together. We had an amazing connection, a bond unlike anything I've experienced before or since.

Then there was the physical stuff, mind-bending sex of the life-altering variety. The memory alone is enough to make my knees weak and my cock hard, even after all this time.

With all that, you'd think we'd have figured out a way to make it work, but we didn't. I was only twenty-six, too young to understand that love like that doesn't come along every day. Besides, I've always been a bit of a whore—in truth, I still am—and it's a side of me that Andy just can't deal with. His love life is the only thing he isn't scattered about; he's monogamous by nature and, after catching me with nine different men, he announced that he'd had it.

Eventually we missed each other and reconnected, but I couldn't stay faithful and he wouldn't accept that, so we decided to be friends. It was tricky at first, but over time our friendship grew into a solid, deep attachment, one I've come to treasure and depend upon.

Usually it was enough, but every so often I'd get to thinking that he was my one true love. It was a depressing notion—that he was The One and I'd let him get away. Months would go by, then something would trigger a memory and I'd be miserable. All it took was a smile….

I cleared my throat. "So, what brings you by at this ungodly hour? I haven't seen you this early in the day since…."

Since we woke up in the same bed, we both finished silently. "I know it's early," Andy apologized, "but there's something I need to talk to you about."

I sent up a prayer of thanks that the hard-bodied personal trainer I'd picked up the night before had departed during the wee hours. "What's up?"

"Well, I have some news." Suddenly his smile was gone. "It's about Hope, actually. That is, about Hope and me."

And I knew, right away. He didn't have to say another word. "Holy shit. You're not."

He looked relieved that he didn't have to say it. "I am. I mean, *we* are." He cleared his throat, then, and said it anyway. "Getting married, that is."

"Holy shit," I repeated and shook my head, dazed. "When did this happen?"

"Last night," he replied. "I asked. She said yes. We're doing it."

"And you're *sure*?" I pressed, not sure what I wanted him to say.

"Positive," he said. "She's The One."

Whatever answer I'd been fishing for, it definitely wasn't that. I didn't want to hear that Hope was The One for Andy, not when *he* was The One for me. A pain flared in my chest, displacing the pleasurable warmth that had resided there since his arrival.

"I wanted you to be the first to know," he said, leaning forward to touch my hand. "I haven't told anyone else, Noah. Not even my family."

"Hey, it's big news." My gaze dropped to his hand, covering mine. "Why the secrecy?"

"I didn't want to risk you finding out from somebody else," he explained. "I wanted you to hear it from me. But Hope…well, she's excited, and started calling people first thing…."

"Does she know?" I interrupted.

"About us?" Andy shook his head. "No. Of course not. I mean, she knows there have been men, but…."

"Don't you think you ought to tell her?" I said, moving my hand out from under his.

"Why?" he asked. "What happened between you and me has nothing to do with Hope."

"But it does," I corrected him. "It's no secret that you and I were lovers. What if somebody else fills her in?"

"She'd understand," he said, although he looked uncertain. "Hope is very open-minded."

"Obviously," I agreed, "since she can deal with your bisexuality. But she might not understand about *this*, because you kept it from her."

"You have a point," he conceded reluctantly, "but I wouldn't want her to feel threatened. You and I were….well, serious and we still see a lot of each other."

"That's why you'd better tell her," I insisted. "You're my best friend, Andy. I don't want to lose that because your future wife suddenly decides she doesn't want me around."

Andy didn't reply, but we both knew I was right. Andy is very passive in some ways, more likely to go along with somebody else's decisions than make his own. Taking steps to end our relationship was the most decisive thing I've ever seen him do, and the fact that he did it is a testament to how much pain I put him through.

Before long he rose to go. He and Hope had a long drive that afternoon, he said. They were going upstate to visit her parents and discuss wedding plans.

I experienced a fresh burst of pain. "I'm happy for you, Andy," I said. "You know I am. But you know I thought….I always thought..."

"I know," he said, and put his arms around me. He doesn't do that often these days and, just for a moment, I pressed against him. The sharp, spicy scent of the lime cologne he always wore brought back memories, ones I'd love to reenact, given half a chance.

I knew he could feel my excitement when he gave my waist a squeeze, then took a step back. "Gotta go," he said across the distance between us. "Just one more thing."

"What's that?"

"Would I be a complete asshole if I asked you to be my best man?"

I know my expression gave him my answer. He took my face in his hands. "I want you to know that I still love you, Noah. I always will. What we had….well, it doesn't go away." He kissed me gently, then smiled that heartbreaking smile.

I watched him walk away, then very quietly closed the door and went back to folding the laundry.

❁❁❁

A few weeks later, I was up to my ass in best man-type wedding crap. They'd chosen to marry quickly, or rather Hope had, and I found myself assigned a number of unexpected responsibilities.

One of them was hosting the rehearsal dinner. Hope asked me herself. "Please?" she begged prettily, fluttering her dark lashes at me. "We'll have it catered and hire a cleaning service, so you won't have to lift a finger. It would mean so much to us, Noah. Your place is so beautiful and, after all, it's where Andy and I first met."

Did I mention that? It was true. They'd met at my New Year's Eve party last year, and they've been inseparable ever since I'd actually introduced the love of my life to the woman he was going to marry. Talk about karma.

Of course I said yes, they could have the dinner at my house. It would be a lovely setting there on the deck overlooking the lake. Besides, Hope is nearly impossible to resist. She's a very persuasive woman, bright, charming, and elegant, and I've known her for years. Even though I was jealous and wanted to hate her I couldn't pull it off, because I liked her too much. Besides, even I had to admit that she and Andy were perfect for each other.

Andy was happier than I'd ever seen him and I wanted to feel good about that.

The dinner turned out to be a merry occasion. There's a certain giddiness that comes over people when they gather together to witness the joining of a truly wonderful couple, and our small group was a jolly one. The food was delicious, the champagne excellent, and the mood festive. It was nice to see Andy's parents again and, if they thought it odd that their son's ex-lover was hosting the rehearsal dinner, they didn't mention it.

The single melancholy moment came when most of the food and drink had been consumed. Andy approached me in the kitchen and laid a hand on my shoulder. "I wanted to thank you privately," he said. "I appreciate all you're doing for us, Noah. I know it isn't easy."

"It's my pleasure," I told him. "Really. I'm your best friend, remember?"

"I'll always remember," he said and smiled, that sunshiny smile that I loved. I touched the hand resting on my shoulder and, just for a moment, he let our fingers entwine. Filled with an ineffable sadness, I took his hand and pressed it against my mouth.

When I noticed Hope watching from across the breakfast bar, I quickly let go of him. She waited a moment, then cleared her throat. "Your parents are leaving, Andy," she said. "Come say good night."

As Andy turned toward her, I offered Hope a weak smile. She smiled back, but her eyes were pensive as she led Andy back to the living room where there were hugs and kisses, excited chatter about the wedding the next day, and directions to the nearby hotels. We ushered everyone out and stepped back while the caterers finished packing up and left.

At Hope's suggestion, the three of us gathered in front of the fire to finish off the last of the champagne. I gulped it nervously, anxious to get them out before she brought up the scene she'd inadvertently witnessed. What had she thought, catching Andy and me in such an intimate tête-à-tête? Was she threatened? Upset? Enraged? Was she planning to mutilate my balls with the sterling silver corkscrew?

"You know," she said, interrupting my mental diatribe. "I was a little shocked when I saw the two of you in the kitchen earlier."

Andy looked perplexed, so I jumped in to explain. "Hope, Andy was just thanking me for having the dinner here," I said quickly. "It was nothing."

"It was hardly nothing, Noah," she corrected me. "I saw the way you were looking at each other."

"Well, Andy and I have a history," I admitted. "I'm not sure how much he told you…."

"Everything," she said. "At least I *thought* he'd told me everything."

"I did," Andy said, frowning. "I didn't hold anything back."

"Yes, you did, or am I the only one who realizes the two of you are still in love with each other?"

Andy didn't respond right away, so I jumped in. "Hope, it's *you* that Andy's marrying."

"I know that, Noah." Hope took a long sip of champagne and stared into the fire. "Don't worry. I'm not about to do anything rash, like call off the wedding. Marrying you, Andy….it's exactly what I want. I have no doubts about it, and I don't want *you* having any either."

"I don't," he said stridently.

Hope got up from the couch and drifted over to the window. She remained there silently for a moment, looking out at the night. "It's all right, Andy," she said without turning around. "I understand. You can't help who you love."

"Hope, I love *you*," Andy insisted. "I would *never* do anything to jeopardize that."

"I'm going to bed," I blurted, wanting to be anywhere but there.

"Why?" Hope turned back from the window. "It's early."

"Because I'm uncomfortable," I snapped. "This conversation is none of my business."

"Oh, but it is," she corrected me, "because apparently I'm not the only one in love with my fiancé."

"Hope, I *introduced* the two of you, remember?" I said, conveniently overlooking how dismayed I'd been when they'd hit it off. "Would I do that if I was still in love with him?"

She left the window and returned to the couch, sinking to her knees in front of me. She's a beautiful woman, dark and exotic with a lovely body, but it was her eyes that held me captive. They were wide, clear, and the color of melted chocolate.

"Perhaps you did it *because* you love him," she replied softly. "Because you wanted him to be happy and you knew I'd be the one to make him that way."

She reached out and touched my chest lightly and I felt some kind of current pass between us. I was frozen, hypnotized by her eyes as she leaned toward me, close enough for her breasts to brush my chest. Her breath was against my face, warm and scented with champagne.

When she kissed me on the corner of my mouth I didn't know what to do. The brush of her lips was very light at first. Then, when I didn't resist, she kissed me more deeply. My body underwent a little shock when I felt her tongue slip past my lips and my eyes shot to Andy's.

Help! I shrieked silently. *Andy, help! What the fuck is she doing to me?*

"Hope," Andy said, seeing my panic, "what the *fuck* are you doing to him?"

Hope broke the kiss and shifted her gaze from me to Andy. "I'm giving you permission to have what you want," she told him. "What you've *been* wanting, all along…."

"I never said….," he began, but she didn't let him finish. Instead she angled toward him, resting a hand on my thigh as she leaned across it. I expected him to pull away, but he instead allowed her to kiss him, much as I had, although he seemed to enjoy it more.

"You didn't have to," she murmured against his lips, then kissed him again. I saw her tongue slip into his mouth and knew he would taste wet and sweet. It excited me that her tongue, which had so recently been inside my mouth, was now inside his.

As weird as the situation was, it was making me hot. My cock was hard as a rock and I knew Hope could feel it, since she was stretched across my lap. I cleared my throat, attempting to inch away from her. "Look, Hope," I said. "I think you ought to take this somewhere else. This is between *the two of you.* I mean, okay, you're right. I still have feelings for Andy. I admit it, but he's marrying *you*, not *me*, so there's no reason for me to be involved in this discussion. If you're trying to get some kind of three-way thing going, then you're on the wrong track. I know Andy, and he would *never*…."

Andy broke the kiss. "Noah," he said. "Would you please shut the hell up?"

He wore a devilish grin. My reply stuck in my throat and, when he kissed me, a line of silken electricity shot through my entire body. He tasted just like I remembered and it suddenly overwhelmed me, just how much I loved this man. I went limp and liquidy, unable to do anything but sit there and let him kiss me. I opened my mouth to let him in and fuzzily wondered what Hope was doing.

I didn't have to wonder long. I felt a series of light touches along the insides of my thighs, zeroing in what I knew was a gigantic erection. "Noah…" Hope breathed. "You are *so* hard."

I buried my face in Andy's chest. The blood pounding in my ears nearly eradicated the sound of her voice and I was glad, glad. I wanted to block her out, wanted this moment to be between Andy and me without Hope intruding on it.

But she wouldn't be banished. Andy eased me back against the couch, his mouth gently licking the inside of mine, and at the same time I felt the pressure of Hope's breasts between my legs. Generally, breasts don't do much for me, but these were the ones that Andy kissed and fondled night after night. Perhaps it was this that made the soft swells so enticing, made them generate twin circles of heat that penetrated deep into my body.

Andy moved his mouth from mine to Hope's and I was sandwiched between them, enveloped by their heat. Her hair tickled my chin, smelling like gardenias. I trailed my fingers through the silky tresses, then slid my hand around to her back. Her skin was smooth and warm. I pressed my hand between her shoulder blades, at the same time thrusting forward with my hips.

I heard Hope's sharp intake of breath as the hardness between my legs pressed against her breasts. Andy kept kissing her—hot, wet kisses—his hand joining mine behind her back. He did something to the strap around her neck, her halter top fell away, and her breasts were bared before me, full and sloping, nipples tawny against her pale skin.

I reached for them, but Andy pushed my hands away. He stopped kissing Hope as he unzipped my pants to reveal my stony erection. Andy took it, ran his palm along its stiff length, then wedged it between Hope's breasts.

I emitted an involuntary groan as her heavy tits encased me. Andy squeezed them together, milking my cock with their rich, lewd warmth. His breath came heavily and I saw the bulge in his pants grow as he jerked me off with his woman's tits.

I hadn't touched a woman's breast in years, but suddenly I wanted that fullness in my mouth, wanted the hot, puckered flesh of her nipples against my tongue. I slid to my knees and Andy lifted the soft globes, presenting them for me. I sucked greedily, feeling her nipples contract against my tongue. I knew full well that my intense craving for them had less to do with the woman possessing them than with the man offering them to me, but that did nothing to lessen the force of my desire.

I reached between Andy's legs as I nuzzled his fiancée's breasts. He was hard as an axe handle as I groped for his zipper and tugged it down. When his cock sprang out I wrapped my hand around its firm length, feeling it thrust and writhe in my grasp. A drop of slippery fluid oozed from his narrow slit.

I gave Hope's tits a final nuzzle, then moved my mouth to Andy's cock. I licked it, savoring the taste of his salty precum, and Hope helped me pull his pants down to his ankles so I could explore the twin sacs between his legs. I felt them tighten and retract in my mouth, then gradually worked my way back up his shaft. Andy's cock is long, elegant, and I took it in deep, deeper, until I felt it nudge the back of my throat.

Andy cupped my head in his hands, his fingers stroking the back of my neck. "Noah." He breathed. "God, Noah."

I knew just what he meant. There were no words for how it felt to make love to him again. There was a comforting familiarity to his smell, the taste of his skin, but at the same time a tantalizing newness, a naughtiness not in the least emphasized by Hope's presence.

From behind me she was unfastening my pants, drawing them down as I sucked Andy's cock. I lifted one leg, then the other, to allow her to remove them. She urged my legs apart, then crept between them and began licking my balls, moving from one to the other with light, tantalizing strokes of her tongue.

I moaned, and Andy squeezed the back of my neck. "Don't forget what you're doing," he warned. I redoubled my efforts at sucking and he sighed, his cock pulsing in and out of my throat in a hot, sultry rhythm.

Meanwhile Hope had engulfed both my balls with her mouth. I moaned again and the sound was muffled, since my mouth was filled with Andy's cock. I saw him smile faintly.

"Play with his ass, babe," he said to Hope. "That's Noah's trigger. It makes him wild, doesn't it, my hot little bottom boy?"

I muttered in response and, a moment later, felt Hope's fingers slide between my buttocks. She prodded my anus and the ring of flesh tightened, but she was gentle. She worked her finger into me with light strokes and my ass quivered, then opened. Andy was pulsing in and out of my throat and Hope was matching his rhythm, finger fucking my ass with deep, firm strokes as she mouthed my balls.

"Give him a little tongue in his ass," Andy directed in a husky voice. His hand tightened on the back of my neck and he pushed deeper into my throat as Hope followed his instructions. When I felt her tongue in my ass I *did* go wild, grinding against her face as she rimmed me, my stiff member bouncing in the air.

I felt a throb deep in my balls and pulled my mouth off Andy's cock. "I'm going to come," I groaned, gripping his cock as if it were a lifeline. "Oh, God, I'm going to come…."

But it was Andy who came. His stiff cock jerked once, twice in my hands, then thick cream spurted from his satiny slit. It erupted with force, splattering onto my face and over my hands.

I was concentrating on cleaning every last drop of slippery jism off Andy's cock. Hope withdrew from between my legs and appeared at my side to help me and I kissed her, feeding her a bit of Andy's cum with my tongue. Her lips were soft, her tongue musky.

"Can we move into the bedroom?" she asked, looking at Andy.

He stood up, extending his hands to both of us. The three of us moved into the bedroom, shedding clothes as we did.

I stripped off the last of my clothing—my socks—and stretched out on the bed. My cock was still stiff and Andy couldn't take his eyes off it as he peeled off his khakis. He crawled in between my legs and began lapping my cock with long, slow strokes of his tongue. My groin tightened as I recalled what great head Andy gave.

He took my cock in his mouth next and began milking it, his lips and tongue kneading me in the special rhythm only he seemed to know. His silky hair tickled the insides of my thighs as I arched upward to receive the ministrations of his talented mouth.

Hope stepped out of her panties and lay down beside me, her expression rapt as she watched Andy suck my cock. "Don't stop," she whispered, spreading her thighs.

She slipped her hand between her legs and I saw she was shaved. I watched her fingers caress the moist, nude slit and longed for the taste of it. I rolled to the side, careful not to disrupt Andy, and touched her lightly with my tongue.

The hairless lips of her pussy were soft as a flower petal as I probed them. They separated invitingly, exposing all the mysterious crevices of her woman's body. The slippery cleft was rich and musky, like olive oil mixed with cumin, and her skin smelled of lavender soap. I found the small, tight bud of her clitoris and wrapped my lips around it, sucking hard.

Hope cried out, whipping her head from side to side, her hips gyrating frantically as I ate her hot, wet pussy. I felt my cock throb again. "I'm going to come," I groaned for the second time, thrusting deeper into Andy's warm, moist mouth.

Immediately he pulled me from between his lips with a wet smack. "Not yet," he commanded. He reached for the nightstand, took a condom from the top drawer, and unrolled it over my penis. "I want to watch you fuck my woman," he told me, and beckoned for Hope.

She murmured eager assent and my own agreement was apparent by my rampant penis, barely contained by the latex sheath. Hope straddled me, lowering herself until my cock was pressed against her slippery lips. She began to move, humping her wet slit against my hard shaft.

I pushed my cock into an upright stance so that Hope could impale herself upon it, but Andy caught her by the waist when her pussy was just shy of my pulsating cock. "How bad do you want her?" he asked me.

"Bad," I groaned, thrusting up with my hips.

He lifted her a bit higher. Hope submitted utterly, rising on her knees, although I could see how excited she was. Her face flushed and dreamy, her pussy swollen and dripping, and she was making small mewling sounds in the back of her throat.

Andy was becoming erect again as he cradled Hope against him, suspending a tantalizing few inches over my throbbing member.

"Isn't she beautiful?" he asked me, fingering her nipple lightly. "Isn't she the hottest woman you've ever seen?"

"She is," I agreed thickly, straining higher with my hips.

"You're so fucking sexy, babe," he whispered to her, clasping her close to his side. "Noah is so hot he can hardly stand it, and it's all because of you."

This wasn't entirely true and Andy knew it. He let his hand slide down over Hope's groin to wrap around my engorged cock, then eased her down a bit. My cock nudged the slippery lips and I reared up, almost crazed with lust. I nearly penetrated the velvety slit but Andy deflected me, blocking the slick opening with his hand.

"For Christ's sake, Andy," I snarled. I grabbed Hope's thighs and pulled her down against me, then yelped as Andy's fingers compressed around my cock.

"Let go of her," he snapped. The pressure eased as soon as I did, though he maintained a snug grip. Next he told me to raise my hands over my head, accompanying these instructions with a firm squeeze to my cock, and I complied. Did I mention that Andy is a passive sort? He is, usually, but there are occasions, very specific moments, when he *insists* on being the one in control.

"Take hold of the headboard," he ordered and I did, squeezing it so tightly that my knuckles turned white.

I saw him smile faintly. "That's a good boy," he said and rewarded me by slowly lowering Hope onto my raging hard-on. As I entered her, inch by inch, Andy kept one hand on my pelvis, letting me know by the pressure of his hand that he wanted me to remain still.

It was pure agony, yet torture of the sweetest kind. Her honeyed walls were slick and wet, constricting around my cock like a taut, soft glove. It required a maximum effort to remain still and I broke out in a sweat from the exertion.

When my cock was entirely encased in slippery flesh, Andy pressed his hand against the small of her back. "Now ride him, babe," he instructed her. "Give it to him good."

Hope began fucking me and it *was* good—*damn* good. I closed my eyes, inching my pelvis as far off the bed as I could without releasing my grip on the bedpost. Her tight pussy pulsated around my hard cock, oiling me in slippery juices. Andy urged her to a slow, measured cadence, her slick pussy creating a delicious friction against my straining cock, and I wanted more, wanted to roll her on her back and fuck the living shit out of her.

Andy could see this, I knew. He was eying me closely, watching for any evidence of disobedience and, when my hips lifted off the bed, he raised one dubious eyebrow.

"Looks like you need a little lesson, Noah. Have you forgotten how to obey?"

I knew what to expect when Andy straddled my face. He pushed his cock into my mouth, shoving it down my throat without any preamble. I wasn't prepared for it and made an attempt to draw back, but Andy's hand clamped onto my nipple and gave it a painful twist.

I made a muffled yelp and choked as he rammed into my throat. "Take it, you little cocksucker," he snarled. "Take *all* of it."

All of it was quite a lot, since Andy's cock is not overly thick but extremely long. I arched my neck to open my throat and took it in, every inch of it. The pressure on my nipple relaxed, became light, teasing caresses as I let him drill into me.

"That's right," he whispered. "Suck it good. You look beautiful with your mouth full of cock, Noah."

Hope's pussy slid over my cock while Andy's hard rod plunged in and out of my throat. My body was tense, tight as a whipcord with the effort of holding still, and my hands ached from their grip on the headboard.

Without warning, Hope pulled herself up and off of me. I cried out, my cock straining up into thin air. A second later Andy pulled his cock from between my lips and I was empty, bereft.

My arms were still over my head, locked into place by Andy's strong thighs. "Are you ready, Noah?" he whispered, his tantalizing cock bobbing just a few scant inches from my hungry mouth.

Ready? I was so hot I couldn't answer. I lunged at his cock, but he pulled back.

"*Are you ready?*" he asked again. I watched, hypnotized, as he cradled his cock in one hand, his fingers lightly stroking the slim, elegant length.

"I'm ready," I groaned, gyrating my hips impatiently. Ready for what I didn't know, but I'd take whatever he wanted to give me.

He rolled off me and I saw Hope lying back against the pillows, her legs spread wide with her pussy yawning open, glistening wet, her fingers touching between her legs. "Fuck me, Noah," she begged. "I want you inside me."

I wanted to be inside her, too, but I hesitated, looking up at Andy. A faint smile creased his face and I could see that my obedience had pleased him.

"Go ahead," he said gently. "You can have her."

I didn't wait for him to change his mind, but rolled on top of Hope and jammed my cock into her dripping pussy. She was hot and tight, and my cock was so hard it felt ready to burst.

I could have come right away, but instead I held back, sliding in and out of her at a slow, steady pace. I wanted to thrust and plunge frantically, but I sensed this was not what Andy wanted.

I was rewarded with a light touch between my buttocks. "I'm going to have *you* now," Andy breathed into my ear.

His fingers separated my cheeks of my ass and prodded delicately at my anus. It opened readily, eagerly, as Andy slipped two fingers deep inside. I kept up my slow, dreamy fuck rhythm as Andy's lips trailed down my body. His tongue traced a sensuous line past my shoulder blades, my waist, the small of my back, and culminated in a tantalizing tickling between my buttocks.

I spread my legs as far as I could to give Andy full access to my hungry hole. I felt his tongue prodding at my back door and when he thrust it into my ass I thought I would lose my mind. It felt so good, his long tongue delving deep into me, that I stopped fucking Hope and concentrated on grinding my ass against Andy's hot mouth.

He stopped. "Jesus, Andy, don't stop," I groaned, pressing my ass against him so hard that I almost slipped out of Hope's cunt. Then I jerked forward as he landed a sharp, stinging slap against my buttocks.

"Don't you dare neglect her," he snapped, and pushed my ass away from his mouth.

I resumed fucking the slippery female form beneath me, but my attention was on Andy. I knew he wasn't through with me yet, and this was confirmed when he reached past me.

"Ohhh." I breathed when I saw him retrieve another condom from the nightstand.

I heard him chuckle softly and a moment later there was a hot throbbing between the cheeks of my ass. "This is what you really want, isn't it, Noah? You might have your cock inside of my woman, but this is what you crave." Andy began swiveling his hips, screwing his cock into my tight asshole. "Isn't it, you little bitch?"

I moaned, my ass stretching wider to accept his cock. "Yes," I told him eagerly. "Yes, this is it…what I want…"

"Little bitch," he hissed softly, then suddenly thrust the full length of his cock up my ass.

My hips leapt forward and Hope yelped as I rammed into her pussy. Then Andy was fucking me with long, wondrous strokes. My ass flowered under the onslaught, and I matched his rhythm, fucking Hope as he fucked me.

The three of us moved together, a hot, thrusting triad of slippery sex. Andy gripped my hips as he fucked my ass and Hope's legs were locked around both of us. "Fuck me, baby," she groaned, and I did, not realizing that she wasn't talking to me until she spoke again. "Do it harder. Fuck me with Noah's cock."

Then she was coming, moaning and thrashing beneath me, and Andy's movements increased. He continued to plow my ass and I could feel pressure building up in my balls. "I'm going to come." I choked, slamming harder and harder against her.

"Do it, baby," Andy whispered in my ear. "Come for us."

I gave one hard, final thrust and my cock exploded inside of Hope's pussy. I cried out, arching my body back, but there was no stopping yet. Andy continued to fuck me, his movements becoming frantic as he built up to a fevered pitch. And when he came it was with a final thrust of such power that he made me cry out.

We were motionless for a moment, fused together, then I felt Andy relax. He eased his cock out of my ass and rolled to the side. I withdrew from Hope, and Andy stretched out between us, so that we could snuggle against him on either side.

We lay that way for a long time, our limbs loosely entwined. Hope was curled up like a cat, the curve of her back pressing against Andy's side, and my head was resting on his chest. I could feel the steady beat of his heart against my cheek. After a while I became aware of the sound of their breathing, slow and measured, and surmised that they both had fallen asleep.

How could they *sleep*? In a few short hours, the three of us would be standing together in front of an altar and I would be a witness as they recited their wedding vows. Weren't they worried about what that would be like? How could they not be? Then again, maybe they did this all the time, or perhaps I had just been a fling, a last hurrah before the two of them settled into the monotony of married life. But what if it hadn't, what if it meant something more, something bigger? Either way, how could they possibly *sleep?*

My uneasy ruminations were suddenly disrupted by a vibration, a rumble emanating from deep within Andy's chest. Startled, I lifted my head and looked at him.

He was laughing. Watching me, and laughing.

"What's so damn funny?" I hissed, whispering so I wouldn't wake Hope.

"*You* are," he whispered back. "I'm wondering how long you're going to lay there obsessing over what just happened before you give up and go to sleep."

"*Dick*." But my lips twitched as he pulled me a little closer. He kissed me gently, cupped my ass in his palm, and snuggled against Hope with me in his arms.

Just as I was drifting off, I was struck with a foreign thought. *Maybe, just maybe, there didn't have to be just One. Maybe there could be Two.*

Or maybe even Three.

Jayden Blake writes in Western Massachusetts, where she lives with her partner, dogs, and two gerbils named Lemmiwinks and Mr. Slave. Her work has appeared in the anthologies Swing!, Mammoth Book of Women's Erotic Fantasies, Best Women's Erotica, *and* Bi Guys, *as well as the web sites* The Erotic Woman, Clean Sheets, Three Pillows, New Camp Horror, *and* The Shadow Sacrament. *By day, she is a reference librarian.*

Cutz 'N' Fadez

R.L. PARKER

The fans were not working. They were only helping circulate the heat more. It didn't help that it was Saturday afternoon in the Midtown Blades barber shop, the hottest barber shop in all of Atlanta. On this day, the title "hottest" was only too real as the air conditioning was on the fritz. The only things providing relief from the heat were the ceiling fans and another smaller but louder fan by the door with a bucket of ice sitting in front of it, blowing water vapors through the small shop. Atlanta was suffering from a heat wave.

Only three barbers manned the tiny shop where the crowd of customers wanting a fresh haircut for summer was ever growing despite the stifling heat. Leon, the Jamaican dread, sat in his chair, spinning it around. Of the three barbers working he was the only one without a customer. Looking over at Borne, the lead and most popular barber's line of customers; and then at Trigg, the Dominican barber's line of customers, mostly Latino, he waited for somebody that was tired of waiting for an opening to come and get in his chair. He counted almost ten people in all waiting for a haircut. After five minutes he gave up.

"How com' nobody wan get in mi chair? I cut like di best of 'em," Leon asked while walking over to the radio and turning it to V103. The latest in urban music filled the air as he walked back over to his chair and admired himself in the mirror. Tall, dark and very slim, Leon played in his dreads that fell halfway down his back. Trigg and Borne both glanced over at Leon as he posed in the mirror.

"Maybe the reason you ain't got any customers is 'cuz you pay more attention to ya'self than them." Trigg laughed. Borne shook his head in agreement.

"Seriously, Leon, man, you too busy actin' like you pretty or something." Leon ignored both as he continued primping himself in the mirror.

"Damn, it's hot in here. The A/C guy s'pose to have been here yesterday," Borne said. "This is ridiculous. I'm 'bout to close shop up early today. We can't be open in the heat like this without air conditioning. That cool with you, Trigg? Leon ain't really got any reason to complain, not like he would lose customers." Borne was finished with his customer and saw that Trigg was almost done as well. Leon sucked his teeth and started taking off his barber's smock and headed to the back room to change.

"Yeah, that sounds good to me. I wanna go meet up with this shorty anyways."

Trigg finished up his customer in the chair and Borne told his customers that they were closing early. A collective groan was heard as he shuffled them out the door. Borne closed the blinds on the windows and locked the door after the last had left. Leon emerged from the back room dressed in a bright green, red, and yellow two-piece short suit with the shirt halfway unbuttoned and his hair wet.

"Aight, fellas. Mi gon take it to da house." Leon stopped in front of the mirror to check himself out again. Leon was not a bad-looking man. His dark chocolate skin contrasted favorably with the loud clothes he was wearing. He had a narrow, clean-shaven face with thick full lips and round brown eyes. Borne gave him a once-over and swore he saw a large print going down Leon's thigh. Thankfully his shorts were long enough to not embarrass himself.

"Cool. I'll let you out, man. I had locked the door. Nice… bright…outfit, by the way. Gonna need some shades to look at you for too long." Borne laughed as he escorted Leon to the door.

"You got jokes. But all di ladies, dem love mi style." This was true as Borne always saw a new woman bringing Leon to work every day.

"Link up wit mi lata, B. Holla at me, Trigg." Leon threw back the peace sign at Trigg as he walked out the shop.

As Leon walked down the sidewalk Borne locked the door and turned to face Trigg standing by his chair facing him with a broom in his hand. Trigg was short, about five feet eight inches and wide with broad shoulders. He was built like an offensive lineman but was very solid and well defined. His face was round and his eyes were a mocha brown. He had thick lips that were framed by a goatee. Borne felt his nature rising as he watched Trigg clean up his area. Trigg had cakes on him that would make even the straightest man look twice. Borne wondered if Trigg got down but was always afraid to ask or find out. He himself was not out but he also wasn't on the 'down low,' either. If any-one wanted to know all they had to do was ask. Borne had to shake himself out of his daze as Trigg had caught him staring. Was that a smile? Is he blushing?

"Yo, Trigg. Don't worry bout cleaning up. I got it covered. You said you had a date, right?"

"A what? Oh yeah! I'm supposed to be meeting up with some-one…but that can wait. I'll help you clean, if you want that is."

Hell yeah, I want your sexy ass to stay, Borne thought to himself. He really did want to holla at Trigg. But he decided that tonight wasn't the night.

"Nah, Trigg. I'm good. Go on ya date, man. I'll clean the shop. Call me tomorrow. We'll hang out. I don't think I'm gonna open back up until the A/C is fixed."

Trigg took off his smock and handed the broom to Borne. "Ight, man, I offered, tho. But I'll definitely hit you up tomorrow." Trigg grabbed his duffle bag that was by his chair and slung it over his shoulder.

"I'll get at you." Borne watched Trigg's ass bounce as he walked toward the door.

"Hey, make sure you lock it on your way out." Borne headed to the backroom of the barbershop. He remembered seeing a beer in the icebox when he was getting ready for work earlier. Having heard the door shut and the lock click, Borne found his beer in the fridge and popped open the can. The cold froth instantly chilled his body against the heat as he drank half the can in one gulp. Borne noticed that he had sweat through his shirt and decided to remove it. The full-length mirror in the corner caught Borne's reflection and he stopped to give himself the once over before resuming cleaning the shop.

Borne stood a good six-four with a medium complexion. His red-brown skin appeared flush from the heat. Borne noticed that he had begun to let himself go. Where his once well-defined six-pack lay was now a bit of a pouch. His chest was also a bit meati-er than he was used to but still held its musculature for the most part. His arms were still big and toned as he flexed in the mirror. Placing his right hand on his newly discovered gut he looked at the open beer in his left. Seeing a direct relation between the two, Borne tossed the beer into a nearby waste basket. The heat of the day returned. Borne leaned against the wall as he watched himself in the mirror touching himself. He slid his hand across his chest and tweaked his own nipple. The combination of the heat along with flashes of Trigg's perfect bubble ass had turned him on. He slowly moved both his hands to his pants and looked at his mirror double as he unbuttoned his pants and pulled down his zipper. Borne moaned slightly as he reached into his pants with one hand and grabbed his nipple again with the other. Borne's nipples proved very sensitive as they sprang to life under his touch. He pinched them harder with his thumb and index finger. A stiffening in his pants let Borne know that his not-so-lil' man was ready to play.

Slowly and carefully, Borne pulled out his awakening member, all while still watching himself in the mirror. A good circumcised nine inches and thick as a Red Bull can, Borne's manhood stood erect, begging for attention. Borne obliged. He began stroking himself, watching his hand glide back and forth over his throbbing shaft. He watched his actions in the mirror taking note of how he looked and breathed; His chest beginning to heave with heavy breaths as he fell deeper and deeper into his trance. Borne's pants began to slip down, exposing the crack of his own plump bubble. Borne pulled out his balls so that they too could enjoy the show. Borne closed his eyes as he continued to stroke. Leaning further back on the wall he began to gyrate his hips to match his hands' movements. Sweat started pouring from his body, all over his face, chest and gut making him gleam. He could feel himself getting more and more excited and knew that release was coming. He started stroking faster, his balls slapping wildly against his pants. A few more moments and he would come.

"Hello?" a male voice asked from within the shop. Borne stopped dead in his tracks and painfully stuffed his now leaking dick back into his pants.

"Yo Trigg, that you? What you forget?" Borne fastened and zippered up his pants as he emerged shirtless from the backroom. The man in the shop was not Trigg.

Borne lost his breath.

"I had come in for a haircut but the shop is empty. The door was open though and the sign in the window still says 'open.'" The man continued as he looked around the empty shop but mostly at Borne's shirtless body.

Thank God, I didn't flip the sign, Borne thought to himself. He still just looked at the man in his shop. The man stood about five-eleven or six-one and was stocky in build. A big boy for sure. He was thick from head to toe. Just how Borne preferred. Under a well kept fro' was the face of an angel. He was chocolate in complexion with hazel eyes and had a small nose and thick full pinkish lips. His face was a bit chubby like a child's, innocent yet unquestionably mischievous. He was wearing a tank top T-shirt over his large frame. It hugged him for dear life as it accentuated his belly and meaty chest. The man's big arms were exposed but they weren't flabby. Borne guessed that the man weighed about 230 pounds but carried it very well. His thick thighs tried but failed to conceal two of the biggest hams Borne had ever seen; only they weren't in the store or on the dinner table but were hidden in the back of the man's gray sweatpants.

"So…um…are you open?" the man asked. Borne wiped the imaginary drool off his face as he shook himself out of his fixation. He saw the man staring at his chest.

"Oh, yeah we're open...no... No actually I am closed. I thought the door was locked…"

"But the sign says different." The man pointed back at the sign in the window.

"Yeah, I didn't get a chance to..." Borne saw a look of disappointment fall on the man's face.

"But it's cool. I can cut you real quick. What type of cut you need?" Borne walked over to his barber's chair and brushed it off, motioning for the man to sit.

"I just want a fade, nothing special." Borne could smell strawberries as the man sat in his chair. He picked up his clippers and turned them on. The man turned back with a surprised look on his face as he stared at Borne's abdomen.

"Where's the smock?" Borne mentally smacked himself for rushing and thought of an excuse.

"Oh. Man! I'm sorry, it's so hot out today and the shop's A/C is broken. I can cut you like this, but if you're uncomfortable, I'll put a shirt on." The man turned back around and relaxed into the chair.

"I was talking about a smock for me. You're fine as is." Borne smacked himself again.

"Oh yeah, sorry about that." Both Borne and the man smiled as Borne put a smock on the man and tied some tissue around his neck to avoid irritation. The smell of strawberries filled his nose again. It came from the man's hair.

"So a fade, huh? I can do that. Any preference? High cut, low, or even all over?" Borne palmed the man's head. His hair was so soft. His manhood jumped in his pants.

"Even all over. The name's Quincy, by the way." Quincy shifted in the chair, moving his arms under the barber's smock.

"I'm Borne."

Borne began cutting Quincy's hair. He wanted to talk with Quincy but did not know where to start or what to say. He wanted to ask him what that fragrance was he was wearing that was turning him on so. How was his day? Where he had been all his life? Borne couldn't decide what to say first. Quincy decided for him.

"Man, this haircut already feels good. I had too much hair for this heat. I don't see how others do it. It's supposed to be even hotter tomorrow. It's already ninety-eight degrees and rising. These Georgia summers. Can't beat them." Borne saw light trickles of perspiration running down Quincy's temples and gently brushed them away.

"Yeah, man. That's why I closed shop. Imma keep it closed too until the damn A/C gets fixed." Borne noticed how Quincy kept shooting glances at him from the corner of his eyes.

"Seriously? I understand that, but hey, my dad is a repairman. I could have him come and look at it for you." Borne brushed up against Quincy. His stomach touched Quincy's face while his erect member, already straining against the thigh of his pants, rested against Quincy's arm. Quincy did not move away. He enjoyed the hardness on his arm and the clammy feel of Borne's stomach on his cheek. Borne swore that Quincy leaned in closer.

"Oh yeah? Leave me his number, man. I will give him a call." Borne continued to grind against Quincy as he finished the haircut. Quincy never objected.

"You got anything to drink? This heat has me dried out." Borne was spinning Quincy in the chair so that he could cut his hairline from a different angle. He stopped to think for a minute with Quincy directly facing him. Borne cut off the clippers and stood upright. His erection was in Quincy's face, daring him to do something.

"Nah, man, I don't. I had a beer but it's gone now. I could get you some water."

Quincy leaned forward and reached for Borne's pants. He pulled them down and grabbed Borne's fully awoke manhood.

"I don't really want any water. I was thinking about something else."

Before Borne could react Quincy had him down his throat, voraciously gobbling up Borne's dick. Borne lost his balance as Quincy pulled him forward as if he were going to swallow him whole. Quincy moaned in pleasure as he grabbed Borne's buttocks and squeezed them with all his strength causing Borne to cringe in pain. *That's going to leave a mark*, Borne thought.

Having regained his balance, Borne stepped all the way out of his pants so that he could better feed Quincy his dick. Quincy took all Borne had without missing a beat. Borne could see himself moving in and out Quincy's mouth and it only made him hornier. He pulled the smock off of Quincy only to find that Quincy's dick was already out and dripping with pre-cum. Borne lifted Quincy's shirt and started twisting his nipples. Quincy moaned in pleasure as Borne played with his chest. Borne started thrusting into Quincy's mouth, feeling his balls slap against Quincy's chin.

"Suck that dick, man. Damn. You gone make me bust in ya mouth."

"Yeah, baby, bust that nutt down my throat." Quincy demanded as he slapped his face with Borne's dick, licking it along the shaft, then sucking on his balls. Borne almost came when Quincy took both his nuts into his mouth but fought it back. He wasn't finished yet. Borne lifted Quincy's shirt all the way off and leaned over to suck on his chest with its half dollar-sized nipples. Quincy grabbed both his and Borne's dicks and rubbed them together while Borne sucked on his tits as if they were giving him life. Borne help Quincy slide his sweats off while sitting in the chair and held Quincy's ass in his hands. He could feel the heat coming off of it as he continued sucking Quincy's chest. He bit down on the nipple in his mouth causing Quincy to scream out in pain and scrape Borne's back with his fingernails. Borne tried slipping a finger into Quincy's hot hole but it was too tight. It would need some loosening up.

Borne dropped to his knees in front of Quincy and placed Quincy's legs up on the armrests of the barber chair. The hole winked at him as it was now exposed. Borne dove in face first. Quincy couldn't control himself as he wiggled about in the chair. Borne's long hard tongue darting in and out his ass in rapid-fire licks had Quincy reaching the breaking point. Quincy clamped down on the back of Borne's head and pulled him farther in his ass. Borne reached and grabbed Quincy's dick while tongue fucking him, jerking it in a hard and rough fashion. Quincy couldn't contain himself anymore. He came in a gush of white cream shooting all over his own gut and chest. Borne continued sucking on his hole as he watched Quincy spasm. He himself was still rock hard and his dick was begging for release. Borne looked over on his barber's stand and saw a tube of Vaseline. He quickly reached for it and scooped some of the thick grease out and rubbed it on his shaft. Standing and pushing Quincy's legs back behind his face, he rammed himself into Quincy's puckered hole. Quincy gasped out in pain as Borne plunged deep into him. Quincy could feel himself stretching as he tried to accommodate Borne's massive member. Borne silenced Quincy's yells by sticking his tongue down his throat. He thrust harder and harder into

Quincy as if he were an animal. Quincy braced himself with the armrests as Borne lay into him. Borne could tell Quincy was enjoying it because his dick had gotten hard again. He could feel it between their stomachs rubbing together as he dug deeper. Borne's balls were getting heavy and had tightened up. He was about to come. Borne pulled all the way out of Quincy for a moment, then plunged all the way back in and could feel Quincy's hole give way. Quincy felt himself about to come again. He pulled Borne over onto him and the two kissed as he shot hot nutt on the both of them, coating their merged skin in dripping juices. Borne bit down hard on Quincy's bottom lip as he tensed up and came inside his hungry hole; shooting wave after wave of pent-up orgasm into Quincy's ass. After squeezing out the last drop, the two collapsed on each other for a moment. Both were breathing heavy from exhaustion. Their closeness combined with the heat soaked them in their own sweat. Quincy wrapped his arms around Borne as he let his legs down. Borne was still inside him. After a few moments more, Borne got up and looked at Quincy. The two smiled at each other.

"So this is how you intended on paying me, huh?" Borne pulled out of Quincy, letting his dick plop out onto his thigh.

"Whatever, negro. I could tell you wanted it when I first saw you."

"This is true." The two laughed an uneasy laugh.

"But for real, I enjoyed myself and I hope you did, too." Before Borne could answer, the door to the shop opened. Borne turned to see Trigg staring at him and Quincy with a dumbfounded look on his face. His jaw was wide open in disbelief. Borne tried to cover himself as Quincy grabbed his clothes and started putting them on.

"I… I, uh just wanted to…never mind." Trigg started but did not finish as he turned and bolted out the door. Borne quickly pulled on his pants and ran after Trigg. He caught up to Trigg just as he was getting into his car. Borne open the passenger door and jumped into the car.

'Trigg, wait... I can explain." Borne was still out of breath from his session with Quincy and then chasing Trigg down the block.

"Yo! Get out my car. You ain't gotta explain." Trigg looked over at Borne with a look of hurt and anger on his face.

"I should have told you before about…about me being a homo… I just thought…" Borne's mind raced as he searched for the words. His heart was racing... but why?

"B, for real, you ain't gotta explain nothing to me. I already knew you was a fa…you were gay. I just never thought I would see you in, you know...the act." Borne's heart was still racing. Trigg was taking this too well.

"Trigg, man…I'm, I'm sorry." Was that all he could manage to say?

"Borne, you got company back in the shop. You should get back to him. I gotta get going. I don't even know why I came back. Get out my car, man! I can't really talk to you right now…I'll talk to you tomorrow at ya crib…"I'll even call first before I stop by," he added sarcastically. "Get out!" Trigg reached over and opened Borne's door. Borne looked over at Trigg and didn't recognize his friend. Trigg appeared to be shivering in anger and his eyes were watering. Borne felt guilty. He slowly got out the car.

"Yo, I'll be at my crib all day tomorrow. You come over whenever you want." Trigg did not say anything. Borne closed the door and Trigg's car, a late-model Mustang, sped off leaving skid marks in its wake.

When Borne got back to the shop he couldn't find any trace of Quincy. There was a note in his barber's chair with Quincy's number on it. It also had the number to Quincy's father's repair shop. Borne collapsed into the chair and threw his head back with a deep sigh.

"What a fucking day."

The next day Borne waited at his house in Decatur for Trigg, who never showed. He called Quincy and apologized for how things ended the previous day. Quincy accepted and the two set up a time to hook up again. Quincy would come by at the end of the week. Borne gave Quincy his address and they said their good-byes. After hanging up with Quincy, Borne tried calling Trigg but was sent straight to voicemail. Ten calls of being sent to voicemail later, Borne gave up in angry frustration and threw the phone against the wall of his living room. Borne called Leon. Leon hadn't heard from Trigg. He was thankful that Trigg hadn't called Leon and outed him, at least not yet. The phone started ringing. Borne quickly answered without waiting for the caller ID.

"Hello?" There was a pause before a recorded message played over the line stating that the appointment to have the air conditioning at the barbershop repaired was cancelled by the technician and needed to be rescheduled…again. Borne cursed loudly as he hung up the phone before the message had finished. He retrieved the paper with Quincy's dad's number on it and called and asked if he could come look at the unit. Midtown Blades had air conditioning by the end of the day.

The next day Borne re-opened the shop. It was a Monday but he figured he needed to make up for lost business. Surprisingly, the shop filled up quickly. The heat had not let up but at least the shop had air again. Leon was back to work and was excited to have customers lining up for him. The customers were Trigg's regulars. Trigg was not there nor had he called in. Borne decided to go and look for him.

"Hey, Leon. I'm leaving the shop for a minute. You'll be okay?" Leon was shocked because he had never been left in charge or alone before.

"Yea mon. Eryting be jus fine. Send ya customers ovr' fi mi'. Leon got it covered." Borne thanked Leon and tossed him the keys to the shop and hurriedly left out in search of Trigg. It was not like Trigg to ever miss a day of work. He figured he had given him time to cool off but he still couldn't understand why Trigg would be mad enough to avoid him, especially after admitting already knowing about him. Borne jumped into his old Chevrolet pickup truck and headed to Trigg's crib in the West End.

Fifteen minutes later Borne was pulling up into Trigg's driveway. Trigg lived alone and had a small but decent pad with a garage, which was half open. A sense of relief rushed over Borne as he saw Trigg in his garage working on a racing motorcycle. Trigg looked up briefly to see who had pulled into his yard. He continued working without acknowledging Borne as he walked up. Borne did not seem to notice through his relief.

"Hey Trigg, man! Where you been? Ya phone off or something?"

"What's up, B? Nah, it's on." Trigg was shirtless with a pair of torn shorts on as he worked on his bike. Borne stopped to look at all of Trigg's stocky body as its muscles moved under his skin, busy at the task at hand. Borne put a hand on Trigg's shoulder to try and get his attention.

"I been trying to call you. I wanted to talk to you about…about the other day."

Trigg turned to face Borne but found himself staring directly at his crotch. Trigg stood up and sat on his bike.

"Man, I told you it's cool. I'm done wit that." He couldn't look Borne in the eyes.

"Then why you don't answer the damn phone? Why you won't come to work? If you are so 'okay' with it, why are you avoiding me?"

"I dunno…I'm sorry. I guess I was just, I dunno, more mad than anything."

Borne stopped and looked at Trigg inquisitively. What could he be mad about? Trigg turned and faced him while still sitting on his bike.

"I was mad…mad because I had come back for you. I cancelled wit my shorty and was gonna chill wit you. Had I known that you would be…with someone else, I wouldn't have bothered." Borne could see tears welling in Trigg's eyes.

"So what exactly are you trying to say, Trigg?" Trigg stared down at the floor for a moment, then back up at Borne.

"Man, I don't know what I'm saying. I just…I guess I just like you. More than just as boys, yo. I knew you got down because I've seen you around. I never was comfortable enough to just come out and tell you. When I saw you wit that other dude tho, that shit hurt me. I just couldn't be around you right then."

Borne walked over to Trigg and stood close enough to smell the sweat and grease coming off Trigg's body. He took Trigg's face in his hand and lifted it to meet his eyes.

"Man…wow…had I known how you felt, then I would have been kickin' it with you. I know you've seen how I been sweatin' you in da shop and when we hang out. Damn, Trigg. All that time gone by…wasted when we could have been…"

"Well, who says we still got to wait? You know how I feel and I know you want me. Let's just go from here. I couldn't take seein' you with somebody else. Be with me."

"You ain't said nothing but a word."

Borne bent over and kissed Trigg as hard as he could. He poured all his passion and wants into Trigg's warm welcoming embrace. Trigg matched Borne's intensity as he finally gave in to his own wantings. While still kissing, Trigg undid Borne's pants and slipped them down to the hot garage floor. He was greeted by Borne's rock-hard manhood, already at full attention. The smell of Borne made Trigg's mouth water as he took Borne all the way into his mouth. Borne could have cum right then. He had always lusted after and wanted Trigg and now he finally had him. Trigg wanted him too though as he digested Borne with deep thrusts and lustful moans.

Borne wanted in on the action as he lowered Trigg down to the concrete and laid him on his back all while never leaving his mouth. He saw Trigg's huge dick straining against his shabby shorts. Borne ripped it free and stared at the thick uncut dick as if it were a new toy before he engulfed all eight inches of it. Trigg moaned in pleasure as he felt Borne's hot wet mouth surround his dick. He sucked on Borne even harder as he started gyrating his dick into Borne's throat. The two of them rolled and rocked about on the floor as they tried to eat each other alive. Borne tasted precum on Trigg's dick and wanted him to finish. He grabbed Trigg's perfectly rounded ass and spread it apart. He fingered the hole for a minute before plunging it deep into Trigg. Trigg let out a muffled cry as Borne searched for his prostate; when he found it, he gently applied pressure to it. Trigg tried to yell in ecstasy but was gagged by Borne's massive tool. Trigg shot off into Borne's mouth, just as Borne wanted. He drank Trigg's orgasm, sucking and licking on his head until it was completely dry.

They got up off the floor, kissing each other with ferocious wet kisses. Trigg leaned back onto his motorcycle and Borne collapsed on top of him; sucking his neck until he knew a mark would be left, then biting Trigg's nipples. Borne tore off Trigg's shorts and wrapped Trigg's thick thighs around him as he planted his feet firmly on the floor on either side of the bike. Trigg arched his back to try and meet Borne halfway.

Borne looked down at the longtime man of his affection. He couldn't believe this was finally happening. Trigg gave him a wanting look while sucking in his bottom lip. Borne's heart skipped a beat. This was more than what it seemed. Without words, Borne eased himself into Trigg's warmth. He was already dripping wet and like a suction device, grabbed hold of Borne and pulled him all the way in.

Neither wanted the moment to end as they kissed and fell into love. The two melted into one as a gentle breeze blew into the garage from outside. They didn't take notice or care that they may be seen by the cars passing by outside nor did they hear the chorus of light taps on the roof as rain began to fall.

The heat wave was broken.

෨ඥ

R.L. Parker is a new voice to be heard in the land of fiction. Flesh to Flesh *will be his first published work but expect more from this promising new talent. He is currently working on a novel follow-up to his story, "Cutz 'N' Fadez." Mr. Parker is currently finishing his bachelor's degree in Atlanta where he resides with his partner.*

Heaven Sent

MICHAEL FLETCHER COOPER

Tonight was going to be my night. It seemed like it had been forever since Corey and I had gone out to the club together for a night of drinking and dancing. The icing on the cake was that my best friend Anthony and his boyfriend Shawn were joining us. I have to admit that at first, I wasn't feeling much like going out. I mean, I had a lot of work to get done and I only had the weekend to do it. The only reason that I decided to go was because Anthony and Shawn had begged me to put the books away for an evening and come spend some time with them. I had been really busy lately having to juggle my school-work with my job at the restaurant, which left little time for hanging out with my friends or spending quality time with Corey. I knew that Corey had been feeling a little neglected lately, so I decided to go out to show my baby that after nine months, he still meant the world to me.

I was just putting my diamond studs in my ears when Corey came into the bathroom.

"Baby, Anthony just called and said that him and Shawn are downstairs waiting. You ready?" he asked me as he kissed me on the cheek and patted me on my ass. "Damn, I love them cakes, Jaylen!" He flashed that goofy grin that I loved so much and looked at me with longing in his eyes as he licked his sexy lips.

"I know you do, baby," I replied as I kissed him, "but like you said, the lovebirds are downstairs waiting on us. And you know if we stay up here much longer, they're liable to leave our asses!"

"Aiight, baby," he said with a hint of disappointment in his voice as he followed me into the foyer, "but you belong to me when we get back, angel."

"Boy, you already know everything I got belongs to you," I said as we stepped out of our one-bedroom apartment into the cool evening air. We rushed down the stairs to Shawn's silver Honda Accord and jumped in the backseat just in time to see Anthony and Shawn ending what appeared to be a very deep and passionate kiss.

"You two can't keep your hands off of each other for even five minutes, can you?" I jokingly asked as Shawn cranked up the car and backed out of the parking space.

"Bitch, you had us waiting for about ten minutes. You know you ain't never on time for nothing," Shawn shot back as he gave Anthony a quick peck on the cheek before pulling out onto the busy street.

"The last time I heard, you only needed ten minutes," I snapped back as I playfully nudged Shawn. "Anyway, how are you doing, Anthony?"

"Girl, I'm hanging in there as always," Anthony answered. "And you?"

"I'm good," I answered back. "You know these English papers have been trying to kick my ass but I figured I would feature ya'll tonight and come on out."

"Well, we're glad that both you and Corey could make some time for lil' ol' us," Shawn said as he pulled onto the interstate. "Corey, my man, you been hanging in there?"

"Yeah, I can't really complain. This one ain't been showin' me no love lately, but everything else is cool," he said playfully as he pulled me close, allowing my head to rest on his muscular chest. Corey and I seemed made for each other, like two pieces of a puzzle that fit together so perfectly and effortlessly. As I lay there, I thought about the past nine months with Corey and where our relationship was going. We had hit a few bumps in the road, but for the moment, all I knew was that I was as in love with him now as I had ever been.

We soon pulled up to the club and immediately noticed all the people in line. I guess we weren't the only ones who had gotten the "Free b4 Midnight" text message because the line was practically wrapped around the building. Shawn parked the car and Anthony and I both proceeded to look ourselves over one more time in our respective mirrors.

"What ya'll gotta look in the mirror for?" Corey asked with a quizzical look on his face. "I mean, who ya'll trying to look good for?" Corey looked toward Shawn for the assist.

"Yeah. I mean, ya'll already know who ya'll are going home with," Shawn said matter-of-factly as Anthony and I jumped out of the car to join our awaiting men.

"This is true," I answered as I applied some ChapStick to my lips to put the finishing touches on my look. I smacked my lips at Corey, and smiled. "It's always important for a young man to look his best. Besides, you never know who you will run into."

Anthony and I walked arm in arm like two giddy girls at their first college party while Shawn and Corey walked close behind us, talking about the latest basketball scores.

As we got closer, I think we noticed all the stares that we as a group were getting. And when I thought about it, we did look kinda fly. For starters, I had on a form-fitting sky-blue hoodie with light-denim, stonewashed jeans, topped of with my white-and-sky-blue Chucks. My Corey had on a matching sky-blue-and-white jersey, which showed off his caramel-colored and divinely chiseled body, and a sky-blue diamond stud in his right ear. Even Anthony and Shawn looked cute in their corresponding red-and-white his and his T-shirts. Anthony's had three-quarter-length sleeves and Shawn's was sleeveless to show off his rippling biceps.

Corey approached me and held me from behind by my waist. I guess he felt as if he had to mark his territory being the alpha male that he was because there were definitely some cuties in line. I followed suit by leaning into Corey and clasping my hands into his. If I didn't know any better, I would have thought that we were in a chocolate factory because there were caramel men, milk chocolate men, dark chocolate men, and from their stares, I'm sure that all of them wanted at least one of us to give them a taste. Even though none of them held a candle to Corey and his "Boris Kodjoe" good looks, there were indeed some fine brothas in our midst. I'm just saying…

When we finally made it to the front of the line, we entered the club and were immediately bombarded by the loud music blasting from the speakers and the multi-colored fluorescent lights beaming down on us from above. We all walked through the lobby area and made our way to the bar on the other side of the club. To start, I ordered a Tropical Martini. Corey ordered a Blue Motherfucker and Anthony and Shawn both had Sex on the Beach. What else, right? After I downed a few more martinis and sipped on everyone else's drinks, I definitely loosened up. I don't know if it was the alcohol or the DJ, but we were all definitely feeling the music, and we let that dance floor have it. If I wasn't making Corey feel my fire by dipping it low to Eve's "Tambourine," I was grinding my pelvis into his in sync with the beat of Destiny's Child's "Lose My Breath." It seemed as if DJ Diamond was using a playlist right out of my head. When he slowed it down with Ruff Endz's "Someone to Love You," Corey held me firmly yet tenderly with his muscular arms, and we melted like ice into each other's arms as we rocked back and forth to the mellow beats.

"I love you, Jaylen," Corey gently whispered in my ear as we swayed back and forth to the soulful stylings of Keyshia Cole's "Heaven Sent," "and I never want to let you go."

"I love you, too, Corey," I answered back. "And if it's up to me, we will hold on to each other forever."

Just as the song ended and we released our embrace, I felt a tap on my shoulder. I whirled around to see the last person whom I expected to see: my ex-boyfriend Marcus.

"Oh my God!" I said, feeling surprised, nervous, and excited all at the same time as I gave him a hug. "When did you move back to Atlanta?"

"I actually moved back about a month ago," Marcus answered as he flashed his pearly whites. "You look good, by the way."

"Aww thanks," I said as I blushed a little bit. Marcus always did have the ability to make me feel so special, but I snapped out of that trance as soon as I looked over at Corey and saw the look on his face. "Marcus, this is Corey."

"Nice to meet you, Corey," Marcus said as he extended his right hand.

"Yeah, you too," Corey said in a flippant manner as he reluctantly shook Marcus' hand.

"Well, I'm gonna get back to my friends," Marcus started. "I just saw you from across the room and thought I would come speak. We should all get together sometime. Maybe go to a movie or something. Anyway, it was good to see you, Jaylen. Nice to meet you, Corey."

As Marcus walked away, I turned to Corey and noticed a look of frustration and anger on his face. I reached for his hand and he quickly yanked it away from me.

"What's wrong with you?" I asked in sheer confusion.

"Jaylen, if you don't know, then it's whatever," Corey answered back with blatant disapproval in his voice.

"Oh my God," I sighed in frustration. "Are you mad because I gave Marcus a hug? Baby, you know I'm yours so I hope that's not what you're tripping about."

"Man, whatever, Jaylen," Corey replied as he threw his hands up and turned his back on me. "You don't even see what the problem is. You know what? I need to walk away for a minute. I'll catch up with you later." Corey walked off the dance floor, leaving me absolutely stunned, not to mention alone.

Is he serious with this? I stood there and thought about what had just happened when I realized that I was sweating up a storm. I walked across the club to the bathroom to freshen up. I headed back to the dance floor and was grooving to a new beat when I felt two familiar arms lock around my waist. To my surprise, I turned to see Marcus smiling at me.

"So, we meet again," Marcus said in a sly manner as he gently caressed my cheek. "Where's your friend?"

"I don't know where he went," I answered hurriedly. A feeling began to come over me that I was trying hard to fight. And I knew that if I stayed around Marcus any longer, I would be in danger of succumbing to it. All the alcohol in my system wasn't helping matters much either.

"I didn't want to take up too much of your time," Marcus said as he looked into my eyes. "I just wanted to say that it was good to see you—really good." He put his hands around my waist, brought me into him, and kissed me gently, yet passionately, on the lips. For a second or two, I felt myself kissing Marcus back, and I instantly pulled away from him.

"I can't, Marcus," I said as I forced myself out of his grasp. "Corey is my boyfriend."

"Oh," Marcus responded with a surprised look on his face. "I had no idea. I didn't mean to disrespect you or your relationship, Jaylen. I promise. Well, you got my number so just get at me sometime, okay?" Marcus gripped my hand tightly one last time before he turned and disappeared into the massive crowd of sweating, gyrating bodies.

I turned around to go search for Corey, but I didn't have to look long to find him; I didn't even have to move an inch. He was standing maybe twenty feet from me, and we were looking directly into each other's eyes. I could see the pained expression on his face and instantly I knew what he had just seen. He turned away from me and walked through the doorway as I stood paralyzed on the edge of the dance floor. When I regained the ability to move, I tried my best to find Corey; I found Anthony instead.

"Have you seen Corey?" I asked Anthony in something of a panic.

"Yeah boo," Anthony answered hesitantly. "He's outside with Shawn and he's definitely more than upset. They sent me to come find you because they are ready to go."

I explained to Anthony what had happened with Marcus as we

walked out of the club to the car. When we got to Shawn's Accord, Corey was sitting in the passenger seat, so Anthony and I climbed in the back. I could tell he was mad just by looking at him through the car window. He didn't even look at me. During the car ride back to our place, Shawn and Anthony tried their hardest to relieve some of the tension in the air, but they were unsuccessful. When Shawn pulled into our apartment complex, Corey quickly said good-bye to everyone and jumped out of the car, somewhat slamming the car door.

"Good luck, honey," Anthony said in a reassuring tone as he gave me a hug. "Go make things right, okay? Even though you hurt him, he definitely loves you, Jaylen. He's stubborn, but he will listen to what you have to say."

"Thanks Anthony," I replied as I exited the car. "Good night, Shawn," I said as I closed the car door.

"Good night," Shawn answered back. "Now go get ya man."

As the headlights of the Accord disappeared into the night, I reluctantly headed up to the second level of our building. I could feel the tension in the air before I even opened the door to our apartment. *He didn't even keep the door open for me?* I thought. As I closed the door behind me, I could hear the television in the bedroom, which I knew from experience meant that Corey was in no mood to talk. As I entered the bedroom, I sat down slowly on the bed next to Corey. I could feel him tense up as if he was suppressing his anger with every fiber in his body. With the *Golden Girls* up to their usual antics on the screen, I attempted to reach out and touch Corey's hand.

"Don't fuckin' touch me!" Corey barked as he snatched his hand away and threw the remote control against the wall. He stormed out of the room. I jumped as the remote control hit the wall, yelled out his name and hurried out the room after him.

When I reached the living room, he was grabbing his car keys. I cut him off at the pass, throwing myself in between him and the apartment door.

"Jaylen, get outta my fuckin' way!" The anger in Corey's voice made me cringe, but I didn't budge.

"Baby, we need to talk," I said calmly as I touched his arms, which were as silky as caramel and muscular out of this world. I have to admit it turned me on a bit.

He shrugged me off and looked at me as if I had made a statement that was impossible for him to grasp. "Oh, so I'm ya 'baby' now?" he asked. "When you introduced me to that muthafucka at the club, I wasn't ya 'baby.' And I damn sure wasn't ya 'baby' when you had that fool's tongue in ya mouth!" He turned his back on me.

"Corey," I started as I put my hand on his back. Even through his jersey, I could feel the well-defined muscles of his back. "You know I love you, Corey. You mean the world to me. I don't know what else to say but I'm sorry. I really am."

"Man, you wasn't even thinking about me, were you? You seemed pretty content with the fact that he was kissing you. I was watchin' you the whole fuckin' time, Jaylen. You kissed him back and we both know it. You don't even have to say shit 'cuz I know you did!" Corey violently pushed my hand away, causing me to lose my footing for a moment.

As I stood there, I could see that Corey was becoming more and more agitated. His veins were practically popping out of his neck and he punched his palm with his fist. I didn't know what else to say, so I just said the first thing that came to my mind.

"Yeah, I kissed him back for a second, Corey," I admitted, "but I instantly stopped. I promise. And I did tell him that you were my boyfriend. I would never jeopardize our relationship on purpose. I was a little tipsy, and besides that, I didn't know that he was going to kiss me, Corey."

"So I'm supposed to excuse ya'll kissin' cuz he didn't give you a warning and 'cuz you was drunk?" Corey snapped back cynically. "Oh, well, excuse the fuck outta me! I didn't realize that alcohol dictated what you did and did not do."

"I guess I deserve that, Corey," I meekly replied, "but trust me when I say that Marcus is an ex and that's what I intend to keep him. You are who and what I want, Corey." I stepped toward him.

"I can't do this with you right now," Corey said as he let out an exhale of frustration and stepped back. "I could really hurt you right now, Jaylen." I could detect a slight whimper in his voice as he headed once again for the door.

"So you're just going to leave me, Corey? We need to talk about this, baby," I said in an exasperated way as I once again stepped in front of the doorway.

"Why don't you call Marcus and talk to him about it?" Corey asked sarcastically as he looked at me with a smug look on his face.

"Maybe I will," I snapped back. Instantly, I regretted saying that. I had wanted to say something that would get to Corey, but I wasn't ready to see the pained expression that appeared on his face.

"What the fuck did you just say to me?" Corey asked with a look of disbelief on his face. "I can't believe you just said that shit to me, you fuckin' bitch!"

"What did you just call me?" I asked like I was in search of clarification. I know he didn't just say that to me.

"I called you a 'fuckin' bitch'…"

Before I knew it, my hand left my side and slapped Corey across the face. Corey didn't even give me a chance to run.

Almost instantly, he grabbed me by my shoulders, hoisted me up, and forcefully pressed my back against the door. I was stunned; we had never been violent with each other before. As I looked at him with both anger and fear in my eyes, my vision became blurred with tears. Instantly, the angry expression on his face softened and I could see the liquid veneer that was beginning to cover his beautiful hazel, almond-shaped eyes. A solitary teardrop fell from my eyes as one drop fell simultaneously from each of his. It was in that instant that I knew what love was.

"Damn, I love you, angel," he said to me as I wiped the tears away from his cheeks.

"I love you too, Corey," I said, another single tear falling on my cheek. I needed to show him how much.

With that, still hoisted off the ground, I wrapped my legs tightly around Corey's waist and drew him close to me. I was determined to show him how much he meant to me. Our lips touched, and at that moment, I knew that tonight was going to be magical. I held onto Corey for dear life as our tongues became intertwined like two strands of a Twizzler candy. He palmed my ass and continued to kiss me passionately as he carried me to the bedroom. Once in the bedroom, he put me down and placed his hands inside of my black-and-red Calvin Kleins, gently squeezing my ass. Simultaneously, I lifted his jersey up over his head and started to nibble on his neck, marking my territory.

"Damn, baby," he moaned in ecstasy as I gently pulled at his neck with my teeth while I ripped off my hoodie. I was going to give Corey all that I had if it was the last thing I did. When I had satisfied his neck, I moved up to his ears. I covered more places on his ear than a Q-tip, licking every crevice of his ear, both inside and out. I traced the inside of his ear with my tongue, making him quiver involuntarily. As I snacked on his ears, he attempted to take my pants off, but I stopped him. He was my prince and I didn't want him to have to lift a finger; I wanted him to sit back and let his angel bless him in ways he never even dreamed about. I wanted him to lift something later on, but his finger wasn't what I had in mind.

With his jersey off, I moved quickly down to his nipples, which I knew were two of his hot spots. I would hit the others later, but for now, I was hungry and Corey's nipples were the perfect appetizer. I started with his right nipple, teasing him by circling my tongue around his nipple's periphery before going in for the kill. Corey liked his nipples bitten and sucked rough, and I was just the man to do it. I pulled, bit, and nibbled at his nipples like I was a newborn baby waiting to be satisfied by his mother's milk. The shakes of Corey's body and the ear-piercing moans that escaped his mouth reassured me that I was indeed doing my job and doing it well. I ran my tongue from the base of his Adam's apple, down the dip created by the perfectly chiseled pecs of his chest, and across the rolling waves of his stomach created by his flawless six-pack. I slowly made my way down to Corey's pelvis, and I pulled the waistband of his boxers down just enough to reveal the top of his crotch as I tickled the spot with my tongue. He shook as I pulled off his briefs, leaving his naked caramel body lying helpless on the bed. His body was my caramel kingdom, and tonight I was in total control of the land. I quickly took off the rest of my clothes and went back to exerting my power and reign over my man's kingdom. I traced the "V" of his pelvis with my tongue as I squeezed his nipples with my fingers. Corey's caramel scepter jumped every time a part of me touched his body, and I was more than ready to devour every single inch of it. Tonight, his every wish was my demand. Staying true to form,

I first teased the head of his dick, licking it ever so gently with my tongue. Spiraling around his caramel scepter, I ran my tongue down the shaft and back, planting gentle kisses along the way. Once I was done teasing him, I went in for the kill and as I did, Corey let out the most sensual "Ahh" that I had ever heard. Corey tasted so good, and even though his dick wasn't an M&M, he melted in my mouth like no other. I slid it in and out of my mouth hard yet gently, working both my mouth and my tongue in ways I never had before. I headed back to the tip of his golden scepter and licked up his sweet nectar, allowing his sexual juices to mix freely with my rushing river of saliva.

He begged for me to stop, but I wasn't done yet. However, I guess he wasn't having it because he sat up, grabbed me, and kissed me passionately. Then, he flipped me over and started to run his tongue down the back of my body all the way to the small of my back. He paused for a moment and gently spanked my ass. I love it when he takes control. He kissed my ass in several places before gently parting it like the Red Sea and soothingly ran his tongue up and down the entryway to my candy shop, causing me to become temporarily paralyzed. To add insult to injury, he blew his soft, sweet breath into my hot, quivering flesh, which he knew drives me crazy. He stuck his tongue in and I couldn't help but tightly clench the down comforter as he devoured my chocolate cake like it was his last meal. I begged for mercy; he showed none. He was driving me wild, his tongue exploring my ass like it was an undiscovered land. As he intensely nibbled on my Georgia peach, licking up its sweet juices in the process, he palmed, caressed, and gently spanked my ass. He spread my legs even wider and shoved his tongue even deeper inside of me, making me call out his name. There was not one spot on either of my chocolate walls that his tongue didn't cover. He circled his tongue around as if it was running laps as he ferociously licked up every grain of sugar and ounce of chocolate that my ass had to offer.

All of a sudden, he picked me up by my legs and carried me over to the wall, continuing to eat me up the whole time. His caramel scepter once again began to call my name. I took the opportunity to answer the call and, wrapping my legs around his neck, sucked his dick like it held a liquid that was vital to my life. After Corey had satisfied his voracious appetite with my dessert, he held me upright so that my legs were wrapped around his waist and my eyes were looking dead into his.

"Are you ready for me, baby?" Corey asked in that deep, sensuous voice that I had fallen in love with.

"You know I am," I answered back as I braced myself to be taken over by the power of his kingdom.

My body was calling out for Corey; I was ready for our bodies to become one. He easily slid his scepter inside of me as if my body was the lock and his the key. I bit my bottom lip in the heat of passion and prepared myself to be ruled all night long. Corey started off slow and gentle at first, palming my ass as he slid it up and down on his dick. While making love to me, he carried me over to the bed and before I knew it, he was on top of me and was in total control of my body. I held onto him for dear life as he thrust his throbbing scepter deeper and deeper inside my candy shop. I called out his name in a fit of ecstasy as I dug my fingers into his back. Our bodies melted together and became one as we made love. He propelled his pulsating dick deeper, harder, and faster inside of me as the sweat generated from our passion ran down our glistening bodies.

"Do you love me, angel?" Corey asked as he looked into my eyes, his dick claiming more and more of my body.

"You know I do," I whispered back, barely able to speak due to the power that was taking over me.

"You better," he said matter-of-factly as he plunged his dick in a rhythmic staccato-like fashion to make his point very clear.

The heat generated by the friction of our bodies was almost as intense as the feeling of ecstasy that ran throughout my body. This feeling was heaven.

"Baby, I'm about to cum," Corey warned as his body tensed up in preparation for the explosion.

"Me too," I responded as I prepared myself for impact. "Make me feel you, *papi*."

Simultaneously, I felt Corey's scepter swell and burst inside me as Corey yelled, "Jaylen!" as I exploded, showering my stomach as well as Corey's with the creamy, hot liquid that shot out like a geyser. I moaned Corey's name as our bodies shuddered and convulsed in unison following the release of our pent-up anger and passion.

A few minutes later, as we lay in the bed cuddled up, I couldn't help but think about the night's events and how my love for Corey far surpassed any romantic love that I had ever known.

"Jaylen?" Corey asked as we sat looking out the balcony window at the beautiful oncoming sunrise.

"Yes, Corey?" I answered as I sat up and looked into those hazel, almond-shaped eyes.

"I love you, angel," he whispered, "and never want to let you go."

"I love you, too, *papi*," I whispered back, "and if it's up to me, we will hold onto each other forever."

As I looked off into the distance at the fiery sun with Corey's arms around me holding me tight, I thanked God for blessing me with my angel.

ဆာ⃝ဃ

Michael Fletcher Cooper, a native of Lithonia, Georgia, is currently a twenty-one-year-old college senior attending Morehouse College. Graduating in May 2008 with a bachelor of arts degree in English and a minor in psychology, Michael has served in many capacities during his time at Morehouse. He is a member of several organizations including the Sigma Tau Delta National English Honor Society and Psi Chi National Psychology Honor Society and is also a resident assistant and an English tutor. As a proud gay African-American man and an aspiring author, "Heaven Sent" is Michael's first step toward achieving his dream of becoming a prominent name in the literary genre of African-American gay fiction. His vivacious and outgoing personality is what has gotten him to this point in his life, and he hopes to continue to make his mark. Michael would love to hear from you, so feel free to contact him at Aries_BoiAngel@yahoo.com.

Blow the Horn
WASHINGTON PARKS

I f he could just relax and breathe, then it would be much easier; but, he couldn't relax and the pain was too much to bear. He braced himself against the wall as he felt his insides light on fire. A hand on the back of his head pushed him into the pillows while the other grabbed his hips firmly and held him in place. He could feel it inside him, ripping its way through him as his inner lining collapsed around the intruder. His partner made no efforts to ease his discomfort as his dick tore its way through him. Sweat dripped from his body as stroke after stroke went into him; would there be no end? Tears had begun to well up in his eyes; he could feel himself bleeding from the penetration…he needed to get away, to escape from…

"Reginald, hit the showers!" screamed Coach Johnson.

The sound of the coach's rugged voice snapped Reginald Graham out of his trip down memory lane. He continued to run around the track and shook off the sound of his name as it echoed across the field. He hated his name. He always told people to call him Reggie or nothing at all. His football coach, Mack Johnson, never seemed to care how much his legal name irked him.

Coach Johnson made Reggie run laps while the rest of the team practiced. It was his punishment for a long night of partying when he should have been resting. Coach Johnson figured that two-and-a-half hours of running was enough for one day and dismissed Reggie to the showers.

Reggie collapsed onto the track that had been his bane. The heat of the sun had made it unbearable to run on pavement in track shoes. He had long since discarded his shirt, revealing his smooth muscular brown frame. He was short for his age of nine-teen—about five feet eight inches—too short for the football team, or at least in Coach Johnson's mind. He never wanted to play Reggie, but the kid was a box of lightning wrapped in dyna-mite. He could always be counted on in a pinch to deliver yards when time was short and field was long.

Nobody on the team acknowledged Reggie as he lay on the track. After a few minutes he finally picked himself up and walked back toward the locker room, dejected. On the practice field adjacent to the game field where the football team was practic-ing, he could hear the marching band getting ready for their performance at the game later that week. They were playing against A&T, which was always a big game for St. Augustine's.

Reggie decided to let the showers wait as he instead walked over to watch the band practice. He took a seat in the stands as he watched his roommate and best friend, TJ, who was on the drum line. Reggie watched from atop the hill as the band played on. He was awed by all the formations and dance movements they exhibited all while never missing a note or step. St. Augustine's Marching Band was nationally ranked and many of its members went on to successful careers in music after college.

Reggie spotted TJ among the sea of shiny instruments and legs. TJ was third chair in the drum line. His quad drums required a strong back and excellent hand-to-eye coordination. TJ's light-skin tone had been reddened by the heat and his tall, wiry frame deceived most from the power he held in his skinny body and long thin arms. He also had an impressive bubble on his backside that bounced with each step. TJ was standing in mid-field with a trumpet player, performing a duet.

Odd combination, trumpet and drum, Reggie thought. But as he listened to the enchanting sounds, he realized the combination worked well. Reggie continued to stare, amazed at the trumpet player: a tall, medium-built brother with thick thighs and high cheekbones with his hair in braids and flowing down his back. As Reggie became more enchanted, the sounds of their concerto faded into the background, he followed the movements of the man with the trumpet with interest. Becoming lost in thoughts and fantasy, as well as his growing erection, he imagined burying his manhood deep into the trumpet player's ass while TJ stroked his mouth. He could see the trumpet player hungrily taking both of their cocks into his mouth at the same time. Reggie began rubbing his erection inside his uniform as he sat back and let his thoughts run wild. After becoming lost in his daydream he hadn't noticed that the band had dispersed. Practice was over. TJ called his name out from the field. Reggie shook off his fantasy and went down to meet his friend. The trumpet player was still there talking with TJ as Reggie approached. His pants grew even tighter as he tried to conceal himself.

"Wassup, fool?" TJ greeted his friend with the customary handshake, pulling Reggie into him.

"Not shit, my dude," Reggie managed to garble out as he cleared his throat. He turned to face the trumpet player.

"My bad. Reggie, this is Caleb. We got a duet together for this new song the band is performing. We debut it for the game on Friday." Caleb reached out his free hand to Reggie who quickly grabbed it.

"Wassup?" Caleb shyly asked.

"Nothing. What's good?" Reggie asked, hoping he wasn't blushing. He would blame it on the heat if it was that obvious. An uncomfortable silence descended on the small group as Reggie and Caleb looked at each other.

"So Caleb, we hooking up tonight to work on this duet right?" TJ asked, finally breaking the silence. Caleb had still been staring at Reggie's chocolate body.

"Oh yeah. Just swing by my place. My roommates won't be there. What time? Around eight p.m.?"

"Yeah, that sounds good. So I guess I'll see you then," TJ replied.

"Okay, bet. I'm gonna get going. See you tonight, TJ. It was good meeting you, Reggie."

Caleb was still staring at Reggie and TJ definitely noticed this time.

"Hey, you too, man," Reggie replied to Caleb as he walked off leaving the two roommates standing on the field. The sun was beginning to set as the stadium lights began to automatically flicker on. TJ smiled slyly at Reggie who gave him a quizzical look in response.

"What?"

"Negro, please. I saw how ya'll was eye-ballin' each other." Reggie couldn't hide his embarrassment.

"Man, whatever. So you think he gets down?"

"Damn. Aren't you straight to the point? But yeah, he does… at least I think so."

"Word? Think you can hook that up for me?" Reggie asked hopefully. TJ stared at him for a minute, looking at him from head to toe. He brushed some grass off of Reggie's shoulder.

"Yeah, I might be able to. Come with me tonight over to his

place. We'll see if we can get something to pop off." Reggie's grin spanned from ear to ear.

The practice field was as empty now as was the football field. Everybody had vacated the premises for better things. TJ motioned for Reggie to follow him back to the band room.

"I gotta put this equipment back before they accuse me of stealing it." TJ laughed. "And you know I ain't having that."

"Cool. We should be getting back, but I'm gonna run over to the locker room real quick and get a shower in. I'll meet you back at the room," Reggie said as he started toward the football team's locker room.

"You know what? We have a shower room too," he said with a devious inflection in his voice. "Nobody ever uses it. Besides, I'm sure everyone has left by now. You could shower there." Reggie paused and considered TJ's idea and smiled. He figured that the band's showers had to be an improvement over the fungus- and disease-infested football locker room.

"Aight, let's go."

The two walked back to the band room together and everybody had indeed left, even the band director. However, the door was still open with a note attached to it for TJ from the director who requested that he put back the equipment and lock the doors.

"Yo, if you put back your drums, how you supposed to practice with dude tonight? We still going, right?" Reggie asked nervously. TJ laughed.

"Damn. You must really be feeling Caleb. Don't worry. We're still going. But you must be a fool if you think I am going to lug these damn drums around. I have a drum pad that I practice on."

"Oh." Football consumed Reggie's free time so much that he never noticed how TJ practiced. TJ continued to laugh at him.

"So, where the showers at?" Reggie asked, looking around the band room. He saw no indication that there was a locker room or even a changing room. He wondered where everybody changed into their band uniforms before games and performances.

"The shower room is actually the director's. It's in his office. Don't worry. I have a key," TJ assured his friend.

"Hmmm, you and the director seem awfully close," Reggie joked. TJ looked over at Reggie with his mouth open in shock.

"Shut up. It ain't even like that."

Reggie laughed hard as TJ put up his equipment. He ogled TJ's ass as he was bending over, putting his drum on the floor.

"Yeah, right. I know that the director be hittin' that phat ass. That's why you enjoying all these privileges."

TJ scoffed at Reggie's remark.

"He wishes—so do you. You of all people know that I'm a strict top. Nobody gets in this right here." TJ rubbed his butt. Reggie sighed loudly in response.

"Yeah…I know. So come on. Show me the shower already." He led Reggie through the band room and into the director's office. Reggie noticed the numerous plaques that lined the walls and trophies adorned the many cases in the office. None were below first place. St. Augustine's band had become known for excellence.

TJ opened up the door to the bathroom. It was a small room with a toilet, a sink and a locker room shower pipe in the middle of the floor. Nothing fancy.

"So, this is the luxury bathroom the great band leader commands. Not impressed." Reggie looked over the cubby hole of a bathroom, disappointed.

"As long as it gets the job done; your shower awaits." TJ pointed to the long metal pipe connecting the ceiling to the floor. It had a shower head sticking from it as well as hot and cold knobs. Reggie figured he would have been just as better off using the football locker room.

His apprehension about using the band director's shower was soon washed away as the relaxing warm water from the shower massaged his flesh. He stood underneath the water with his eyes closed. He just wanted to feel the wetness of it all; his hard body becoming softer under the endless stream of droplets. As he reached for his soap on a rope, he heard the footsteps of someone behind him. Turning, he saw TJ standing there, completely naked with his manhood standing long and tall.

"I figured that you might want some company," TJ uttered. His voice was low, almost a whisper as he approached Reggie.

Reggie's own sex instantly rose as he made room for TJ without saying anything. He reached out to touch TJ's body and started lathering him up with the soap. TJ did the same in return. The two created their own heat as the water fell on their muscular frames. Slowly, Reggie lathered the soap all over TJ's chest and stomach, sliding his hand around to his sides to squeeze and clean them. Reggie rhythmically applied the lather on TJ, stepping in closer so that they could feel each other's hardness. Neither said a word as they bathed each other. TJ slid his bar of soap across the back of Reggie's broad shoulders, down to the small of his back and into his heavenly crack. He spread Reggie's cheeks as he cleaned each one separately and meticulously. Reggie's hole tightened at the attention as TJ's finger found its way to it, scrubbing it clean. The two turned and faced each other. They could no longer control their hands as they automatically grabbed for each other's lust. They embraced as they stroked the other. As roommates and both tops, this is all that they could offer each other; but it was more than enough. Reggie kissed and licked TJ's pink nipples, biting them to get him to moan as TJ sucked on Reggie's neck, careful not to leave a mark. They could feel each other tighten and knew that it was close to finish. The soap had provided a warm wet lather as they sped up their strokes. They came together and their lust was released out onto their wet bodies and to the bathroom floor as they tongue kissed each other passionately. Reggie got weak for a moment, but TJ was there to steady him as he regained his footing.

"I got you, baby boy. I'll always have you," TJ said as they hugged once again. Reggie looked up at TJ with a bit of sadness in his eyes.

"Man, why you gotta keep doing this to me? You know I can't resist your sexy ass," Reggie said.

"I dunno. You doing a great job of it in other areas...resisting, that is." Reggie knew what TJ meant; he wanted to penetrate him.

"I told you about that. You are a top...I'm a top...that wouldn't work out. Besides, I would be willing to let you hit if you did the same for me. But you won't. I can't get down like that. You won't even go down on a brotha!" TJ loosened his hold on Reggie as the same old conversation resurfaced.

"Reggie, I ain't into that! You know that about me and you know it won't change. Why can't you just deal with it already?" TJ stepped out of the shower in a huff and went to dry himself off and put on his clothes. Reggie followed.

"Yeah, yeah. You expect me to just 'deal' with it while I go against myself and serve up the ass for you? Picture that! You know what? I'm dropping the topic for now. On to more urgent concerns...are we going to see this kat or not?"

"Yeah. It's still on. Hell, fucking around with you, I might be late. Let's get going."

"You should call him and let him know we're still coming," Reggie eagerly suggested.

"Yeah, I will on the way."

The two finished dressing and left the band room, locking the doors behind them. In the student parking lot, TJ climbed into his Chevy Impala while Reggie jumped into his Dodge Magnum. He followed TJ to Caleb's crib in downtown Raleigh. The student parking lot was locked overnight and any cars remaining would be towed, so they couldn't ride together. Dropping one car off at the dorm would cause them to be late so they decided to take different cars.

✪✪✪

The sun had set causing the lights of the city to illuminate the sky. Raleigh was a beautiful city at night. It held a Northern ambiance all while proudly stating its Southern roots. Reggie followed TJ down the streets of the city, taking in the sights and the people of the night that roamed the town looking for fun at the club or food from the nearest diner.

When they reached Caleb's apartment, they walked the pathway leading to the building and up three flights of stairs until finally reaching Caleb's door. Reggie began to feel apprehensive about inviting himself along. He didn't play an instrument and really had no reason to be here, other than to look at Caleb again. As they waited for Caleb to come to the door after Reggie knocked, TJ played with his drum pad, a flat rectangular rubber pad with circular shapes embedded into it. They could both hear a muted trumpet playing inside the apartment. After waiting a few more minutes Reggie knocked again, louder. The trumpet stopped playing. Reggie looked over at TJ who was still tapping beats on his drum pad. Reggie rolled his eyes at his friend. He was still upset with him from the shower room. He felt that TJ was being stubborn and selfish. How could he ask someone to do something that he would not do himself?

Finally sounds could be heard close to the door from within the apartment. After a brief pause Reggie and TJ could hear Caleb taking the locks off the door. Three sets. The boy was cautious. He opened the door wide, smiling at the two visitors. Reggie smiled back, blushing as he gave Caleb the once-over. Caleb looked as if he were ready for bed. He was dressed in a tight white tank top that molded to his wide frame and some flannel pajama bottoms with no socks on his feet. TJ cleared his throat as he prepared to speak.

"Hey Caleb, I uh, brought Reggie with me. I hope it isn't a problem," TJ pleaded. Caleb shrugged off the notion of another guest. He didn't mind at all.

"Oh, it's no problem. Come on in, you guys." He moved aside to let them enter into his home.

"Hey Reggie," Caleb said shyly as Reggie walked past him, following TJ.

"Hey," Reggie replied.

"TJ, we can practice in the living room. There is more space in there. Reggie, you can go to my room if you want so you don't have to hear us. I have video games and cable plus some CDs if you wanna listen to some music."

"Yeah, that would be great," Reggie said.

TJ plopped down on Caleb's sofa, a giant red leather contraption that engulfed him. He climbed out of it enough to put his drum pad on the coffee table in front of the sofa and pull his drumsticks from out of his pockets. Caleb's silver trumpet was already on the table with a muting device lodged into it. TJ pulled out some rolled-up sheet music and began to make notes on it. He was ready for practice. Caleb went into the kitchen and brought back some sodas for his guests. He handed one to TJ and the other to Reggie, who had just been standing in the middle of the living room looking around the apartment. He saw pictures all over the place of people who weren't Caleb. He also noted that the place looked to have been decorated by men but, there was something feminine about the overall design, as if a female had come in later and tried to spruce up the place. Frilly curtains hung from the bay window and candles were scattered about the coffee table and the bookshelf in the corner of the room. "Hey, come on. I'll show you my room."

Reggie followed closely behind Caleb as they walked down the hallway to his room. Caleb smelled clean, as if he had just stepped out of the shower. His long braids had been tied into a ponytail as they hung down his back. Reggie saw that he didn't have on underwear under his pajamas as they pressed firmly around his ample cheeks, being pulled deeper and deeper into his crack as he walked. Reggie had to make himself look away for fear of jumping on him right then and there.

When they got to Caleb's room after walking down the long hallway, Reggie was impressed that it was impeccably clean. Everything looked like it was in place. The boy's room could have been in one of those magazines for housewives about good living and pre-arranged homes. Unlike the living room, there were no pictures on the walls or on the desk or nightstand, only posters of musicians and artwork. Caleb had a small twin bed in the corner of the room but a giant comfortable-looking recliner sat in front of the bed. It had drink holders in it as well as controller hooks for his video games. Clearly, he loved his video games.

"Well, here it is. It isn't much, but it's mine. You are welcome to it. Feel free to play any game you like. I have plenty." That was an understatement. The kid had three stacks of video games that were floor to ceiling high beside his dresser with the thirty-two-inch flat-panel television. Caleb pointed to his stereo.

"I also have music if you want to drown us out, or you can just watch television." Caleb turned to return to the living room.

"Hey, thanks, Caleb," Reggie called out. "I know I kind of invited myself along. You didn't have to let me stay, but I appreciate it."

"It's cool, man, seriously. Besides, if I ain't want you to be here, then you wouldn't be. So, just chill. Play a game or watch TV, or something. I'll be back to check on you in a few."

And just like that, he was gone. Reggie went to the door and cracked it to listen to what TJ and Caleb were doing. He hoped that he'd hear TJ putting in a good word with Caleb about him. After hearing them make small talk for a few minutes, he heard them start to play their song. Reggie was upset even more at TJ now for not setting him up with Caleb like he said he would. Reggie sighed loudly and closed the door. He was already bored. He had never been much of a video-game person nor did he watch television. He always read books or worked out. He decided to check out Caleb's music collection. He was glad to find out that they shared similar tastes in music and chose a Sade CD to listen to. Reggie went over and sat in the large recliner. He reclined back as Sade's smooth voice filled the room with her melancholy sound. Tired from the long day of school and practice,

Reggie closed his eyes to rest them at first but soon was asleep.

✿✿✿

As Reggie slept, TJ and Caleb continued to practice. TJ, growing tired of tapping out beats on his drum pad, threw the sticks down and slumped back into the couch. Caleb stopped and sat next to him.

"What's wrong?" Caleb asked. TJ looked at him with a devilish smirk as he pulled down his basketball shorts and revealed his eleven-inch red snake. Caleb's jaw dropped in shock.

"I want you to play my trumpet." TJ grabbed the back of Caleb's head and forced him down on his shiny red cane. Caleb didn't protest as he took it all the way down his throat. TJ stood up off of the couch, letting his shorts drop to the floor and Caleb sat down directly in front of him with his back against the seat cushions. TJ grabbed the back of the couch as he began to fuck Caleb's mouth, feeding him dick. Caleb began to struggle to keep up with TJ's strokes, gagging as the massive dick invaded his mouth and snaked its way toward his stomach. TJ didn't care as he continued his violent thrusts. Caleb's eyes watered with tears. He grabbed TJ's thighs to try and push him away but he only thrust harder. TJ could feel himself about to come but he was not ready as he abruptly stopped and pulled out of Caleb's mouth. Caleb desperately tried to regain his breath but was lifted off of the floor and turned over on the couch by TJ's surprisingly strong arms. Caleb was dizzied as his face and upper torso lay across the couch, his arms outstretched. His long hair fell into his face as he lay stunned. He felt TJ pull his pajamas down, exposing his big round brown mounds. TJ spat on Caleb's hole and then his own shaft as he lubed it. Regaining composure, Caleb looked back at TJ and tried to get up, but TJ only pushed him back down on the couch.

"What are you doing?" Caleb began to ask. TJ didn't respond but soon Caleb had his answer as he could feel himself splitting apart as TJ battered his way inside him. Caleb screamed loudly as TJ fucked him. He had never felt such pain before as TJ slapped his cheeks and continued to violate him. TJ moved fast; he could feel the orgasm coming. He grabbed Caleb's hips and pulled him all the way back onto his raging erection. Caleb let out another yelp as TJ began to unload into him. Caleb felt the hot juices shooting inside of his anus and coating his walls. TJ roared with satisfaction as he collapsed on Caleb's back.

"Whose ass is this, bitch?" he demanded.

"Reggie's," Caleb answered. TJ gave a look of disgust.

"Whose?"

A hand brushed gently across Reggie's arm, lightly caressing it, slowly. He moved in response, mumbling something unintelligible.

"Reggie," Caleb whispered. Reggie snored softly as Caleb stared at him. Caleb took in his frame, admiring his solid build as it lay dormant in his chair. He grabbed Reggie's shoulder, more firmly this time.

"Reggie!" he repeated. Reggie awoke startled from his sleep. He saw Caleb staring at him and quickly sat up, wiping his mouth to check if he had any drool. Caleb smiled at him as he rubbed his eyes. Was that a dream? Had that actually happened?

"Hey, man. How long was I sleep?" he said, yawning.

"For a while. It's okay though. You were tired." Caleb sat on the arm of the chair beside Reggie.

"Man, I just had the wildest dream," he said as he stretched. Caleb stared down at Reggie's hard-on outlining his pants.

"Really? What about?" Caleb asked as Reggie checked the time on his cell phone. It was almost ten. He suddenly remembered TJ and looked around for him.

"Where is TJ?" he asked.

"Gone," Caleb answered still sitting on the chair looking at him. Reggie blushed.

"Gone? What do you mean? He just left me?" Reggie started to get up.

"You're funny. No. He left to go get us some food. He'll be back, eventually. He's been gone for a hot minute, though," Caleb said as he got up from the chair and walked over to his television. "You wanna watch some TV?"

Reggie leaned back into the recliner, feeling more relaxed and at ease now that he knew where TJ was, or rather, where he wasn't.

"Yeah, I guess. What's on?"

"I dunno." Caleb switched the receiver on and returned to the chair, sitting on the arm of it again. Reggie felt comfortable with Caleb being so close and didn't question it. They sat and stared at the television blankly before Reggie cleared his throat.

"What was that?" Caleb asked.

"Huh? Oh nothing. I didn't say anything. Was just clearing my throat," Reggie clarified, embarrassed.

Caleb was still staring at him.

"So, Reggie, why did you come here tonight?" The question caught Reggie off guard. He struggled to find an answer as Caleb saw him squirming in his chair. "I mean, it's okay that you did. I actually am glad that you did."

Reggie looked up at Caleb who was blushing. They both smiled. Reggie laughed.

"You are? Why is that?"

"I saw you staring at me on the practice field today. I also saw you playing with yourself," Caleb stated as a matter of fact. Reggie's embarrassment was obvious on his face. Caleb put his hand on Reggie's thigh. "But I liked it. I was checking you, too, trust. So, I'm glad that you are here."

"Yeah," Reggie said as he leaned farther back into the recliner. "I'm glad I came, too. I was feeling you and wanted to get to know you better. I ain't know if you got down, but I had a feeling you did, at least I hoped you did."

Caleb laughed as he moved his hand from Reggie's thigh to his zipper, playing with it.

"I had always thought that you and TJ were a couple. I been watching you for a long time but every time I see you, I see TJ. So I figured that I would never get my chance."

Reggie laughed sarcastically.

"Oh no, me and TJ are roommates and best friends. We don't get down, at least not together. We're both tops." Caleb's ears perked up.

"Both tops? Wow, that must be interesting. So, you're saying that you have never bottomed?" Reggie fell quiet and Caleb instantly regretted his question. "Hey, it's cool if you don't want to talk about it." Reggie sat up in the chair and looked at Caleb.

"No, it's okay. I can answer it. To be honest with you, yes I have bottomed before…it just wasn't a pleasant experience for me." Caleb moved over to his bed and motioned for Reggie to follow. Caleb stretched out on the bed, lying back on his pillows.

"I understand what you are saying, man. It hurts—a lot—especially when the guy doesn't know what he is doing."

Reggie sighed.

"Yeah, it does. I actually had to go to the hospital. He had ruptured my inner lining and I was hemorrhaging. So every time something is about to jump off with him, I remember that and stop it before it goes too far."

"Wow. That's messed up. So this guy…you must still talk to him? Since things still 'jump off.' Does he know what he did to you?"

Reggie lay down next to Caleb. They both were silent as they stared at the ceiling for an eternity before Reggie answered:

"Yeah, he knows." Caleb raised his eyebrows in interest as he turned on his side to face Reggie.

"He does? It's TJ, isn't it?" Reggie closed his eyes and blew out air as he nodded his head in response.

"I figured that. You love him, don't you?"

"Yeah, I do. But I won't get into anything else with him. The most we do is jack off together but we don't have sex." Caleb moved closer to Reggie, gently rubbing his arm.

"Because you don't want to bottom anymore?"

"No, that's not it, not entirely. I would bottom again for him. But he won't do it for me. He won't even do oral. So as long as he is like that, then I'll be the same way. That's why I am all top now."

"Have you even topped before?" Caleb asked, moving even closer to Reggie, their lips touching. Reggie smiled at Caleb's question.

"No. I haven't. I have only had one sexual encounter, but I would like to give it a try. Why? Are you a bottom? Since we have basically discussed my whole history, you ever take dick before?"

"I do. Actually I'm *all* bottom. What do you plan to do about it?"

Reggie grabbed Caleb's hand and together they unzipped his pants. He looked up at Caleb with sex in his eyes; he lowered his voice to a deep whisper.

"I was hoping that since you play the trumpet and all that you would be able to help me out with my instrument. I can't get it to play." Reggie pulled out his hard-on for Caleb to see. Caleb's eyes lit up in response as he licked his lips. It was like déjà vu, but Reggie was determined to be nothing like TJ.

"In that dream I had earlier—at least I think it was a dream—you and TJ were fucking it." Caleb choked on air in response.

"Damn, that must have been some dream. Me and TJ? Eww. You ain't gotta worry about that. He ain't my type." Reggie looked relieved. He didn't know whether he was jealous of Caleb or TJ, perhaps both. Caleb grabbed Reggie's sex to get his attention again.

"So, back to the subject at hand. You want me to blow your horn for you? See if I can get it to work?" he asked as he positioned himself between Reggie's legs and lowered himself to his knees. Reggie had a drop of pre-cum forming on his head.

"Let's make our own duet."

Caleb smiled as he jumped on top of Reggie, straddling him. Reggie squeezed his hips as Caleb ground into him.

"I think I can make your instrument play. But, first I wanna show you how to play my trumpet."

Caleb pulled apart the fly to his pajamas and let his semi-erect dick plop out onto Reggie's chest. Reggie watched it grow and Caleb moved toward his face. Caleb rubbed his dick head on Reggie's lips, wetting them with his pre-cum before Reggie opened up and finally took him in all the way down his throat. Caleb braced himself on the wall as he rode Reggie's face, massaging his windpipe. Reggie's own manhood throbbed with anticipation as he started jerking it. Caleb turned to see Reggie madly stroking and pushed his hands away. Leaving Reggie's mouth for a quick second, Caleb turned around and started sucking Reggie's dick. The two wrapped around each other, becoming a mass of arms and legs as they rolled about on Caleb's bed. Caleb could feel himself getting ready to cum and pulled himself out of Reggie's mouth and got up off the bed.

"Damn, yo. I underestimated them head skills," Caleb said as he stroked his dick while staring back at Reggie who laughed. "Let's do this then, since you all about business tonight. Take them clothes off."

Reggie quickly got undressed as Caleb removed his pajama bottoms and tank top revealing a solid thick frame. He turned around to show off his assets to Reggie who jumped him, knocking him back onto the bed. Reggie aimed his manhood at Caleb's hole and tried to force it in with all his might, Caleb yelled in protest.

"Fuck! Calm down, Reggie! That shit hurts! Didn't we just talk about that? We got all the time we need, baby boy. I sent TJ way across town for the food."

"I'm sorry. I just thought that this was how it's done," Reggie apologized as he wiped sweat from his brow.

"Nah yo. You got to ease it in, slowly. Trust me that it feels better to both of us when you start slow. It's an ass, not a pussy, can't just be ramming into it. Here, let me get you some lube." Caleb reached over to his nightstand and opened the top drawer, removing a bottle of Wet lubrication. He handed it to Reggie.

Reggie's heartbeat was racing. He couldn't believe that this was happening. He wanted to live out every one of his porn star dreams with Caleb at that moment but realized he had to slow down. He didn't want to hurt Caleb. Not like he had been. Sensing Reggie's hesitation, Caleb turned over and pulled Reggie down on top of him. The two met in a flurry of kisses to lips, necks, nipples and bites to the cheek. They held each other as if it would be the last time they ever would hold another person, grinding and grunting into each other. Caleb knew what Reggie wanted, reaching into his nightstand again, pulling out a condom.

"Strap up, big boy."

Caleb flipped over and pushed his ass into the air, spreading his cheeks apart so that Reggie could see his hole winking at him. Reggie squirted out the lube and gently applied it to Caleb's puckered spot. He slid a finger into it and Caleb's ass greedily sucked it in up to his knuckle. Caleb moaned in response. Reggie slid his finger in and out of the hole, loosening it as Caleb continued to moan in pleasure and approval. Reggie's tool had gotten so hard that it looked swollen. His eight-inch looked to be sixteen. He rolled the condom onto it and braced himself behind Caleb. Reggie applied a small amount of lube onto the condom as he began to press into Caleb. Slowly, but surely, Caleb's resistance gave way until Reggie was completely immersed inside him. Caleb's walls gripped down tightly on Reggie as he fought back his urge to come. Caleb began throwing his ass back at Reggie, riding his rod. Reggie leaned his muscular frame back while pushing his groin forward so that Caleb could get the most penetration. He reached around and grabbed Caleb's own erection with his greased hand and let it slide back and forth in his palm as Caleb continued his rocking. Caleb began to rock faster and harder as Reggie squeezed. Reggie could feel himself about to come as Caleb shot hot fluid into his hand and onto the bed. Reggie pulled out of Caleb and ripped off the condom as he began to release. Caleb quickly turned around and swallowed Reggie's cock. He hungrily suckled as Reggie unleashed his orgasm down his throat. They lay on top of each for a few moments to catch their breath before they moved to the bathroom to clean up.

Moments later in the bathroom, Reggie was once again inside

Caleb and he had Caleb's right leg lifted on top of the bathroom counter over the sink as Reggie waxed Caleb's ass, while licking his ear when they heard a knock at the front door. TJ had returned with the food. The two quickly got dressed as they both rushed into the living room. Caleb opened the door to let TJ in, who was carrying pizzas and a bag of Chinese food.

"I couldn't decide which so I got both," he said as he placed the food on the kitchen table. TJ looked suspiciously at both Reggie and Caleb while sitting down at the table. Caleb pretended not to notice as he pulled out the paper plates.

"Good, cuz I am starved, yo," Reggie said as he sat at the table, reaching for pizza and an egg roll. He also ignored TJ's stares. The three sat and ate silently before Reggie spoke up between bites of pepperoni and teriyaki chicken.

"You know, that duet you two have is off da chain. I never did ask what the name of it was." '

"'Blow the Horn,'" TJ replied. They all stopped what they were doing for a moment before breaking out in laughter.

After the three had eaten dinner, TJ and Reggie prepared to leave. As TJ went into the living room to collect his things, Caleb and Reggie gave each other knowing looks. They both smiled. Caleb got up and walked toward the door.

"So, TJ, I heard you was all top," Caleb said abruptly. TJ walked back into the kitchen area.

"Yeah, fo sho.' Why do you ask?" TJ asked while grabbing his large member through his pants. Reggie stood up and went behind TJ, rubbing and caressing his chest and stomach from behind.

"Well, we figured that since you are all top that we could all try an experiment tonight." Reggie growled seductively into TJ's ear. TJ leaned his head back, giving in to Reggie's touch.

"Oh yeah, baby boy? What did ya'll have planned?" TJ slid his basketball shorts to the floor, letting his swollen sex plop out and stand at attention. "We 'bout to get into a threesome?"

"Something like that," Caleb said as he turned and locked the door. "In fact, that actually sounds pretty good. But, first we decided to teach you a lesson in giving."

TJ gave Caleb a quizzing look before suddenly being pushed over the kitchen table. Before TJ knew what was going on, Caleb grabbed his outstretched arms, holding him down on the table. Reggie stood behind TJ and kicked his legs apart, spreading his bubble-shaped ass cheeks apart.

"Oh shit!" TJ exclaimed. "No, wait! We can't do this!" He tried squirming and breaking free but Caleb only held onto him tighter.

"Oh. But we can. And we will," Caleb said calmly. His crotch was directly in front of TJ's face. A sneaky smile formed in the corners of TJ's mouth, a secret smile that gave his tacit consent.

"Yeah, TJ, just relax, yo. I'm 'bout to bang the drum slowly, pa. Don't worry. You'll warm up to the beat," Reggie said as he aimed his hard-on for TJ's hole. He rammed his dick inside TJ's virgin ass, causing TJ to wince. As TJ opened his mouth to scream, Caleb filled it with his dick.

"Shhhh, can't be too loud. Here, blow this horn."

Reggie and Caleb smiled as they stroked each end of TJ, and after a while, so did TJ.

ஒஐ

Washington Parks resides in Crown Heights, New York and is an avid fan of dancehall music. He is a work-from-home sex-operator and spends his free time with his dog, Trumpet. He hopes to one day fashion an erotic fantasy set in the world of Jamaican Dancehall.

Between 6 and 8

GEORGE KEVIN JORDAN

What the hell was I supposed to say? I knew what I wanted to say: Hell Naw. But when your rival at work asks you over for dinner with his wife, deliberately in front of your co-workers, you don't refuse. You nod your head, show all your teeth, and say, "I appreciate that man, thanks."

Cornell Levy was the only person at work who got under my skin. I mean, like most people, I hated my job and some days wished I could set the whole floor on fire; but in general, everyone else in the office was pretty cool. There were minor squabbles when a looming deadline approached, but for the most part I had no problems with anyone else. Cornell was different.

Maybe it's because he went to Yale, and I went to a state school in Ohio, and we have the same position; maybe it's because while he seems to display some type of tangible glee in organizing spreadsheets and PowerPoint presentations, I spend most of my days surfing IMDb for the latest Will Smith movie; maybe it's because he wishes he could care a little less about the day job, and I wish I could care a little more. Whatever the reason, whenever we got into a room for more than a few minutes, there was instant tension.

Normal, playful, vocal tones escalated into harsh, loud, *Ima-*

kickyoass screaming matches. Both our bosses pulled us in for peer mediation meetings. Because we are the only two black VPs working at the firm, I knew it scared them to see us fighting. *Good God, the coloreds are acting up again.* And to be honest, I was ashamed that word of our petty bickering got up to our bosses, but Cornell had a way of just saying my name that made me want to leap over the desk and smash his face.

But I'll be damn if he didn't trump me—asking me to dinner in front of everyone in the global staff meeting. Sure the meeting was over and many people had headed out, but both our bosses were still gabbing about their Atkins diet plans when Cornell pulled me aside and spoke in a decibel so loud I was sure April at the reception desk heard him.

"Hey Miles, man, you should really come over for dinner this Thursday." His smile was half teeth, half curled-up lips. If smug was a body odor, it exuded from his pores. "My wife makes the best grilled chicken fajitas, and we can chill and watch the game afterward."

I was trapped. If I refused, everyone in the office would think that I was the troublemaker. They would have a scapegoat, and I would be looking for a new job. But, if I accepted, I would have to spend time outside of the office with Cornell.

The irony was, in another universe, Cornell would be the perfect catch. He was six feet tall, with a physique that stretched his form-fitting dress shirts and slacks just right. His sandalwood-colored skin was without a flaw. And his lips, the lips that he used daily to berate my performance and skills as a manager, looked soft, moist and pouty all the time. But I didn't need to look at the imprint that pressed against his pants to know he was a dick.

In the business world, however, being political is often more important than being honest. So there I was at *Mr.-immaculately-knotted-ties'* front door, bottle of wine in hand, pride in check. I rang the doorbell, praying I was in one of those action drama movies where the entire house blows up after you push the buzzer. I closed my eyes for a second of hope, and opened them when I heard rustling from the other side of the door. There would be no explosion, no spies to whisk me off and make me a part of their band of assassins. I had to admit to myself that, one, I watch too much television, and two, I was in for one long, boring night.

When the door opened I expected to see Valerie–*oh-please-call-me-Val*—Levy. She was the uberbougie ying to his obnoxious yang. I met her last year at the Christmas party. She spent the whole night sipping on club soda, and bragging about how she could never handle a work schedule like her husband's. It was like she was reading cue cards he wrote. Disgusting. When the door swung open, it was Cornell, in another one of his muted gray, confining sweater vests.

"Hey man, come on in." As I stepped inside the marble-tiled foyer, he handed me a drink and smiled. "It's vodka. I hope you like it."

"That's fine. Thanks," I said as I surveyed his home. Actually it looked more like a museum, with original art on the walls, and statues of Greek, African and Oriental gods and goddesses in every corner. It was definitely the abode of a successful person. I pondered why this guy had the equivalent of the MoMA exhibit in his house, and I could barely balance my checkbook. He led me to the living room.

"Where is Val?" I questioned, imaging her upstairs sucking the blood out of their maid so she could sustain her beauty and vitality for the night.

"She had an emergency come up, and she went to see her folks out of town." Cornell guided me to the couch and we both sat down. I set the wine bottle down on the coffee table.

"But she did leave us the fajitas." We both gave tired chuckles for a tired joke. There was a beat of silence that extended to what seemed a symphony of quiet, until finally Cornell placed his glass on its coaster, rested his arms on his legs and interlocked his fingers.

"We have some issues we need to resolve." The smile evaporated from his face, and Cornell seemed to be studying me.

"I agree," I said. "There is just too much tension."

"Well, tonight, we're going to work it out." He did not move.

"Cool," I said, when what I really wanted to say was just stop being a punk-ass bitch, whining and complaining about everything.

"My wife and I got a divorce two months ago," Cornell blurted out.

Suddenly all the drama was explained. He was in a bad marriage. It was stressing him out, and he was taking it out on me at work.

Okay! "I'm sorry, man." I had to admit relief at finally resolving our tension.

"Fuck her. I don't care about her." He picked up his glass again, and I felt my eyes widen. Okay, obviously he still had some separation issues.

"Have you thought about seeing someone?" I don't know why I lowered my voice like I was telling a secret. We both knew he was crazy and needed either a shrink or Jesus.

"I don't need a doctor," he said. "And this isn't about my wife. My issue is with you."

Suddenly, I felt goose bumps ride up my arms. This fool was crazy. Even though I was starving, the fajitas were admittedly becoming less and less important.

"Look, man," I tried to reason with him, "obviously we both want what's best for the company. We just need to work together to give it to them."

My best PR answer. Cornell stared at me. He didn't blink. He leaned in and said, "You need to learn how to take orders when I give them to you."

Now I was hot. "You aren't my boss," I blurted out. "And even if you were, you're an idiot. Half the shit you have us doing is ineffective and a waste of peoples' time."

"You think you know everything with your little Acme college degree. You think you're fine with your little pretty faggot ass."

It was like the words beat against my chest; like they were physical embodiments of rage trying to beat me down. Did this fool really just call me a "faggot"?

"You stupid muthafucka!" I yelled. "You just lost a job."

I headed for the door, and Cornell made a beeline to cut me off. He grabbed my arm from behind. I turned around expecting an apology, him pleading for me to forgive his indiscretion. Instead, I felt a huge hand slam against my face. It was so hard, it caught me off balance and I tumbled to the floor. I needed to get up, because now I was ready to whip this fool's ass. But he was already on top of me. Literally, his body was pinning mine in place. His hand grabbed my face. "You need to learn to do as you're told."

"What?" I was confused and trying to break free when I felt something that didn't fit. In the mid region, I felt him pressed up against my pelvis. Was he...hard? He slapped me back into reality, and I grabbed his neck. He was strong. I tried to move him off of me, and as we writhed on the ground, his erection was confirmed. And then he leaned down and kissed me.

His lips locked with mine, and he explored my mouth with his tongue like a scavenger searching for meat in the desert. There was nothing untouched. To my shame, I started to feel myself getting excited, but then came another slap.

"You gon' do what I say?" he whispered in my ear. "You gon' be my little bitch?"

I laughed out loud. Okay, this was an office prank or something.

"Enough, Cornell." I laughed again, hoping the game would end. "You scared me, ooh."

I moved to stand up, but he pushed me back down. He gripped my shirt with his hand, and then I heard a rip so loud it echoed in the house. The seams of my clothes tore apart, and he pulled the shirt right off of me. His lips were on my neck now, sucking hard like he was trying to give me a hickey.

His right hand moved from pinning my left hand to pinching my nipples. If there was a time to resist, this was it. I had a free hand. I could have hit him. I could have pushed him off. Instead, I put my hand on his chest, in a superficial attempt to push him off, but more so to find his nipples.

I pinched them, and he moaned. He moved his hand up to my neck and started strangling me. I thought I was suffocating. He was going to kill me. But suddenly my body tingled in places that never moved before, and I moaned.

"I been watching yo' ass walking around at my company like you run shit," he mumbled. "I'm gonna show you who runs shit." With one fluid move he unbuckled my belt and unzipped my pants. As he turned me over he pulled my pants down so they were just below my ass cheeks. His two hands gripped and separated the flesh, and suddenly I felt a breeze and shivered. Then, there was a wet tongue pushing through my inner walls, showing no mercy circling around the top. I squirmed and tried hard to remember why I didn't like this guy.

"Open it for me." He moaned as he continued munching and I tried to regain my composure. Both my hands were free now, but I was locked in a mental battle between my flesh and my common sense. He slapped my ass and spit inside, and my common sense was knocked out in the first round. The warmth of his muscular body against mine was sending me over the edge. I felt sweat gathering on the small of my back.

Cornell rose up, pulling me up by my waist. As I rose, he pushed my pants down until I was completely naked in front of him. He swung me around and pushed me against the wall. A hard hand pummeled my face again, but this time I got my own slap out. Cornell laughed and grabbed my neck. He pounded my chest with his fists. Not in an overtly hard way, just enough to make me hit him back.

"Yeah," he moaned. I helped him take off his clothes. He rewarded me by biting my ears. I felt his dick riding up my thigh. He bent down and pushed my legs apart. Then he wrapped his arm around my waist and lifted me in the air.

The anticipation was always the worst. But when he finally pushed the head in, I was high from the experience. I relaxed my muscles and allowed more of him to come inside. When he was all the way in, he balanced my thighs on his forearm and pumped with a fury that almost knocked me unconscious. Cornell was whispering in my ears, but I couldn't hear a thing. There was nothing but the beating of my heart, and the steady pounding of flesh. He carried me into the bedroom, still inside, and once my back hit the mattress, he went to work. The rhythm was like a jazz song—up-tempo one moment, slow the next, staccato in the middle, and manic at the end.

"You gon' do what daddy say now?" Cornell managed to ask between grunts, and the only thing I could do to keep him going was to nod yes.

"Uhn!" I felt my ass tighten and react to Cornell's thick dick as it jerked and pulsated until he finally released the ghost inside. He shook and moaned until there was nothing left his body could do. He collapsed on top of me.

"I got you. Don't worry," he whispered, before he pulled out and dragged me to the top of the bed with him. We lay there in darkness, the stillness almost as dramatic as the action before it. He guided me into his arms and held me tight. We slept for hours.

A vibrating phone woke us both. Cornell grabbed it and coughed out, "Hello."

He moaned a little, and then said, "Aight" into the phone and hung up. He pulled me back into his arms again. A few minutes later the doorbell rang, and Cornell got up, bent over to kiss my neck and walked out of the room.

Several minutes later, three figures entered the room. I stood up. I spotted Cornell between two naked bodies. They all approached the bed. The shortest one with the thick horse legs and ass that didn't move bent over in front of me. His hot mouth slid up and down on my dick.

"You work under me, yo'," Cornell said. "I found someone to work under you." The man began sucking with such ferociousness, I was afraid I would pass out. He stopped just short of my climax and stood up. Then he straddled me and sat down. It was burning up, and I felt dizzy with each bounce his body took up and down. I looked at Cornell, who was being serviced by the other man. Then, the little man on top of me flexed his muscles, and he received all of my attention again. I grabbed his waist and lifted him up to change positions. He positioned his soft feet over my shoulders as I practiced my speed and momentum. The man didn't say a word, but I could see him sucking his lips with each stroke. My legs began shaking, and I knew the time had arrived. He must have too, because he squeezed just tight enough to force me to explode.

"Damn, damn...damn." They were the only words I could muster. I barely got a chance to pull out before the other guy, the one I could see clearly in the light now, grabbed my arm. He was taller and more muscular than Cornell, but his face looked younger, like he had just graduated from college, and this was his initiation into manhood. He got off the bed and spread my legs. He stood behind me and entered with no warning or care for how it felt. He pounded away—slapping my ass each time I tried to adjust for the pain.

"Wait," I pleaded, needing a chance to catch my breath.

"Tell him to shut up and take it," the man said to Cornell.

"He's a good boy," Cornell said. "He'll take it." I looked up as Cornell bent over and kissed me on the lips. He winked at me and then straddled the little man with the killer ass. The big man grunted and slapped my ass while the little one sucked my dick as Cornell fucked him. It didn't take long before I felt the big man's pace pick up, and his grunting transformed into yelling.

"Yeah—yeah!" He shook, and then fell back and out of me. The little man rose up and pulled out of my mouth. He jacked his stick until he released his milk onto the sheets. Seconds later, Cornell moaned and moaned until he was done.

We all took showers and cleaned house. The two men got dressed and departed as quietly and mysteriously as they entered. I figured that was my cue to leave, but Cornell wrapped his arms around me and led me back to the bed. We lay down, and he kept me in a bear hug the entire night.

My internal clock beat the sun by thirty minutes. It was 5:30 a.m., and I had to get home. I was not about to be caught wearing the same clothes as the day before.

"I gotta go." I tried to wiggle my way out of Cornell's vise grip.

"No you don't," he said and hugged me tighter.

"Yeah, I have to read the agenda for your boring-ass meeting this morning." We both looked at each other and laughed.

He let me go and followed me to the door. I wanted to ask what the hell happened. How did we go from being enemies to sharing bodily fluids and cuddling all night? So many questions all stopped by his kiss.

"Hurry up and get home." He smiled. "'Cause I will call you out if you're late to my meeting."

I shook my head and walked out.

"Hey man," Cornell said. "I don't think I have any more beef with you."

"Me neither." I was surprised by my answer.

"Well, just in case, I think we should meet up again tonight to make sure our points are made clear."

"I agree," I said.

"So, you gone let me be the boss?" he asked.

I looked at him and smiled. "You're still not my boss. But I don't think you're a dick anymore."

"Naw." He smiled. "I'm your dick."

I still could not explain that night. But I do know we had a new weekly meeting. And Cornell and I never once argued at work again.

The Christian Discount

C.J. LIVINGSTON

When I moved to a steep, dry, volcanic-formed Caribbean island, there were things I had to get used to: not having the home delivery of mail, or pizza; not having a gay bar or even a cruisy area to pick up men; six months of arid, hot weather (to contrast the six rainy months of hurricane season); and the adventurous sexual antics of island fever, enflamed during heat spells or long periods of time spent alone on the same small rock. There was also a code that governed the sliding scale of the costs of things, from the prices charged mega-rich charter yachters to what you might charge the ecotourist to the discounts that varied with the degree one was considered a "local."

We were in the middle of a spring heat wave and a tough drought, and I hadn't been off the rock in eight months. It had been almost as long since it rained. Water trucks were jamming up traffic, slowly climbing the island's steep hillsides and negotiating its narrow, hairpin turns. I was already jealous that my landlord, Melynda Ray, was away on vacation to the modern conveniences of the United States mainland when our cistern ran dry. I was just about to take a quick sailor's shower, knowing we needed to conserve water since it hadn't rained in so long, and had just flushed the morning's contents of the toilet. As the tank was filling back up with water I heard the agonizing telltale sounds, the groaning of the house's water pipes and the painful shuddering within the walls. The toilet tank began to retch in dry heaves.

Luckily, my landlord picked up her cell phone when I called, and she telephoned the water company from her vacation. I knew the way the hose had to enter Melynda's half of the split house we shared to fill the cistern, so she called me back and said that all I had to do was let the Thomas Brothers in that afternoon at 3:30 and make sure everything was done right: the lid put back on the cistern, a check written for which she would reimburse me for half, and her half of the house locked up after they left.

My landlord was a beautiful woman in her fifties, and I imagined her as my private Mrs. Madrigal, gardening incessantly and harvesting delightful and magical tropical herbs. She told me that she was from the United States; that she intended to live like she was in the United States; and that she expected me to live like I was in the States as well. Melynda said she expected me to take showers as long as I liked, and to wash my jeep whenever I wanted. We had a washer and a dryer, she said, that was almost constantly running. She said that if it didn't rain enough and we ran out of water, we'd buy a truckload and halve the cost. Melynda watered her garden twice a day.

She also divulged to me one night over a dinner on her patio— a dinner at which we drank chilled Pinot Grigio with each serving, something she might not soberly share—that she sometimes "carried on" with the carpenter for discounted handiwork around the house, as well as for the sheer thrill of it. One glass of wine later she told me she sometimes got a discount on the water—with Jelani Thomas, the older brother and a "Rastaman," she said.

Melynda said it started when Jelani noticed her pot plants growing on the side of the house as he climbed the hill from the road. She rolled a joint quickly and they smoked it out back while his clean-cut younger brother crouched over and held the hose filling the cistern. "My bruddah's a Chris-jun," Jelani had said, nodding toward the water truck's advertisement on its tanks: "Thomas Brothers Water Co.—In God We Trust." She said Jelani gave her a "Christian discount" and was back to her house alone before the buzz wore off.

I was impressed. I'd seen the mahogany hunk sitting in his water truck. I'd seen him climb the steep hill up from the road with the heavy hose in his hand. I'd seen his muscles ripple under his sweaty shirt, and the way his dreadlocks—wrapped into a red, green and yellow crocheted kufi—bounced with each strong step. And that day the cistern ran dry when Melynda was out of town, I saw the muscles and skin and everything else I could ever dare dream of.

The Thomas Brothers were scheduled for 3:30 so I decided to limber up at two o'clock. I planned a nice hour for a yoga workout in my homemade hotbox, with thirty minutes to cool off and work on a horny buzz myself. I was betting on a bisexual rush this afternoon—with its heat dry-roasting everyone's skin taut, hormones swimming in blood near its boiling point, even the Caribbean Sea as warm as a bath; I was going for the Christian discount.

I closed the windows and the sliding glass door of my bedroom, opened the curtains wide so the full sun could come in, unfolded my workout mat on the tile, and put in a thirty-minute chanting tape I knew a strenuous routine to. I turned up the volume and let my shorts drop to the floor, and I lay back on the yoga mat in my jock strap. As I stretched my hands over my head, I smelled the light musk of my armpits. And as I raised my torso, sitting up and spreading my thighs, I felt the sweat start to slide along my sides and back, soaking into the elastic of the straps that framed my tan line. A rivulet of sweat streamed down the crack of my white ass.

At 2:35 the heat had steamed up the sliding glass doors and sweat was running from every pore. I lay with my legs rolled back over my head, feet on the floor behind it: the plow position, a self-fellatio pose when I was younger, and still a great view to watch my ass get eaten or pounded by a rough stud. The mantra and music thundered through the stereo, then suddenly, the pounding stuttered and I saw, through the triangle of my ass crevice and thighs, the outline of Jelani Thomas, the water man, peering through the foggy glass door. "Inside!" he called as he knocked, and I jumped up and yelled that I was coming.

I turned off the radio and quickly tied a sarong around my waist. I was a little bewildered: No one ever arrived early in the West Indies. But I was thankful that a long cold shower would be the reward at the end of this thirty-minute ordeal. By the time I got my windows opened and was outside, Jelani had gone back to the truck and his assistant, a lean nugget with a short afro and the name "Lincoln" embroidered onto his navy work shirt, had climbed the hill with the thick canvas hose. I let him in Melynda's back door and he knelt below her desk at the lid of the cistern. He knelt on the terra-cotta tile and pulled the heavy lid off, his round ass in loose Levi's. Lincoln wore no belt and the wide denim waist gaped open, displaying his smooth slender back where his shirt slid up toward his shoulders. His head had disappeared into the echoing cavern.

He looked up, bringing with him a cloud of mosquitoes that he blew away with gusts of hot breath, but I tried not to get excited: my landlord had said the little one was the goody-two-shoes. He screwed the foot-long metal nozzle onto the end of the hose and yelled, "Ready!" back over his shoulder. I didn't care if Lincoln was a Christian, as long as I could stand over him and look at his young black ass while he held the hose steady and kept if from soaking Melynda's house.

Down the hill, Jelani turned a gauge on the truck and the flat hose engorged with the rush of water. My dick got hard watching Lincoln struggle with the water pressure, and I was glad the tight jockstrap controlled my own water snake beneath the thin sarong. And when the hose stilled and poured forth the steady stream of water, Lincoln kept crouched over it to hold it in place. Out the door, I watched Jelani walk along the top of the truck's tank. He also wore dungarees, but his jeans were darker blue and tighter than Lincoln's. His skin was lighter, like sorghum honey, and his thighs bulged as he bent to release the tank's air drafts. Then Jelani jumped down and climbed the hill up toward me with his clipboard and a book of receipts.

"Afternoon," he said when he reached Melynda's balcony, and he apologized for being early. "Look like you was getting a good stretch over there," he said, motioning toward my place with his head. "A fine halasana for true."

I was impressed: Jelani knew his yoga. "Good afternoon," I returned. "It was the plow posture. And thanks! You follow yoga?"

"I like to stretch t'ings, mehson," he said. "Stretching treat ya right, ya know." He bent over and touched his toes. I smiled. "It boiling today!"

I said the heat was almost unbearable, and we went inside Melynda's to get out of the sun. Lincoln grunted to acknowledge we'd come in, but as far as I was concerned, he was just show-casing that gorgeous ass of his. I sat on Melynda's love seat, and Jelani looked at my leg where the pareja's fabric had parted. I was proud of my legs' hard-earned tone, and I had shaved them both smooth for a triathlon; the sun glinted from the shiny perspiration. Jelani said he liked my sarong. I was thinking of him stretching things.

"Melynda mentioned that you liked plants," I said, now stand-ing because my hard-on was getting strained and uncomfortable. "Come out the front door."

At this Lincoln looked over his shoulder and said, "Don't be gone long." He smiled like he was well aware of what I had in mind. Outside, I led Jelani to the budding beauties Melynda had left me in charge of. He pulled a branch to his nose and inhaled.

"Red skunk," he said approvingly. "Got any dried up?"

I pulled out a honker of a cigar I had rolled, a spliff you usually see around here only at beach concerts and carnival. I offered him the blunt and he stuck it in between his lips. God, I imagined my dick pulled on by those swollen suckers. He rolled the joint around his mouth and licked the paper at the end. As I leaned in with the lighter, wind-protected with my cupped hand, Jelani stared straight into my blue eyes behind the flame between us. The tip flamed and lit, and Jelani's quick tokes got the cherry nice and hot.

Behind the blue cloud of smoke he stared at me. I hadn't even smoked anything and I was getting dizzy. He handed me the joint and I stayed close to him as I pulled on it, coughing imme-diately at the large volume of smoke I took in. Jelani laughed and took it back. He dragged long and slow, his enormous chest ex-panding and bringing us inches closer to touching, and then he held his breath. Jelani didn't say anything; he just looked in my eyes. Then he put the joint down in an orchid pot and pulled my head so our lips were within an inch of each other's. His strong thumbs pressed lightly into my jaw so that I opened my mouth and he sealed the gap between us with his thick lips, exhaling the smoke inside me.

His steady hands on my head and face were enough to send me over the edge and down the hill. I didn't force a kiss on him; I just let his smoke-filled breath flow into me. I could taste him sweet behind the cloud, and when his lungs were empty, his lips closed with mine softly near a kiss. "Close your eyes," he said, and I did. "Open your mouth and don't hold your breath."

"Just let everyt'ing open," Jelani said. And then he put his broad hand flat against my stomach and told me to open my eyes. I couldn't believe the amount of smoke I exhaled as he gently pushed his hand up my bare belly, expelling the smoke as he pressed over my abs and chest muscles, and I didn't even cough.

His hand stayed on my pecks and he rubbed the hard nipples. Jelani kept me close to him pulling on my tits and his other hand reached around and found my ass beneath the sarong. His thick fingers pulled at the elastic straps of my jock and let them snap hard against my cheeks. He snapped them over and over while squeezing my nipple tighter and tighter. He leaned in close to me and whispered, "Bwoy, you want de Chris-jun discount?"

I couldn't believe the beauty in his lips when he spoke. I wanted to suck on his pink tongue each time it darted from the wet cave of his mouth, and his breath was intoxicating—its skunky smoke and, I swear I could detect some previous sex at some point in his day. I knelt down, my bare knees on the leather-topped steel toes of Jelani's dusty black work boots. My face nuzzled the nine-inch outline of his thick cock through his dark jeans. He moaned and pulled me to his feet. "Inside," he groaned, and I thought about Lincoln in Melynda's house alone. I was getting stoned and greedy: I wanted to taste them both.

Jelani picked up the joint and followed me into Melynda's. Lincoln still crouched over the hose, his head and shoulders down below Melynda's desk; his ass, which seemed to have grown more fantastic while we were outside, still high in the air; the canvas hose still thick and pulsing with pressure.

"Taste dis," Jelani told Lincoln, kicking the sole of his work boot lightly, and then he nudged me. "Hold it for him," he said.

I took the big spliff, stirring from the hit Jelani had blown inside me, and got down on the floor with Lincoln. I crawled behind him, but the desk's legs were too narrow to let me beside him. I got my knees on the inside and outside of his, and I had to lean against his back to reach my right hand to his mouth. With my hips against his ass, I was in perfect penetration position, and I had to keep my balance by hugging onto his solid torso with my left arm. His lips brushed my fingers as they found the joint, and it flared in the shadows under the desk as he stoked the fire with quick puffs, each pushing me closer against him, holding on tighter so he didn't throw me off. My dick now edged past the tight elastic waistband and stood rock hard against my stomach, against Lincoln's ass through the back of his jeans.

Now Jelani couldn't see this fact, but he told me to stay there and take a hit off the joint. He told me to take it slow and not to cough. He told Lincoln to stay still and hold on to the hose. And as I took a slow drag of dense smoke, I felt Jelani's large hands raise the sarong up over my ass. I relaxed and remembered what he said: I tried to let everything open as I inhaled and slowed my breath. I held the joint back to Lincoln who arched his back, pushing the seam of his jeans against my cock. Again his lips brushed my fingers, and this time, I felt his tongue when he blew out the smoke.

Jelani was whispering into my asshole, enchanting island words to open it, brushing it with his rough fingers, stroking it gently, massaging my ass muscles with his palms and then he buried his tongue deep inside me. I knocked Lincoln forward but he caught his balance and pushed me back against Jelani's hungry mouth.

I almost dropped the big joint down into the wet cistern when Jelani pulled at my ass with his teeth. Lincoln took the smoker and tamped it out on the lid to the other side of him. Jelani pushed his face into my ass and bit lightly as he probed. He pulled me against his chin by the jock's straps, lathering my crack with his devotion, and stretching the waistband tight against my throbbing cock. I licked at Lincoln's ears and he raised his ass against me. "Come," Jelani said, and pulled me back from under the desk with Lincoln.

As I turned I saw that he had freed his huge dick from his jeans and was stroking it with his hand. His shirt was unbuttoned and his chocolate chest was covered with tiny curls of black fur. His tits were big melons, and a pearly string of pre-cum drooled from his foreskin. He pushed his jeans down around his feet and sat on the loveseat while I tried to stretch my mouth around his monster cock. Once I got my lips and teeth around the thick head, I could only take the width and length into my throat by remembering to stay open. I kneeled before him and let him slip off my jockstrap as I sucked him. He squatted and shuffled toward me, prodding me backward toward the desk with his cock against my throat.

Without losing his dick from the vacuum of my mouth, he knelt and started pulling at Lincoln's boots, maneuvering him quickly out of his socks and then his trousers. He pushed Lincoln's shirt up to his shoulders. Jelani fucked my mouth with his big cock, and I pulled at my own, felt Lincoln's now bare ass with my other hand. I was aching to be sandwiched between these two hot fucks. I felt Jelani thicken and quicken his thrust so I pushed him away and watched his big dick twitch up and down in my face.

By the time I found Melynda's condoms (Jelani knew where she kept them), he had taken off his own boots and jeans and stood towering like a big tree above me. His whole body, but especially his dick, was unreal. He was completely naked except for the globe of yarn that held his braids. He was simply colossus. Overpowering. But gentle as he took a condom and unrolled it over my steel-rigid dick. He took out another and I watched it stretch over his fucklog. I couldn't believe that it was going to fit inside me but, oh, how I knew that it was. I knew it was going to rake me. It was going to slam me and I was going to beg for more and more and more.

He turned me around and guided my dick into Lincoln, whose ass was tight and it clamped around me, but Jelani coaxed him through it. I felt sorry for Lincoln, having to hold onto the hose as it filled the cistern. I mean, he was getting fucked, getting started, but he couldn't turn around and watch. He just faced that damn dark cavern, with its mosquitoes and spiders. But he took my dick, all seven inches of it, and loosened as Jelani gripped and released his ass cheeks. It drove me crazy to see Jelani's light-brown hands rubbing the black ass my white dick in an orange condom was now rutting into. I reached over to nudge Jelani behind me. He happily obliged and I felt his stud body position against me.

I had to push Lincoln far beneath the desk and nearly squat upright against Jelani, but he got his hard cockhead against my hole and pushed into me. I silent-screamed like in a nightmare and tears ripped from my eyes. Jelani held me still, tight around the chest with his left arm. He held Lincoln against me with his right arm. He was all the way inside me and I bit my finger, praying I could take it.

We didn't move, just felt the hose's rush of hydraulic pressure, entwined with us like an extra arm or leg or giant dick. I felt Jelani's right arm begin to move, and I knew by the motion that he was jacking Lincoln off. Lincoln started gently rocking his ass against me, his hole grabbing for more of my cock, and next my own ass started to open. Jelani felt it too and he pushed deeper into me.

"Oh fuck!" I yelled, and he took this exclamation as a command and humped harder into me. "Oh fuck!" I whimpered, and he bucked me, my own performance inside Lincoln involuntary, just an echo of the pummel inside me, but Lincoln was moaning and fucking back against me.

Jelani let us go and grabbed both my nipples with his fingers. He held me like that, twisting them as he fucked me into oblivion. Having his thick cock filling my innards prevented me from coming, because otherwise I would have blasted into the rubber separating me from Lincoln's soul. I was being stuffed, fucking delirious, stretched open, and so close to exploding. Lincoln was there too, and he started coming in staccato spurts I heard hit the tile floor, splash into the rising water lever of the cistern, his ass clutching at my dick, sucking on it, his yells echoing back to us.

Jelani must have been about to come in my ass too, because he quickly pulled out of me, his heavy dick thumping against my back, and I relaxed, let my breathing calm and ease the churning in my balls. We rested a minute, catching our breath as we listened to the water gush into the well. Three-thousand seven-hundred gallons we were getting. Our cistern was bone dry. And so were our mouths.

Melynda had left half a pitcher of fresh soursop juice in the fridge and I poured us each a glassful. It did quench our thirst, even if Lincoln had to drink his in the awkward angle beneath the desk. I couldn't remember what his face looked like, but his ass shone like twin dark planets under a full moon. Jelani had Lincoln toss the joint, still huge, back to us from the cistern lid, and he lit it and blew smoke out across the room. He was like a dragon sitting there, I thought, or a volcano.

He turned the joint around so its lit end was in his mouth and then he pulled my lips close to his and started blowing smoke into my face. I caught right on to what he wanted me to do and put my lips around the small protruding end. I opened up my air passages again, letting the smoke fill me. He pushed me back and turned the joint around, getting down on the floor and holding it for Lincoln. Jelani's dick hung between his legs as he leaned over Lincoln, and I crawled over and put my face in his big hairy ass.

He opened his cheeks to me and pressed his hole against my mouth. My tongue flashed inside, and I loved the taste of this hunky man. I chewed at him, licking and sticking my tongue deep inside him. "Fuck me," I heard, but it was Lincoln's voice echoing from the filling cistern. "Fuck me again," he said.

Jelani backed up and moved me in front of him. "Fuck him again," he said. I said that I thought Lincoln wanted to try Jelani's big dick this time, that I just wanted to lick Jelani's ass more than anything. "I can't fuck wid him," Jelani explained. "We related."

"Come," Jelani told me, and put another condom on my dick. He helped me lie on my back and then slide my legs out on either side of Lincoln, so Lincoln could sit on my dick and ride me. Jelani then squatted above my face and slowly lowered the entrance to his heavenly body around the pole of my tongue. Lincoln bounced against my dick and I licked up and down Jelani's brown crack, letting the threads of his short ass hair scratch my face as I slid against him. My nostrils filling with his musky scent of island manhood, I plunged my tongue as far as it would stretch, and at the same time thrust my dick deep into Lincoln's ass. I was already close to shooting into Lincoln, but I wanted to wait until I felt the ropes of Jelani's hot come stream across my stomach. I swirled my tongue inside him and felt the convulsions of the water hose choke beside me.

"Oh yeah," Lincoln said. "De truck cummin' too!" and the hose flinched and emptied in huge spurts like a giant getting off. Each surge of ejection threw Lincoln off balance and he hunkered his ass down on to my dick to ground him. I couldn't see anything. Jelani's ass was my sole dark vision and occupation but I felt Lincoln rise off me and crawl from beneath Melynda's desk. I heard him stand up and say, "Head rush," before he straddled me again and sat back down. I could tell he was facing me now, facing Jelani, and I was inside both of these brothers' asses. I could feel them pounding their sweaty dicks as I probed and dug at them, both of them bouncing and grinding their asses against me.

"Free your hair, 'Lani!" Lincoln urged. "Soak up dis good stuff!" I could feel Jelani shift his weight on my face and I stretched up to see beyond his writhing ass, my vision scaling the slick muscles of his back, to see the crocheted netting lift off his hair and the mane of this Zionic feline rain down like a fountain. I imagined

I was kissing a lion, imagined the firm globes of his ass in my hands were the cheeks of a jungle cat. I imagined the tangy fruit I desired was inside the lion's dangerous mouth. But even though the scene had grown more and more acrobatic, this was no circus act. I could smell the ocean in the long dreadlocks that fell and caged my head like a spider. I could smell the wind. I was in an unexpected island paradise, inside a waterfall of rich blessings, and I was kissing a lion.

Above me, Jelani and Lincoln began bouncing against me in unison. They started groaning and chanting and soon I was moaning with the growing explosion. We all came together, releasing the tension of the hot day, exhausting the last dregs of energy in seemingly choreographed convulsive spurts, mine trapped inside the condom in the annals of Lincoln, and their white stripes crossing each other on my tan torso marking their territory. And I was theirs: every sweat-, cum- and ass-covered part of me. Jelani's giant dick already marked me. He marked my ass and he marked my throat. And he and Lincoln rose from my body and stood. Jelani pulled the condom from my dick and poured my heavy load into the middle of their sticky mess.

I lay there thanking God for my luck, watching these beautiful men get their clothes together, their dicks still swollen and dripping stringy trails of post-come. I hated to see them step into their jeans, but I smiled when I saw Jelani put the receipt pad in his back pocket. Lincoln nodded at me as he went outside, where he unscrewed the nozzle and started to wrap the hose around the length between his wrist and elbow. He climbed over the balcony rail and started easing his way down the hill, flattening and rolling the hose tightly as he went. I lay on my back, on Melynda's floor, one hand behind my head and the other stroking my still semi-hard dick, flipping it back and forth, playing in the three loads of hot cum, and I asked Jelani what I owed him.

He shook his head. "Dis God's water. You ain't pay nuttin.'"

I rolled up off the floor and took my sarong from where it had been thrown in melee, and I followed Jelani to the back door. I was puzzled: I knew Melynda had gotten the water at half price and so I asked why I was getting the bigger discount.

"Two for none, Gentile," Jelani said, and winked those thick eyelashes at me before he climbed over the balcony. I tied the sarong around my waist and followed him down the hill. Lincoln had the hose put away, closed the valves and drafts, and was climbing into the passenger seat. He didn't look at me.

"Lincoln volunteered his commission too," Jelani said, and he knocked on the windshield in front of Lincoln and Lincoln nodded. Lincoln had a handsome face; I was sorry I hadn't been able to see more of it, but I was grateful for the time I could spend with his ass.

"Hey, Jelani," I whispered as he climbed into the cab. I figured Lincoln could hear me but I didn't care. "I thought your brother was a Christian," I said.

Jelani threw his head back and laughed. "My bruddah *is* ah Chris-jun, mehson." Lincoln slapped his denim-covered thigh and laughed too. "Dis here Lincoln is my cousin, bwoy." He reached out the window and pinched my cheek. "You don't go wastin' dat water now, son."

I stood there and watched Jelani and Lincoln make their slow way up the road in the big truck, its motor roaring at the steep incline, its shiny tanks gleaming in the late afternoon sun. "In God We Trust," I read as the truck disappeared, and I said my own version of a little hallelujah. I massaged my chest as I stood there, sweating, enjoying the sweet burn as my palms rubbed my sore nipples.

Then I went inside, of course, and took a very, very long cool shower: I was thankful for a paradise with the natural system of checks and balances; thankful for a way to get water delivered when one couldn't even get a Domino's pizza or his mail; and thankful for a landlord who believed in watering the garden, taking long showers, flushing toilets, and washing clothes and cars.

ৡৎ৩

CJ Livingston writes fiction and poetry in New York City. His work has appeared in Bloom, The Gay & Lesbian Review, Velvet Heat, Bar Stories, and McSweeney's, among other journals and anthologies.

Pretty in the Hood
FRED TOWERS

"Ugh. Not another ketchup sandwich," I said, throwing the bread onto the counter and slamming the empty fridge shut. "I gotta get some real grub."

I stomped through my studio apartment to my dresser and searched for some clothes to throw on. "This'll have to do," I said as I wiggled out of my underwear and slid into the short shorts I found. After I fastened them, I adjusted my cock so the tip peeked out from under the frayed edge. I smiled because I knew my dates always drooled over it no matter how straight they swore they were.

Out on the street it didn't take long for a car to circle around the block. "Hey, darlin', lookin' for company?" I flipped my braids and sauntered on as if I didn't hear him. "Come on," he said as he passed me again. I turned into an alley as he pulled up to me again. I heard him creeping his car behind me.

I turned and put my hands on my hips. "May I help you?"

He looked me up and down and smiled. I noticed him lick his lips as if my cock tip were a piece of chocolate candy when he saw it.

"You sure are pretty," he said as he motioned to his sedan's passenger door. "Need a ride?"

"Maybe." Even though my stomach grumbled, I continued to play the cat and mouse game. "What are you after?"

"Well, uh." He fumbled with his zipper and pulled out his cock.

Even though I preferred dark meat like mine, I noticed that he had a decent one for a white boy. I smiled at his thick tool, and said, "What about it?"

"Get in and find out." He motioned to his door again. "I got it covered."

I understood that to mean he had money, but he didn't know if I was a cop.

"I ain't no shield, baby," I said, sliding into the passenger seat. "What about you?"

"No, I'm definitely not one." He brushed his hand along my thigh and pumped his hand on his cock until precum drizzled out of his slit. "Will this do?" He glanced at a twenty he had sticking out of the ashtray.

"Yeah. That'll be fine." I licked my lips to let him know that it covered a blow, and he smiled. "Mmmm," I said as I reached across and took his cock from him and pumped it some more.

"Oh, yeah," he said, throwing his head back against the headrest.

I slid his cock into my mouth and teased the tip with my tongue ring. I felt him jerk and grab my braids. He brushed them away from my face and held them in a fist so he could watch me in action.

"Oh, yeah, baby. Suck it good." He panted and moaned. "Oh, God. Oh, yes."

Tiring of the teasing, I swallowed him into my throat. He grunted as his thick meat stretched my mouth wide and slammed down my throat. I pumped my face up and down as he guided me with his hand in my braids.

"Take it. Yeah, take it deep."

Every time I swallowed him, his wiry hairs tickled my nose, and I smelled his musky sweat. His scent caused my cock to strain against my shorts. I devoured his cock like it was my last meal.

"Mmm," I moaned and hummed around his cock.

"Here it comes. Oh, God. Oh, yeah," he said as he shot his load into my mouth.

After a couple of minutes, he glanced at his watch. "Gotta go. You'll be seeing me around." He winked at me as he patted my shorts next to my cock.

I noticed precum on my tip, wiped it off with my finger, and licked it off. "Later, darlin.' It's been fun." Flipping my braids, I grabbed the twenty from the ashtray and jumped out of the car.

After I ate some grub at Betsie's Diner, I decided to cut through Brook Park to get back to my apartment.

"Yo, girlie boy."

Hearing those words, I hurried through the parking lot and hoped I made it to the swings. At that point, he'd have to be on foot also. I knew my twinkie ass could outrun him because I'd run track in high school.

"Yo," he said, pulling his car up beside me. "Slow down. I don't mean no harm."

I glanced over to the car and saw his long, thin cock poking out of his pants.

"Come on, baby. Help a fella out."

"What the fuck?" I stopped and stared at him. "Are you for real?"

"Yeah." He stroked it and looked around. "I ain't no fag, but…" He glanced down at his cock as if it'd urge him on. "But I need some."

"Need some what?"

"A tight hole to milk me dry, baby."

I looked around and wondered if I should run.

"Come on, baby. It won't take long." He reached over to the passenger seat and grabbed something.

I froze, even though my brain yelled for me to run.

"I gots money," he said, holding up his wallet.

I wondered if I should grab it and run, but I breathed out the air I held instead.

"Condoms, too." He held up an unopened box. "How much will it take? I got paid today, baby." I heard the urgency in his voice and thought about letting him beg longer, but I crawled into the car instead.

"I don't talk money," I said, looking around the park for cops.

He grabbed out a fifty and laid it on the seat between us. I slid my butt on top of it and reached for his cock.

"Where you wanna go?" I asked. "I ain't goin' to do it out in the open."

He glanced around the park and sighed. "Don't know. Any suggestions? How about your crib?"

"No, not an option." I thought for a minute and said, "How about over in the woods?"

"No one'll see us? Will they?" He glanced nervously toward the woods.

"Nah. Park over there." I pointed to a spot near the tree opening. "We can go under the bridge."

After I stroked his cock a few times, he said, "Okay." His breathy voice wavered as if he wasn't sure, but his cock told him to follow.

As we walked the trail, he jumped at each cracking twig. I noticed used condoms and wrappers thrown about the farther we went. As we neared the bridge, I took his hand, pulled him to a spot, and realized him staring down at our hands.

"How you want me?" I stopped, released his hand, and looked up at him. "You want me from behind? Or legs in the air?"

He glanced at me and then, back where we'd come from.

"Changing your mind?" I patted the pocket I'd slid the money into as we exited the car. "I don't do refunds."

"Nah," he said, going macho male on me. "Just bend over."

I dropped my shorts and bent over. I heard him rip open a condom and spit out the packet that broke off in his mouth. He spit on my hole and slid in a finger. I pushed back onto his finger and moaned.

"Slow down, baby." He pulled his finger out and left my ass begging to be filled. He massaged my ass cheeks, pulling them wide apart and releasing them.

"Please, fill me. I need you." I wiggled my ass, begging for his lean, dark meat to slam home.

He spit on my hole again and inched his cock in. As it entered, his cock felt bigger than it'd looked. My hole expanded to take it in. Once I swallowed the last inch of him into my ass, he gripped my hips and pounded in and out. His balls slapped against mine with each thrust.

"Oh, yeah. Uhhhh," I moaned and pushed back onto him.

Behind me I heard a hissing sound. As he neared coming, the noise grew louder until it exploded along with him into a deep growl. Remaining inside me, he stood still, held onto my hips, and panted. I groaned and shot my load onto the ground ahead of us.

Feeling dazed, I panicked when I heard a ringing. I looked around and wondered what it was.

He pulled out, and the ringing stopped. "Yeah."

At that moment I returned to reality and realized that the noise was his cell phone.

"I'm fixin' to go, baby," he said, throwing the used condom onto the ground and tucking his cock into his pants. "I'm on my way to the car now." He walked away from me to follow the trail back. "Is fried chicken okay for dinner?" After a short pause, he said, "Pickin' some up now."

As we walked out of the woods, he hung up with the caller and rushed to phone someone else. "Hey, Boo. Can you throw together a bucket of chicken for me to pick up in five?" He chuckled. "Yeah, took a detour." He listened to his friend and said, "Man, gotta hurry. Old lady chewing up my ass." Without saying a word to me, he jumped into his car and rushed away.

"So much for romance," I said to the retreating car.

Later that night, I folded the money I'd made and tucked it into the sandwich bag I'd buried in the laundry detergent. Hearing a knock at my door, I brushed the detergent off my hands and straightened my clothes.

"Hi, baby," Richard said, sashaying into my studio. "Are you ready?" He turned toward me, and put his hands on his hips. "Girl, why aren't you dressed?"

"For what?"

"The clubs, honey. It's Saturday night. The queens are feelin' frisky tonight," he said, prancing around my sofa.

"I ain't," I said, plopping down onto the sofa.

"Girl, get your black ass off that couch," he said, standing in front of me with his hands on his hips.

"Whatever," I said, rolling my eyes. "Why don't you go with Freddie?"

"He got busted."

"For what?" I sat up straighter as he sat to talk.

"Selling." He looked around my apartment as if cops might be right behind him.

"Ass or drugs?"

"Drugs." He looked at me again and grinned. "That queen gives it away too easily for free. What are you talking about?"

I laughed. "Yeah, you're right." I looked around my tiny apartment and decided I did need to get out for more than work. "Okay. I'll go," I said, jumping up.

"Good." He drew out the word as if it had a thousand syllables. "Let's go get us some mens, baby. Mmmmm."

"Girl, you're so bad," I said, digging through my drawers for some clothes.

"Honey, you need some romance in your life." He jumped off the sofa and pranced around like he does when he lectures. "Selling is fine and dandy for payin' the bills, but sometimes, you need a man to cuddle up to. Men don't pay for cuddlin.'" He wiggled his finger at me as he said, "You listen to your momma. You hear."

I grinned and shook my head.

"What the hell is takin' you so long?" He pushed me aside and searched through my clothes. "Girl, you need some new clothes. What is this crap?"

"Hey." I tore a pair of my underwear away from him. "They were a present."

"From when?" He looked at the underwear and me. "Your first husband in your last life?"

"Fuck you," I said, tucking them under a cushion as he dove back into my drawers. "My first lover, if you must know, Ms. Thang."

"What about these?" He held up a tight, cropped shirt and short shorts. "These will surely get you some action." He threw them at me. "Get dressed."

"What happened to cuddling?" I asked, holding up the outfit.

"Girl, you have to set the trap first." He giggled. "Then, you cuddles," he said, wrapping his arms around himself.

I rolled my eyes.

Once we arrived at the club, he pushed his way onto the dance floor. I perched on a bar stool, watched him rub against all the men within inches of his dance spot, and nursed a cocktail.

"May I?"

My head snapped around at the question. When I saw the sexy stud before me, I said, "Sure, darlin.' Be my guest." I twisted on the seat to face him. "You new here?"

"No. I travel a lot." He motioned to the bartender to refill our drinks. "I don't get out much." He adjusted his dress slacks, and I noticed his package stretched against the pants. When I finally glanced up, he smiled at me. I giggled, and he chuckled. "I'm Terrence," he said, extending his hand.

"Mike. My friends call me, 'Mickey.' So, what do you do?" I asked, taking a sip of my refreshed drink.

"Consulting." He nodded his head like that explained everything. "What about you?" He reached forward and placed his hand on my leg.

"Sales." I nodded my head and hoped he wouldn't want details.

"Good." He turned from me and glanced toward the dance floor. "Your friend's having fun." He smiled and looked back at me.

Realizing he'd been watching me since we arrived, I smiled. "Yeah."

"Will he get upset if we leave?"

"Nah," I said, taking another drink.

As we left, Richard waved, blew kisses, and said, "Have fun." He winked at me before he turned back to his groupies.

At my apartment, Terrence glanced around and asked, "Where's your bed?"

I patted the sofa. "Under here. Well, make yourself comfortable. I'm goin' to tinkle."

When I returned, he stood in the kitchenette, staring into the empty fridge. "What do you eat?" He held up the mustard and ketchup bottles. "Nothin' to drink either?"

"Why? You hungry?" I paused and waited for him to answer. "I need to go to the store. I just got paid."

"Oh," he said, replacing the condiments. "We'll have to go tomorrow." He grabbed a glass from the cabinet and filled it up with tap water as he spoke.

I raised an eyebrow at him and said, "We ain't married yet."

He twirled around at my words. "I didn't mean." He paused. "I wasn't implying. I just meant we're going to have to eat after tonight." He walked toward me during that statement with a romantic look in his eyes.

"Will we?" I raised an eyebrow again, swung my right hip up and placed my hand on it, giving him my best femme pose.

He chuckled and said, "Oh, yeah." I melted, when he wrapped me up in his arms, pulled me against his teddy bear bod, and kissed me. He directed us down onto the floor with me on top of him. As he massaged my ass with his large hands and our cocks rubbed against each other through our clothes, I panted and moaned. Pulling my shirt above my head, he nibbled my nipples.

I pulled him away from them and kissed him, exploring his mouth with my tongue. Pulling away, I licked his full lips, and he bit my lower one.

I nuzzled his neck and said, "I need you inside me."

"Not yet." He laced his fingers in my braids and pulled me in for another kiss. "I want to take my time. We've got all night."

"Oh, God," I said as he pushed my shorts down. My cock plopped onto his pants with precum drizzling out of my slit.

"Lick it for me, baby," he said, looking down at it. I balanced myself, dipped my finger into it, and licked it off my finger. He watched in a trance as if I were licking his cock. "Mmmmm. That's it, baby. Suck it." I performed my best skills on my finger for him, licking and sucking.

I nuzzled down to his chest and unbuttoned his shirt with my mouth. When I exposed his charcoal-colored chest, I licked and nibbled it. "You taste delicious," I said before I sucked his nipple into my mouth.

"Ohhh." He pushed my head into his chest. "Harder." I bit and sucked harder at his request, and he growled. "Oh, yeah, baby. That's it."

He reached down and grabbed my cock. I threw my head back as he pumped me. My breathing quickened, and I tensed, holding myself up with my arms. As I panted, he pumped harder. I flung my braids forward and moaned. My load shot onto his chest as I grunted.

"Lick it, baby. Clean me up," he said, looking down at his chest.

My load covered his chest and stomach, and I noticed a pearl of it on his right cheek. I started the clean-up with the drop on his face and worked my way down to the top of his pants with him watching.

Undoing his leather belt, I licked my lips and bit the lower one. Instead of nudging his pants down, I reached into the hole of his boxers and pulled his thick, dark cock out. At the sight of it, I moaned.

"I have a condom in my pocket," he said, looking down at me.

I dove into his pockets in response and ripped open the packet with my teeth when I found it. I eased it out and rolled it down his huge dick. Once I had it in place, I teased his tip with my tongue ring.

"Wow, I didn't know you were pierced," he said, moaning and panting from my teasing. "Oh, shit. That feels good."

I swallowed him into the back of my throat. It stretched my mouth wide and pounded my throat as I worked it in and out. I struggled to breathe and knew my jaw and throat were going to hurt later, but I didn't care. I wanted him inside me and wanted to drain him.

"Oh, fuck. Oh, yeah. Uhh." He pushed my head up and down, causing me to gag. "Oh, shit. Here I come."

I continued to swallow him, milking him dry.

"That's enough. Come up here," he said, pulling on my arm.

I crawled up him, and he wrapped his arms around me, holding my head against his chest. I listened to his heartbeat and relaxed my weight on him. I fell asleep.

"Wake up, baby. I'm ready for some more loving," he said, nudging me.

Groggy, I raised my head, wiped my braids out of my face, and rubbed my eyes.

"Are you awake?" He looked down at me.

"Did you sleep?"

"A little." He tipped my head back and kissed me. "You ready for the next round?"

"I don't know. I ain't awake yet," I said, sitting up.

He kissed my back, brushed my braids to one side, and nibbled the curve of my neck. "I want you," he whispered into my ear. I shivered as his warm breath brushed across my ear. "Want to be inside you," he continued.

"Does sound good," I said, turning toward him.

He rolled me onto my back, stood to remove his pants, and threw them on top of our discarded clothes. After he opened the packet he'd pulled from his pocket, he rolled it onto his stiff cock.

"Come here," I said, stretching my arms and legs up to him.

He lowered himself on top of me and kissed me as I wrapped my limbs around him, pulling him closer. After a moment of cuddling, he pulled away from me, and I reached under the sofa for lube.

I moaned when he dipped a lubed finger into my ass. After he pumped it in and out a few times, he added another finger.

"Oh, please. Give me your cock."

He smiled and teased me with his fingers for a while longer.

"Oh, please."

"Demanding little thing. Aren't you?" He chuckled as he removed his fingers and changed positions to enter me. He nudged his tip forward and back several times, teasing me open and leaving me empty again.

"Oh, please." I grunted and flipped my head up to look down at his cock. "Quit teasing me. Give it to me," I said as if I spoke directly to it.

He chuckled. "Okay. Here you go." He pushed it in, and I moaned as my ass stretched to take all of him in. "Is that what you wanted, baby?" he whispered into my ear.

I shivered. "Oh, yeah."

At first, he pumped in and out, letting me feel every inch of him leaving me and filling me again. As my breathing quickened to a pant, he lifted my legs higher and slammed in and out. I felt my balls jiggle as his slapped against my ass.

"Pump yourself. I want you to come with me." In response, I grabbed and pounded it. "That's it, baby. Do it hard." He clenched his teeth and grunted.

Feeling the urge to blow, I bit my lower lip and pushed it back. I wanted to save it, so we could come at the same time. I struggled to breathe as I held it back.

"Come with me." He struggled to speak through his panting and grunting.

I released my load, and it shot across my chest and up onto my face. I imagined it was his come shooting across my face. I licked up the drops on my lips as he collapsed on top of me.

We cuddled the rest of the night, ate breakfast at Betsie's, and went grocery shopping the next day. The honeymoon ended before the next weekend.

"I'll be home this weekend. Yeah, I've missed you, too," Terrence said into his cell phone. "I wish I didn't have to make these business trips either."

I stood at the bathroom door and listened to his end of the conversation. After he snuck into the bathroom every time his phone rang, I had decided to snoop on him to see what he was hiding.

"I love you, too, honey. How's the baby? Is she sleeping through the night?"

Hearing him ending the call, I stepped away from the door and waited for him with my hands on my hips.

He opened the door and smiled. "Hi, baby. What's up?"

"I thought you were going on a business trip?" I stared at him and waited for his response.

"I am. Detroit. I told you that." He stepped forward and leaned in to kiss me, but I clenched my jaw and turned my head. "Baby, what's wrong?"

"Your wife and kid in Detroit?" He paused at my words. After a minute, he lowered his head. "I asked you a question."

"We ain't married. So what's your problem?" He stomped past me. "I've kept you fed and fucked."

"I can keep myself fed and fucked." I turned to look at him. "I don't need a man moving in, thinking he's taking care of my ass."

"How you gonna feed yourself?" He threw his clothes into his suitcase. "Working the streets?" He zipped it closed.

"What's it to you?"

"I felt sorry for your ho ass." He picked up his suitcase and walked toward the door.

"Well, don't. I don't need some two-timing fucker feeling sorry for me." I walked toward him. "You need to accept yourself, ass-hole."

"I know I'm bi, baby. I've accepted that."

"But have you told your wife?" He snapped his head around, and I knew he hadn't. "Get the fuck out."

He sighed and left, slamming the door behind him.

For about two weeks, I stowed away in my tiny apartment like a jail cell. When the groceries ran out, I decided I needed to snap out of it and get to work.

"I'll show you, Mr. Two Timing Terrence. I'm a survivor, baby," I said to the mirror as I pulled a slinky, little shirt over my head and wiggled into my short shorts. "I'm back in action." I winked at my reflection and tossed my braids.

A little later, I opened the door to Ma and Pa's neighborhood grocery store and smiled as Pa glanced up at the bell jingling above the door.

"Been missin' in action. New fella?" He smiled.

Instead of answering him, I wiggled over to the edge of the counter and asked, "Miss me?" I flipped my braids and leaned over the counter in my flirtatious queen pose.

"Sure, have," Pa said, walking around the counter and grabbing my ass. "Go into the back room. I'll be there in a minute."

I pranced off, knowing he was locking the front door like he always did for our encounters. He didn't want Ma or a customer walking in on us. Once in the small stock room, I pulled my shorts down and bent over some boxes.

"Mmm. I sure have missed this cute, little ass. Pretty thing," he said, slapping it.

In response, I wiggled it and smiled. Behind me, I heard him rip a condom packet and unzip his jeans. I felt him push in and fill me up. He wasn't as big as Terrence, but his movements were familiar. He pumped me harder than any man had, slamming my cock against the box as he claimed my ass.

"Oh, yeah. Fuck me good."

He grabbed my shoulders to hold me still as he shoved in and out. I heard his body slap against mine. After a few minutes, he grunted, came and pulled out.

When I turned around, I saw him throwing the condom into the toilet, flushing it, and tucking his cock into his jeans.

"Grab you some groceries on your way out, little one," he said, walking back up front.

Feeling used, but cared for, I smiled and pulled up my shorts. Sometimes, I wondered if there were other queens Pa cared for, but I never asked. Instead, I picked up a hand basket and filled it with groceries.

Pa bagged them, slid me some bills as if he were returning some change, and said, "Don't be away so long."

"I won't. I promise." I smiled, picked up my groceries, and flipped my braids.

On the street, I swished my hips to signal that I was looking for some action. It didn't take long for a car to pull up beside me.

"Hey, pretty. Lookin' sexy today."

"Hey, yourself," I said, smiling at Mr. Thick Dick White Boy.

"I told you I'd be around again."

I raised my eyebrows. "Yeah, you did." At that moment, I decided that I'd stick to selling until the day my heart flutters before my dick does. "Repeat?"

"Oh, yeah," he said as I slid into his car.

ॐ

Fred Towers lives in Indiana with his husband of ten years, Mel. He was published in Bearotica *(Alyson Publications),* Muscle Worshipers *(Starbooks Press), and* Ultimate Gay Erotica 2008 *(Alyson). He writes book reviews for gay male fiction for the Rainbow Reviews website. Besides his gay FTM superhero story in* UGE *2008, he'd hoped to write another superhero story for Superqueeroes, but hopes there is another one. Let him know what you think of his writing, by emailing him at fredtowers@yahoo.com*

Flesh to Flesh

LEE HAYES

Kevin Davis sprang out of the cab just as soon as it screeched to a halt at the curb at Ronald Reagan Washington National Airport, right outside of Washington, D.C. Kevin shoved a fifty-dollar bill through the window separating the cab driver from his riders, grabbed his suitcase, slammed the car door and raced toward the terminal. Even though the fare was only $13.75, Kevin didn't have time to wait for change. Plus, he wanted to reward the driver for getting him to the airport as quickly as possible, in spite of the snow that had suddenly fallen from wounded skies and snarled the already congested traffic.

Once inside, Kevin made his way to the terminal, shoved his credit card into the kiosk, printed his boarding pass and checked his luggage at the counter. He then raced through the terminal, the tails of his trench coat fluttering behind him as he remained resolute in his intent to make his flight—even though the flight was moments away from departing. He sailed down the escalator, weaving past people posted on either side of the moving staircase—people who were completely oblivious of his need to make this flight. He *needed* to escape D.C. and its wretched memories and relax in New Orleans, one of his favorite cities, and he wasn't about to let a few tourists stand in his way.

As he brushed past the pedestrians, he uttered a perfunctory and panicked "excuse me" as he advanced toward his destination. Sweat had formed on his brow and his breathing quickened. Kevin, a former collegiate track star, was almost ashamed that this little run had tired him so; he knew the extra ten pounds he had put on during the last few months had had an effect on his fitness level. Overall, he knew he still looked good; yet, he made a mental note to get back to the gym as soon as he got back to D.C.

While brushing past folks, his mind drifted back to his last trip to New Orleans some years ago when he and a group of friends took an impromptu road trip from Houston to the Crescent City. He thought about the wild time they had shaking their asses with complete abandon in any one of many blues and jazz clubs on Bourbon Street. He remembered drinking Hurricanes at eleven o'clock in the morning and indulging in Crawfish Etouffee for lunch and devouring delightful beignets as the sun set. He had not visited post-Katrina New Orleans, but he hoped the city would give him what he needed.

As he made his way through the airport, he tried to remain unfazed by the holiday decorations. He couldn't wait to be lifted out of the city because he didn't want to spend the Christmas holiday in D.C.; it would be a painful reminder of his very painful breakup with his lover Daryl that still left a pain in his heart—a full two years later. Occasionally, he and Daryl would speak on the phone to check in with each other, or sometimes he'd walk through a crowd and smell a familiar scent and look around for Daryl only to be staring in the face of a complete stranger. The last time he saw Daryl was a couple months ago at a black-tie function for the Human Rights Campaign. Kevin looked up and saw Daryl from across the room and they smiled politely at each other as if they were mere acquaintances instead of friends-turned-lovers-turned-ex-lovers. The moment he saw Daryl across the room, through the sea of entangled bodies wrapped in stiff conversation, his heart skipped a beat. It was love. In spite of Daryl's lies; despite his past indiscretions, love resided in Kevin's heart for that man, but he had learned to love from a distance. As hard as it was for him to admit, he missed his touch, his caress, his scent, his taste and his feel. A part of him wished that he could go back in time to that exact moment when Daryl decided that he needed something that he wasn't getting from Kevin so that Kevin could be that need. He wished he could have been more loving, more attentive, more sexual, more giving, less proud, less demanding, less needy so that Daryl would have stayed with him. He had spent countless hours thinking he "coulda, shoulda, woulda" done something differently, if only he had known. But all that wouldn't change the fact that Daryl stepped out on him and broke the one thing Kevin didn't think could be broken—his faith.

That was then. This is now.

Before he knew it, Kevin had successfully navigated his way through security and was ensconced in the comfort of his first-class seat, cocktail in his hand, listening to the perky flight attendant who announced that the plane would depart on schedule. Kevin, along with the rest of the passengers, breathed a sigh of relief; a little snow on the ground wasn't going to keep him from his destiny.

Just when he delighted in the thought of having an empty seat next to him, a disheveled, but attractive man, emerged from the shadows of the jetway, breathing hard and looking as if he had run a marathon.

"Good afternoon, sir," the flight attendant said. "Let me help you to your seat," she said as she looked at the boarding pass in his hand and ushered him into seat 2B, the window seat next to Kevin. "Here you are, sir. Would you like something to drink?"

"Yes," the man uttered between huffs of breath. "I'll have a Jack and Coke," he said, right before collapsing in the seat. Kevin looked over at the tousled-looking man, smiled at him and handed him a napkin to wipe the sweat that had gathered like raindrops on his forehead.

Have we met before, maybe in a past life? Kevin thought to himself.

"Let me guess," Kevin began, "you got caught up in the traffic mess, right?"

"Man, I don't know what's wrong with these idiots. The snow is not even sticking to the roads but I saw four accidents on I-395," he said while wiping away the sweat. "A trip to the airport that normally takes me twenty minutes took almost two hours today—that's some bullshit."

"Man, I feel you. I almost missed this flight, too. You know these folks can't drive when it rains, so when it snows all hell breaks loose," Kevin said as he leaned back and took a sip of his drink. "Well, just relax, you made it, we're gonna have a safe and smooth flight. Before you know it, we'll be on the ground in New Orleans."

"I hope you're right," he said just as the flight attendant returned with his drink. He opened the small bottle of liquor, mixed it with a dab of Coke and raised his plastic cup. "Here's to a safe flight." Kevin grabbed his cup and touched it to his before taking a sip of his beverage. "By the way, I'm Gabriel—Gabriel Kaine."

"It's nice to meet you, Gabriel. I'm Kevin Davis." For a split second, their eyes met and in that infinitesimally small unit of time, secrets were revealed as they both coyly smiled as if to say to each other *I see you, too.* Kevin surreptitiously eyed this beautiful stranger as Gabriel glanced out of the window and watched the ground beneath them slowly fade out of view. For Kevin, this stranger's bronzed skin and Caesar-like haircut made him look like something out of Greek mythology, something mysterious and enticing.

"Is New Orleans your final stop?" Gabriel asked suddenly.

"Yeah. I was supposed to meet a few friends there for the holiday, but they all canceled on me, but I'm going anyway."

"Ah, an independent man—I like that."

Kevin smiled. *Is he flirting with me?*

"What about you? Is New Orleans your final destination?"

"Yeah, one of my good friends plays the trumpet and he is making his Bourbon Street debut with a jazz band. I have to go and support him; plus, he is a brilliant player. And, like you, I didn't want to be in D.C. for the holiday, either. I just needed to get away. It's been a rough year."

"I feel you on that one," Kevin said. "You should let me know when and where your friend is playing. Maybe I'll drop in."

"That would be nice. Maybe, if you're not too busy, you could squeeze time out of your vacation and have a drink with me. I know this wonderful little bar on Canal Street."

I'd like to squeeze more than time.

"Are you asking me out on a date?" Kevin fearlessly and playfully asked. Gabriel, seemingly taken aback by Kevin's bold words, smiled as his face became reddened.

"Hmmm? A date? I hadn't thought about that. Thanks for asking. Yes, I'll go out with you," he said, turning the tables on Kevin.

"You're pretty smooth, aren't you, pretty boy?"

"You gotta be smooth to be in my line of business."

"Line of business? What are you, a gigolo? If so, I think I have some spare change in my pockets." Kevin pretended to dig into his pockets.

"No, funny man. I'm not a hooka—I'm a journalist."

Suddenly, the truth flashed before Kevin's face like lightning.

"Oh shit. I know who you are. I've seen you on TV. You covered that serial killer, what was his name?"

"He was called 'The Messiah,'" Gabriel said in a sliver of a voice.

"Yeah, that's it. I saw you on CNN a couple of times. I knew you looked familiar when I first saw you, but I didn't know why. Wow, I'm sitting next to a celebrity. Can I have your autograph?" Kevin said, with feigned excitement.

"If you play your cards right, you might get more than my autograph," Gabriel said with a wink. "But, if you don't mind, I'd rather not talk about that case. It's still a little hard for me." Kevin took notice of the sullen expression that commandeered Gabriel's distinctive face. Kevin, having survived an abusive lover and a cheating partner, connected with Gabriel's pain and honored his wishes.

"Not a problem at all. Hey, are you staying at a hotel or with friends?"

"A hotel—the InterContinental on Saint Charles."

Kevin let out a chuckle. "Are you serious? That's my hotel." Kevin tried to not show his excitement, but his enthusiasm showed all over his face. He had not felt a sudden wave of passion for anyone in a very long time and, for him, a part of this trip was meant to re-ignite the part of him that died when his last relationship expired. He didn't want to spend the rest of his life closed off and alone, so a part of him knew that he needed to reconnect with life in a place known for its powerful embrace of celebration and merriment. As he pondered this new development with Gabriel, he suddenly felt as if he had been delivered into the fate's favor; but, past experiences told him to not put too much hope in this serendipitous twist of fate. He took a deep breath, turned his head and tried to slow the rapid pace of his heartbeat.

Gabriel looked over at Kevin whose chocolate skin glowed, leaned in so close that Kevin could smell the whiskey on his breath and whispered, "Do you believe in fate, Mr. Davis?"

Kevin smiled. *I want to believe in you, Mr. Kaine.*

❀❀❀

Once they arrived by cab at the hotel located a few blocks from the French Quarter, they grabbed their bags and walked into the four-star hotel. When the bellman opened the door for them, they walked in and ascended the black and gold carpeted staircase that led to the main lobby. Kevin intentionally fell behind Gabriel as he climbed the stairs. He took a long, lustful look at Gabriel's round ass and powerful thighs as they climbed higher and higher, and his head was assaulted by thoughts of debauchery and lust. He watched Gabriel's muscles flexing beneath his pair of jeans and he imagined what his ass looked like naked. Was it hairy or smooth? Soft like cotton or hard like stone? Or, something in between?

"You getting an eyeful?" Gabriel asked as he turned around and caught Kevin staring just as they reached the final step.

"Uhhhh, something like that. I apologize," Kevin said, trying to shield his embarrassment.

"Don't apologize. Trust me, it's all good."

"I hope to find out," Kevin muttered underneath his breath.

"What was that?"

"Oh, nothing," he said with an impish grin.

Once they reached the guest check-in desk, Gabriel stepped up to the counter, pulled out his identification and credit card and checked in with no problem. He stepped to the side and made room for Kevin to do the same. At the counter, Kevin pulled out his driver's license and credit card and set them on the counter. The desk clerk picked them up and turned his attention to the computer screen in front of him.

"I hope they have a good gym here. I gotta keep my workout up; I just lost thirty pounds," Gabriel stated. "I don't want to lose the momentum now."

"Maybe we can work out together when we get back."

"Sure, but you look pretty together right now."

"I have some toning to do, but I'm aight." Kevin turned his attention to the desk clerk as Gabriel continued looking at him as if he was trying to read Kevin's vibe and energy.

"What?"

"Nothing. Just checking you out, that's all."

"Mr. Davis," the clerk interjected. "I don't have a reservation for you. By any chance could it be under another name or would you have the confirmation number?"

"Excuse me? I made this reservation months ago. No, I don't have a confirmation number and no, it would not be under another name."

"I'm sorry, sir, but I don't have you in our system. Are you sure you booked at this hotel?"

"Of course I'm sure," Kevin said, raising his voice a bit. Not wanting to go completely ballistic in the lobby, Kevin took a deep breath. "Okay, fine. Just give me a room and we'll straighten this mess out later. I can't believe this," he said, righteous indignation spewing from his mouth. "I didn't expect this kind of treatment from this hotel."

"Sir, I do apologize, but the hotel is completely booked through the weekend."

"What? Look here, Brenda," he said as he read her name tag. "I have just traveled from Washington, D.C. and I need a room. I am tired, hungry and I don't have time or patience for this mess. I need to speak with a manager—now."

"I am truly sorry, sir. I'll get one for you." Brenda's tone softened, as did Kevin's demeanor.

"I can't believe this shit." Kevin shook his head from side to side. He looked over at Gabriel whose squinted brow gave the appearance that he was in deep thought.

"I have an idea," he began, "why don't you stay with me?"

Kevin turned and looked into Gabriel's eyes in an effort to ascertain his sincerity. He also needed to know if he could trust this stranger from the plane. Sharing a few cocktails and enjoying each other's conversation in first-class is a huge difference from sharing a room for the weekend, but then Gabriel flashed his perfect teeth and Kevin melted. "Come on, it'll be fun. And, just so you know, I'm not a serial killer—I only write about them." He gave Kevin a playful nudge in his abdomen.

"Are you sure? I don't want to impose." Kevin looked at Gabriel curiously while trying to keep the titillating thought of what could happen if he shared a room with this man at bay. He stared at Gabriel, who met his unbroken gaze, and found his answer. He smiled seductively, shook his head as if to say "yes" and reached down for his bag.

"Good evening, sir. I'm Jerod Bailey, the manager on duty. I understand there is a problem with your reservation," the manager said in a stoic tone as the duo turned to leave.

Without so much as a glance at the manager, Kevin spoke. "No, there's no problem at all." He and Gabriel then walked leisurely to the elevator.

I can't believe I'm doing this. I don't even know him. Kevin tried to reconcile his conflicting feelings as the elevator whisked them to the top floor.

"You know, if you're uncomfortable with this, we can figure something else out."

"Nah, I'm cool if you're cool. I just don't want you to get the wrong impression of me. I don't want you to think I make a habit of staying with strange men in hotels."

Gabriel stepped closer, invading Kevin's personal space. His eyes slowly moved up and down Kevin's body as he bit on his bottom lip.

"I feel perfectly fine with sharing a room—not necessarily a bed—with you. So far, I like the man standing before me and I get a good feeling about you. Let's just get settled in, enjoy this magical city and see what happens." As Gabriel spoke, he moved closer and closer into Kevin's face until the space between their lips was almost non-existent. As he listened to Gabriel's strong voice, he closed his eyes and briefly lost himself in the possibility.

❂❂❂

At 7:15 that night, Kevin was fully dressed in black slacks and a form-fitting black turtleneck sweater by the time Gabriel emerged from the bathroom, covered only by a white towel. Kevin did not try to contain the smile that spread across his eager face as he watched Gabriel race across the room in an attempt to pull it together in order to make the eight o'clock show of his friend. Gabriel mentioned that his friend was playing at Blues City, a lounge on Bourbon Street. Listening to Gabriel rave about the talent of his friend filled Kevin with anticipation.

Gabriel darted across the wide space, decorated in earthy tones, in an almost panicked state. He paid little attention to Kevin, who had taken a seat in the lush lounge chair that occupied a corner near the window; he crossed his legs and watched the show. He watched Gabriel's body, paying special attention to his torso, which didn't contain too many extra pounds of muscle. He had just the right balance of muscle and flesh for Kevin's taste and he loved the way Gabriel moved, taking long, sleek strides as he virtually glided across the room, completely comfortable in his own skin. Kevin admired that quality.

"How about I pour you a drink?" Kevin offered as he got up and moved toward the mini-bar before Gabriel could respond.

"Oh, thank you—make it strong," he said in an almost desperate voice. Kevin dropped a few cubes of ice from the bucket into a glass and opened a small bottle of Jack Daniel's he removed from the mini-bar.

As Kevin poured the whiskey, he looked up over in Gabriel's direction just in time to see Gabriel turn his back and drop his towel to put on a pair of boxer briefs. Kevin's eyes threatened to bulge out his head as he got a complete view of Gabriel's full and meaty ass. His round humps looked like a couple of mounds of yellow cake, soft and moist, just waiting to be devoured. The tribal tattoo that spanned the length of his lower back made Kevin want to trace the design with his tongue.

As Kevin stared, Gabriel turned around and winked at him.

"You see something you like?" he asked as he walked over to Kevin, took his drink and disappeared into the bathroom.

You have no idea.

It had been several months since Kevin had been intimate with anyone and that experience left a lot to be desired. One thing he missed about being with Daryl was their explosive love-making and how they knew each other's hot spots and erogenous zones, unlike making love with a stranger where you have to figure things out as you go.

What have I gotten myself into?

❋❋❋

From the outside of Blues City, the sound of music emanating from the club clashed harshly with the other sounds given voice by Bourbon Street. The sound of obnoxious revelers and music blaring from speakers from an endless line of bars and clubs that lined both sides of the street created an urban dissonance that did not land pleasantly on Kevin's ears. He scurried behind Gabriel who walked into the dimly lit, smoke-soaked lounge, paid the five-dollar cover charge for them both and proceeded to the back to a blue velvet couch marked "Reserved" and took a seat. Gabriel motioned for Kevin to join him. A few seconds later, a scantily clad waitress with a long black ponytail and even longer, smooth, sinewy legs walked up to the table, leaned in and asked for their drink order.

"I'll have a Jack and Coke and he'll have…"

"I'll have the same." She nodded and then moved to the bar.

"You tryna step with the big dogs, huh? I hope you can handle it."

"Well, if I can't, I know you got my back," Kevin said with a wink. Gabriel placed his hand on Kevin's thigh and gave him a licentious look before moving closer to him. Kevin, a bit uncomfortable with Gabriel's public advances, smiled nervously but decided to go with the moment. After all, what happens in New Orleans, stays in New Orleans.

"I know this is going to sound crazy, but I feel a strong connection to you—as if we were meant to meet. I mean, I would never allow a stranger to stay with me in a hotel, particularly after my last relationship; but there is something about you that puts me at ease. I felt it as soon as I sat next to you on the plane. It's crazy, but it's like something brought us together."

"I know. This is really weird because I was thinking the same thing about you. I can't explain what it is that I feel or what this connection is, but it's definitely something. And, without going into detail, but just so you know, I haven't had the best of luck with men. I have spent the better part of the last couple of years reeling from a bad breakup and an even worse breakup before that one. I decided this was the trip I was going to reconnect with life and get back to living. I think I was *supposed* to meet you— for whatever reason—so I'm throwing caution to the wind and just going to enjoy you, in this place, in this time."

"Well said, my brother, well said." Gabriel continued stroking Kevin's thigh just as the thunderous sound of drums filled the room. The rest of the band joined the music and before they knew it, a full ensemble was on stage, playing, drumming, banging, blowing, and singing. Gabriel pointed to the attractive young trumpet player who seemed totally immersed in the hypnotic sounds spewing from his golden instrument.

"That's my boy, Jazz McKinney," Gabriel screamed out over

the music. The waitress returned with the drinks and Kevin took a quick shot as Gabriel jumped to his feet and moved hypnotically to the sounds of the band. The vocalist wailed and scatted and hummed and sang notes of passion, pleasure and pain. Kevin didn't know what song she sang, but it sounded as if it was rooted deeply in the Louisiana bayous. Finally, when the smooth trumpeter blew out his last note triumphantly, Kevin jumped to his feet, too, in recognition of the wonderful display of sight and sound. Kevin could not contain the feeling of joy which moved his stale spirit. The power of that note was felt in equal measure throughout the tightly packed lounge and it diffused throughout the small venue, hanging in air like the promise of a new day, taking up space and casting a spell on the enchanted and partially intoxicated crowd. The sound of the music, along with Gabriel's sultry movements and the magic in the air, took a hold of Kevin. He grabbed Gabriel by the hand and pulled him into the restroom, which was down the hall from where he sat, and locked the door.

"Hey, what's going—" Before he could finish his sentence, Kevin pushed him against the wall and kissed him wildly and passionately. Their hands rubbed each other's body, running the length of their frames, as they groped and pulled at each other. The heat they generated scorched the hair on their bodies and Kevin felt his soul being pulled into Gabriel's body by the powerful suction from his ample lips.

"Damn," Kevin said, finally pulling away. "I don't know what came over me, but we better stop before I rape you in this bathroom."

"You can't rape the willing," he said between breaths. "Shit, I have not been kissed like that in…in—I can't remember the last time I had a kiss like that."

"I don't know what's going on with us, but I like it."

"You'll like this even better," Gabriel said as he dropped to his knees and unbuttoned Kevin's pants.

"Oh shit. We can't do that in here," Kevin said without much weight to his words. Gabriel ignored his anemic caution and proceeded to pull out Kevin's smooth and hardened dick. He looked at it as it throbbed only inches from his face. He looked up into Kevin's eyes.

"You want this?" he asked. "Huh, I can't hear you."

"Yeah—hell yeah!" Kevin uttered right before Gabriel devoured him. The warm feeling of Gabriel's mouth wrapped around his pulsating member sent shockwaves all throughout Kevin's body. His knees got weak and he felt as if he was going to buckle and collapse to the floor. Gabriel's masterful technique bordered on feeling divine. He inhaled Kevin's dick, taking him fully into his mouth and down his throat. He licked, pulled, yanked, sucked, teased and tickled Kevin until he could no longer contain the ecstasy and released his pent-up frustration in streams of white-hot liquid that shot out across the room and landed in splats on the floor. Kevin continued to lean against the wall, his chest heaving and his heart threatening to burst through his chest.

Gabriel moved over to the sink and washed his hands, before taking a wet paper towel and washing the residual semen off Kevin's deflated manhood.

"Was that good for you?" he asked, already knowing the answer.

"It was so much better than good," Kevin said as he pulled up his pants. "I can't believe we just did that—in a public bathroom!" Kevin moved over to Gabriel and kissed him once again, their tongues wrapping around each other. Kevin slid his hand down Gabriel's thigh and stopped at the pipe in his pants. Kevin started to unzip his pants, but Gabriel stopped him.

"Not now, baby. Let's get back to the hotel so we can do this right," he said anxiously. He took Kevin by the hand and led him out of the bathroom, back into the darkened club. He dropped a twenty-dollar bill on the table to pay for the drinks and they were out the door.

"Wait, are you gonna let your friend know we're leaving?"

"I'll send him a text. Right now, what I have in mind is far more important."

They barely made it into the hotel room before their lips locked in a heated embrace. They stumbled through the room, bumping into tables and chairs, tearing off clothes before they tumbled onto the bed. They rolled around naked on the king-sized bed, their hands fully exploring each other's body. Kevin pulled Gabriel to his feet and continued their kisses. He pushed Gabriel into the chair, his erection pointing to the heavens and Kevin slid down onto the floor. He wasted no time in inserting Gabriel into his mouth and Gabriel let out a deep moan that filled the room. Gabriel pinched and pulled at his own nipples while Kevin fully worked over his dripping erection. Gabriel then pulled Kevin into his face and forcefully inserted his tongue into his mouth.

"Oh my God, you taste so good." Gabriel pushed Kevin off him and forced him to sit down in the chair. Gabriel stood above him and started moving his body as if he were a stripper. His body contorted and rolled and popped seductively and Kevin watched every move.

"I wanna see you jack off," he stated while he danced. Kevin gripped his dick and started working the shaft as he eyed Gabriel. Gabriel turned his back to him and bent over so that Kevin would get a full view of his plump ass. Without saying a word,

Gabriel moved over to his small bag, pulled out a condom and lube. He seductively tore open the package with his teeth and put the condom in his mouth. Kneeling again before Kevin, he used his mouth to wrap Kevin's dick in plastic while he lubed his opening. Kevin moaned as the condom slid over his dick. Gabriel straddled Kevin, positioning his dick within inches of his hole.

'Be gentle," he said before easing his way down Kevin's pole. Slowly, Kevin felt the warm, tightness engulf him and his eyes rolled to the back of his head. Gabriel let out a deep breath as Kevin entered him and he did not move for a few seconds to give his body time to adjust to Kevin. Then, he started bouncing up and down, slowly and then with more force and authority until he was riding like a champion jockey. The tempo of Gabriel's movements blended perfectly with the pace of Kevin's thrusts and their writhing bodies fused together in unbridled passion. The sound of the zeal of their sex crashed against the walls in loud thumps and reverberated against the windows. Using the power of his legs, Kevin stood up—still inside Gabriel—and continued to thrust deeply. Gabriel locked his arms around Kevin's neck and his legs around his waist and held on. Kevin then pulled out of him and Gabriel moved over to the window, threw open the curtains and motioned for Kevin to come closer. The view of New Orleans from their twenty-fifth-floor window was spectacular.

Gabriel turned around, his face pressed against the window, and allowed Kevin to enter him from the back. Without pause or hesitation, Kevin continued his assault of Gabriel in the open window. The thought of a voyeur possibly watching from another window intensified their lust. They were locked together, body to body, flesh to flesh, in a powerful exchange of energy. Kevin took a quick look out of the window into the Louisiana night right as he pressed deeper into Kevin. His scrotum tightened, sending chills throughout his body. He knew it was that time. He pulled out of Gabriel, yanked the condom off and exploded all over Gabriel's ass, his hot semen running down Gabriel's legs. Gabriel turned around and grabbed Kevin's dick and continued to jerk it until the pleasure turned to a sweet pain. Gabriel pushed Kevin onto the bed and straddled him. He leaned in and sucked on Kevin's tongue while simultaneously stroking his own dick. Kevin felt Gabriel's body shake and within seconds, he shot quick bursts of cum all over Kevin's chest and face. Gabriel let out a wail before collapsing onto Kevin's chest, sealing them together with his love juice.

"Damn, I love this city," Kevin said. Gabriel rolled off Kevin and onto his back. He turned his head and looked Kevin directly in the eyes.

"What happens when we get back to D.C.?"

Kevin took a breath and pondered Gabriel's question. "Well, I'm not sure, but 'I dwell in possibility,'" he said, quoting Emily Dickinson.

For a brief second, an image of Daryl flashed through Kevin's head. Then, he thought about Gabriel and the warm feeling he felt toward him.

Daryl, who?

ೞೞ

Lee Hayes is a graduate of The Bernard M. Baruch College, City University of New York, where he received his masters of public administration degree in 2005. He is the author of Passion Marks *and* A Deeper Blue: Passion Marks II. *He currently lives in Washington, D.C. Visit the author at www.leehayes.info*

IF YOU ENJOYED THE STORIES IN THIS COLLECTION,
CHECK OUT

PASSION MARKS

BY LEE HAYES

AVAILABLE FROM STREBOR BOOKS

CHAPTER 1

The black cordless phone slammed against the right side of my face with such force that it sent my entire body reeling over the white sofa. I rolled over it and onto the coffee table, shattering the glass top. Instantly, my face went numb. I lay on the floor in a daze, trying to ascertain the extent of the damage: the pain was intense. I rubbed my face with my hands while I tried to ignore the warm feel of blood as it oozed out of my back and soaked my shirt. When I found the strength, I looked above me and saw him looming like a volcano suddenly compelled to erupt. His savagely contorted face burned with the fire of his words and the anger that dripped from his thick breath. When I attempted to sit up, I felt his shoe in my chest, kicking me back to the carpet. His words failed to convey any meaning through the depth of my pain, but the anger on his face spoke volumes. I closed my eyes, praying this nightmare would end; instead of ending, his body suddenly pressed down on my chest, and unrelenting fists pounded my face. I tried to shield my face from his blows with my arms, even while his frame weighed heavily upon me.

By this time, my lungs were on the verge of collapse and I gasped desperately for air. I was far too weak to force him off me, and when I struck him in the eye with my fist, it only made him pound harder. Through his anger, and between the unbroken chains of profanity, he yelled something about blood on the carpet, *as if it was my fault*, and then pulled me up from where I lay like a rag doll. He stood me up so I could look directly in his brown eyes, and then he slapped me so hard across the face that I crashed into the wall, narrowly escaping the flames of the fireplace. Just as he raced toward me, I stood up, and with all the force I could muster, I slammed my fist into his face. He stumbled. I threw my body into him with the force of a line-backer. He tried to withstand the force, but he lost his balance, and we both tumbled onto the floor. His head hit the side of the entertainment center, and blood began to run down his face from the open wound. I pounded his face with my fist, and then slammed his head onto the floor repeatedly like a man possessed. He looked worn out. It was over.

I rolled off him and onto my back, taking a moment to breathe as I looked up at the ceiling. Slowly, I moved away from him. That's when I felt his fist connect with the back of my head. He plowed into me like a truck from behind, and I flew into the fifty-gallon aquarium, shattering the glass and sending the helpless fish to the floor. They flipped and flopped, gasping for air; within moments they'd be dead. He grabbed my left leg and pulled me with ease across the carpet, unmoved by my struggle for freedom. My attempt at liberation from his massive hands proved futile, and he continued dragging me across the white carpet, leaving behind a trail the color red.

When we reached the staircase, he gave my body a tremendous yank to assert his control. With sudden prowess, he moved behind me, pushed my body down, and forced my stomach into the stairs. I could feel his gigantic hands on the back of my neck as he pressed my face into the carpet. I was pinned down, unable to move. He ripped off my bloodstained shirt and tossed it aside. As he whispered something in my ear, his hands grabbed my ass. The heat of his breath scalding my neck was far worse than the words he spoke. He grabbed me by the waist and raised my body up just enough for him to undo my belt. As he pulled down my pants and underwear in one swift motion, I braced myself. His accelerated breathing became louder and louder in anticipation. I tried to prepare myself for the violation. I knew that he would do everything in his power to make it hurt—to make me scream for mercy. He had a special affinity for delivering pain. This time I would deny him the perverse pleasure of hearing me scream.

Behind me, I heard him unzip his pants; that was the catalyst that brought tears to my eyes. I would not let them fall. My tears would only add to his callous joy, so I withheld them. My legs were then forced apart, and I knew there was no turning back. With his arm still pressed against the back of my neck, and my face forcibly held against the floor, I felt his thick flesh force its way into me, connecting in a vile union. The pain of that first thrust when it broke through my barrier almost caused me to let out a loud scream, but I held it in. His bursts rocked my body, and the pain increased the longer he stayed in me. I reached my hands behind my back and tried to push him off me, but my effort proved pointless. He pushed harder and harder, while his inhuman grunts filled the room, like the howl of a wolf in the darkness of night. The force of his thrusts rolled my body back and forth, back and forth, back and forth, for what seemed like an endless moment in time. My face dug deeper into the stair, and the burn from the carpet on my face was becoming painful. His panting was vicious, much like an animal that suddenly realized the extent of its power and its victory. All the while, his voice shouted despicable words, and with each debilitating push from his body into mine, his voice became louder. *This had to end.* All of the hurt my body suffered now went to my head, and I could feel myself losing consciousness. He turned my head toward him, forcing me to look into his hollow eyes. Blood stained his face. His muscles inside of me began to contract, and I knew it would be over soon. He pushed harder, faster, harder, and still faster, until I felt the release of his hot fluids. He pulled out of my body while still enjoying his eruption. His juices spilled on my back, and then rolled down my side. It was over. From behind, he wrapped his hands around my waist and pulled me into his powerful chest. He held me there for a few seconds, gently kissed the back of my neck, and released me. *"Clean up this mess,"* he said as he motioned toward the war-torn room. He climbed over me, and made his way up the staircase. When I looked up, I saw the back of his naked body reach the top of the stairs and disappear into darkness.

There were no words with enough power to capture the way I felt. I remained laying face down in the carpet, naked except for one sock dangling off my foot, unwilling—perhaps unable—to move. I felt stinging sensations pulsating on my back from the glass still buried beneath my skin. I tried to check my back to see if it had stopped bleeding, but I really wasn't concerned about those cuts; my attention was singularly focused on bigger issues. My entire body, wrapped in a throbbing blanket of pain, felt limp. After a few deep breaths, I managed to regain some control of my tattered frame, and forced myself to slide slowly to the bottom of the staircase, where I pulled my knees into my chest, and rested in the corner like a small child hiding from monsters under the bed. The sweet smell of jasmine still clung in the air, much like a damp mist over a lake in the early morning. With my right hand, I caressed my face—the swelling had already begun. I needed to crawl into the kitchen to get some ice, but that distance seemed unconquerable. The dimly lit house, once full of noise, now sat quiet as if the weakened sky had nothing left to give after its storm. The only audible sounds came from the rain lightly pounding against the windows, and the murmur of the rolling thunder. The lightning flashes offered a brief illumination, but I longed for the darkness to bury my shame.

The entire evening replayed in my head like a big-screen horror movie. I paid close attention to the details to see if I could figure out where it went wrong. Alluring candles, sweet incense, and a basket full of fabulous seafood in front of the fireplace. Sexy love ballads from the stereo, expensive wine, and vases full of freshly cut colorful roses all over the house. It all seemed so perfect. James and I had held each other closely while staring seductively in each other's eyes; this was the man that I adored. The evening conversation had been full of love and comforting smiles. His soothing caresses brought me to the ultimate state of relaxation. I thought the dark days were long behind us, forever sealed by the hands of time. For the first time in months, it seemed that we could be the happy couple I envisioned.

This wasn't the first time I had felt his fists and been burned by his quick temper. Throughout the course of our relationship, violence was not uncommon, especially during his times of stress related to his firm, Lancaster Computer Systems. A year ago LCS made an acquisition of a smaller computer firm in Austin; this transaction brought out the worst in James. Some nights when he came home, I feared for my safety, and at times, for my life, not knowing what to expect when he walked through the door. It was like rolling the dice.

Partly, it was my fault. I knew this. Sometimes, maybe out of boredom, I would intentionally antagonize him just to get a reaction. I wanted to see how far I could push him. I wanted to know whether or not I had the power to make him lose control. During stressful times, instead of being supportive and appreciative, I managed to say or do the wrong thing. But this attack was by far one of the most vicious outbursts I'd suffered at his hands.

Over and over again, I replayed the evening. The phone rang and he picked up. While he was on the phone, I decided to go into the kitchen for more wine, and when I returned something in him had changed. He seemed irritable and ended the phone call by slamming the phone on its base. As I approached him, the phone rang again. I answered it without thinking. By the time I heard his commands to let it ring, it was too late. I should have noticed the look on his face. I should have heard his words. I should not have let anything interrupt the mood. He stood up and held his hand out for the phone, and I innocently gave it to him. That's when everything changed. *It was my fault*. If only I hadn't answered that call. If only I had listened to him. I would have to start paying more attention to his needs. The phone call could have waited.

As I dragged myself up from the corner with considerable effort, I wondered how many men and women were in situations similar to mine. The lyrics to that old song "How Could You Hurt the One You Love?" came to mind. I managed to limp slowly to the restroom without losing my balance. I held a firm grip on the black sink for support, and when I flipped the light switch on, I let out a shriek as I looked at the broken and tattered image that stood before me in the mirror. *Surely, this wasn't me.* The mirror played a cruel joke. My eyes were beginning to close from the swelling, and bloodstains covered my face. My swollen lips pulsated with a heavy pain. Numerous purple and black bruises covered my chest, and the gentlest touch of my passion marks caused a horrible sensation. Still holding onto the sink, I turned to examine my back in the mirror, but when I turned, a sudden explosion of pain enveloped my body. The room started to spin, and before I even realized what was happening, I collapsed to the floor in a fit of pain. The plush mauve rug did little to break my fall. I heard the sound and felt the thump as my head hit the porcelain tub, and everything went black.

✖ ✖ ✖

"Sometimes, Kevin, you reap what you sow." I was startled by the familiar voice and when I opened my eyes the apparition stood before me, part flesh and part fantasy, and then vanished into the darkness.

"Keevan? Where are you?" I asked in fright. My heart palpitated with the rapid speed of hummingbird wings, and it felt as if it would beat through my chest.

"I came back." I followed the voice into the den. Keevan stood there, dressed in the same clothing he wore when I found him dead. I walked slowly toward him, with carefully chosen steps. "I'm your brother. I came back." His words haunted me and his expressions taunted me while his eyes mocked, offering no absolution. He vanished in the same mystery that allowed him to come forth.

CHAPTER 2

After what seemed like only moments, I opened my eyes. I looked around and realized that I was upstairs in our bedroom. The green silk sheets were damp and sticky from my sweat. Slowly, I sat up in the bed and wiped some of the moisture from my forehead. James stood in front of the mirror, adding a few last-minute touches to his appearance. His blue Armani suit fit his frame perfectly, and the shiny, metallic silver tie provided the perfect contrast with the dark background. He wore success casually like a pair of expensive shoes with a polished shine. His persona projected an image of confidence and coolness, but that was a mask he wore for others. Only I knew the real James, full of paranoia, pain, suspicion, rage, love, hate, mystery, magic, confusion, all deeply rooted in an overwhelming fear of failure; that's why he pushed himself so hard. He needed to prove that he could successfully overcome his humble beginnings from the projects of the 5th Ward of Houston, and the dire predictions of those who doomed him to fail.

As soon as he realized that I was awake he rushed over to the bed, and my body contracted as I braced for sudden impact. He took a seat on the bed next to me, his brown eyes filled with sorrow, and stroked my forehead lovingly and with compassion.

"Baby, lie back down and put this on your face. It'll keep the swelling down." He placed an ice pack on my forehead. "I found you last night on the bathroom floor downstairs, so I cleaned you up and put you to bed. What were you dreaming about? You kept mumbling something about Keevan. I haven't seen you sweat this much in awhile." I watched his lips move with quiet grace. I loved him, loathed him, hurt for him, cried for him, despised him, wanted to kill him, wanted to hold him, wanted to be held by him, wanted to see him succeed, longed for his failure, but ultimately, I needed him. I needed his attention. I needed his love. I needed his support. He was the only consistent thing in my life since my brother died. He grabbed my hand and held it as he spoke. "I'm sorry. I know that doesn't make up for what happened. I don't know what to say. Maybe it was the wine that made me snap. I promise you this will never happen again, and I'll never drink again. I never want to hurt you again. You are my world. I will never raise my hand to hit you. I'll make it up to you," he said as tears replaced the usual sparkle in his eyes, and then a small stream of tears ran down his face. I released his grip, and tried to wipe the tears from his face.

"You've made that promise before, but it keeps happening," I said in a low, almost inaudible childlike voice.

"I know I have, but this time I promise it's different," he said with the sincerest expression on his face. Through his eyes, I searched his soul for honesty and sorrow. I knew he wanted to do right, to be better, but I wasn't sure he was capable of such remarkable change.

"I'm sorry I made you act like that," I muttered, trying to find the strength to force a small smile, and trying to find words to absolve his guilt.

"Baby, it's not your fault. Don't apologize for me." He wiped the moisture from his face with his left hand, and caressed my arm with the right. "I have to go to work now. I wish I could stay and take care of you, but I have a meeting that can't be missed. If you need anything, just call me and leave a message with Deborah, okay?" I smiled as best as I could as he walked out of the room. I heard his heavy footsteps bounce down the stairs in their usual rhythmic pattern. Part of me was glad to see him go, but the other part longed for the gentleness of the man who just left the room. Sometimes, I felt there were no limits to what I would do for his love; in spite of his obvious faults, he loved me, and that's what I needed.

✖ ✖ ✖

I lay back in the bed, lost in space and time, hearing chaotic voices crying out from the dark corners in my mind. I heard my brother's voice. I needed to find relief from his razor-like words.

No one could haunt me like that. Even James' blows failed to hurt as much as my brother's words. The images of him I often saw were more than mere dreams, more concrete than fantasies. He started appearing to me right after his death. Initially, his words served to comfort me and urge me to continue living, even without him. More recently, his words took a sinister twist and became more and more accusatory. I used to want to go to sleep so that I could be reunited with my other half, but the last few weeks' sleep became more and more disturbing. Born eight minutes and fourteen seconds before me, Keevan was technically the oldest twin, and felt a need to protect me. But I let him down when he needed me the most. For that, I would never forgive myself.

I turned my head to the right, and on top of the marble fireplace, in a neat silver frame, was a picture that I would treasure always. A picture of Keevan and me, dressed in white T-shirts and blue jeans, flashing our fraternity hand sign. I thought about the four weeks, four days, eight hours, and nineteen minutes we spent pledging with our other line brothers. I didn't think anything could be much worse than pledging, but his strength carried me through. He picked me up when I fell and when I couldn't stand, he stood for us both. There were times when he weathered my storms without hesitation. He was there for me when I needed him; he was my strength and my rock. I could not have done it without him, but when he needed to be carried, I was nowhere to be seen.

The day we found him he was supposed to pick Tony and me up from the airport in Houston after spending New Year's 2000 in D.C. When our flight landed, Tony and I waited at the gate for him, but Keevan was not there. He was fanatical in his promptness, so when he didn't show up within the first few minutes, I began to worry; I knew something out of the ordinary had happened. After an hour of waiting and calling the apartment, I knew something was wrong. We took a cab from the airport to his apartment, and his car was parked on the back row. We raced frantically to his apartment and I tried to use my spare key to enter, but the keyless deadbolt was locked from the inside. Tony and I banged on the door, but still no movement from the inside could be detected. No television, no radio, no sound emanated from the interior of the apartment at all. We rushed to the other side of the apartment and Tony kicked in the window, slowly removing the jagged glass so that he could enter without harming himself. I watched him bend over and step inside the apartment through the window. He told me to go to the front door and as soon as he got inside, he'd let me in.

The smell. A suffocating odor escaped from the apartment in a nauseating whirlwind. Within seconds, the thick vapors permeated every inch of our clothing with an incomprehensible stench. When I inhaled, the indigestible stench took a defensive position in my throat, making it difficult to breathe, and forcing me to cough. I ran to the back of the apartment toward the bedroom. My heart pounded. Sweat dripped from the palms of my hands in foreboding. Without hesitation, I threw open the door. There he lay, on his stomach, in the middle of his bedroom floor, a few inches from the phone. With outstretched hands, it appeared he was reaching for help. His body, already decomposing, was hardly recognizable. Around his mouth, a thick white foamy matter had begun to grow. A deep rumbling grew in my stomach, and my legs suddenly weakened. I tried to steady myself to exit the room, but I stumbled into the wall. Finally, I managed a small measure of control and made my way out of the crypt.

Once outside the apartment, a stream of tears flowed from my eyes, almost blinding me to the crowd now gathered outside.

Tony tried to comfort me, but his words provided no consolation. While I was off partying in D.C., my brother lay dying—alone. How could I have been so careless as to let him die alone? I should have been there to protect him, to help him, but I wasn't. The whole right half of my body went limp, like a physical part of me died. A vast emptiness swallowed my soul and my descent into darkness began.